D1108448

FAVOURITE TALES
FROM GRIMM AND ANDERSEN

FAVOURITE TALES FROM GRIMM AND ANDERSEN

Illustrated by Jiří Trnka

B. Mitchell

© Artia, Prague 1959, 1961
This combined edition first published in English by
Orbis Publishing, London 1983
Reprinted 1984

Printed in Czechoslovakia by Polygrafia, Prague
1/01/43/51−04

CONTENTS

BRIAR ROSE

A long time ago there lived a King and Queen, who said every day, 'If only we had a child!' but for a long time they had none.

And then one day, as the Queen was bathing, a frog crept out of the water on to the land, and said to her: 'Your wish shall be fulfilled; before a year has passed you shall bring a daughter into the world.'

The frog's words came true. The Queen had a little girl who was so beautiful that the King could not contain himself for joy, and prepared a great feast. He invited not only his relations, friends and acquaintances, but the fairies, in order that they might be favourably and kindly disposed towards the child. There were thirteen of them in the kingdom, but as the King had only twelve golden plates for them to eat from, one of the fairies had to stay at home.

The feast was held with all splendour, and when it came to an end the fairies all presented the child with a magic gift. One gave her virtue, another beauty, a third riches, and so on, with everything in the world that she could wish for.

When eleven of the fairies had said their say, the thirteenth suddenly appeared. She wanted to revenge herself for not having been invited. Without greeting anyone, or even glancing at the company, she called out in a loud voice: 'The Princess shall prick herself with a distaff in her fifteenth year and shall fall down dead.' And without another word she turned and left the hall.

Everyone was terror-struck; but the twelfth fairy, whose wish was still un-spoken, stepped forward. She could not cancel the curse, but could only soften it, so she said: 'It shall not be death, but a deep sleep lasting a hundred years, into which your daughter shall fall.'

The King was so anxious to guard his dear child from the misfortune, that he sent out a command that all the distaffs in the whole kingdom should be burned.

As time went on all the promises of the fairies came true. The Princess grew up to be so beautiful, modest, kind and clever that everyone who saw her could not but love her. Now it happened that on the very day when she was fifteen years old the King and Queen were away from home, and the Princess was left quite alone in the castle. She wandered about over the entire place, looking at rooms and halls as she pleased, and at last she came to an old tower. She ascended a narrow, winding staircase and reached a little door. A rusty key was sticking in the lock, and when she turned it, the door flew open. In a little room sat an old woman with a spindle, spinning her flax busily.

'Good day, Granny,' said the Princess, 'what are you doing?'

'I am spinning,' said the old woman, and nodded her head.

'What is the thing that whirls round so merrily?' asked the Princess; and she took the spindle and tried to spin too.

But she had scarcely touched it before the curse was fulfilled, and she pricked her finger with the spindle. The instant she felt the prick she fell upon the bed which was standing near, and lay still in a deep sleep which spread over the whole castle.

The King and Queen, who had just come home and had stepped into the hall, went to sleep, and all their courtiers with them. The horses went to sleep in the stable, the dogs in the yard, the doves on the roof, the flies on the wall; yes, even the fire flickering on the hearth grew still and went to sleep, and the roast meat stopped crackling. The cook, who was pulling the scullion's hair because he had made some mistake, let him go and went to sleep. The wind dropped, and on the trees in front of the castle not a leaf stirred.

Round the castle a hedge of briar roses began to grow up; every year it grew higher, till at last it surrounded the whole castle so that nothing could be seen of it, not even the flags on the roof.

But there was a legend in the land about the lovely sleeping Briar Rose, as the King's daughter was called, and from time to time princes came and tried to force a way through the hedge into the castle. They found it impossible, for the thorns, as though they had hands, held them fast, and the princes remained caught in them without being able to free themselves, and so died a miserable death.

After many, many years a Prince came again to the country and heard an old man tell of the castle which stood behind the briar hedge, in which a most beautiful maiden called Briar Rose had been asleep for the last hundred years, and with her slept the King, Queen, and all the courtiers. He knew also, from his grandfather, that many princes had already come and sought to pierce through the briar hedge, and had remained caught in it and died a sad death.

Then the young Prince said, 'I am not afraid; I am determined to go and look upon the lovely Briar Rose.'

The good old man did all in his power to dissuade him, but the Prince would not listen to his words.

Now, however, the hundred years were just ended, and the day had come when Briar Rose was to wake up again. When the Prince approached the briar hedge it was in blossom, and was covered with beautiful large flowers, which made way for him of their own accord and let him pass unharmed, and then closed up again into a hedge behind him.

In the courtyard he saw the horses and brindled hounds lying asleep; on the roof sat the doves with their heads under their wings. And when he went into the house the flies were asleep on the walls, and near the throne lay the King and Queen. In the kitchen was the cook, with his hand raised as though about to strike the scullion, and the maid sat with the black fowl in her lap which she was about to pluck.

He went on further, and all was so still that he could hear his own breathing. At last he reached the tower, and opened the door into the little room where Briar Rose was asleep. There she lay, looking so beautiful that he could not take his eyes off her; he bent down and gave her a kiss. As he touched her, Briar Rose opened her eyes and looked lovingly at him.

Then they went down together; and the King woke up, and the Queen, and all the courtiers, and looked at each other with astonished eyes. The horses in the stable stood up and shook themselves, the hounds leaped about and wagged their tails and the doves on the roof lifted their heads from under their wings, looked round, and flew into the fields. The flies on the walls began to crawl again, the fire in the kitchen roused itself and blazed up and cooked the food, the meat began to crackle, and the cook boxed the scullion's ears so soundly that he screamed aloud, while the maid finished plucking the fowl. Then the wedding of the Prince and Briar Rose was celebrated with all splendour, and they lived happily till the end of their days.

Once upon a time there was a dear little girl who was loved by everyone who looked at her, but most of all by her grandmother, and there was nothing she would not have given to the child. Once she gave her a little hood of red velvet, which suited her so well that she would never wear anything else; so she was always called 'Little Red Riding-Hood'.

One day her mother said to her, 'Come, Little Red Riding-Hood, here is a piece of cake and a bottle of wine. Take them to your grandmother; she is ill and weak, and they will do her good. Set out before it gets hot, and when you are going, walk nicely and quietly and do not run off the path, or you may fall and break the bottle, and then your grandmother will get nothing; and when you go into her room, don't forget to say "Good-morning", and don't peep into every corner before you do it.'

'I will take great care,' said Little Red Riding-Hood to her mother, and gave her hand on it.

The grandmother lived out in the wood, half a league from the village, and just as Little Red Riding-Hood entered the wood, a wolf met her. Little Red Riding-Hood did not know what a wicked creature he was, and was not at all afraid of him.

'Good-day, Little Red Riding-Hood,' said he.

'Thank you kindly, wolf.'

'Whither away so early, Little Red Riding-Hood?'

'To my grandmother's.'

'What have you got in your apron?'

'Cake and wine; yesterday was baking-day, so poor sick grandmother is to have something good, to make her stronger.'

'Where does your grandmother live, Little Red Riding-Hood?'

'A good quarter of a league farther on in the wood; her house stands under the three large oak-trees; the nut-trees are just below. You surely must know it,' replied Little Red Riding-Hood.

The wolf thought to himself, 'What a tender young creature! what a nice plump mouthful! She will be better to eat than the old woman. I must act craftily, so as to catch both.' So he walked for a short time by the side of Little Red Riding-Hood, and then he said, 'See, Little Red Riding-Hood, how pretty the flowers are about here—why do you not look round? I believe, too, that you do not hear how sweetly the little birds are singing; you walk gravely along as if you were going to school, while everything else out here in the wood is merry.'

Little Red Riding-Hood raised her eyes, and when she saw the sunbeams dancing here and there through the trees, and pretty flowers growing everywhere, she thought, 'Suppose I take grandmother a fresh nosegay; that would please her too. It is so early in the day that I shall still get there in good time.' And so she ran from the path into the wood to look for flowers. And whenever she had picked one, she fancied that she saw a still prettier one farther on, and ran after it, and so got deeper and deeper into the wood.

Meanwhile, the wolf ran straight to the grandmother's house and knocked at the door.

'Who is there?'

'Little Red Riding-Hood,' replied the wolf. 'She is bringing cake and wine; open the door.'

'Lift the latch,' called out the grandmother, 'I am too weak, and cannot get up.'

The wolf lifted the latch, the door flew open, and without saying a word he went straight to the grandmother's bed and devoured her. Then he put on her clothes, dressed himself in her cap, laid himself in bed and drew the curtains.

Little Red Riding-Hood, however, had been running about picking flowers, and when she had gathered so many that she could carry no more, she remembered her grandmother, and set out on the way to her.

She was surprised to find the cottage door standing open, and when she went into the room, she had such a strange feeling that she said to herself, 'Oh dear! how uneasy I feel today, and at other times I like being with grandmother so much.' She called out 'Good-morning', but received no answer; so she went to the bed and drew back the curtains. There lay her grandmother with her cap pulled far over her face, and looking very strange.

'Oh! grandmother,' she said, 'what big ears you have!'

'The better to hear you with, my child,' was the reply.

'But, grandmother, what big eyes you have!' she said.

'The better to see you with, my dear.'

'But, grandmother, what large hands you have!'

'The better to hug you with.'

'Oh! but, grandmother, what a terrible big mouth you have!'

'The better to eat you with.'

And scarcely had the wolf said this, than with one bound he was out of bed and had swallowed up Red Riding-Hood.

When the wolf had appeased his appetite, he lay down again in the bed, fell asleep and began to snore very loud. The huntsman was just passing the house, and thought to himself, 'How the old woman is snoring! I must just see if she wants anything.' So he went into the room, and when he came to the bed he saw that the wolf was lying in it. 'Do I find you here, you old sinner!' said he. 'I have long sought you!' Then just as he was going to fire at him, it occurred to him that the wolf might have devoured the grandmother and that she might still be saved, so he did not fire, but took a pair of scissors and began to cut open the stomach of the sleeping wolf.

When he had made two snips, he saw the little red hood shining, and then he made two snips more, and the little girl sprang out, crying, 'Ah, how frightened I have been! How dark it was inside the wolf!' And after that the aged grandmother came out alive also, but scarcely able to breathe. Little Red Riding-Hood, however, quickly fetched great stones with which they filled the wolf's body, and when he awoke, he wanted to run away, but the stones were so heavy that he fell down at once, and fell dead.

Then all three were delighted. The huntsman drew off the wolf's skin and went home with it; the grandmother ate the cake and drank the wine which Red Riding-Hood had brought, and revived, but Red Riding-Hood thought to herself, 'As long as I live, I will never by myself leave the path, to run into the wood, when my mother has forbidden me to do so.'

It is also related that once when Little Red Riding-Hood was again taking cakes to the old grandmother, another wolf spoke to her and tried to entice her from the path. Red Riding-Hood was, however, on her guard, and went straight forward on her way, and told her grandmother that she had met the wolf, and that he had said 'good-morning' to her, but with such a wicked look in his eyes that if they had not been on the public road she was certain he would have eaten her up. 'Well,' said the grandmother, 'we will shut the door, that he may not come in.'

Soon afterwards, the wolf knocked, and cried, 'Open the door, grandmother, I am Little Red Riding-Hood, and am fetching you some cakes.' But they did not speak or open the door, so the grey-beard stole twice or thrice round the house, and at last jumped on the roof, intending to wait until Red Riding-Hood went home in the evening and then to steal after her and devour her in the darkness.

But the grandmother saw what was in his thoughts. In front of the house was a great stone trough, so she said to the child, 'Take a pail, Red Riding-Hood; I made some sausages yesterday, so carry the water in which I boiled them to the trough.'

Red Riding-Hood carried until the great trough was quite full. Then the smell of the sausages reached the wolf, and he sniffed and peeped down, and at last stretched out his neck so far that he could no longer keep his footing and began to slip, and slipped down from the roof straight into the great trough, and was drowned.

But Red Riding-Hood went joyously home, and from that time was safe from harm.

CINDERELLA

The wife of a rich man fell sick, and as she felt that her end was drawing near she called her only daughter to her bedside and said, 'Dear child, be good and pious, and then the good God will always protect you, and I will look down on you from heaven and be near you.' Thereupon she closed her eyes and departed.

Every day the girl went out to her mother's grave and wept, and she remained pious and good. When winter came the snow spread a white sheet over the grave, and when the spring sun had drawn it off again, the man had taken another wife.

The woman had brought two daughters into the house with her, who were beautiful and fair of face, but vile and black of heart. Now a bad time began for the poor stepchild. 'Is the stupid goose to sit in the parlour with us?' they said. 'He who wants to eat bread must earn it; out with the kitchen-wench.' They took her pretty clothes away from her, put an old grey bed-gown on her, and gave her wooden shoes. 'Just look at the proud princess, how decked out she is!' they cried, and laughed, and led her into the kitchen.

There she had to do hard work from morning till night: get up before daybreak, carry water, light fires, cook and wash. Besides this, the sisters did her every imaginable injury—they mocked her, and emptied her peas and lentils into the ashes, so that she was forced to sit and pick them out again. In the evening, when she had worked till she was weary, she had no bed to go to, but had to sleep by the fireside in the ashes. And as on that account she always looked dusty and dirty, they called her Cinderella.

It happened that the father was going to the fair, and he asked his two step-daughters what he should bring back for them. 'Beautiful dresses,' said one; 'Pearls and jewels,' said the second.

'And you, Cinderella, what would you like?'

'Father, break off for me the first branch which knocks against your hat on the way home.'

So he bought beautiful dresses, pearls and jewels for his two stepdaughters, and on his way home, as he was riding through a green thicket, a hazel twig brushed against him and knocked off his hat. Then he broke off the branch and took it with him.

When he reached home he gave his stepdaughters the things which they had wished for, and to Cinderella he gave the branch from the hazel-bush. Cinderella thanked him, went to her mother's grave and planted the branch on it, and wept so much that the tears fell down on it and watered it. It grew, and became a handsome tree. Three times a day Cinderella went and sat beneath it, and wept and prayed, and a little white bird always came on the tree; and if Cinderella expressed a wish, the bird threw down to her what she had wished for.

It happened, however, that the King ordered a festival which was to last three days, and to which all the beautiful young girls in the country were invited, in order that his son might choose himself a bride. When the two stepsisters heard that they, too, were to appear among the number, they were delighted, called Cinderella, and said, 'Comb our hair for us, brush our shoes and fasten our buckles, for we are going to the festival at the King's palace.'

Cinderella obeyed, but wept, because she too would have liked to go with them to the dance; and she begged her stepmother to allow her to do so. 'You go, Cinderella!' said she; 'dusty and dirty as you are, you would go to the festival? You do not have clothes and shoes, and yet you would dance?' As, however, Cinderella went on asking, the stepmother at last said, 'I have emptied a dish of lentils into the ashes for you; if you have picked them out again in two hours, you shall go with us.'

The girl went through the back door into the garden, and called, 'You tame pigeons, you turtle-doves, and all you birds beneath the sky, come and help me to pick

> The good into the pot,
> The bad into the crop.'

Then two white pigeons came in by the kitchen window, and afterwards the turtle-doves, and at last all the birds beneath the sky, came whirring and crowding in, and alighted amongst the ashes. And the pigeons nodded with their heads and began to pick, pick, pick, pick, and the rest began also to pick, pick, pick, pick, and gathered all the good grains into the dish. Hardly had one hour passed before they were finished, and all flew out again. Then the girl took the dish to her stepmother, and was glad, and believed that now she would be allowed to go with them to the festival. But the stepmother said, 'No, Cinderella, you have no clothes and you cannot dance; you would only be laughed at.' And as Cinderella wept at this, the stepmother said, 'If you can pick two dishes of lentils out of the ashes for me in one hour, you shall go with us.' And she thought to herself, 'That she most certainly cannot do.'

When the stepmother had emptied the two dishes of lentils amongst the ashes, the girl went through the back door into the garden and cried, 'You tame pigeons, you turtle-doves, and all you birds under heaven, come and help me to pick

> The good into the pot,
> The bad into the crop.'

Then two white pigeons came in by the kitchen window, and afterwards the turtle-doves, and at length all the birds beneath the sky, came whirring and crowding in, and alighted amongst the ashes. And the doves nodded with their heads and began to pick, pick, pick, pick, and the others began also to pick, pick, pick, pick, and gathered all the good seeds into the dishes, and before half an hour was over they had already finished, and all flew out again. Then the girl carried the dishes to the stepmother and was delighted, and believed that she might now go with them to the festival. But the stepmother said, 'All this will not help you; you shall not go with us, for you have no clothes and cannot dance; we should be ashamed of you!' With this she turned her back on Cinderella, and hurried away with her two proud daughters.

As no one was now at home, Cinderella went to her mother's grave beneath the hazel-tree, and cried:

'Shiver and quiver, my little tree,
Silver and gold throw down over me.'

Then the bird threw a gold-and-silver dress down to her, and slippers embroidered with silk and silver. She put on the dress with all speed, and went to the festival. Her stepsisters and the stepmother, however, did not know her, and thought she must be a foreign princess, for she looked so beautiful in the gleaming dress. They never once thought of Cinderella, and believed that she was sitting at home in the dirt, picking lentils out of the ashes. The Prince went to meet her, took her by the hand and danced with her. He would dance with no other maiden, and never let go of her hand, and if anyone else came to invite her, he said, 'This is *my* partner.'

She danced till it was evening, and then she wanted to go home. But the King's son said, 'I will go with you and bear you company,' for he wished to see to whom the beautiful girl belonged. She escaped from him, however, and sprang into the pigeon-house. The King's son waited until her father came, and then he told him that the strange maiden had leapt into the pigeon-house. The old man thoughtt 'Can it be Cinderella?' and they had to bring him an axe and a pickaxe so that he might hew the pigeon-house to pieces, but no one was inside it.

And when they got home, Cinderella lay in her dirty clothes among the ashes, and a dim little oil-lamp was burning on the mantelpiece, for Cinderella had jumped quickly down from the back of the pigeon-house and had run to the little hazel-tree, and there she had taken off her beautiful clothes and laid them down, and the bird had taken them away again, and then she had placed herself in the kitchen amongst the ashes in her grey gown.

Next day, when the festival began afresh and her parents and the stepsisters had gone once more, Cinderella went to the hazel-tree and said:

'Shiver and quiver, my little tree,
Silver and gold throw down over me.'

Then the bird threw down a much more beautiful dress than on the preceding day. And when Cinderella appeared at the festival in this dress, everyone was astonished at her beauty. The King's son had waited until she came, and instantly took her by the hand and danced with no one but her. When others came and invited her, he said, 'She is *my* partner.'

When evening came she wished to leave, and the King's son followed her and wished to see into which house she went. But she sprang away from him, and into the garden behind the house. There stood a beautiful tall tree on which hung the most magnificent pears. She clambered so nimbly between the branches, like a squirrel, that the King's son did not know where she was gone. He waited until her father came, and said to him, 'The strange maiden has escaped from me, and I believe she has climbed up the pear-tree.'

The father thought, 'Can it be Cinderella?' and had an axe brought and cut the tree down, but no one was on it.

And when they got into the kitchen, Cinderella lay there amongst the ashes, as usual, for she had jumped down on the other side of the tree, had taken the beautiful dress to the bird in the little hazel-tree, and put on her grey gown.

On the third day, when her parents and sisters had gone, Cinderella once more went to the little tree and said:

'Shiver and quiver, my little tree,
Silver and gold throw down over me.'

And now the bird threw down to her a dress which was more splendid and magnificent than any she had yet had, and the slippers were golden. And when she went to the festival in this dress, no one knew how to speak for astonishment. The King's son danced with her only, and if anyone invited her to dance, he said, 'She is *my* partner.'

When evening came, Cinderella wished to leave, and the King's son was anxious to go with her, but she escaped from him so quickly that he could not follow her. The King's son had, however, used a stratagem, and had caused the whole staircase to be smeared with pitch, and there, when she ran down, the girl's left slipper remained sticking. The King's son picked it up, and it was small and dainty, and all golden.

Next morning, he went with it to the father, and said to him, 'No one shall be my wife but she whose foot this golden slipper fits.'

Then the two sisters were glad, for they had pretty feet. The eldest went with

the shoe into her room and wanted to try it on, and her mother stood by. But she could not get her big toe into it, and the shoe was too small for her. Then her mother gave her a knife, and said, 'Cut the toe off; when you are Queen you will have no more need to go on foot.'

The girl cut the toe off, forced the foot into the shoe, swallowed the pain, and went out to the King's son. Then he took her on his horse as his bride and rode away with her. They were, however, obliged to pass the grave, and there, on the hazel-tree, sat the two pigeons and cried:

> 'Turn and peep, turn and peep,
> There's blood within the shoe,
> The shoe it is too small for her,
> The true bride waits for you.'

Then he looked at her foot and saw how the blood was flowing from it. He turned his horse round and took the false bride home again, and said she was not the true one, and that the other sister was to put the shoe on.

Then this one went into her chamber and got her toes safely into the shoe, but her heel was too large. So her mother gave her a knife, and said. 'Cut a bit off your heel; when you are Queen you will have no more need to go on foot.'

The maiden cut a bit off her heel, forced her foot into the shoe, swallowed the pain, and went out to the King's son. He took her on his horse as his bride and rode away with her, but when they passed by the hazel-tree, two little pigeons sat on it and cried,

> 'Turn and peep, turn and peep,
> There's blood within the shoe,
> The shoe it is too small for her,
> The true bride waits for you.'

Then he looked down at her foot and saw how the blood was running out of her shoe, and how it had stained her white stocking. Then he turned his horse and took the false bride home again. 'This also is not the right one,' said he, 'have you no other daughter?'

'No,' said the man, 'there is only a little stunted kitchen-wench which my late wife left behind her, but she cannot possibly be the bride.'

The King's son said he was to send her up to him; but the mother answered, 'Oh no, she is much too dirty; she cannot show herself!'

He absolutely insisted on it, and Cinderella had to be called. She first washed her hands and face clean, and then went and bowed down before the King's son, who gave her the golden shoe. Then she seated herself on a stool, drew her foot out of the heavy wooden shoe, and put it into the slipper, which fitted like a glove. And when she rose up and the King's son looked at her face, he recognised the beautiful maiden who had danced with him, and cried, 'That is the true bride!'

The stepmother and the two sisters were terrified and became pale with rage; the King's son, however, took Cinderella on his horse and rode away with her. As they passed by the hazel-tree, the two white doves cried,

'Turn and peep, turn and peep,
No blood is in the shoe,
The shoe is not too small for her,
The true bride rides with you.'

and when they had cried that, the two came flying down and placed themselves on Cinderella's shoulders, one on the right, the other on the left, and remained sitting there, until she reached the palace.

THE WISHING-TABLE, THE GOLD-ASS
AND THE CUDGEL IN THE SACK

There was once upon a time a tailor who had three sons, and only one goat. But as the goat supported the whole of them with her milk, she was obliged to have good food, and to be taken every day to pasture. The sons, therefore, did this in turn. Once the eldest took her to the churchyard, where the finest herbs were to be found, and let her eat and run about there. At night when it was time to go home he asked, 'Goat, have you had enough?' The goat answered,

> 'I have eaten so much,
> Not a leaf more I'll touch, meh! meh!'

23

'Come home, then,' said the youth, and took hold of the cord round her neck, led her into the stable and tied her up securely.

'Well,' said the old tailor, 'has the goat had as much food as she ought?'

'Oh,' answered the son, 'she has eaten so much, not a leaf more she'll touch.'

But the father wished to satisfy himself, and went down to the stable, stroked the dear animal and asked, 'Goat, are you satisfied?' The goat answered,

> 'Wherewithal should I be satisfied?
> Among the graves I leapt about,
> And found no food, so went without, meh! meh!'

'What do I hear?' cried the tailor, and ran upstairs and said to the youth, 'Hollo, you liar; you said the goat had had enough, and have let her hunger!' and in his anger he took the yard-measure from the wall, and drove him out with blows.

Next day it was the turn of the second son, who looked out for a place in the fence of the garden, where nothing but good herbs grew, and the goat cleared them all off. At night when he wanted to go home, he asked, 'Goat, are you satisfied?' The goat answered,

> 'I have eaten so much,
> Not a leaf more I'll touch, meh! meh!'

'Come home, then,' said the youth, and led her home and tied her up in the stable.

'Well,' said the old tailor, 'has the goat had as much food as she ought?'

'Oh,' answered the son, 'she has eaten so much, not a leaf more she'll touch.'

The tailor would not rely on this, but went down to the stable and said, 'Goat, have you had enough?' The goat answered,

> 'Wherewithal should I be satisfied?
> Among the fences I leapt about,
> And found no food, so went without, meh! meh!'

'The godless wretch!' cried the tailor, 'to let such a good animal hunger,' and he ran up and drove the youth out of doors with the yard-measure.

Now came the turn of the third son, who wanted to do the thing well, and sought out some bushes with the finest leaves, and let the goat devour them. In the evening, when he wanted to go home, he asked, 'Goat, have you had enough?' The goat answered,

> 'I have eaten so much,
> Not a leaf more I'll touch, meh! meh!'

'Come home, then,' said the youth, and led her into the stable and tied her up

'Well,' said the old tailor, 'has the goat had a proper amount of food?'

'She has eaten so much, not a leaf more she'll touch.'

The tailor did not trust to that, but went down and asked, 'Goat, have you had enough?' The wicked beast answered,

> 'Wherewithal should I be satisfied?
> Among the fields I leapt about,
> And found no leaves, so went without, meh! meh!'

'Oh, the brood of liars!' cried the tailor, 'each as wicked and forgetful of his duty as the other! You shall no longer make a fool of me,' and, quite beside himself with anger, he ran upstairs and belaboured the poor young fellow so vigorously with the yard-measure that he sprang out of the house.

The old tailor was now alone with his goat. Next morning he went down into the stable, caressed the goat, and said, 'Come, my dear little animal, I will take you to feed myself.' He took her by the rope and conducted her to green hedges, and amongst milfoil, and whatever else goats like to eat. 'There you may for once eat to your heart's content,' said he to her, and let her browse till evening. When he asked, 'Goat, are you satisfied?' she replied,

> 'I have eaten so much,
> Not a leaf more I'll touch, meh! meh!'

'Come home, then,' said the tailor, and led her into the stable and tied her fast. When he was going away, he turned round again and said, 'Well, are you satisfied for once?' But the goat did not behave better to him, and cried,

> 'Wherewithal should I be satisfied?
> Among the fields I leapt about,
> And found no leaves, so went without, meh! meh!'

When the tailor heard that, he was shocked, and saw clearly that he had driven away his three sons without cause. 'Wait, you ungrateful creature,' cried he, 'it is not enough to drive you forth, I will mark you so that you will no more dare to show yourself amongst honest tailors.' In great haste he ran upstairs, fetched his razor, lathered the goat's head, and shaved her as clean as the palm of his hand. And as the yard-measure would have been too good for her, he brought the horse-whip, and gave her such cuts with it that she ran away in violent haste.

When the tailor was thus left quite alone in his house he fell into great grief, and would gladly have had his sons back again, but no one knew whither they were gone.

The eldest had apprenticed himself to a joiner, and learnt industriously and indefatigably, and when the time came for him to go travelling his master presented him with a little table which had no particular appearance, and was made of common wood, but it had one good property; if anyone set it out, and said, 'Little table, spread thyself,' the good little table was at once covered with a clean little cloth, and a plate was there, and a knife and fork beside it, and dishes with boiled meats and roasted meats, as many as there was room for, and a great glass of red wine shone so that it made the heart glad. The young journeyman thought, 'With this thou hast enough for thy whole life,' and went joyously about the world and never troubled himself at all whether an inn was good or bad, or if anything was to be found in it or not. When it suited him he did not enter an inn at all, but in the plain, in a wood, a meadow, or wherever he fancied, he took his little table off his back, set it down before him, and said, 'Spread thyself,' and then everything appeared that his heart desired.

At length he took it into his head to go back to his father, whose anger would now be appeased, and who would willingly receive him with his wishing-table. It came to pass that, on his way home, he came one evening to an inn which was filled with guests. They bade him welcome, and invited him to sit and eat with them, for otherwise he would have difficulty in getting anything. 'No,' answered the joiner, 'I will not take the few bites out of your mouths; rather than that, you shall be my guests.'

They laughed, and thought he was jesting with them; he, however, placed his wooden table in the middle of the room, and said, 'Little table, spread thyself.' Instantly it was covered with food, so good that the host could never have procured it, and the smell of it ascended pleasantly to the nostrils of the guests. 'Fall to, dear friends,' said the joiner, and the guests, when they saw that he meant it, did not need to be asked twice, but drew near, pulled out their knives and attacked it valiantly. And what surprised them the most was that when a dish became empty a full one instantly took its place of its own accord. The innkeeper stood in one corner and watched the affair; he did not at all know what to say, but thought, 'You could easily find a use for such a cook as that in your kitchen.'

The joiner and his comrades made merry until late into the night; at length they lay down to sleep, and the young apprentice also went to bed, and set his magic table against the wall.

The host's thoughts, however, let him have no rest; it occurred to him that there was a little old table in his lumber-room, which looked just like the apprentice's, and he brought it out quite softly, and exchanged it for the wishing-table.

Next morning the joiner paid for his bed, took up his table, never thinking that he had got a false one, and went his way. At mid-day he reached his father, who received him with great joy. 'Well, my dear son, what have you learnt?' said he to him.

'Father, I have become a joiner.'

'A good trade,' replied the old man, 'but what have you brought back with you from your apprenticeship?'

'Father, the best thing I have brought back with me is this little table.'

The tailor inspected it on all sides and said, 'You did not make a masterpiece when you made that; it is a bad old table.'

'It is a table which furnishes itself,' replied the son. 'When I set it out and tell it to cover itself, the most beautiful dishes stand on it, and a wine also, which gladdens the heart. Just invite all our relations and friends; they shall refresh and enjoy themselves for once, for the table will give them all they require.'

When the company was assembled, he put his table in the middle of the room and said, 'Little table, spread thyself,' but the little table did not bestir itself, and remained just as bare as any other table which did not understand language. Then the poor apprentice became aware that his table had been changed, and was ashamed at having to stand there like a liar. The relations, however, mocked him, and were forced to go home without having eaten or drunk. The father brought out his patches again, and went on tailoring, but the son went to a master in the craft.

The second son had gone to a miller and had apprenticed himself to him. When his years were over, the master said to him, 'As you have conducted yourself so well, I give you an ass of a peculiar kind, which neither draws a cart nor carries a sack.'

'To what use is he put, then?' asked the young apprentice.

'He lets gold drop from his mouth,' answered the miller. 'If you set him on a cloth and say "Bricklebrit", the good animal will drop gold-pieces for you.'

'That is a fine thing,' said the apprentice, and thanked the master, and went out into the world. When he had need of gold, he had only to say 'Bricklebrit' to his ass, and it rained gold-pieces, and he had nothing to do but pick them off the ground. Wheresoever he went, the best of everything was good enough for him, and the dearer the better, for he had always a full purse. When he had looked about the world for some time he thought, 'You must seek out your father; if you go to him with the gold-ass he will forget his anger and receive you well.'

It came to pass that he came to the same public-house in which his brother's table had been exchanged. He led his ass by the bridle, and the host was about to take the animal from him and tie him up, but the young apprentice said, 'Don't trouble yourself; I will take my grey horse into the stable, and tie him up myself, too, for I must know where he stands.'

This struck the host as odd, and he thought that a man who was forced to look

27

after his ass himself could not have much to spend; but when the stranger put his hand in his pocket and brought out two gold-pieces, and said he was to provide something good for him, the host opened his eyes wide and ran and sought out the best he could muster.

After dinner the guest asked what he owed. The host did not see why he should not double the reckoning, and said the apprentice must give two more gold-pieces. He felt in his pocket, but his gold was just at an end. 'Wait an instant, sir host,' said he, 'I will go and fetch some money,' but he took the tablecloth with him. The host could not imagine what this could mean, and being curious, stole after him, and as the guest bolted the stable-door, he peeped through a hole left by a knot in the wood. The stranger spread out the cloth under the animal and cried, 'Bricklebrit', and immediately the beast began to let gold-pieces fall, so that it fairly rained down money on the ground.

'Eh, my word,' said the host, 'ducats are quickly coined there! A purse like that is not amiss.'

The guest paid his score and went to bed, but in the night the host stole down into the stable, led away the master of the mint, and tied up another ass in his place.

Early next morning the apprentice travelled away with the ass and thought that he had his gold-ass. At mid-day he reached his father, who rejoiced to see him again, and gladly took him in. 'What have you made of yourself, my son?' asked the old man.

'A miller, dear father,' he answered.

'What have you brought back with you from your travels?'

'Nothing else but an ass.'

'There are asses enough here,' said the father, 'I would rather have had a good goat.'

'Yes,' replied the son, 'but it is no common ass, but a gold-ass; when I say "Bricklebrit", the good beast opens its mouth and drops a whole sheetful of gold-pieces. Just summon all our relations hither, and I will make them rich folks.'

'That suits me well,' said the tailor, 'for then I shall have no need to torment myself any longer with the needle,' and ran out himself and called the relations together.

As soon as they were assembled, the miller bade them make way, spread out his cloth, and brought the ass into the room. 'Now watch,' said he, and cried 'Bricklebrit', but no gold-pieces fell, and it was clear that the animal knew nothing of the art, for every ass does not attain such perfection. Then the poor miller pulled a long face, saw that he was betrayed, and begged pardon of the relatives, who went home as poor as they came. There was no help for it—the old man had to betake him to his needle once more, and the youth hired himself to a miller.

The third brother had apprenticed himself to a turner, and, as that is skilled labour, he was the longest in learning. His brothers, however, told him in a letter how badly things had gone with them, and how the innkeeper had cheated them of their beautiful wishing-gifts on the last evening before they reached home. When the turner had served his time and had to set out on his travels, as he had conducted himself so well, his master presented him with a sack and said, 'There is a cudgel in it.'

'I can put on the sack,' said he, 'and it may be of good service to me, but why should the cudgel be in it? It only makes it heavy.'

'I will tell you why,' replied the master; 'if anyone has done anything to injure you, do but say, "Out of the sack, Cudgel!" and the cudgel will leap forth among the people and play such a dance on their backs that they will not be able to stir or move for a week, and it will not leave off until you say, "Into the sack, Cudgel!"'

The apprentice thanked him, put the sack on his back, and when any one came too near him, and wished to attack him, he said, 'Out of the sack, Cudgel!' and instantly the cudgel sprang out, and dusted the coat or the jacket of one after the other on their backs, and never stopped until it had stripped it off them, and it was done so quickly that before anyone was aware it was already his own turn.

In the evening the young turner reached the inn where his brothers had been cheated. He laid his sack on the table before him, and began to talk of all the wonderful things he had seen in the world. 'Yes,' said he, 'people may easily find a table which will cover itself, a gold-ass, and things of that kind—extremely good things which I by no means despise—but these are nothing in comparison to the treasure which I have won for myself and am carrying about with me in my sack here.'

The innkeeper pricked up his ears; 'What in the world can that be?' thought he, 'the sack must be filled with nothing but jewels. I ought to get them cheap, too, for all good things go in threes.'

When it was time for sleep, the guest stretched himself on the bench and laid his sack beneath him for a pillow. When the innkeeper thought his guest was lying in a sound sleep, he went to him, and pushed and pulled quite gently and carefully at the sack to see if he could possibly draw it away and lay another in its place. The turner had, however, been waiting for this for a long time, and now just as the innkeeper was about to give a hearty tug, he cried, 'Out of the sack, Cudgel!' Instantly the little cudgel came forth and fell on the innkeeper, and gave him a sound thrashing.

The host cried for mercy; but the louder he cried, so much the more heavily the cudgel beat the time on his back, until at length he fell to the ground exhausted. Then the turner said, 'If you do not give back the table which covers itself, and the gold-ass, the dance shall begin afresh.'

'Oh, no,' cried the host, quite humbly, 'I will gladly produce everything, only make the accursed kobold creep back into the sack.'

Then said the apprentice, 'I will let mercy take the place of justice, but beware of getting into mischief again!' So he cried, 'Into the sack, Cudgel!' and let him have rest.

Next morning the turner went home to his father with the wishing-table and the gold-ass. The tailor rejoiced when he saw him once more, and asked him likewise what he had learned in foreign parts. 'Dear father,' said he, 'I have become a turner.'

'A skilled trade,' said the father. 'What have you brought back with you from your travels?'

'A precious thing, dear father,' replied the son, 'a cudgel in the sack.'

'What!' cried the father, 'a cudgel! That's worth your trouble, indeed! From every tree you can cut yourself one.'

'But not one like this, dear father. If I say "Out of the sack, Cudgel!" the cudgel springs out and leads any one who means ill with me a weary dance, and never stops until he lies on the ground and prays for fair weather. Look you, with this cudgel have I got back the wishing-table and the gold-ass which the thievish innkeeper took away from my brothers. Now let them both be sent for, and invite all our kinsmen. I will give them to eat and to drink, and will fill their pockets with gold into the bargain.'

The old tailor would not quite believe him, but nevertheless got the relatives together. Then the turner spread a cloth in the room and led in the gold-ass, and said to his brother, 'Now, dear brother, speak to him.'

The miller said 'Bricklebrit', and instantly the gold-pieces fell down on the cloth like a thunder-shower, and the ass did not stop until everyone of them had so much that he could carry no more. (I can see in your face that you also would have liked to be there.)

Then the turner brought the little table, and said, 'Now, dear brother, speak to it.' And scarcely had the carpenter said, 'Table, spread thyself,' than it was spread and amply covered with the most exquisite dishes. Then such a meal took place as the good tailor had never yet known in his house, and the whole party of kinsmen stayed together till far in the night, and were all merry and glad. The tailor locked away needle and thread, yard-measure and goose, in a press, and lived with his three sons in joy and splendour.

What, however, became of the goat who was to blame for the tailor driving out his three sons? That I will tell you. She was ashamed that she had a bald head, and ran to a fox's hole, and crept into it. When the fox came home, he was met by two great eyes shining out of the darkness, and was terrified and ran away. A bear met him, and as the fox looked quite disturbed, he said, 'What is the matter with you, brother Fox, why do you look like that?'

'Ah,' answered Redskin, 'a fierce beast is in my cave and stared at me with its fiery eyes.'

'We will soon drive him out', said the bear, and went with him to the cave and looked in, but when he saw the fiery eyes, fear seized on him likewise; he would have nothing to do with the furious beast, and took to his heels.

The bee met him, and as she saw that he was ill at ease, she said, 'Bear, you are really pulling a very pitiful face; what has become of all your gaiety?'

'It is all very well for you to talk,' replied the bear. 'A furious beast with staring eyes is in Redskin's house, and we can't drive him out.'

The bee said, 'Bear, I pity you; I am a poor weak creature whom you would not turn aside to look at, but still, I believe I can help you.' She flew into the fox's cave, lighted on the goat's smoothly shorn head, and stung her so violently that she sprang up, crying 'Meh, meh,' and ran forth into the world as if mad, and to this hour no one knows where she has gone.

TOM THUMB

A poor peasant sat one evening by his hearth and poked the fire, while his wife sat opposite spinning. He said: 'What a sad thing it is that we have no children; our home is so quiet, while other folks' houses are noisy and cheerful.'

'Yes,' answered his wife, and she sighed; 'even if it were an only one, and if it were no bigger than my thumb, I should be quite content, and we would love it with all our hearts.'

Now some time after this, she had a little boy who was strong and healthy, but was no bigger than a thumb. Then they said: 'Our wish has been fulfilled, and, small as he is, we will love him dearly.' And because of his tiny stature they called him Tom Thumb. They let him want for nothing, yet the child grew no bigger, but remained the same size as when he was born. Still, he looked out on the world with intelligent eyes, and soon showed himself a clever and agile creature, who was lucky in all he attempted.

One day, when the peasant was preparing to go into the forest to cut wood, he said to himself, 'I wish I had someone to bring the cart after me.'

'Oh, father!' said Tom Thumb, 'I will soon bring it. You leave it to me; it shall be there at the appointed time.'

Then the peasant laughed, and said, 'How can that be? You are much too small even to hold the reins.'

'That doesn't matter, if only mother will harness the horse,' answered Tom. 'I will sit in his ear and tell him where to go.'

'Very well,' said the father, 'we will try it for once.'

When the time came, the mother harnessed the horse, set Tom in his ear, and then the little creature called out 'Gee-up' and 'Whoa' in turn, and directed the horse where to go. It went quite well, just as though it were being driven by its master; and they went the right way to the wood. Now it happened that while the cart was turning a corner, and Tom was calling to the horse, two strange men appeared on the scene.

'My goodness,' said one, 'what is this? There goes a cart, and a driver is calling to the horse, but there is nothing to be seen.'

'That is very peculiar,' said the other; 'we will follow the cart and see where it stops.'

The cart went on deep into the forest, and arrived quite safely at the place where the wood was cut.

When Tom spied his father, he said, 'You see, father, here I am with the cart;

now lift me down.' The father held the horse with his left hand, and took his little son out of its ear with the right. Then Tom sat down quite happily on a straw.

When the two strangers noticed him, they did not know what to say for astonishment.

Then one drew the other aside, and said: 'Listen, that little creature might make our fortune if we were to show him in the town for money. We will buy him.'

So they went up to the peasant, and said: 'Sell us the little man; he shall be well looked after with us.'

'No,' said the peasant, 'he is the delight of my eyes, and I will not sell him for all the gold in the world.'

But Tom Thumb, when he heard the bargain, crept up by the folds of his father's coat, placed himself on his shoulder, and whispered in his ear, 'Father, let me go; I will soon come back again.'

Then his father gave him to the two men for a fine piece of gold.

'Where will you sit?' they asked him.

'Oh, put me on the brim of your hat; then I can walk about and observe the neighbourhood without falling down.'

They did as he wished, and when Tom had said good-bye to his father, they went away with him.

They walked on till it was twilight, when the little man said, 'You must lift me down.'

'Stay where you are,' answered the man on whose head he sat.

'No,' said Tom 'I will come down. Lift me down immediately.'

The man took off his hat and set the little creature in a field by the wayside. He jumped and crept about for a time, here and there among the sods, then slipped suddenly into a mouse-hole which he had discovered.

'Good evening, gentlemen, just you go home without me,' he called out to them in mockery.

They ran about and poked with sticks into the mouse-hole, but all in vain. Tom crept further and further back, and, as it soon got quite dark, they were forced to go home, full of anger and with empty purses.

When Tom noticed that they were gone, he crept out of his underground hiding-place again. 'It is dangerous walking in this field in the dark,' he said, 'one might easily break one's leg or one's neck.' Luckily, he came to an empty snail shell. 'Thank goodness,' he said, 'I can pass the night in safety here,' and he sat down.

Not long after, just when he was about to go to sleep, he heard two men pass by. One said: 'How shall we set about stealing the rich parson's gold and silver?'

'I can tell you,' interrupted Tom.

'What was that?' said one robber in a fright. 'I heard someone speak.'

They remained standing and listened.

Then Tom spoke again: 'Take me with you and I will help you.'

'Where are you?' they said.

'Just look on the ground and see where the voice comes from,' he answered.

At last the thieves found him, and lifted him up. 'You little urchin, are *you* going to help us?'

'Yes,' he said; 'I will creep between the iron bars in the pastor's room, and will hand out to you what you want.'

'All right,' they said, 'we will see what you can do.'

When they came to the parsonage, Tom crept into the room, but called out immediately with all his strength to the others: 'Do you want everything that is here?'

The thieves were frightened, and said, 'Do speak softly, and don't wake anyone.'

But Tom pretended not to understand, and called out again, 'What do you want? Everything?'

The cook, who slept above, heard him and sat up in bed and listened. But the thieves were so frightened that they retreated a little way. At last they summoned up courage again, and thought to themselves, 'The little rogue wants to tease us.' So they came back and whispered to him, 'Now, do be serious, and hand us out something.'

Then Tom called out again, as loud as he could, 'I will give you everything if only you will hold out your hands.'

The maid, who was listening intently, heard him quite distinctly and jumped out of bed and stumbled to the door. The thieves turned and fled, running as though wild huntsmen were after them. But the maid, seeing nothing, went to get a light. When she came back with it, Tom, unperceived, slipped out into the barn, and the maid, after she had searched every corner and found nothing, went to bed again thinking she had been dreaming with her eyes and ears open.

Tom Thumb climbed about in the hay, and found a splendid place to sleep. There he determined to rest till day came, and then to go home to his parents. But he had other experiences to go through first. Indeed, this world is full of trouble and sorrow!

The maid got up in the grey dawn to feed the cows. First she went into the barn, where she piled up an armful of hay, the very bundle in which poor Tom was asleep. But he slept so soundly that he knew nothing till he was almost in the mouth of the cow, who was eating him up with the hay.

'Heavens!' he said, 'however did I get into this mill?' But he soon saw where he was, and the great thing was to avoid being crushed between the cow's teeth. At last, whether he liked it or not, he had to go down the cow's throat.

'The windows have been forgotten in this house,' he said. 'The sun does not shine into it, and no light has been provided.'

Altogether he was very ill-pleased with his quarters, and, worst of all, more and more hay came in at the door, and the space grew narrower and narrower. At last he called out, in his fear, as loud as he could, 'Don't give me any more food. Don't give me any more food.'

The maid was just milking the cow, and when she heard the same voice as in the night, without seeing anyone, she was frightened and slipped from her stool and spilt the milk. Then, in the greatest haste, she ran to her master, and said: 'Oh Your Reverence, the cow has spoken!'

'You are mad,' he answered; but he went into the stable himself to see what was happening. Scarcely had he set foot in the cow-shed before Tom began again: 'Don't bring me any more food.'

Then the pastor was terrified too, and thought that the cow must be bewitched; so he ordered it to be killed. It was accordingly slaughtered, but the stomach, in which Tom was hidden, was thrown into the manure heap. Tom had the greatest trouble in working his way out. Just as he stuck out his head, a hungry wolf ran by and snapped up the whole stomach with one bite. But still Tom did not lose courage. 'Perhaps the wolf will listen to reason,' he said. So he called out, 'Dear wolf, I know where you could find a magnificent meal.'

'Where is it to be had?' asked the wolf.

'Why, in such and such a house,' answered Tom. 'You must squeeze through the grating of the store-room window, and there you will find cakes, bacon and sausages, as much as you can possibly eat.' And he went on to describe his father's house.

The wolf did not wait to hear this twice, and at night forced himself in through the grating and ate to his heart's content. When he was satisfied, he wanted to go away again; but he had grown so fat that he could not get out the same way. Tom had reckoned on this, and began to make a great commotion inside the wolf's body, struggling and screaming with all his might.

'Be quiet,' said the wolf, 'you will wake up the people of the house.'

'All very fine,' answered Tom. 'You have eaten your fill, and now I am going to make merry.' And he began to scream again with all his might.

At last his father and mother woke up, ran to the room, and looked through the crack of the door. When they saw a wolf, they went away, and the husband fetched his axe, and the wife a scythe.

'You stay behind,' said the man, as they came into the room. 'If my blow does not kill him, you must attack him and rip up his body.'

When Tom Thumb heard his father's voice, he called out: 'Dear father, I am here, inside the wolf's body.'

Full of joy, his father cried, 'Heaven be praised! our dear child is found again,' and he bade his wife throw aside the scythe that it might not injure Tom.

Then he gathered himself together, and struck the wolf a blow on the head, so that it fell down lifeless. Then with knives and shears they ripped up the body, and took their little boy out.

'Ah,' said his father, 'how troubled we have been about you.'

'Yes, father, I have travelled about the world, and I am thankful to breathe fresh air again.'

'Wherever have you been?' they asked.

'Down a mouse-hole, in a cow's stomach and in a wolf's maw,' he answered; 'and now I shall stay with you.'

'And we will never sell you again, for all the riches in the world,' they said, kissing and fondling their dear child.

Then they gave him food and drink, and had new clothes made for him, as his own had been spoilt in his travels.

THE SPIRIT IN THE BOTTLE

There was once a poor woodcutter who toiled from early morning till late night. When at last he had laid by some money he said to his boy, 'You are my only child; I will spend the money which I have earned by the sweat of my brow on your education. If you learn some honest trade you can support me in my old age, when my limbs have grown stiff and I am obliged to stay at home.'

Then the boy went to a high school and learned diligently so that his masters praised him, and he remained there a long time. When he had worked through two classes, but was still not yet perfect in everything, the little pittance which the father had earned was all spent, and the boy was obliged to return home to him.

'Ah,' said the father sorrowfully, 'I can give you no more, and in these hard times I cannot earn a farthing more than will suffice for our daily bread.'

'Dear father,' answered the son, 'don't trouble yourself about it; if it is God's will it will turn to my advantage. I shall soon accustom myself to it.'

When the father wanted to go into the forest to earn money by helping to pile and stack wood and also to chop it, the son said, 'I will go with you and help you.'

'Nay, my son,' said the father, 'that would be hard for you; you are not accustomed to rough work, and will not be able to bear it, besides I have only one axe and no money left wherewith to buy another.'

'Just go to the neighbour,' answered the son, 'he will lend you an axe until I have earned one for myself.'

The father then borrowed an axe of the neighbour, and next morning at break of day they went out into the forest together. The son helped his father and was quite merry and brisk about it. But when the sun was right over their heads, the father said, 'We will rest and have our dinner, and then we shall work as well again.'

The son took his bread in his hands and said, 'Just you rest, father, I am not tired; I will walk up and down a little in the forest, and look for birds' nests.'

'Oh, you fool,' said the father, 'why should you want to run about there? Afterwards you will be tired, and no longer able to raise your arm; stay here, and sit down beside me.'

The son, however, went into the forest, ate his bread, was very merry, and peered in among the green branches to see if he could discover a bird's nest anywhere. So he went up and down until at last he came to a great dangerous-looking oak, which certainly was already many hundred years old, and which five men could not have spanned. He stood still and looked at it, and thought, 'Many a bird must have built its nest in that.'

Then all at once it seemed to him that he heard a voice. He listened and became aware that someone was crying in a very smothered voice, 'Let me out! Let me out!' He looked around but could discover nothing; nevertheless, he fancied that the voice came out of the ground.

Then he cried, 'Where are you?'

The voice answered, 'I am here down amongst the roots of the oak-tree. Let me out! Let me out!'

The scholar began to loosen the earth under the tree and search among the roots, until at last he found a glass bottle in a little hollow. He lifted it up and held it against the light, and then saw a creature shaped like a frog springing up and down in it.

'Let me out! Let me out!' it cried anew, and the scholar, thinking no evil, drew the cork out of the bottle. Immediately a spirit ascended from it, and began

to grow, and grew so fast that in a very few moments he stood before the scholar, a terrible fellow as big as half the tree by which he was standing.

'Know you,' he cried in an awful voice, 'what your wages are for having let me out?'

'No,' replied the scholar fearlessly, 'how should I know that?'

'Then I will tell you,' cried the spirit; 'I must strangle you for it.'

'You should have told me that sooner,' said the scholar, 'for I should then have left you shut up, but my head shall stand fast for all you can do; more persons than one must be consulted about that.'

'More persons here, more persons there,' said the spirit. 'You shall have the wages you have earned. Do you think that I was shut up there for such a long time as a favour? No, it was a punishment for me. I am the mighty Mercurius. Whoso releases me, him must I strangle.'

'Softly,' answered the scholar, 'not so fast. I must first know that you really were shut up in that little bottle, and that you are the right spirit. If, indeed, you can get in again, I will believe, and then you may do as you will with me.'

The spirit said haughtily, 'That is a very trifling feat,' drew himself together, and made himself as small and slender as he had been at first, so that he crept through the same opening, and right through the neck of the bottle in again. Scarcely was he within than the scholar thrust the cork he had drawn back into the bottle, and threw it among the roots of the oak into its old place, and the spirit was betrayed.

And now the scholar was about to return to his father, but the spirit cried very piteously. 'Ah, do let me out! Ah, do let me out!'

'No,' answered the scholar, 'not a second time! He who has once tried to take my life shall not be set free by me, now that I have caught him again.'

'If you will set me free,' said the spirit, 'I will give you so much that you will have plenty all the days of your life.'

'No,' answered the scholar, 'you would cheat me as you did the first time.'

'You are playing away your own good luck,' said the spirit; 'I will do you no harm, but will reward you richly.'

The scholar thought, 'I will venture it; perhaps he will keep his word, and anyhow he shall not get the better of me.'

Then he took out the cork, and the spirit rose up from the bottle as he had done before, stretched himself out and became as big as a giant.

'Now you shall have your reward,' said he, and handed the scholar a little bag just like a plaster, and said, 'If you spread one end of this over a wound it will heal, and if you rub steel or iron with the other end it will be changed into silver.'

'I must try that,' said the scholar, and went to a tree, tore off the bark with his axe, and rubbed it with one end of the plaster. It immediately closed together and was healed. 'Now it is all right,' he said to the spirit, 'and we can part.' The spirit thanked him for his release, and the scholar thanked the spirit for his present, and went back to his father.

'Where have you been racing about?' said the father; 'why have you forgotten your work? I said at once that you would never get on with anything.'

'Be easy, father, I will make it up.'

'Make it up, indeed,' said the father angrily, 'there's no art in that.'

'Take care, father, I will soon hew that tree there, so that it will split.'

Then he took his plaster, rubbed the axe with it, and dealt a mighty blow, but as the iron had changed into silver, the edge turned. 'Hullo, father, just look what a bad axe you've given me; it has become quite crooked.'

The father was shocked, and said, 'Ah, what have you done? Now I shall have to pay for that, and have not the wherewithal, and that is all the good I have got by your work.'

'Don't get angry,' said the son, 'I will soon pay for the axe.'

'Oh, you blockhead,' cried the father, 'how will you pay for it? You have nothing but what I give you. These are students' tricks that are sticking in your head, but you have no idea of wood-cutting.'

After a while the scholar said, 'Father, I can really work no more; we had better take a holiday.'

'Eh, what!' answered he. 'Do you think I will sit with my hands lying in my lap like you? I must go on working, but you may take yourself off home.'

'Father, I am here in this wood for the first time; I don't know my way alone. Do go with me.'

As his anger had now abated, the father at last let himself be persuaded and went home with him. Then he said to the son, 'Go and sell your damaged axe, and see what you can get for it, and I must earn the difference, in order to pay the neighbour.'

The son took the axe and carried it into town to a goldsmith, who tested it, laid it in the scales, and said, 'It is worth four hundred thalers; I have not so much as that by me.'

The son said, 'Give me what you have; I will lend you the rest.'

The goldsmith gave him three hundred thalers, and remained a hundred in his debt. The son thereupon went home and said, 'Father, I have got the money; go and ask the neighbour what he wants for the axe.'

'I know that already,' answered the old man, 'one thaler, six groschen.'

'Then give him two thalers, twelve groschen—that is double and enough; see, I have money in plenty,' and he gave the father a hundred thalers, and said, 'You shall never know want; live as comfortably as you like.'

'Good heavens!' said the father, 'how have you come by these riches?'

The scholar then told how all had come to pass, and how he, trusting in his luck, had made such a good hit. But with the money that was left, he went back to the high school and went on learning more, and as he could heal all wounds with his plaster, he became the most famous doctor in the whole world.

THE GRAVE-MOUND

A rich farmer was one day standing in his yard inspecting his fields and gardens. The corn was growing up vigorously and the fruit-trees were heavily laden with fruit. The grain of the year before still lay in such immense heaps on the floors that the rafters could hardly bear it. Then he went into the stable, where were well-fed oxen, fat cows and horses bright as looking-glass. At length, he went back into his sitting-room, and cast a glance at the iron chest in which his money lay.

Whilst he was thus standing surveying his riches, all at once there was a loud knock close by him. The knock was not at the door of his room, but at the door of his heart. It opened, and he heard a voice which said to him, 'Have you done good to your family with it? Have you considered the necessities of the poor? Have you shared your bread with the hungry? Have you been contented with what you have, or did you always desire to have more?'

The heart was not slow in answering, 'I have been hard and pitiless, and have never shown any kindness to my own family. If a beggar came, I turned away my eyes from him. I have not troubled myself about God, but have thought only of increasing my wealth. If everything which the sky covers had been my own, I should still not have had enough.'

When he was aware of this answer he was greatly alarmed, his knees began to tremble, and he was forced to sit down.

Then there was another knock, but the knock was at the door of his room. It was his neighbour, a poor man who had a number of children whom he could no longer satisfy with food. 'I know,' thought the poor man, 'that my neighbour is rich, but he is as hard as he is rich. I don't believe he will help me, but my children are crying for bread, so I will venture it.' He said to the rich man, 'You do not readily give away anything that is yours, but I stand here like one who feels the water rising above his head. My children are starving; lend me four measures of corn.'

The rich man looked at him long, and then the first sunbeam of mercy began to melt away a drop of the ice of greediness. 'I will not lend you four measures,' he answered, 'but I will make you a present of eight, but you must fulfil one condition.'

'What am I to do?' said the poor man.

'When I am dead, you shall watch for three nights by my grave.'

The peasant was disturbed in his mind at this request, but in the need in which he was, he would have consented to anything; he accepted, therefore, and carried the corn home with him.

It seemed as if the rich man had foreseen what was about to happen, for when three days were gone by, he suddenly dropped down dead. No one knew exactly how it came to pass, but no one grieved for him. When he was buried, the poor man remembered his promise; he would willingly have been released from it, but he thought, 'After all, he acted kindly by me. I have fed my hungry children with his corn, and even if that were not the case, where I have once given my promise I must keep it.'

At nightfall, he went into the churchyard, and seated himself on the grave-mound. Everything was quiet; only the moon appeared above the grave, and frequently an owl flew past and uttered her melancholy cry. When the sun rose, the poor man betook himself in safety to his home, and in the same manner the second night passed quietly by. On the evening of the third day he felt a strange uneasiness; it seemed to him that something was about to happen. When he went out he saw, by the churchyard wall, a man whom he had never seen before. He was no longer young, had scars on his face, and his eyes looked sharply and eagerly around. He was entirely covered with an old cloak, and nothing was visible but his great riding-boots. 'What are you looking for here?' asked the peasant. 'Are you not afraid of the lonely churchyard?'

'I am looking for nothing,' he answered, 'and I am afraid of nothing! I am like the youth who went forth to learn how to shudder, and had his labour for his pains, but got the King's daughter to wife and great wealth with her, but I remained poor. I am nothing but a paid-off soldier, and I mean to pass the night here, because I have no other shelter.'

'If you are without fear,' said the peasant, 'stay with me, and help me to watch that grave there.'

'To keep watch is a soldier's business,' he replied; 'whatever we fall in with here, whether it be good or bad, we will share it between us.' The peasant agreed to this and they seated themselves on the grave together.

All was quiet until midnight, when suddenly a shrill whistling was heard in the air, and the two watchers perceived the Evil One standing bodily before them.

'Be off, you ragamuffins!' cried he to them, 'the man who lies in that grave belongs to me; I want to take him, and if you don't go away I will wring your necks!'

'Sir with the red feather,' said the soldier, 'you are not my captain, I have no need to obey you, and I have not yet learned how to fear. Go away, we shall stay sitting here.'

The Devil thought to himself, 'Money is the best thing with which to get hold of these two vagabonds.' So he began to play a softer tune, and asked quite kindly if they would not accept a bag of money and go home with it?

'That is worth listening to,' said the soldier, 'but one bag of gold won't serve us;

if you will give as much as will go into one of my boots, we will quit the field for you and go away.'

'I have not so much as that about me,' said the Devil, 'but I will fetch it. In the neighbouring town lives a money-changer who is a good friend of mine, and will readily advance it to me.'

When the Devil had vanished the soldier took his left boot off, and said, 'We will soon pull the charcoal-burner's nose for him; just give me your knife, comrade.' He cut the sole off the boot, and put it in the high grass near the grave on the edge of a hole that was half overgrown. 'That will do,' said he; 'now the chimney-sweep may come.'

They both sat down and waited, and it was not long before the Devil returned with a small bag of gold in his hand.

'Just pour it in,' said the soldier, raising up the boot a little, 'but that won't be enough.'

The Black One shook out all that was in the bag; the gold fell through and the boot remained empty. 'Stupid Devil,' cried the soldier, 'it won't do! Didn't I say so at once? Go back again and bring more.'

The Devil shook his head, went, and in an hour's time came with a much larger bag under his arm.

'Now pour it in,' cried the soldier, 'but I doubt the boot will be full.' The gold clinked as it fell, but the boot remained empty. The Devil looked in himself with his burning eyes, and convinced himself of the truth.

'You have shamefully big calves to your legs!' cried he, and made a wry face.

'Do you think,' replied the soldier, 'that I have a cloven foot like you? Since when have you been so stingy? See that you get more gold together, or our bargain will come to nothing!'

The Wicked One went off again. This time he stayed away longer, and when at length he appeared he was panting under the weight of a sack which lay on his shoulders. He emptied it into the boot, which was just as far from being filled as before. He became furious, and was just going to tear the boot out of the soldier's hands, but at that moment the first ray of the rising sun broke forth from the sky, and the Evil Spirit fled away with loud shrieks. The poor soul was saved.

The peasant wished to divide the gold, but the soldier said, 'Give what falls to my lot to the poor. I will come with thee to thy cottage, and together we will live in rest and peace on what remains, as long as God is pleased to permit.'

THE MASTER-THIEF

One day an old man and his wife were sitting in front of a miserable house resting a while from their work. Suddenly a splendid carriage with four black horses came driving up, and a richly-dressed man descended from it. The peasant stood up, went to the great man, and asked what he wanted, and in what way he could be useful to him. The stranger stretched out his hand to the old man, and said, 'I want nothing but to enjoy for once a country dish; cook me some potatoes in the way you always have them, and then I will sit down at your table and eat them with pleasure.'

The peasant smiled and said, 'You are a count or a prince, or perhaps even a duke; noble gentlemen often have such fancies, but you shall have your wish.'

The wife went into the kitchen and began to wash and rub the potatoes, and to make them into balls, as they are eaten by the country-folks. Whilst she was busy with this work, the peasant said to the stranger, 'Come into my garden with me for a while; I have still something to do there.' He had dug some holes in the garden and now wanted to plant some trees in them.

'Have you no children,' asked the stranger, 'who could help you with your work?'

'No,' answered the peasant, 'I had a son, it is true, but it is long since he went out into the world. He was a ne'er-do-well, sharp and knowing, but he would learn nothing and was full of bad tricks. At last he ran away from me, and since then I have heard nothing of him.'

The old man took a young tree, put it in a hole, drove in a post beside it, and when he had shovelled in some earth and had trampled it firmly down, he tied the stem of the tree above, below, and in the middle, fast to the post by a rope of straw.

'But tell me,' said the stranger, 'why don't you tie that crooked knotted tree, which is lying in the corner there bent down almost to the ground, to a post also that it may grow straight as well as these?'

The old man smiled and said, 'Sir, you speak according to your knowledge; it is easy to see that you are not familiar with gardening. That tree there is old and mis-shapen; no one can make it straight now. Trees must be trained while they are young.'

'That is how it was with your son,' said the stranger; 'if you had trained him while he was still young, he would not have run away. Now he, too, must have grown hard and mis-shapen.'

'Truly it is a long time since he went away,' replied the old man, 'he must have changed.'

'Would you know him again if he were to come to you?' asked the stranger.

'Hardly by his face,' replied the peasant, 'but he has a mark about him, a birthmark on his shoulder, that looks like a bean.'

When he said that the stranger pulled off his coat, bared his shoulder, and showed the peasant the bean.

'Good God!' cried the old man, 'thou art really my son!' and love for his child stirred in his heart. 'But,' he added, 'how canst thou be my son, thou hast become a great lord and livest in wealth and luxury? How hast thou contrived to do that?'

'Ah, father,' answered the son, 'the young tree was bound to no post and has grown crooked; now it is too old—it will never be straight again. How have I got all that? I have become a thief; but do not be alarmed, I am a master-thief. For me there are neither locks nor bolts; whatsoever I desire is mine. Do not imagine that I steal like a common thief; I only take some of the superfluity of the rich. Poor people are safe—I would rather give to them than take anything from them. It is the same with anything which I can have without trouble, cunning and dexterity—I never touch it.'

'Alas, my son,' said the father, 'it still does not please me. A thief is still a thief; I tell thee it will end badly.'

He took him to his mother, and when she heard that this was her son, she wept for joy, but when he told her that he had become a master-thief, two streams flowed down over her face. At length she said, 'Even if he has become a thief, he is still my son, and my eyes have beheld him once more.'

They sat down to table, and once again he ate with his parents the wretched food which he had not eaten for so long.

The father said, 'If our lord, the count up there in the castle, learns who thou art and what trade thou followest, he will not take thee in his arms and cradle thee in them as he did when he held thee at the font, but will cause thee to swing from a halter.'

'Be easy, father, he will do me no harm, for I understand my trade. I will go to him myself this very day.'

When evening drew near, the master-thief seated himself in his carriage and drove to the castle. The count received him civilly, for he took him for a distinguished man. When, however, the stranger made himself known, the count turned pale and was quite silent for some time. At length he said, 'You are my godson, and on that account mercy shall take the place of justice, and I will deal leniently with you. Since you pride yourself on being a master-thief, I will put your art to the proof, but if you do not stand the test, you must marry the ropemaker's daughter, and the croaking of the raven must be your music on the occasion.'

'Lord Count,' answered the master-thief, 'think of three things, as difficult as you like, and if I do not perform your tasks, do with me what you will.'

The count reflected for some minutes, and then said, 'Well, then, in the first place, you shall steal the horse I keep for my own riding out of the stable; in the next, you shall steal the sheet from beneath the bodies of my wife and myself when we are asleep, without our observing it, and the wedding-ring of my wife as well; thirdly and lastly, you shall steal away out of the church the parson and clerk. Mark what I am saying, for your life depends on it.'

The master-thief went to the nearest town; there he bought the clothes of an old peasant-woman, and put them on. Then he stained his face brown and painted wrinkles on it as well, so that no one could have recognised him. Then he filled a small cask with old Hungary wine in which was mixed a powerful sleeping-drink. He put the cask in a basket, which he took on his back, and walked with slow and tottering steps to the count's castle.

It was already dark when he arrived. He sat down on a stone in the courtyard and began to cough like an asthmatic old woman, and to rub his hands as if he were cold. In front of the door of the stable some soldiers were lying round a fire; one of them observed the woman, and called out to her, 'Come nearer, old mother, and warm yourself beside us. After all, you have no bed for the night, and must take one where you can find it.'

The old woman tottered up to them, begged them to lift the basket from her back, and sat down beside them at the fire.

'What have you got in your cask, old lady?' asked one.

'A good mouthful of wine,' she answered. 'I live by trade; for money and fair words I am quite ready to let you have a glass.'

'Let us have it here, then,' said the soldier, and when he had tasted one glass, he said, 'When wine is good, I like another glass,' and had another poured out for himself, and the rest followed his example.

'Hallo, comrades,' cried one of them to those who were in the stable, 'here is an old goody who has wine that is as old as herself; take a draught, it will warm your stomachs far better than our fire.'

The old woman carried her cask into the stable. One of the soldiers had seated himself on the saddled riding-horse, another held its bridle in his hand, and a third had laid hold of its tail. She poured out as much as they wanted until the spring ran dry. It was not long before the bridle fell from the hand of the one, and he fell down and began to snore; the other left hold of the tail, lay down, and snored still louder. The one who was sitting in the saddle did remain sitting, but bent his head almost down to the horse's neck, and slept, and blew with his mouth like the bellows of a forge. The soldiers outside had already been asleep for a long time, and were lying on the ground motionless, as if dead.

When the master-thief saw that he had succeeded, he gave the first a rope in his hand instead of the bridle, and the other who had been holding the tail, a wisp of straw, but what was he to do with the one who was sitting on the horse's back? He did not want to throw him down, for he might have awakened and have uttered a cry. He had a good idea; he unbuckled the girths of the saddle, tied a couple of ropes which were hanging to a ring on the wall fast to the saddle, and drew the sleeping rider up into the air on it. Then he twisted the rope round the posts, and made it fast. He soon unloosed the horse from the chain, but if he had ridden over the stony pavement of the yard they would have heard the noise in the castle. So he wrapped the horse's hoofs in old rags, led him carefully out, leapt upon him, and galloped off.

When day broke, the master galloped to the castle on the stolen horse. The count had just got up, and was looking out of the window. 'Good morning, Sir Count,' he cried to him, 'here is the horse, which I have got safely out of the stable! Just look, how beautifully your soldiers are lying there sleeping; and if you will but

go into the stable, you will see how comfortable your watchers have made it for themselves.'

The count could not help laughing; then he said, 'For once you have succeeded, but things won't go so well the second time, and I warn you that if you come before me as a thief, I will handle you as I would a thief.'

When the countess went to bed that night, she closed her hand with the wedding-ring tightly together, and the count said, 'All the doors are locked and bolted; I will keep awake and wait for the thief, but if he gets in by the window, I will shoot him.'

The master-thief, however, went in the dark to the gallows, cut a poor sinner who was hanging there down from the halter, and carried him on his back to the castle. Then he set a ladder up to the bedroom, put the dead body on his shoulders, and began to climb up. When he had got so high that the head of the dead man showed at the window, the count, who was watching in his bed, fired a pistol at him, and immediately the master let the poor sinner fall down and hid himself in one corner.

The night was sufficiently lighted by the moon for the master to see distinctly how the count got out of the window on to the ladder, came down, carried the dead body into the garden, and began to dig a hole in which to lay it. 'Now,' thought the thief, 'the favourable moment has come,' and he stole nimbly out of his corner, and climbed up the ladder straight into the countess's bedroom.

'Dear wife,' he began in the count's voice, 'the thief is dead, but, after all, he is my godson, and has been more of a scapegrace than a villain. I will not put him to open shame; besides, I am sorry for the parents. I will bury him myself before daybreak in the garden, that the thing may not be known, so give me the sheet. I will wrap up the body in it, and bury him as a dog buries things by scratching.' The countess gave him the sheet.

'I tell you what,' continued the thief, 'I have a fit of magnanimity on me; give me the ring, too—the unhappy man risked his life for it, so he may take it with him into his grave.' She would not gainsay the count, and although she did it unwillingly she drew the ring from her finger and gave it to him.

The thief made off with both these things and reached home safely before the count in the garden had finished his work of burying.

What a long face the count did pull when the master came next morning, and brought him the sheet and the ring. 'Are you a wizard?' said he. 'Who has fetched you out of the grave in which I myself laid you, and brought you to life again?'

'You did not bury me,' said the thief, 'but the poor sinner on the gallows,' and he told him exactly how everything had happened. And the count was forced to own to him that he was a clever, crafty thief.

'But you have not reached the end yet,' he added, 'you have still to perform the third task, and if you do not succeed in that, all this is of no use.' The master smiled and returned no answer.

When night had fallen he went with a long sack on his back, a bundle under his arms, and a lantern in his hand, to the village church. In the sack he had some crabs, and in the bundle, short wax candles. He sat down in the churchyard, took out a crab, and stuck a wax candle on his back. Then he lighted the little light, put the crab on the ground, and let it creep about. He took a second out of the sack, and treated it in the same way, and so on until the last was out of the sack. Hereupon he put on a long black garment that looked like a monk's cowl, and stuck a grey beard on his chin. When at last he was quite unrecognisable, he took the sack in which the crabs had been, went into the church, and ascended the pulpit.

The clock in the tower was just striking twelve; when the last stroke had sounded, he cried with a loud and piercing voice, 'Hearken, sinful men, the end of all things has come! The last day is at hand! Hearken! Hearken! Whosoever wishes to go to heaven with me must creep into the sack. I am Peter, who opens and shuts the gates of heaven. Behold how the dead outside there in the churchyard are wandering about collecting their bones. Come, come, and creep into the sack; the world is about to be destroyed!'

The cry echoed through the whole village. The parson and the clerk, who lived nearest to the church, heard it first, and when they saw the lights which were moving about the churchyard, they observed that something unusual was going on, and went into the church. They listened to the sermon for a while, and then the clerk nudged the parson, and said, 'It would not be amiss if we were to use the opportunity together, and before the dawning of the last day, find an easy way of getting to heaven.'

'To tell the truth,' answered the parson, 'that is what I myself have been thinking, so if you are inclined, we will set out on our way.'

'Yes,' answered the clerk, 'but you, the parson, have the precedence; I will follow.'

So the parson went first, and ascended the pulpit where the master opened his sack. The parson crept in first, and then the clerk. The master immediately tied up the sack tightly, seized it by the middle, and dragged it down the pulpit-steps, and whenever the heads of the two fools bumped against the steps, he cried, 'We are going over the mountains.' Then he drew them through the village in the same way, and when they were passing through puddles, he cried, 'Now we are going through wet clouds,' and when at last he was dragging them up the steps of the castle, he cried, 'Now we are on the steps of heaven, and will soon be in the outer court.' When he had got to the top, he pushed the sack into the pigeon-house, and when the pigeons fluttered about, he said, 'Hark how glad the angels are, and how they are flapping their wings!' Then he bolted the door upon them and went away.

60

Next morning he went to the count, and told him that he had performed the third task also, and had carried the parson and clerk out of the church.

'Where have you left them?' asked the lord.

'They are lying upstairs in a sack in the pigeon-house, and imagine that they are in heaven.'

The count went up himself, and convinced himself that the master had told the truth. When he had delivered the parson and clerk from their captivity, he said, 'You are an arch-thief, and have won your wager. For once you escape with a whole skin, but see that you leave my land, for if ever you set foot on it again, you may count on your elevation to the gallows.'

The arch-thief took leave of his parents, once more went forth into the wide world, and no one has ever heard of him since.

THE NIX OF THE MILL-POND

There was once upon a time a miller who lived with his wife in great contentment. They had money and land, and their prosperity increased year by year more and more. But ill-luck comes like a thief in the night; as their wealth had increased, so did it again decrease, year by year, and at last the miller could hardly call the mill in which he lived his own. He was in great distress, and when he lay down after his day's work, found no rest, but tossed about in his bed, full of care.

One morning he rose before daybreak and went out into the open air, thinking that perhaps there his heart might become lighter. As he was stepping over the mill-dam the first sunbeam was just breaking forth, and he heard a rippling sound in the pond. He turned round and perceived a beautiful woman rising slowly out of the water. Her long hair, which she was holding off her shoulders with her soft hands, fell down on both sides and covered her white body. He soon saw that she was the nix of the mill-pond, and in his fright did not know whether he should run away or stay where he was. But the nix made her sweet voice heard, called him by his name, and asked him why he was so sad? The miller was at first struck dumb, but when he heard her speak so kindly he took heart and told her how he had formerly lived in wealth and happiness, but that now he was so poor that he did not know what to do.

'Be easy,' answered the nix, 'I will make you richer and happier than you have ever been before, only you must promise to give me the young thing which has just been born in your house.'

'What else can that be,' thought the miller, 'but a young puppy or kitten?' and he promised what she desired.

The nix descended into the water again, and he hurried back to his mill, consoled and in good spirits. He had not yet reached it, when the maid-servant came out of the house and cried to him to rejoice, for his wife had given birth to a little boy. The miller stood as if struck by lightning; he saw very well that the cunning nix had been aware of it and had cheated him. Hanging his head, he went up to his wife's bedside, and when she said, 'Why do you not rejoice over the fine boy?' he told her what had befallen him, and what kind of a promise he had given to the nix.

'Of what use to me are riches and prosperity?' he added, 'if I am to lose my child; but what can I do?'

Even the relations, who had come thither to wish them joy, did not know what to say.

In the meantime, prosperity again returned to the miller's house. All that he

undertook succeeded; it was as if presses and coffers filled themselves of their own accord, and as if money multiplied nightly in the cupboards. It was not long before his wealth was greater than it had ever been before. But he could not rejoice over it untroubled; the bargain which he had made with the nix tormented his soul. Whenever he passed the mill-pond, he feared she might ascend and remind him of his debt. He never let the boy himself go near the water. 'Beware,' he said to him, 'if thou dost but touch the water, a hand will rise, seize thee, and draw thee down.'

But as year after year went by and the nix did not show herself again, the miller began to feel at ease. The boy grew up to be a youth and was apprenticed to a huntsman. When he had learnt everything, and had become an excellent huntsman, the lord of the village took him into his service. In the village lived a beautiful and true-hearted maiden, who pleased the huntsman, and when his master perceived that, he gave him a little house; the two were married, lived peacefully and happily, and loved each other with all their hearts.

One day the huntsman was chasing a roe; and when the animal turned aside from the forest into the open country, he pursued it and at last shot it. He did not notice that he was now in the neighbourhood of the dangerous mill-pond, and went, after he had disembowelled the roe, to the water, in order to wash his blood-stained hands. Scarcely, however, had he dipped them in than the nix ascended, smilingly wound her dripping arms around him, and drew him quickly down under the waves, which closed over him.

When it was evening and the huntsman did not return home, his wife became alarmed. She went out to seek him, and as he had often told her that he had to be on his guard against the snares of the nix and dared not venture into the neighbourhood of the mill-pond, she already suspected what had happened. She hastened to the water, and when she found his hunting-pouch lying on the shore, she could no longer have any doubt of the misfortune. Lamenting her sorrow and wringing her hands, she called on her beloved by name, but in vain. She hurried across to the other side of the pond and called him anew; she reviled the nix with harsh words, but no answer followed. The surface of the water remained calm; only the crescent moon stared steadily back at her. The poor woman did not leave the pond. With hasty steps she paced round and round it, without resting a moment, sometimes in silence, sometimes uttering a loud cry, sometimes softly sobbing.

At last her strength came to an end, and she sank down to the ground and fell into a heavy sleep. Presently a dream took possession of her. She was anxiously climbing upwards between great masses of rock; thorns and briars caught her feet, the rain beat in her face, and the wind tossed her long hair about. When she reached the summit, quite a different sight presented itself to her; the sky was blue, the air soft, and the ground sloped gently downwards, and on a green meadow, gay with flowers of every colour, stood a pretty cottage. She went up to it and opened the door; there sat an old woman with white hair, who beckoned to her kindly.

At that very moment the poor woman awoke. Day had already dawned, and she at once resolved to act in accordance with her dream. She laboriously climbed the mountain; everything was exactly as she had seen it in the night. The old woman received her kindly, and pointed out a chair on which she might sit. 'You must have met with a misfortune,' she said, 'since you have sought out my lonely cottage.'

With tears, the woman related what had befallen her.

'Be comforted,' said the old woman, 'I will help you. Here is a golden comb for you. Tarry till the full moon has risen, then go to the mill-pond, seat yourself on the shore, and comb your long black hair with this comb. When you have done, lay it down on the bank, and you will see what will happen.'

The woman returned home, but the time till the full moon came passed slowly. At last the shining disc appeared in the heavens. Then she went out to the mill-pond, sat down and combed her long black hair with the golden comb, and when she had finished, she laid the comb down at the water's edge. It was not long before there was a movement in the depths; a wave rose, rolled to the shore, and bore the comb away with it. In not more than the time necessary for the comb to sink to the bottom, the surface of the water parted and the head of the huntsman arose. He did not speak, but looked at his wife with sorrowful glances. At the same instant, a second wave came rushing up and covered the man's head. All had vanished; the mill-pond lay peaceful as before, and nothing but the face of the full moon shone on it.

Full of sorrow, the woman went back, but again the dream showed her the cottage of the old woman. Next morning she again set out and complained of her woes to the wise woman. The old woman gave her a golden flute, and said, 'Tarry till the full moon comes again, then take this flute; play a beautiful air on it, and when you have finished, lay it on the sand; then you will see what will happen.'

The wife did as the old woman told her. No sooner was the flute lying on the sand than there was a stirring in the depths, and a wave rushed up and bore the flute away with it. Immediately afterwards, the water parted, and not only the head of the man, but half of his body also arose. He stretched out his arms longingly towards her, but a second wave came up, covered him, and drew him down again. 'Alas, what does it profit me?' said the unhappy woman, 'that I should see my beloved, only to lose him again!'

Despair filled her heart anew, but the dream led her a third time to the house of the old woman. She set out, and the wise woman gave her a golden spinning-wheel, consoled her and said, 'All is not yet fulfilled; tarry until the time of the full moon, then take the spinning wheel, seat yourself on the shore, and spin the spool full, and when you have done that, place the spinning-wheel near the water, and you will see what will happen.'

The woman obeyed all she said exactly. As soon as the full moon showed itself, she carried the spinning-wheel to the shore, and spun industriously until the flax came to an end and the spool was quite filled with the threads. No sooner was the wheel standing on the shore than there was a more violent movement than before in the depths of the pond, and a mighty wave rushed up and bore the wheel away with it. Immediately the head and the whole body of the man rose into the air, in a water-spout. He quickly sprang to the shore, caught his wife by the hand and fled. But they had scarcely gone a very little distance, when the whole pond rose with a frightful roar and streamed out over the open country. The fugitives already saw death before their eyes, when the woman in her terror implored the help of the old woman, and in an instant they were transformed, she into a toad, he into a frog.

The flood which had overtaken them could not destroy them, but it tore them apart and carried them far away. When the water had dispersed and they both touched dry land again, they regained their human form, but neither knew where the other was; they found themselves among strange people, who did not know their native land. High mountains and deep valleys lay between them. In order to keep themselves alive, they were both obliged to tend sheep.

For many long years they drove their flocks through field and forest and were full of sorrow and longing. When spring had once more broken forth on the earth, they both went out one day with their flocks, and as chance would have it, they drew near each other. They met in a valley but did not recognise each other; yet they rejoiced that they were no longer so lonely. Henceforth they each day drove their flocks to the same place; they did not speak much, but they felt comforted.

One evening when the full moon was shining in the sky and the sheep were already at rest, the shepherd pulled the flute out of his pocket and played on it a beautiful but sorrowful air. When he had finished he saw that the shepherdess was weeping bitterly. 'Why are you weeping?' he asked.

'Alas,' answered she, 'thus shone the full moon when I played this air on the flute for the last time, and the head of my beloved rose out of the water.'

He looked at her, and it seemed as if a veil fell from his eyes and he recognised his dear wife, and when she looked at him, and the moon shone in his face, she knew him also. They embraced and kissed each other, and no one need ask if they were happy.

IRON HANS

There was once a King whose castle was surrounded by a forest full of game. One day he sent a huntsman out to shoot a deer, but he never came back.

'Perhaps an accident has happened to him,' said the King.

Next day he sent out two more huntsmen to look for him, but they did not return either.

On the third day he sent for all his huntsmen, and said to them, 'Search the whole forest without ceasing, until you have found all three.'

But not a single man of all these, or one of the pack of hounds they took with them, ever came back. From this time forth no one would venture into the forest; so there it lay, wrapped in silence and solitude, with only an occasional eagle or hawk circling over it.

This continued for several years, and then one day a strange huntsman sought an audience of the King, and offered to penetrate into the dangerous wood. The King, however, would not give him permission, and said, 'It's not safe, and I am afraid if you go in that you will never come out again, any more than all the others.'

The huntsman answered, 'Sire, I will take the risk upon myself. I do not know fear.'

So the huntsman went into the wood with his dog. Before long the dog put up some game and wanted to chase it; but hardly had he taken a few steps when he came to a deep pool, and could go no further. A naked arm appeared out of the water, seized him, and drew him down.

When the huntsman saw this, he went back and fetched three men with pails to empty the pool. When they got to the bottom they found a wild man, whose body was as brown as rusty iron, and whose hair hung down over his face to his knees. They bound him with cords, and carried him away to the castle. There was great excitement over the wild man, and the King had an iron cage made for him in the courtyard. He forbade anyone to open the door of the cage on pain of death, and the Queen had to keep the key in her own charge.

After this, anybody could walk in the forest with safety.

The King had a little son eight years old, and one day he was playing in the courtyard. In his play his golden ball fell into the cage. The boy ran up, and said, 'Give me back my ball.'

'Not until you have opened the door,' said the wild man.

'No; I can't do that,' said the boy, 'my father has forbidden it,' and then he ran away.

Next day he came again, and asked for his ball. The man said, 'Open my door,' but he would not.

On the third day the King went out hunting, and the boy came again, and said, 'Even if I would, I could not open the door. I have not got the key.'

Then the wild man said, 'It is lying under your mother's pillow. You can easily get it.'

The boy, who was very anxious to have his ball back, threw his scruples to the winds, and fetched the key. The door was very stiff, and he pinched his fingers in opening it. As soon as it was open the wild man came out, gave the boy his ball, and hurried away. The boy was now very frightened, and cried out, 'Oh, wild man, don't go away, or I shall be beaten!'

The wild man turned back, picked up the boy, put him on his shoulder, and walked hurriedly off into the wood.

When the King came home he saw at once the cage was empty, and asked the Queen how it had come about. She knew nothing about it, and went to look for the key, which was of course gone. They called the boy, but there was no answer. The King sent people out into the fields to look for him, but all in vain; he was gone. The King easily guessed what had happened, and great grief fell on the royal household.

When the wild man got back into the depths of the dark forest he took the boy down off his shoulder and said, 'You will never see your father and mother again; but I will keep you here with me, because you had pity on me and set me free. If you do as you are told, you will be well treated. I have treasures and gold enough and to spare, more than anybody in the world.'

He made a bed of moss for the boy, on which he went to sleep. Next morning the man led him to a spring and said, 'You see this golden well is bright and clear as crystal? You must sit by it, and take care that nothing falls into it, or it will be contaminated. I shall come every evening to see if you have obeyed my orders.'

The boy sat down on the edge of the spring to watch it; sometimes he would see a gold fish or a golden snake darting through it, and he guarded it well, so that nothing should fall into it. One day as he was sitting like this his finger pained him so much that involuntarily he dipped it into the water. He drew it out very quickly, but saw that it was gilded, and although he tried hard to clean it, it remained golden. In the evening Iron Hans came back, looked at the boy, and said, 'What has happened to the well today?'

'Nothing, nothing!' he answered, keeping his finger behind his back so that Iron Hans should not see it.

But he said, 'You have dipped your finger into the water. It does not matter this time, but take care that nothing of the kind occurs again.'

Early next morning the boy took his seat by the spring again to watch. His

71

finger still hurt very much, and he put his hand up above his head; but, unfortunately, in so doing he brushed a hair into the well. He quickly took it out, but it was already gilded. When Iron Hans came in the evening, he knew very well what had happened.

'You have let a hair fall into the well,' he said. 'I will overlook it once more, but if it happens for the third time the well will be polluted, and you can no longer stay with me.'

On the third day the boy again sat by the well; but he took good care not to move a finger, however much it might hurt. The time seemed very long to him as he looked at his face reflected in the water. As he bent over further and further to look into his eyes, his long hair fell over his shoulder right into the water. He started up at once, but not before his whole head of hair had become golden, and glittered like the sun. You may imagine how frightened the poor boy was. He took his pocket-handkerchief and tied it over his head, so that Iron Hans should not see it. But he knew all about it before he came, and at once said, 'Take that handkerchief off your head,' and then all the golden hair tumbled out. All the poor boy's excuses were no good. 'You have not stood the test, and you can no longer stay here. You must go out into the world, and there you will learn the meaning of poverty. But as your heart is not bad, and as I wish you well, I will grant you one thing. When you are in great need, go to the forest and cry "Iron Hans", and I will come and help you. My power is great, greater than you think, and I have gold and silver in abundance.'

So the King's son left the forest, and wandered over trodden and untrodden paths till he reached a great city. He tried to get work, but he could not find any; besides, he knew no trade by which to make a living. At last he went to the castle and asked if they would employ him. The courtiers did not know what use they could make of him, but they were taken with his appearance, and said he might stay. At last the cook took him into his service, and said he might carry wood and water for him and sweep up the ashes.

One day, as there was no one else at hand, the cook ordered him to carry the food up to the royal table. As he did not want his golden hair to be seen, he kept his cap on. Nothing of the sort had ever happened in the presence of the King before, and he said, 'When you come into the royal presence, you must take your cap off.'

'Alas, Sire,' he said, 'I cannot take it off, because I have a bad wound on my head.'

Then the King ordered the cook to be called, and asked how he could take such a boy into his service, and ordered him to be sent away at once. But the cook was sorry for him, and exchanged him with the gardener's boy.

Now the boy had to dig and hoe, plant and water, in every kind of weather.

One day in the summer when he was working alone in the garden it was very hot, and he took off his cap for the fresh air to cool his head. When the sun shone on his hair it glittered so that the beams penetrated right into the Princess's bedroom, and she sprang up to see what it was. She discovered the youth, and called to him, 'Bring me a nosegay, young man.'

He hurriedly put on his cap, picked a lot of wild flowers, and tied them up. On his way up to the Princess, the gardener met him, and said, 'How can you take such poor flowers to the Princess? Quickly cut another bouquet, and mind they are the choicest and rarest flowers.'

'Oh, no,' said the youth. 'The wild flowers have a sweeter scent, and will please her better.'

As soon as he went into the room the Princess said, 'Take off your cap; it is not proper for you to wear it before me.'

He answered again, 'I may not take it off, because I have a wound on my head.'

But she took hold of the cap, and pulled it off, and all his golden hair tumbled over his shoulders in a shower. It was quite a sight. He tried to get away, but she took hold of his arm and gave him a handful of ducats. He took them, but he cared nothing for the gold and gave it to the gardener for his children to play with.

Next day the Princess again called him to bring her a bunch of wild flowers, and when he brought it she immediately clutched at his cap to pull it off; but he held it on with both hands. Again she gave him a handful of ducats, but he would not keep them, and gave them to the gardener's children. The third day the same thing happened, but she could not take off his cap, and he would not keep the gold.

Not long after this the kingdom was invaded. The King assembled his warriors. He did not know whether they would be able to conquer his enemies or not, as they were very powerful and had a mighty army. Then the gardener's assistant said, 'I have been brought up to fight; give me a horse, and I will go too.'

The others laughed and said, 'When we are gone, find one for yourself. We will leave one behind in the stable for you.'

When they were gone, he went and got the horse out; it was lame in one leg, and hobbled along, humpety-hump, humpety-hump. Nevertheless, he mounted it and rode away to the dark forest. When he came to the edge of it, he called three times, 'Iron Hans' as loud as he could, till the trees resounded with it.

The wild man appeared immediately, and said, 'What do you want?'

'I want a strong horse to go to the war.'

'You shall have it, and more besides.'

The wild man went back into the wood, and before long a groom came out, leading a fiery charger with snorting nostrils. Behind him followed a great body of warriors all in armour, and their swords gleaming in the sun. The youth handed over his three-legged steed to the groom, mounted the other, and rode away at the head of the troop.

When he approached the battle-field a great many of the King's men had already fallen, and before long the rest must have given in. Then the youth, at the head of his iron troop, charged, and bore down the enemy like a mighty wind, smiting everything in the way. They tried to fly, but the youth fell upon them, and did not stop while one remained alive.

Instead of joining the King, he led his troop straight back to the wood and called Iron Hans again.

'What do you want?' asked the wild man.

'Take back your charger and your troop, and give me back my three-legged steed.'

His request was granted, and he rode his three-legged steed home.

When the King returned to the castle his daughter met him and congratulated him on his victory.

'It was not I who won it,' he said; 'but a strange knight, who came to my assistance with his troop.' His daughter asked who the strange knight was, but the King did not know, and said, 'He pursued the enemy, and I have not seen him since.'

She asked the gardener about his assistant, but he laughed and said, 'He has just come home on his three-legged horse, and the others made fun of him and said, "Here comes our hobbler back again," and asked which hedge he had been sleeping under. He answered, "I did my best, and without me things would have gone badly." Then they laughed at him more than ever.'

The King said to his daughter, 'I will give a great feast lasting three days, and you shall throw a golden apple. Perhaps the unknown knight will come among the others to try and catch it.'

When notice was given of the feast, the youth went to the wood and called Iron Hans.

'What do you want?' he asked.

'I want to secure the King's golden apple,' he said.

'It is as good as yours already,' answered Iron Hans. 'You shall have a tawny suit, and ride a proud chestnut.'

When the day arrived the youth took his place among the other knights, but no one knew him. The Princess stepped forward and threw the apple among the knights, and he was the only one who could catch it. As soon as he had it he rode away.

On the second day Iron Hans fitted him out as a white knight, riding a gallant grey. Again he caught the apple; but he did not stay a minute, and, as before, hurried away.

The King now grew angry, and said, 'This must not be; he must come before me and give me his name.'

He gave an order that if the knight made off again he was to be pursued and brought back.

On the third day the youth received from Iron Hans a black outfit, and a fiery black charger.

Again he caught the apple; but as he was riding off with it, the King's people chased him, and one came so near that he wounded him in the leg. Still he escaped, but his horse galloped so fast that his helmet fell off, and they all saw that he had golden hair. So they rode back, and told the King what they had seen.

Next day the Princess asked the gardener about his assistant.

'He is working in the garden. The queer fellow went to the feast, and he only came back last night. He has shown my children three golden apples which he won.'

The King ordered him to be brought before him. When he appeared he still wore his cap. But the Princess went up to him and took it off; then all his golden hair fell over his shoulders, and it was so beautiful that they were all amazed by it.

'Are you the knight who came to the feast every day in a different colour and caught the three golden apples?' asked the King.

'Yes,' he answered, 'and here are the apples,' bringing them out of his pocket, and giving them to the King. 'If you want further proof, here is the wound in my leg given me by your people when they pursued me. But I am also the knight who helped you to conquer the enemy.'

'If you can do such deeds you are no gardener's boy. Tell me who is your father?'

'My father is a powerful King, and I have plenty of gold—as much as I ever want.'

'I see very well,' said the King, 'that we owe you many thanks. Can I do anything to please you?'

'Yes,' he answered; 'indeed, you can. Give me your daughter to be my wife!'

The maiden laughed, and said, 'He does not beat about the bush; but I saw long ago that he was no gardener's boy.'

Then she went up to him and kissed him.

His father and mother came to the wedding, and they were full of joy, for they had long given up all hope of ever seeing their dear son again. As they were all sitting at the wedding feast, the music suddenly stopped, the doors flew open, and a proud King walked in at the head of a great following. He went up to the bridegroom, embraced him, and said, 'I am Iron Hans, who was bewitched and changed into a wild man; but you have broken the spell and set me free. All the treasure that I have is now your own.'

GODFATHER DEATH

A poor man had twelve children and was forced to work night and day to give them even bread. When, therefore, the thirteenth came into the world, he knew not what to do in his trouble, but ran out into the great highway, and resolved to ask the first person he met to be godfather. The first to meet him was the good God who already knew what filled his heart, and said to him, 'Poor man, I pity thee. I will hold thy child at its christening, and will take charge of it and make it happy on earth.'

The man said, 'Who art thou?'

'I am God.'

'Then I do not desire to have thee for a godfather,' said the man; 'thou givest to the rich, and leavest the poor to hunger.' Thus spoke the man, for he did not know how wisely God apportions riches and poverty. He turned, therefore, away from the Lord, and went farther.

Then the Devil came to him, and said, 'What seekest thou? If thou wilt take me as a godfather for thy child, I will give him gold in plenty, and all the joys of the world as well.'

The man asked, 'Who art thou?'

'I am the Devil.'

'Then I do not desire to have thee for godfather,' said the man; 'thou deceivest men and leadest them astray.'

He went onwards, and then came Death striding up to him with withered legs, and said, 'Take me as godfather.'

The man asked, 'Who art thou?'

'I am Death, and I make all equal.'

Then said the man, 'Thou art the right one, thou takest the rich as well as the poor, without distinction; thou shalt be godfather.'

Death answered, 'I will make thy child rich and famous, for he who has me for a friend can lack nothing.'

The man said, 'Next Sunday is the christening; be there at the right time.'

Death appeared as he had promised, and stood godfather quite in the usual way.

When the boy had grown up, his godfather one day appeared and bade him go with him. He led him forth into a forest, and showed him a herb which grew there, and said, 'Now shalt thou receive thy godfather's present. I will make thee a celebrated physician. When thou art called to a patient, I will always appear to thee. If I stand by the head of the sick man, thou mayst say with confidence that thou wilt make him well again, and if thou givest him of this herb he will recover; but if I stand by the patient's feet, he is mine, and thou must say that all remedies are in vain, and that no physician in the world could save him. But beware of using the herb against my will, or it will fare ill with thee.'

It was not long before the youth was the most famous physician in the whole world. 'He had only to look at the patient and he knew his condition at once, and if he would recover, or must needs die.' So they said of him, and from far and wide people came to him, sent for him when they had anyone ill, and gave him so much money that he soon became a rich man.

Now it so befell that the King became ill, and the physician was summoned, and was to say if recovery were possible. But when he came to the bed, Death was standing by the feet of the sick man, and the herb did not grow which could save him. 'If I could but cheat Death for once,' thought the physician; 'he is sure to take it ill if I do, but, as I am his godson, he will shut one eye; I will risk it.' He therefore took up the sick man and laid him the other way, so that now Death was standing by his head. Then he gave the King some of the herb, and he recovered and grew healthy again.

But Death came to the physician, looking very black and angry, threatened him with his finger, and said, 'Thou hast overreached me; this time I will pardon it, as thou art my godson. But if thou venturest it again, it will cost thee thy neck, for I will take thee thyself away with me.'

Soon afterwards the King's daughter fell into a severe illness. She was his only child, and he wept day and night, so that he began to lose the sight of his eyes, and he caused it to be made known that whosoever rescued her from death should be her husband and inherit the crown. When the physician came to the sick girl's bed, he saw Death by her feet. He ought to have remembered the warning given by his godfather, but he was so infatuated by the great beauty of the King's daughter, and the happiness of becoming her husband, that he flung all thought to the winds. He did not see that Death was casting angry glances on him, that he was raising his hand in the air and threatening him with his withered fist. He raised up the sick girl, and placed her head where her feet had lain. Then he gave her some of the herb, and instantly her cheeks flushed red, and life stirred afresh in her.

When Death saw that for a second time he was defrauded of his own property, he walked up to the physician with long strides, and said. 'All is over with thee, and now the lot falls on thee,' and seized him so firmly with his ice-cold hand that he could not resist, and led him into a cave below the earth. There he saw how thousands and thousands of candles were burning in countless rows, some large, others half-sized, others small. Every instant some were extinguished, and others again burnt up, so that the flames seemed to leap hither and thither in perpetual change. 'See,' said Death, 'these are the lights of men's lives. The large ones belong to children, the half-sized ones to married people in their prime, the little ones belong to old folk; but children and young folks likewise have often only a tiny candle.'

'Show me the light of my life,' said the physician, and he thought that it would still be very tall. Death pointed to a little end which was just threatening to go out, and said, 'Behold, it is there.'

'Ah, dear godfather,' said the horrified physician, 'light a new one for me, do it for love of me, that I may enjoy my life, be King, and the husband of the King's beautiful daughter.'

'I cannot,' answered Death, 'one must go out before a new one is lighted.'

'Then place the old one on a new one, that will go on burning at once when the old one has come to an end,' pleaded the physician.

Death behaved as if he were going to fulfil his wish, and took hold of a tall new candle; but as he desired to revenge himself he purposely made a mistake in fixing it, and the little piece fell down and was extinguished. Immediately the physician fell on the ground, and now he himself was in the hands of Death.

There was once a young huntsman who went into the forest to lie in wait. He had a fresh and joyous heart, and as he was going thither, whistling upon a leaf, an ugly old crone came up who spoke to him and said, 'Good-day, dear huntsman, truly you are merry and contented, but I am suffering from hunger and thirst; do give me an alms.'

The huntsman had compassion on the poor old creature, felt in his pocket, and gave her what he could afford. He was then about to go further, but the old woman stopped him and said, 'Listen, dear huntsman, to what I tell you; I will make you a present in return for your kindness. Go on your way now, but in a little while you will come to a tree whereon nine birds are sitting which have a cloak in their claws, and are plucking at it. Take your gun and shoot into the midst of them; they will let the cloak fall down to you, but one of the birds will be hurt and will drop down dead. Carry away the cloak. It is a wishing-cloak; when you throw it over your shoulders you only have to wish to be in a certain place and you will be there in the twinkling of an eye. Take out the heart of the dead bird and swallow it whole, and every morning early, when you get up, you will find a gold piece under your pillow.'

The huntsman thanked the wise woman, and thought to himself, 'Those are fine things that she has promised me, if all does but come true.' And verily, when he had walked about a hundred paces, he heard in the branches above him such a screaming and twittering that he looked up and saw there a crowd of birds who were tearing a piece of cloth about with their beaks and claws, and tugging and fighting as if each wanted to have it all to himself. 'Well,' said the huntsman, 'this is wonderful; it has really come to pass just as the old wife foretold!' and he took the gun from his shoulder, aimed, and fired right into the midst of them, so that the feathers flew about. The birds instantly took to flight with loud outcries, but one dropped down dead, and the cloak fell at the same time. Then the huntsman did as the old woman had directed, cut open the bird, sought the heart, swallowed it down, and took the cloak home with him.

Next morning when he awoke the promise occurred to him, and he wished to see if it also had been fulfilled. When he lifted up the pillow, the gold piece shone in his eyes, and next day he found another, and so it went on, every time he got up. He gathered together a heap of gold, but at last he thought, 'Of what use is all my gold to me if I stay at home? I will go forth and see the world.'

He then took leave of his parents, buckled on his huntsman's pouch and gun, and went out into the world.

It came to pass that one day he travelled through a dense forest, and when he came to the end of it, in the plain before him stood a fine castle. An old woman was standing with a wonderfully beautiful maiden, looking out of one of the windows.

The old woman, however, was a witch, and said to the maiden, 'There comes one out of the forest who has a wonderful treasure in his body; we must filch it from him, my dear daughter, it is more suitable for us than for him. He has a bird's heart about him, by means of which a gold piece lies every morning under his pillow.' She told her what she was to do to get it, and what part she had to play, and finally threatened her and said with angry eyes, 'And if you do not attend to what I say, it will be the worse for you.'

Now when the huntsman came nearer he descried the maiden, and said to himself, 'I have travelled about for such a long time, I will take a rest for once, and enter that beautiful castle. I have certainly money enough.' Nevertheless, the real reason was that he had caught sight of the beautiful girl.

He entered the house, and was well received and courteously entertained. Before long he was so much in love with the young witch that he no longer thought of anything else, and only saw things as she saw them, and did what she desired.

The old woman then said, 'Now we must have the bird's heart; he will never miss it.' She prepared a drink, and when it was ready poured it into a cup and gave it to the maiden, who was to present it to the huntsman. She did so, saying, 'Now, my dearest, drink to me.'

So he took the cup, and when he had swallowed the draught, he brought up the heart of the bird. The girl had to take it away secretly and swallow it herself, for the old woman would have it so. Thenceforward, he found no more gold under his pillow, but it lay instead under that of the maiden, from whence the old woman fetched it away every morning; but he was so much in love and so befooled, that he thought of nothing else but of passing his time with the girl.

Then the old witch said, 'We have the bird's heart, but we must also take the wishing-cloak away from him.'

The girl answered, 'We will leave him that; he has lost his wealth.'

The old woman was angry and said, 'Such a mantle is a wonderful thing, and is seldom to be found in this world. I must and will have it!' She gave the girl several blows, and said that if she did not obey it should fare ill with her. So she did the old woman's bidding, placed herself at the window and looked on the distant country, as if she were very sorrowful.

The huntsman asked, 'Why dost thou stand there so sorrowfully?'

'Ah, my beloved,' was her answer, 'over yonder lies the Garnet Mountain, where the precious stones grow. I long for them so much that when I think of them I feel quite sad, but who can get them? Only the birds; they fly and can reach them, but a man, never.'

'Hast thou nothing else to complain of?' said the huntsman. 'I will soon remove that burden from thy heart. '

With that, he drew her under his mantle, wished himself on the Garnet Mountain, and in the twinkling of an eye they were sitting on it together. Precious stones were glistening on every side, so that it was a joy to see them, and together they gathered the finest and costliest of them. Now the old woman had, through her sorceries, contrived that the eyes of the huntsman should become heavy. He said to the maiden, 'We will sit down and rest awhile; I am so tired that I can no longer stand on my feet.' Then they sat down, and he laid his head in her lap and fell asleep. When he was asleep, she unfastened the mantle from his shoulders and wrapped herself in it, picked up the garnets and stones, and wished herself back at home with them.

But when the huntsman had had his sleep out and awoke, and perceived that his sweetheart had betrayed him and left him alone on the wild mountain, he said, 'Oh, what treachery there is in the world!' and sat down there in care and sorrow, not knowing what to do. But the mountain belonged to some wild and monstrous giants who dwelt thereon and lived their lives there, and he had not sat long before he saw three of them coming towards him, so he lay down as if he were sunk in a deep sleep.

Then the giants came up, and the first kicked him with his foot and said, 'What sort of an earth-worm is lying curled up here?'

The second said, 'Step upon him and kill him.'

But the third said, 'That would indeed be worth your while. Just let him live, he cannot remain here; and when he climbs higher, towards the summit of the mountain, the clouds will lay hold of him and bear him away.'

So saying, they passed by.

But the huntsman had paid heed to their words, and as soon as they were gone, he rose and climbed up to the summit of the mountain, and when he had sat there a while a cloud floated towards him, caught him up, carried him away, and travelled about for a long time in the heavens. Then it sank lower, and let itself down on a great cabbage-garden, girt round by walls, so that he came softly to the ground on cabbages and vegetables.

Then the huntsman looked about him and said, 'If I had but something to eat! I am so hungry, and my hunger will increase in course of time; but I see here neither apples nor pears, nor any other sort of fruit—everywhere nothing but cabbages.' But at length he thought, 'At a pinch I can eat some of the leaves; they do not taste particularly good, but they will refresh me.' With that, he picked himself out a fine head of cabbage and ate it, but scarcely had he swallowed a couple of mouthfuls than he felt very strange and quite different.

Four legs grew on him, a large head and two thick ears, and he saw with horror that he was changed into an ass. Still, as his hunger increased every minute, and as the juicy leaves were suitable to his present nature, he went on eating with great zest. At last he arrived at a different kind of cabbage, but as soon as he had swallowed it he again felt a change, and reassumed his former shape.

Then the huntsman lay down and slept off his fatigue. When he awoke next morning, he broke off one head of the bad cabbages and another of the good ones, and thought to himself, 'This shall help me to get my own again and punish treachery.' Then he took the cabbages with him, climbed over the wall, and went forth to seek for the castle of his sweetheart. After wandering about for a couple of days he was lucky enough to find it again. He dyed his face brown, so that his own mother would not have known him, and begged for shelter: 'I am so tired,' said he, 'that I can go no further.'

The witch asked, 'Who are you, countryman, and what is your business?'

'I am a King's messenger, and was sent out to seek the most delicious salad that grows beneath the sun. I have even been so fortunate as to find it, and am carrying it about with me; but the heat of the sun is so intense that the delicate cabbage threatens to wither, and I do not know if I can carry it any further.'

When the old woman heard of the exquisite salad, she was greedy, and said, 'Dear countryman, let me just taste this wonderful salad.'

'Why not?' answered he, 'I have brought two heads with me, and will give you one of them,' and he opened his pouch and handed her the bad cabbage.

The witch suspected nothing amiss, and her mouth watered so for this new dish that she herself went into the kitchen and dressed it. When it was prepared she could not wait until it was set on the table, but took a couple of leaves at once; but hardly had she swallowed them than she was deprived of her human shape, and she ran out into the courtyard in the form of an ass.

Presently the maidservant entered the kitchen, saw the salad standing there ready prepared, and was about to carry it up; but on the way, according to habit, she was seized by the desire to taste, and she ate a couple of leaves. Instantly, the magic power showed itself, and she likewise became an ass and ran out to the old woman, and the dish of salad fell to the ground.

Meantime the messenger sat beside the beautiful girl, and as no one came with the salad and she also was longing for it, she said, 'I don't know what has become of the salad.'

The huntsman thought, 'The salad must have already taken effect,' and said, 'I will go to the kitchen and enquire about it.' As he went down he saw the two asses running about in the courtyard; the salad, however, was lying on the ground.

'All right,' said he, 'the two have taken their portion,' and he picked up the other leaves, laid them on the dish, and carried them to the maiden. 'I bring you the delicate food myself,' said he, 'in order that you may not have to wait longer.'

Then she ate of it, and was, like the others, immediately deprived of her human form, and ran out into the courtyard in the shape of an ass.

After the huntsman had washed his face, so that the transformed ones could recognise him, he went down into the courtyard and said, 'Now you shall receive the wages of your treachery,' and bound them together, all three with one rope, and drove them along until he came to a mill. He knocked at the window; the miller put out is head, and asked what he wanted.

'I have three unmanageable beasts,' answered he, 'which I don't want to keep any longer. Will you take them in and give them food and stable room, and manage them as I tell you, and I will pay what you ask.'

The miller said, 'Why not? but how am I to manage them?'

The huntsman then said that he was to give three beatings and one meal daily to the old donkey, and that was the witch; one beating and three meals to the younger one, which was the servant-girl; and to the youngest, which was the maiden, no beatings and three meals, for he could not bring himself to have the maiden beaten. After that he went back into the castle and found therein everything he needed.

After a couple of days, the miller came and said he must inform him that the old ass which had received three beatings and only one meal daily was dead; 'the two others,' he continued, 'are certainly not dead, and are fed three times daily, but they are so sad that they cannot last much longer.'

The huntsman was moved to pity, put away his anger, and told the miller to drive them back again to him. And when they came, he gave them some of the good salad, so that they became human again.

The beautiful girl fell on her knees before him, and said, 'Ah, my beloved, forgive me for the evil I have done you; my mother drove me to it; it was done against my will, for I love you dearly. Your wishing-cloak hangs in a cupboard, and as for the bird's heart, I will take a vomiting potion.'

But he thought otherwise, and said, 'Keep it; it is all the same, for I will take thee for my true wife.'

So the wedding was celebrated, and they lived happily together until their death.

THE BREMEN TOWN-MUSICIANS

Once upon a time a man had an ass which for many years carried sacks to the mill without tiring. At last, however, its strength was worn out; it was no longer of any use for work. Accordingly, its master began to ponder as to how best to cut down its keep; but the ass, seeing there was mischief in the air, ran away and started on the road to Bremen. There he thought he could become a town-musician.

When he had been travelling a short time, he fell in with a hound, who was lying panting on the road as though he had run himself off his legs.

'Well, what are you panting so for, Growler?' said the ass.

'Ah,' said the hound, 'just because I am old, and every day I get weaker, and

91

also because I can no longer keep up with the pack, my master wanted to kill me, so I took my departure. But now, how am I to earn my bread? '

'Do you know what,' said the ass, 'I am going to Bremen, and shall there become a town-musician; come with me and take your part in the music. I shall play the lute, and you shall beat the kettle-drum.'

The hound agreed, and they went on.

A short time after they came upon a cat, sitting in the road, with a face like three rainy days.

'Well, what has been crossing you, Whiskers?' asked the ass.

'Who can be cheerful when he is out at elbows?' said the cat. 'I am getting on in years and my teeth are blunted, and I prefer to sit by the stove and purr instead of hunting round after mice. Just because of this my mistress wanted to drown me. I made myself scarce, but now I don't know where to turn.'

'Come with us to Bremen,' said the ass. 'You are a great hand at serenading, so you can become a town-musician.'

The cat consented, and joined them.

Next the fugitives passed by a yard where a cock was sitting on the door, crowing with all its might.

'You crow so loud you pierce one through and through,' said the ass. 'What is the matter?'

'Why! didn't I prophesy fine weather for Lady Day, when Our Lady washes the Christ Child's little garment and wants to dry it? But, notwithstanding this, because Sunday visitors are coming tomorrow, the mistress has no pity and she has ordered the cook to make me into soup, so I shall have my neck wrung tonight. Now I am crowing with all my might while I have the chance.'

'Come along, Red-comb,' said the ass; 'you had much better come with us. We are going to Bremen, and you will find a much better fate there. You have a good voice, and when we make music together there will be quality in it.'

The cock allowed himself to be persuaded, and they all four went off together. They could not, however, reach the town in one day, and by evening they arrived at a wood, where they determined to spend the night. The ass and the hound lay down under a big tree; the cat and the cock settled themselves in the branches, the cock flying right up to the top, which was the safest place for him. Before going to sleep he looked round once more in every direction; suddenly it seemed to him that he saw a light burning in the distance. He called out to his comrades that there must be a house not far off, for he saw a light:

'Very well,' said the ass, 'let us set out and make our way to it, for the entertainment here is very bad.'

The hound thought some bones or meat would suit him too, so they set out in the direction of the light, and soon saw it shining more clearly and getting bigger and bigger, till they reached a brightly-lighted robbers' den. The ass, being the tallest, approached the window and looked in.

'What do you see, old Jackass?' asked the cock.

'What do I see?' answered the ass, 'why, a table spread with delicious food and drink, and robbers seated at it enjoying themselves.'

'That would just suit us,' said the cock.

'Yes; if we were only there,' answered the ass.

Then the animals took counsel as to how to set about driving the robbers out. At last they hit upon a plan.

The ass was to take up his position with his forefeet on the window-sill, the hound was to jump on his back, the cat to climb up on to the hound, and last of all the cock flew up and perched on the cat's head. When they were thus arranged, at a given signal they all began to perform their music: the ass brayed, the hound barked, the cat mewed, and the cock crowed; then they dashed through the window, shivering the panes. The robbers jumped up at the terrible noise; they thought nothing less than that a demon was coming in upon them, and fled into the wood in the greatest alarm. Then the four animals sat down to table, and helped themselves according to taste, and ate as though they had been starving for weeks. When they had finished they extinguished the light and looked for sleeping places, each one to suit his nature and taste.

The ass lay down on the manure heap, the hound behind the door, the cat on the hearth near the warm ashes, and the cock flew up to the rafters. As they were tired from the long journey, they soon went to sleep.

When midnight was past, and the robbers saw from a distance that the light was no longer burning and that all seemed quiet, the chief said:

'We ought not to have been scared by a false alarm,' and ordered one of the robbers to go and examine the house.

Finding all quiet, the messenger went into the kitchen to kindle a light, and taking the cat's glowing, fiery eyes for live coals, he held a match close to them so as to light it. But the cat would stand no nonsense; it flew at his face, spat and scratched. He was terribly frightened and ran away.

He tried to get out by the back door, but the hound, who was lying there, jumped up and bit his leg. As he ran across the manure heap in front of the house, the ass gave him a good sound kick with his hind legs, while the cock, who had awoken at the uproar quite fresh and gay, cried out from his perch: 'Cock-a-doodle-doo.'

Thereupon the robber ran back as fast as he could to his chief, and said: 'There is a gruesome witch in the house, who breathed on me and scratched me with her long fingers. Behind the door there stands a man with a knife, who stabbed me; while in the yard lies a black monster, who hit me with a club; and upon the roof the judge is seated, and he called out, "Bring the rogue here," so I hurried away as fast as could.'

Thenceforward the robbers did not venture again to the house, which, however, pleased the four Bremen musicians so much that they never wished to leave it again.

And he who last told the story has hardly finished speaking yet.

THE GOOSE-GIRL

There was once an old Queen whose husband had been dead for many years, and she had a very beautiful daughter. When she grew up she was betrothed to a Prince in a distant country. When the time came for the maiden to be sent into this distant country to be married, the old Queen packed up quantities of clothes and jewels, gold and silver, cups and ornaments, and, in fact, everything suitable to a royal outfit, for she loved her daughter very dearly.

She also sent a waiting-woman to travel with her, and to put her hand into that of the bridegroom. They each had a horse. The Princess's horse was called Falada, and it could speak.

When the hour of departure came, the old Queen went to her bedroom, and with a sharp little knife cut her finger and made it bleed. Then she held a piece of white cambric under it, and let three drops of blood fall on to it. This cambric she gave to her daughter, and said, 'Dear child, take good care of this; it will stand you in good stead on the journey.' They then bade each other a sorrowful farewell. The Princess hid the piece of cambric in her bosom, mounted her horse, and set out to her bridegroom's country.

When they had ridden for a time the Princess became very thirsty, and said to the waiting-woman, 'Get down and fetch me some water in my cup from the stream. I must have something to drink.'

'If you are thirsty,' said the waiting-woman, 'dismount yourself, lie down by the water and drink. I don't choose to be your servant.'

So, in her great thirst, the Princess dismounted and stooped down to the stream and drank, as she might not have her golden cup. The poor Princess said, 'Alas!' and the drops of blood answered, 'If your mother knew this, it would break her heart.'

The royal bride was humble, so she said nothing, but mounted her horse again. Then they rode several miles further; but the day was warm, the sun was scorching, and the Princess was soon thirsty again.

When they reached a river she called out once more to her waiting-woman, 'Get down, and give me some water in my golden cup!'

She had forgotten all about the rude words which had been said to her. But the waiting-woman answered more haughtily than ever, 'If you want to drink, get the water for yourself. I won't be your servant.'

Being very thirsty, the Princess dismounted, and knelt by the flowing water. She cried, and said, 'Ah me!' and the drops of blood answered, 'If your mother knew this, it would break her heart.'

While she stooped over the water to drink, the piece of cambric with the drops of blood on it fell out of her bosom and floated away on the stream; but she never noticed this in her great fear. The waiting-woman, however, had seen it, and rejoiced at getting more power over the bride, who, by losing the drops of blood, had become weak and powerless.

Now, when she was about to mount her horse Falada again, the waiting-woman said, 'By rights, Falada belongs to me; this jade will do for you!'

The poor Princess was obliged to give way. Then the waiting-woman, in a harsh voice, ordered her to take off her royal robes and to put on her own mean garments. Finally, she forced her to swear before heaven that she would not tell a creature at the Court what had taken place. Had she not taken the oath she would have been killed on the spot. But Falada saw all this and marked it.

The waiting-woman then mounted Falada and put the real bride on her poor jade, and they continued their journey.

There was great rejoicing when they arrived at the castle. The Prince hurried towards them, and lifted the waiting-woman from her horse, thinking she was his bride. She was led upstairs, but the real Princess had to stay below.

The old King looked out of the window and saw the delicate, pretty little creature standing in the courtyard; so he went to the bridal apartments and asked the bride about her companion who was left standing in the courtyard, and wished to know who she was.

'I picked her up on the way, and brought her with me for company. Give the girl something to do to keep her from idling.'

But the old King had no work for her, and could not think of anything. At last he said, 'I have a little lad who looks after the geese; she may help him.'

The boy was called little Conrad, and the real bride was sent with him to look after the geese.

Soon after, the false bride said to the Prince, 'Dear husband, I pray you do me a favour.' He answered, 'That will I gladly.'

'Well, then, let the knacker be called to cut off the head of the horse I rode; it angered me on the way.'

Really, she was afraid that the horse would speak, and tell of her treatment of the Princess. So it was settled, and the faithful Falada had to die.

When this came to the ear of the real Princess, she promised the knacker a piece of gold if he would do her a slight service. There was a great dark gateway to the town, through which she had to pass every morning and evening: would he nail up Falada's head in this gateway, so that she might see him as she passed?

The knacker promised to do as she wished, and when the horse's head was cut off, he hung it up in the dark gateway. In the early morning, when she and Conrad went through the gateway, she said in passing:

'Alas! dear Falada, there thou hangest!'

And the head answered:

'Alas! Queen's daughter, there thou gangest!
If thy mother knew thy fate,
Her heart would break with grief so great.'

Then they passed on out of the town, right into the fields, with the geese. When they reached the meadow, the Princess sat down on the grass and let down her hair. It shone like pure gold, and when little Conrad saw it, he was so delighted that he wanted to pluck some out; but she said:

'Blow, blow, little breeze,
And Conrad's hat seize.
Let him join in the chase
While away it is whirled,
Till my tresses are curled
And I rest in my place.'

Then a strong wind sprang up, which blew away Conrad's hat right over the fields, and he had to run after it. When he came back, she had finished combing her hair and it was all put up again; so he could not get a single hair. This made him very sulky, and he would not say another word to her. And they tended the geese till evening, when they went home.

Next morning, when they passed under the gateway, the Princess said:

'Alas! dear Falada, there thou hangest!'

Falada answered:

'Alas! Queen's daughter, there thou gangest!
If thy mother knew thy fate,
Her heart would break with grief so great.'

Again, when they reached the meadows, the Princess undid her hair and began combing it. Conrad ran to pluck some out but she said quickly:

'Blow, blow, little breeze,
And Conrad's hat seize.

Let him join in the chase
While away it is whirled,
Till my tresses are curled
And I rest in my place.'

The wind sprang up and blew Conrad's hat far away over the fields, and he had to run after it. When he came back the hair was all put up again, and he could not pull a single hair out. And they tended the geese till the evening. When they got home Conrad went to the old King, and said, 'I won't tend the geese with that maiden again.'

'Why not?' asked the King.

'Oh, she vexes me every day.'

The old King then ordered him to say what she did to vex him.

Conrad said, 'In the morning, when we pass under the dark gateway with the geese, she talks to a horse's head which is hung up on the wall. She says:

"Alas! Falada, there thou hangest!"

and the head answers:

"Alas! Queen's daughter, there thou gangest!
If thy mother knew thy fate,
Her heart would break with grief so great." '

Then Conrad went on to tell the King all that happened in the meadow, and how he had to run after his hat in the wind.

The old King ordered Conrad to go out next day as usual. Then he placed himself behind the dark gateway, and heard the Princess speaking to Falada's head. He also followed her into the field, and hid himself behind a bush, and with his own eyes he saw the goose-girl and the lad come driving the geese into the field. Then, after a time, he saw the girl let down her hair, which glittered in the sun. Directly after this, she said:

'Blow, blow, little breeze,
And Conrad's hat seize.
Let him join in the chase
While away it is whirled,
Till my tresses are curled
And I rest in my place.'

Then came a puff of wind, which carried off Conrad's hat and he had to run after it. While he was away, the maiden combed and did up her hair; and all this the old King observed. Thereupon he went away unnoticed; and in the evening, when the goose-girl came home, he called her aside and asked her why she did all these things.

'That I may not tell you, nor may I tell any human creature; for I have sworn it under the open sky, because if I had not done so I should have lost my life.'

He pressed her sorely, and gave her no peace, but he could get nothing out of her. Then he said, 'If you won't tell me, then tell your sorrows to the iron stove there,' and he went away.

She crept up to the stove, and, beginning to weep and lament, unburdened her heart to it, and said: 'Here I am, forsaken by all the world, and yet I am a Princess. A false waiting-woman brought me to such a pass that I had to take off my royal robes. Then she took my place with my bridegroom, while I have to do mean service as a goose-girl. If my mother knew this it would break her heart.'

The old King stood outside by the pipes of the stove, and heard all that she said. Then he came back and told her to go away from the stove. He caused royal robes to be put upon her, and her beauty was a marvel. The old King called his son, and told him that he had a false bride—she was only a waiting-woman; but the true bride was here, the so-called goose-girl.

The young Prince was charmed with her youth and beauty. A great banquet was prepared, to which all the courtiers and good friends were bidden. The bride-groom sat at the head of the table, with the Princess on one side and the waiting-woman at the other; but she was dazzled, and did not recognise the Princess in her brilliant apparel.

When they had eaten and drunk and were all very merry, the old King put a riddle to the waiting-woman. 'What does a person deserve who deceives his master?' telling the whole story, and ending by asking, 'What doom does he deserve?'

The false bride answered, 'No better than this. He must be put stark naked into a barrel stuck with nails, and be dragged along by two white horses from street to street till he is dead.'

'That is your own doom,' said the King, 'and the judgment shall be carried out.'

When the sentence was fulfilled, the young Prince married his true bride, and they ruled their kingdom together in peace and happiness.

There was once a father who had two sons. One was clever and sensible, and always knew how to get on. But the younger one was stupid, and could not learn anything, and he had no imagination.

When people saw him, they said: 'His father will have plenty of trouble with him.'

Whenever there was anything to be done, the eldest one always had to do it. But if his father sent him to fetch anything late in the evening, and the way lay through the churchyard or any other dreary place, he would answer: 'Oh no, father, not there; it makes me shudder!' For he was afraid.

In the evening, when stories were being told round the fire which made one's flesh creep, and the listeners said: 'Oh, you make me shudder!' the youngest son, sitting in the corner listening, could not imagine what they meant. 'They always say "It makes me shudder!" And it doesn't make me shudder a bit. It must be some art which I can't understand.'

Now it happened one day that his father said to him: 'I say, you in the corner there, you are growing big and strong. You must learn something by which you can earn a living. See what pains your brother takes, but you are not worth your salt.'

'Well, father,' he answered, 'I am quite ready to learn something; nay, I should very much like to learn how to shudder, for I know nothing about that.'

The elder son laughed when he heard him, and thought: 'Good heavens! what a fool my brother is; he will never do any good as long as he lives.'

But his father sighed, and answered: 'You will easily enough learn how to shudder, but you won't make your bread by it.'

Soon after, the sexton came to the house on a visit, and the father confided his troubles about his son to him. He told him how stupid he was, and how he could never learn anything. 'Would you believe that when I asked him how he was going to earn his living, he said he would like to learn how to shudder?'

'If that's all,' said the sexton, 'he may learn that from me. Just let me have him, and I'll soon put the polish on him.'

The father was pleased, for he thought: 'Anyhow, the lad will gain something by it.'

So the sexton took him home with him, and he had to ring the church-bells.

A few days after, the sexton woke him at midnight and told him to get up and ring the bells. 'You shall soon be taught how to shudder!' he thought, as he crept stealthily up the stairs beforehand.

When the lad got up into the tower and turned round to catch hold of the bell rope, he saw a white figure standing on the steps opposite the belfry window.

'Who is there?' he cried; but the figure neither moved nor answered.

'Answer,' cried the lad, 'or get out of the way. You have no business here in the night.'

But so that the lad should think he was a ghost, the sexton did not stir.

The lad cried for the second time: 'What do you want here? Speak if you are an honest fellow, or I'll throw you down the stairs.'

The sexton did not think he would go to such lengths, so he made no sound, and stood as still as if he were made of stone.

Then the lad called to him the third time, and, as he had no answer, he took a run and threw the ghost down the stairs. It fell down ten steps and remained lying in a corner.

Then he rang the bells, went home, and, without saying a word to anybody, went to bed and was soon fast asleep.

The sexton's wife waited a long time for her husband, but, as he never came back, she got frightened, and woke up the lad.

'Don't you know what has become of my husband?' she asked. 'He went up into the church tower before you.'

'No,' answered the lad. 'There was somebody standing on the stairs opposite the belfry window, and, as he would neither answer me nor go away, I took him to be a rogue and threw him downstairs. Go and see if it was your husband; I should be sorry if it were.'

The woman hurried away and found her husband lying in the corner, moaning with a broken leg. She carried him down, and then hastened with loud cries to the lad's father.

'Your son has brought about a great misfortune; he has thrown my husband downstairs and broken his leg. Take the good-for-nothing fellow away, out of our house.'

The father was horrified, and, going back with her, gave the lad a good scolding.

'What is the meaning of this inhuman prank? The Evil One must have put it into your head.'

'Father,' answered the lad, 'just listen to me. I am quite innocent. He stood there in the dark, like a man with some wicked design. I did not know who it was, and I warned him three times to speak, or to go away!'

'Alas!' said his father, 'you bring me nothing but disaster. Go away out of my sight. I will have nothing more to do with you.'

'Gladly, father. Only wait till daylight; then I will go away, and learn to shudder. Then, at least, I shall have one art to make my living by.'

'Learn what you like,' said his father. 'It's all the same to me. Here are fifty thalers for you. Go out into the world, and don't tell a creature where you come from, or who your father is, for you will only bring me to shame.'

'Just as you please, father. If that is all you want, I can easily fulfil your desire.'

At daybreak, the lad put his fifty thalers into his pocket and went out along the high road, repeating over and over to himself as he went: 'If only I could shudder, if only I could shudder.'

A man came by and overheard the words the lad was saying to himself, and when they had gone a little further, and came within sight of the gallows, he said; 'See, there is the tree where those seven have been wedded to the ropemaker's daughter, and are now learning to fly. Sit down below them, and when night comes you will soon learn to shudder.'

'If nothing more than that is needed,' said the lad, 'it is easily done. And if I learn to shudder as easily as that, you shall have my fifty thalers. Come back to me early tomorrow morning.'

Then the lad went up to the gallows, and sat down under them to wait till night came.

As he was cold he lighted a fire, but at midnight the wind grew so cold that he did not know how to keep himself warm. The wind blew the men on the gallows backwards and forwards, and swung them against each other, so he thought: 'Here am I freezing by the fire, how much colder they must be up there.'

And as he was very compassionate, he mounted the ladder, undid them, and brought all seven down, one by one. Then he blew up the fire, and placed them round it to warm themselves. They sat there and never moved, even when the fire caught their clothing.

'Take care, or I will hang you all up again.'

The dead men, of course, could not hear, and remained silent while their few rags were burnt up.

Then he grew angry, and said: 'If you won't take care of yourselves, I can't help you, and I won't be burnt with you.'

So he hung them all up again in a row, and sat down by the fire and went to sleep again. Next morning, the man, wanting to get his fifty thalers, came to him and said: 'Now do you know what shuddering means?'

'No,' he said, 'how should I have learnt it? Those fellows up there never opened their mouths, and they were so stupid they let the few poor rags they had about them burn.'

Then the man saw that no thalers would be his that day, and he went away, saying: 'Never in my life have I seen such a fellow as this.'

The lad also went on his way, and again began saying to himself: 'Oh, if only I could learn to shudder, if only I could learn to shudder.'

A carter, walking behind him, heard this, and asked: 'Who are you?'

'I don't know,' answered the youth.

'Who is your father?'

'That I must not say.'

'What are you always mumbling in your beard?'

'Ah,' answered the youth, 'I want to learn to shudder, but no one can teach me.'

'Stop your silly chatter,' said the carter. 'Just you come with me, and I'll see that you have what you want.'

The youth went with the carter, and in the evening they reached an inn, where they meant to pass the night. He said, quite loud, as they entered: 'Oh, if only I could learn to shudder, if only I could learn to shudder.'

The landlord, who heard him, laughed, and said: 'If that's what you want, there should be plenty of opportunity for you here.'

'I will have nothing to say to it,' said the landlady. 'So many a prying fellow has already paid the penalty with his life. It would be a sin and a shame if those bright eyes should not see the light of day again.'

But the youth said: 'I will learn it somehow, however hard it may be. I have been driven out for not knowing it.'

He gave the landlord no peace till he told him that there was an enchanted castle a little way off, where anyone could be made to shudder if he would pass three nights in it. The King had promised his daughter to wife to anyone who dared do it, and she was the prettiest maiden the sun had ever shone on. There were also great treasures hidden in the castle, watched over by evil spirits, enough to make any poor man rich who could break the spell. Already many had gone in, but none had ever come out.

Next morning the youth went to the King, and said: 'By your leave, I should like to spend three nights in the enchanted castle.'

The King looked at him, and, as he took a fancy to him, he said: 'You may ask three things to take into the castle with you, but they must be lifeless things.'

He answered: 'Then I ask for a fire, a turning-lathe, and a cooper's bench with the knife.'

The King had all three carried into the castle with him.

When night fell, the youth went up to the castle and made a bright fire in one of the rooms. He put the cooper's bench with the knife near to the fire, and seated himself on the turning-lathe.

'Oh, if only I could shudder,' he said, 'but I shan't learn it here either.'

Towards midnight he wanted to make up the fire, and as he was blowing it up, something in one corner began to shriek: 'Miau, miau, how cold we are!'

'You fools!' he cried. 'What do you shriek for? If you are cold, come and warm yourselves by the fire.'

As he spoke, two big black cats bounded up and sat down, one on each side of him, and stared at him with wild, fiery eyes.

After a time, when they had warmed themselves, they said: 'Comrade, shall we have a game of cards?'

'Why not?' he answered, 'but show me your paws first.'

Then they stretched out their claws.

'Why,' he said, 'what long nails you've got. Wait a bit; I must cut them for you.'

He seized them by the scruff of their necks, lifted them on to the cooper's bench, and screwed their paws firmly to it.

'I have looked at your fingers, and the desire to play cards with you has passed.'

Then he killed them and threw them out into the moat.

But no sooner had he got rid of these two cats, and was about to sit down by his fire again, than crowds of black cats and dogs swarmed out of every corner, more and more of them. They howled horribly, and trampled on his fire, and tried to put it out.

For a time he looked quietly on, but when it grew too bad he seized his cooper's knife and cried: 'Away with you, you rascally pack,' and let fly among them right and left. Some of them sprang away; the others he killed and threw out into the water.

When he came back he scraped the embers of his fire together again, and warmed himself. He could hardly keep his eyes open, and felt the greatest desire to go to sleep. He looked round, and in one corner he saw a big bed.

'That's the very thing,' he said, and lay down in it. As soon as he closed his eyes the bed began to move, and soon it was tearing round and round the castle. 'Very good!' he said. 'The faster the better!' The bed rolled on as if it were dragged by six horses—over thresholds and stairs, up and down.

Suddenly it went hop, hop, hop, and turned topsy-turvy, so that it lay upon him like a mountain. But he pitched the pillows and blankets into the air, slipped out of it, and said: 'Now anyone may ride who likes.'

Then he lay down by his fire and slept till daylight.

In the morning the King came, and when he saw him lying on the floor, he thought the ghosts had killed him and he was dead. So he said: 'It's a sad pity for such a handsome fellow.'

But the youth heard him and sat up, saying: 'It has not come to that yet.'

The King was surprised and delighted, and asked him how he had got on.

'Pretty well!' he answered. 'One night is gone; I suppose I shall get through the others too.'

When the landlord saw him he opened his eyes and said: 'I never thought I should see you alive again. Have you learnt how to shudder now?'

'No,' he answered, 'it's all in vain. If only someone would tell me how.'

The second night came, and up he went again and sat down by the fire and began his old song: 'Oh, if only I could learn to shudder.'

In the middle of the night a great noise and uproar began, first soft, and then growing louder; then for a short time there would be silence.

At last, with a loud scream, half the body of a man fell down the chimney in front of him.

'Hullo!' he said, 'another half is wanting here; this is too little.'

The noise began again, and, amidst shrieks and howls, the other half fell down.

'Wait a bit,' he said, 'I'll blow up the fire.'

When this was done, and he looked round, the two halves had come together, and a hideous man sat in his place.

'We didn't bargain for that,' said the youth. 'The bench is mine.'

The man wanted to push him out of the way, but the youth would not have it, flung him aside, and took his own seat.

Then more men fell down the chimney, one after the other, and they fetched nine human shin-bones and two skulls, and began to play skittles. The youth felt inclined to join them, and cried: 'I say, can I play too?'

'Yes, if you've got any money.'

'Money enough,' he answered, 'but your balls aren't quite round.'

Then he took the skulls and turned them on the lathe till they were· quite round. 'Now they will roll better,' he said. 'Here goes! The more, the merrier!'

So he played with them and lost some money, but when it struck twelve everything disappeared. He lay down and was soon fast asleep.

Next morning the King came again to look after him, and said: 'Well, how did you get on this time?'

'I played skittles,' he answered, 'and lost a few coins.'

'Didn't you learn to shudder?'

'Not I. I only made merry. Oh, if I could but find out how to shudder.'

On the third night he again sat down on his bench, and said quite savagely: 'If only I could shudder!'

When it grew late, six tall men came in carrying a bier, and he said: 'Hullo there! That must be my cousin who died a few days ago.' And he beckoned and said: 'Come along, cousin, come along.'

The men put the coffin on the floor, and he went up and took the lid off, and there lay a dead man. He felt the face, and it was as cold as ice. 'Wait,' he said, 'I will warm him.'

Then he went to the fire and warmed his hand and laid it on the dead man's face, but the dead man remained cold. He took him out of the coffin, sat down by the fire and took him on his knees, and rubbed his arms to make the blood circulate.

But it was all no good. Next, it came into his head that if two people were in bed together, they warmed each other. So he put the dead man in the bed, covered him up, and lay down beside him.

After a time the dead man grew warm and began to move.

Then the youth said: 'There, you see, cousin mine, have I not warmed you?'

But the man rose up and cried: 'Now I will strangle you!'

'What!' said he, 'are those all the thanks I get? Back you go into your coffin then.' So saying, he lifted him up, threw him in, and fastened down the lid. Then the six men came back and carried the coffin away.

'I cannot shudder,' he said, 'and I shall never learn it here.'

Just then a huge man appeared. He was frightful to look at, old, and with a long white beard.

'Oh, you miserable wight!' he cried. 'You shall soon learn what shuddering is, for you shall die.'

'Not so fast,' said the youth. 'If I am to die, I must be present.'

'I will make short work of you,' said the old monster.

'Softly! softly! don't you boast. I am as strong as you, and very likely much stronger.'

'We shall see about that,' said the old man. 'If you are the stronger, I will let you go. Come; we will try.'

Then he led him through numberless dark passages to a smithy, took an axe, and with one blow struck one of the anvils into the earth.

'I can better that,' said the youth, and went to the other anvil. The old man placed himself near to see, and his white beard hung over.

Then the youth took the axe and split the anvil with one blow, catching the old man's beard in it at the same time.

'Now, I have you fast,' said the youth, 'and you will be the one to die.'

Then he seized an iron rod and belaboured the old man with it till he shrieked for mercy, and promised him great riches if he would stop.

Then the youth pulled out the axe and released him, and the old man led him back into the castle and showed him three chests of gold in a cellar.

'One is for the poor,' he said, 'one for the King, and one for you.'

The clock struck twelve, and the ghost disappeared, leaving the youth in the dark.

'I must manage to get out somehow,' he said, and groped about till he found his way back to his room, where he lay down by the fire and went to sleep.

Next morning the King came and said: 'Now you must have learnt how to shudder.'

'No,' said he. 'What can it be? My dead cousin was there, and an old man with a beard came and showed me a lot of gold. But what shuddering is, that no man can tell me.'

Then said the King: 'You have broken the spell on the castle, and you shall marry my daughter.'

'That is all very well,' he said; 'but still I don't know what shuddering is.'

The gold was got out of the castle, and the marriage was celebrated, but, happy as the young King was, and much as he loved his wife, he was always saying: 'Oh, if only I could learn to shudder, if only I could learn to shudder.'

At last his wife was vexed by it, and her waiting-woman said: 'I can help you; he shall be taught the meaning of shuddering.'

And she went out to the brook that ran through the garden and got a pail full of cold water and little fishes.

At night, when the young King was asleep, his wife took the coverings off and poured the cold water over him, and all the little fishes flopped about him.

Then he woke up, and cried: 'Oh, how I am shuddering, dear wife, how I am shuddering! Now I know what shuddering is!'

Once there was a miller who was poor, but who had a beautiful daughter. Now it happened that he had to go and speak to the King, and in order to make himself appear important he said to him, 'I have a daughter who can spin straw into gold.'

The King said to the miller, 'That is an art which pleases me well; if your daughter is as clever as you say, bring her tomorrow to my palace, and I will try what she can do.'

And when the girl was brought to him he took her into a room which was quite full of straw, gave her a spinning-wheel and a reel, and said, 'Now set to work, and if by tomorrow morning early you have not spun this straw into gold during the night, you must die.' Thereupon he himself locked up the room, and left her in it alone. So there sat the poor miller's daughter, and for her life could not tell what to do; she had no idea how straw could be spun into gold, and she grew more and more miserable, until at last she began to weep.

But all at once the door opened, and in came a little man and said, 'Good evening, Mistress Miller; why are you crying so?'

'Alas!' answered the girl, 'I have to spin straw into gold, and I do not know how to do it.'

'What will you give me,' said the manikin, 'if I do it for you?'

'My necklace,' said the girl.

The little man took the necklace, seated himself in front of the wheel, and whirr, whirr, whirr, three turns, and the reel was full; then he put another on, and whirr, whirr, whirr, three times round, and the second was full too. And so it went on until the morning, when all the straw was spun and all the reels were full of gold.

By daybreak the King was already there, and when he saw the gold he was astonished and delighted, but his heart became only more greedy. He had the miller's daughter taken into another room full of straw, which was much larger, and commanded her to spin that also in one night if she valued her life. The girl knew not how to help herself, and was crying, when the door again opened, and the little man appeared, and said, 'What will you give me if I spin the straw into gold for you?'

'The ring on my finger,' answered the girl.

The little man took the ring, again began to turn the wheel, and by morning had spun all the straw into glittering gold.

The King rejoiced beyond measure at the sight, but still he had not gold enough; and he had the miller's daughter taken into a still larger room full of straw, and said, 'You must spin this, too, in the course of this night; but if you succeed, you shall be my wife.'

'Even if she be a miller's daughter,' thought he, 'I could not find a richer wife in the whole world.'

When the girl was alone the manikin came again for the third time, and said, 'What will you give me if I spin the straw for you this time also?'

'I have nothing left that I could give,' answered the girl.

'Then promise me, if you should become Queen, your first child.'

'Who knows whether that will ever happen?' thought the miller's daughter; and, not knowing how else to help herself in this strait, she promised the manikin what he wanted, and for that he once more spun the straw into gold.

And when the King came in the morning and found all as he had wished, he took her in marriage, and the pretty miller's daughter became a Queen.

A year after, she had a beautiful child, and she never gave a thought to the manikin. But suddenly he came into her room, and said, 'Now give me what you promised.'

The Queen was horror-struck, and offered the manikin all the riches of the kingdom if he would leave her the child.

But the manikin said, 'No, something that is living is dearer to me than all the treasures of the world.'

Then the Queen began to weep and cry, so that the manikin pitied her. 'I will give you three days' time,' said he; 'if by that time you find out my name, then you shall keep your child.'

So the Queen thought the whole night of all the names that she had ever heard, and she sent a messenger to inquire, far and wide, for any other names that there might be. When the manikin came the next day, she began with Caspar, Melchior, Balthazar, and said all the names she knew, one after another; but to every one the little man said, 'That is not my name.'

On the second day she had enquiries made in the neighbourhood as to the names of all the people there, and she repeated to the manikin the most uncommon and curious. 'Perhaps your name is Shortribs, or Sheepshanks, or Laceleg?' but he always answered, 'That is not my name.'

On the third day the messenger came back again, and said, 'I have not been able to find a single new name, but as I came to a high mountain at the end of the forest, where the fox and the hare bid each other good night, there I saw a little house, and before the house a fire was burning, and round about the fire quite a ridiculous little man was jumping; he hopped upon one leg, and shouted:

' "Today I bake, tomorrow I brew,
    The next I'll have the young Queen's child.

113

Ha! glad am I that no one knew,
That Rumpelstiltskin I am styled." '

You may think how glad the Queen was when she heard the name! And when soon afterwards the little man came in and asked, 'Now, Mistress Queen, what is my name?' at first she said, 'Is your name Conrad?'

'No.'

'Is your name Harry?'

'No.'

'Perhaps your name is Rumpelstiltskin?'

'The Devil has told you that! the Devil has told you that!' cried the little man, and in his anger he plunged his right foot so deep into the earth that his whole leg went in; and then in rage he pulled at his left leg so hard with both hands that he tore himself in two.

JORINDA AND JORINGEL

There was once an old castle in the middle of a vast thick wood; in it there lived an old woman quite alone, and she was a witch. By day she made herself into a cat or a screech-owl, but regularly at night she became a human being again. In this way she was able to decoy wild beasts and birds, which she would kill, and boil or roast. If any man came within a hundred paces of the castle, he was forced to stand still and could not move from the place till she gave the word of release; but if an innocent maiden came within the circle, she changed her into a bird, and shut her up in a cage which she carried into a room in the castle. She must have had seven thousand cages of this kind, containing pretty birds.

Now, there was once a maiden called Jorinda who was more beautiful than all other maidens. She had promised to marry a very handsome youth named Joringel, and it was in the days of their courtship, when they took the greatest joy in being alone together, that one day they wandered out into the forest. 'Take care,' said Joringel; 'do not let us go too near the castle.'

It was a lovely evening. The sunshine glanced between the tree-trunks of the dark greenwood, while the turtle-doves sang plaintively in the old beech trees. Yet Jorinda sat down in the sunshine and could not help weeping and bewailing, while Joringel, too, soon became just as mournful. They both felt miserable as if they had been going to die. Gazing round them, they found they had lost their way, and did not know how they should find the path home.

Half the sun still appeared above the mountain; half had sunk below. Joringel peered into the bushes and saw the old walls of the castle quite close to them; he was terror-struck, and became pale as death. Jorinda was singing:

> 'My birdie with its ring so red
> Sings sorrow, sorrow, sorrow;
> My love will mourn when I am dead,
> Tomorrow, morrow, mor—jug, jug.'

Joringel looked at her, but she was changed into a nightingale who sang 'Jug, jug.'

A screech-owl with glowing eyes flew three times round her, and cried three times 'Shu hu-hu.' Joringel could not stir; he stood like a stone without being able to speak, or cry, or move hand or foot. The sun had now set. The owl flew into a bush, out of which appeared almost at the same moment a crooked old woman, skinny and yellow; she had big, red eyes and a crooked nose whose tip reached her chin. She mumbled something, caught the nightingale, and carried it away in her hand. Joringel could not say a word nor move from the spot, and the nightingale was gone. At last the old woman came back, and said in a droning voice: 'Greeting to thee, Zachiel! When the moon shines upon the cage, unloose the captive, Zachiel!'

Then Joringel was free. He fell on his knees before the witch, and implored her to give back his Jorinda; but she said he should never have her again, and went away. He pleaded, he wept, he lamented, but all in vain. 'Alas! what is to become of me?' said Joringel.

Finally he went away, and arrived at a strange village, where he spent a long time as a shepherd. He often wandered round about the castle, but did not go too near it. At last he dreamt one night that he found a blood-red flower, in the midst of which was a beautiful large pearl. He plucked the flower, and took it to the castle. Whatever he touched with it was made free of enchantment. He dreamt, too, that by this means he had found his Jorinda again.

In the morning when he awoke he began to search over hill and dale, in the hope of finding a flower like this; he searched till the ninth day, when he found the flower early in the morning. In the middle was a big dewdrop, as big as the finest pearl. This flower he carried day and night, till he reached the castle. He was not held fast as before when he came within the hundred paces of the castle, but walked straight up to the door.

Joringel was filled with joy; he touched the door with the flower, and it flew open. He went in through the court, and listened for the sound of birds. He went on and found the hall, where the witch was feeding the birds in the seven thousand cages. When she saw Joringel she was angry, very angry—scolded, and spat poison and gall at him. He paid no attention to her, but turned away and searched among the bird-cages. Yes, but there were many hundred nightingales; how was he to find his Jorinda?

While he was looking about in this way he noticed that the old woman was secretly removing a cage with a bird inside, and was making for the door. He sprang swiftly towards her, touched the cage and the witch with the flower, and then she no longer had power to exercise her spells. Jorinda stood there, as beautiful as before, and threw her arms round Joringel's neck. After that he changed all the other birds back into maidens again, and went home with Jorinda, and they lived long and happily together.

MOTHER HOLLE

There was once a widow who had two daughters—one of whom was pretty and industrious, whilst the other was ugly and idle. But she was much fonder of the ugly and idle one, because she was her own daughter; and the other, who was a stepdaughter, was obliged to do all the work, and be the Cinderella of the house. Every day the poor girl had to sit by a well in the highway, and spin and spin till her fingers bled.

Now it happened that one day the shuttle was marked with her blood, so she dipped it in the well, to wash the mark off; but it dropped out of her hand and fell to the bottom. She began to weep, and ran to her stepmother and told her of the mishap. But she scolded her sharply, and was so merciless as to say, 'Since you have let the shuttle fall in, you must fetch it out again'.

So the girl went back to the well and did not know what to do; and in the sorrow of her heart she jumped into the well to get the shuttle. She lost her senses; and when she awoke and came to herself again, she was in a lovely meadow where the sun was shining and many thousands of flowers were growing. Along this meadow she went, and at last came to a baker's oven full of bread, and the bread cried out, 'Oh, take me out! take me out! or I shall burn; I have been baked a long time!' So she went up to it, and took out all the loaves one after the other with the bread shovel.

After that she went on till she came to a tree covered with apples, which called out to her, 'Oh, shake me! shake me! we apples are all ripe!' So she shook the tree till the apples fell like rain, and went on shaking till they were all down, and when she had gathered them into a heap, she went on her way.

At last she came to a little house, out of which an old woman peeped; but she had such large teeth that the girl was frightened, and was about to run away. But the old woman called out to her, 'What are you afraid of, dear child? Stay with me; if you will do all the work in the house properly, you shall be the better for it. Only you must take care to make my bed well, and to shake it thoroughly till the feathers fly—for then there is snow on the earth. I am Mother Holle.'

As the old woman spoke so kindly to her, the girl took courage and agreed to enter her service. She attended to everything to the satisfaction of her mistress, and always shook her bed so vigorously that the feathers flew about like snow-flakes. So she had a pleasant life with her; never an angry word and boiled or roast meat every day.

She stayed some time with Mother Holle, and then she became sad. At first she did not know what was the matter with her, but found at length that it was homesickness; although she was many thousand times better off here than at home, still she had a longing to be there. At last she said to the old woman, 'I have a longing for home, and however well off I am down here, I cannot stay any longer; I must go up again to my own people.'

Mother Holle said, 'I am pleased that you long for your home, and as you have served me so truly, I myself will take you up again.' Thereupon she took her by the hand, and led her to a large door. The door was opened, and just as the maiden was standing beneath the doorway, a heavy shower of golden rain fell, and all the gold remained sticking to her, so that she was completely covered over with it.

'You shall have that because you are so industrious,' said Mother Holle; and at the same time she gave her back the shuttle which she had let fall into the well. Thereupon the door closed, and the maiden found herself up above upon the earth, not far from her mother's house.

And as she went into the yard the cock was standing by the well-side, and cried:

> 'Cock-a-doodle-doo!
> Your golden girl's come back to you!'

So she went in to her mother, and as she arrived thus covered with gold, she was well received, both by her and her sister.

The girl told all that had happened to her; and as soon as the mother heard how she had come by so much wealth, she was very anxious to obtain the same good luck for the ugly and lazy daughter, who now had to seat herself by the well and spin. And in order that the shuttle might be stained with blood, she stuck her hand into a thorn bush and pricked her finger. Then she threw her shuttle into the well, and jumped in after it.

She came, like the other, to the beautiful meadow and walked along the very same path. When she got to the oven the bread again cried, 'Oh, take me out! take me out! or I shall burn; I have been baked a long time!' But the lazy thing answered, 'As if I had any wish to make myself dirty?' and on she went.

Soon she came to the apple tree, which cried, 'Oh, shake me! shake me! we apples are all ripe!' But she answered, 'I like that! one of you might fall on my head,' and so went on.

When she came to Mother Holle's house she was not afraid, for she had already heard of her big teeth, and she hired herself to her immediately.

The first day she forced herself to work diligently, and obeyed Mother Holle when she told her to do anything, for she was thinking of all the gold that she would give her. But on the second day she began to be lazy, and on the third day still more so, and then she would not get up in the morning at all. Neither did

she make Mother Holle's bed as she ought, and did not shake it so as to make the feathers fly up.

Mother Holle was soon tired of this, and gave her notice to leave. The lazy girl was willing enough to go, and thought that now the golden rain would come. Mother Holle led her, too, to the great door; but while she was standing beneath it, instead of the gold a big kettleful of pitch was emptied over her. 'That is the reward of your service,' said Mother Holle, and shut the door.

So the lazy girl went home; but she was quite covered with pitch, and the cock by the well-side, as soon as he saw her, cried out:

> 'Cock-a-doodle-doo!
> Your pitchy girl's come back to you!'

But the pitch stuck fast to her, and could not be got off as long as she lived.

SNOW-WHITE AND ROSE-RED

There was once a poor widow who lived in a lonely cottage. In front of the cottage was a garden wherein stood two rose-trees, one of which bore white and the other red roses. She had two children who were like the two rose-trees, and one was called Snow-white and the other Rose-red. They were as good and happy, as busy and cheerful as ever two children in the world were, only Snow-white was more quiet and gentle than Rose-red. Rose-red liked better to run about in the meadows and fields seeking flowers and catching butterflies; but Snow-white sat at home with her mother, and helped her with her housework, or read to her when there was nothing to do.

The two children were so fond of each other that they always held each other by the hand when they went out together, and when Snow-white said, 'We will not leave each other,' Rose-red answered, 'Never so long as we live,' and their mother would add, 'What one has she must share with the other.'

They often ran about the forest alone and gathered red berries, and no beasts did them any harm, but came close to them trustfully. The little hare would eat a cabbage-leaf out of their hands, the roe grazed by their side, the stag leapt merrily by them, and the birds sat still upon the boughs and sang whatever they knew.

No mishap overtook them; if they stayed too late in the forest, and night came on, they laid themselves down near one another upon the moss and slept until morning came, and their mother knew this and had no distress on their account.

Once when they had spent the night in the wood and the dawn had roused them, they saw a beautiful child in a shining white dress sitting near their bed. He got up and looked quite kindly at them, but said nothing and went away into the forest. And when they looked round they found that they had been sleeping quite close to a precipice, and would certainly have fallen into it in the darkness if they had gone only a few paces further. And their mother told them that it must have been the angel who watches over good children.

Snow-white and Rose-red kept their mother's little cottage so neat that it was a pleasure to look inside it. In the summer Rose-red took care of the house and every morning laid a wreath of flowers by her mother's bed before she awoke, in which was a rose from each tree. In the winter Snow-white lit the fire and hung the kettle on the wrekin. The kettle was of copper and shone like gold, so brightly was it polished. In the evening, when the snow-flakes fell, the mother said, 'Go, Snow-white, and bolt the door,' and then they sat round the hearth, and the mother took her spectacles and read aloud out of a large book, and the two girls listened as they sat and span. And close by them lay a lamb upon the floor, and behind them upon a perch sat a white dove with its head hidden beneath its wings.

One evening, as they were thus sitting comfortably together, someone knocked at the door as if he wished to be let in. The mother said, 'Quick, Rose-red, open the door; it must be a traveller who is seeking shelter.' Rose-red went and pushed back the bolt, thinking that it was a poor man, but it was not; it was a bear that stretched his broad, black head within the door.

Rose-red screamed and sprang back, the lamb bleated, the dove fluttered, and Snow-white hid herself behind her mother's bed. But the bear began to speak and said, 'Do not be afraid, I will do you no harm! I am half-frozen and only want to warm myself a little beside you.'

'Poor bear,' said the mother, 'lie down by the fire, only take care that you do not burn your coat.' Then she cried, 'Snow-white, Rose-red, come out; the bear will do you no harm, he means well.' So they both came out, and by-and-by the lamb and dove came nearer, and were not afraid of him. The bear said, 'Here, children, knock the snow out of my coat a little;' so they brought the broom and swept the bear's hide clean; and he stretched himself by the fire and growled contentedly and comfortably. It was not long before they grew quite at home, and played tricks with their clumsy guest. They tugged his hair with their hands, put their feet upon his back and rolled him about, or they took a hazel-switch and beat him, and when he growled they laughed. But the bear took it all in good part, only when they were too rough he called out, 'Leave me alive, children,

> Snowy-white, Rosy-red,
> Will you beat your lover dead?'

When it was bed-time, and the others went to bed, the mother said to the bear, 'You can lie there by the hearth, and then you will be safe from the cold and the bad weather.' As soon as day dawned the two children let him out, and he trotted across the snow into the forest.

Henceforth the bear came every evening at the same time, laid himself down by the hearth, and let the children amuse themselves with him as much as they liked; and they got so used to him that the doors were never fastened until their black friend had arrived.

When spring had come and all outside was green, the bear said one morning to Snow-white, 'Now I must go away, and cannot come back for the whole summer.'

'Where are you going, then, dear bear?' asked Snow-white.

'I must go into the forest and guard my treasures from the wicked dwarfs. In the winter, when the earth is frozen hard, they are obliged to stay below and cannot work their way through; but now, when the sun has thawed and warmed the earth, they break through it, and come out to pry and steal; and what once gets into their hands and in their caves, does not easily see daylight again.'

Snow-white was quite sorry for his going away, and as she unbolted the door for him, and the bear was hurrying out, he caught against the bolt and a piece of his hairy coat was torn off, and it seemed to Snow-white as if she had seen gold shining through it, but she was not sure about it. The bear ran away quickly and was soon out of sight behind the trees.

A short time afterwards the mother sent her children into the forest to get firewood. There they found a big tree which lay felled on the ground, and close by the trunk something was jumping backwards and forwards in the grass, but they could not make out what it was. When they came nearer they saw a dwarf with an old, withered face and a snow-white beard a yard long. The end of the beard was caught in a crevice of the tree, and the little fellow was jumping backwards and forwards like a dog tied to a rope, and did not know what to do.

He glared at the girls with his fiery, red eyes and cried, 'Why do you stand there? Can you not come here and help me?'

'What are you about there, little man?' asked Rose-red.

'You stupid, prying goose!' answered the dwarf; 'I was going to split the tree to get a little wood for cooking. The little bit of food that one of us wants gets burnt up directly with thick logs; we do not swallow so much as you coarse, greedy folk. I had just driven the wedge safely in, and everything was going as I wished, but the wretched wood was too smooth and suddenly sprang asunder, and the tree closed so quickly that I could not pull out my beautiful white beard; so now it is tight in and I cannot get away, and the silly, sleek, milk-faced things laugh! Ugh! how odious you are!'

The children tried very hard, but they could not pull the beard out, it was caught too fast. 'I will run and fetch someone,' said Rose-red.

'You senseless goose!' snarled the dwarf; 'why should you fetch someone? You are already two too many for me; can you not think of something better?'

'Don't be impatient,' said Snow-white, 'I will help you,' and she pulled her scissors out of her pocket, and cut off the end of the beard.

As soon as the dwarf felt himself free he laid hold of a bag which lay amongst the roots of the tree, and which was full of gold, and lifted it up, grumbling to himself, 'Uncouth people, to cut off a piece of my fine beard. Bad luck to you!' and then he swung the bag upon his back, and went off without even once looking at the children.

Some time after that Snow-white and Rose-red went to catch a dish of fish. As they came near the brook they saw something like a large grasshopper jumping towards the water, as if it were going to leap in. They ran to it and found it was the dwarf.

'Where are you going?' said Rose-red; 'you surely don't want to go into the water?'

'I am not such a fool!' cried the dwarf; 'don't you see that the accursed fish wants to pull me in?' The little man had been sitting there fishing, and unluckily the wind had twisted his beard with the fishing-line; just then a big fish bit, and the feeble creature had not strength to pull it out. The fish kept the upper hand and pulled the dwarf towards him. He held on to all the reeds and rushes, but it was of little good; he was forced to follow the movements of the fish and was in urgent danger of being pulled into the water.

The girls came just in time; they held him fast and tried to free his beard from the line, but all in vain—beard and line were entangled fast together. Nothing was left but to bring out the scissors and cut the beard, whereby a small part of it was lost.

When the dwarf saw that he screamed out, 'Is that civil, you toadstool, to disfigure one's face? Was it not enough to clip off the end of my beard? Now you have cut off the best part of it. I cannot let myself be seen by my people. I wish you had been made to run the soles off your shoes!' Then he took out a sack of pearls which lay in the rushes, and without saying a word more he dragged it away and disappeared behind a stone.

It happened that soon afterwards the mother sent the two girls to the town to buy needles and thread, and laces and ribbons. The road led them across a heath upon which huge pieces of rock lay strewn here and there. Now they noticed a large bird hovering in the air, flying slowly round and round above them; it sank lower and lower, and at last settled near a rock not far off. Directly afterwards they heard a loud, piteous cry. They ran up and saw with horror that the eagle had seized their old acquaintance the dwarf, and was going to carry him off.

The children, full of pity, at once took tight hold of the little man, and pulled against the eagle so long that at last he let his booty go. As soon as the dwarf had recovered from his first fright he cried with his shrill voice, 'Could you not have done it more carefully? You dragged at my brown coat so that it is all torn and full of holes, you helpless, clumsy creatures!' Then he took up a sack of precious stones, and slipped away again under the rock into his hole. The girls, who by this time were used to his thanklessness, went on their way and did their business in the town.

As they crossed the heath again on their way home they surprised the dwarf, who had emptied out his bag of precious stones in a clean spot, and had not thought that anyone would come there so late. The evening sun shone upon the brilliant stones; they glittered and sparkled with all colours so beautifully that the children stood still and looked at them.

'Why do you stand gaping there?' cried the dwarf, and his ashen-grey face became copper-red with rage. He was going on with his bad words when a loud growling was heard, and a black bear came trotting towards them out of the forest. The dwarf sprang up in a fright, but he could not get to his cave, for the bear was already close. Then in the dread of his heart he cried, 'Dear Mr Bear, spare me, I will give you all my treasures; look, the beautiful jewels lying there! Grant me my life. What do you want with such a slender little fellow as I? You would not feel me between your teeth. Come, take these two wicked girls; they are tender morsels for you, fat as young quails; for mercy's sake, eat them!'

The bear took no heed of his words, but gave the wicked creature a single blow with his paw, and he did not move again.

The girls had run away, but the bear called to them, 'Snow-white and Rose-red, do not be afraid; wait, I will come with you.' Then they knew his voice and waited, and when he came up to them suddenly his bearskin fell off, and he stood there a handsome man, clothed all in gold. 'I am a King's son,' he said, 'and I was bewitched by that wicked dwarf, who had stolen my treasures; I have had to run about the forest as a savage bear until I was freed by his death. Now he has got his well-deserved punishment.'

Snow-white was married to him, and Rose-red to his brother, and they divided between them the great treasure which the dwarf had gathered together in his cave. The old mother lived peacefully and happily with her children for many years. She took the two rose-trees with her, and they stood before her window, and every year bore the most beautiful roses, white and red.

THE WATER OF LIFE

There was once a King who was so ill that it was thought impossible his life could be saved. He had three sons, and they were all in great distress on his account, and they went into the castle gardens and wept at the thought that he must die. An old man came up to them and asked the cause of their grief. They told him that their father was dying, and nothing could save him. The old man said, 'There is only one remedy which I know; it is the Water of Life. If he drinks of it he will recover, but it is very difficult to find.'

The eldest son said, 'I will soon find it,' and he went to the sick man to ask permission to go in search of the Water of Life, as that was the only thing to cure him.

'No,' said the King. 'The danger is too great. I would rather die.'

But he persisted so long that at last the King gave his permission.

The Prince thought, 'If I bring this water I shall be the favourite, and I shall inherit the kingdom.'

So he set off, and when he had ridden some distance he came upon a dwarf standing in the road, who cried, 'Whither away so fast?'

'Stupid little fellow,' said the Prince, proudly; 'what business is it of yours?' and rode on.

The little man was very angry, and made an evil vow.

Soon after, the Prince came to a gorge in the mountains, and the further he rode the narrower it became, till he could go no further. His horse could neither go forward nor turn round for him to dismount; so there he sat, jammed in.

The sick King waited a long time for him, but he never came back. Then the second son said, 'Father, let me go and find the Water of Life,' thinking, 'if my brother is dead I shall have the kingdom.'

The King at first refused to let him go, but at last he gave his consent. So the Prince started on the same road as his brother, and met the same dwarf, who stopped him and asked where he was going in such a hurry.

'Little Snippet, what does it matter to you?' he said, and rode away without looking back.

But the dwarf cast a spell over him, and he, too, got into a narrow gorge like his brother, where he could neither go backwards nor forwards.

This is what happens to the haughty.

As the second son also stayed away, the youngest one offered to go and fetch the Water of Life, and at last the King was obliged to let him go.

When he met the dwarf, and he asked him where he was hurrying to, he stopped

133

and said, 'I am searching for the Water of Life, because my father is dying.'

'Do you know where it is to be found?'

'No,' said the Prince.

'As you have spoken pleasantly to me, and not been haughty like your false brothers, I will help you and tell you how to find the Water of Life. It flows from a fountain in the courtyard of an enchanted castle; but you will never get in unless I give you an iron rod and two loaves of bread. With the rod strike three times on the iron gate of the castle, and it will spring open. Inside you will find two lions with wide-open jaws, but if you throw a loaf to each they will be quiet. Then you must make haste to fetch the Water of Life before it strikes twelve, or the gates of the castle will close and you will be shut in.'

The Prince thanked him, took the rod and the loaves, and set off. When he reached the castle all was just as the dwarf had said. At the third knock the gate flew open, and when he had pacified the lions with the loaves, he walked into the castle. In the great hall he found several enchanted Princes, and he took the rings from their fingers. He also took a sword and a loaf, which were lying by them. On passing into the next room he found a beautiful maiden, who rejoiced at his coming. She embraced him, and said that he had saved her, and should have the whole of her kingdom; and if he would come back in a year she would marry him. She also told him where to find the fountain with the enchanted water; but, she said, he must make haste to get out of the castle before the clock struck twelve.

Then he went on, and came to a room where there was a beautiful bed freshly made, and as he was very tired he thought he would take a little rest; so he lay down and fell asleep. When he woke it was striking a quarter to twelve. He sprang up in a fright, ran to the fountain and took some of the water in a cup which was lying near, and then hurried away. The clock struck just as he reached the iron gate, and it banged so quickly that it took off a bit of his heel.

He was rejoiced at having got some of the Water of Life, and hastened on his homeward journey. He again passed the dwarf, who said, when he saw the sword and the loaf, 'Those things will be of much service to you. You will be able to strike down whole armies with the sword, and the loaf will never come to an end.'

The Prince did not want to go home without his brothers, and he said, 'Good dwarf, can you not tell me where my brothers are? They went in search of the Water of Life before I did, but they never came back.'

'They are both stuck fast in a narrow mountain gorge. I cast a spell over them because of their pride.'

Then the Prince begged so hard that they might be released that at last the dwarf yielded; but he warned him against them and said, 'Beware of them; they have bad hearts.'

He was delighted to see his brothers when they came back, and told them all that had happened to him; how he had found the Water of Life, and brought a goblet full with him. How he had released a beautiful Princess, who would wait a year for him and then marry him, and he would become a great Prince.

Then they rode away together, and came to a land where famine and war were raging. The K...g thought he would be utterly ruined, so great was the destitution.

The Prince went to him and gave him the loaf, and with it he fed and satisfied his whole kingdom. The Prince also gave him his sword, and he smote the whole army of his enemies with it, and then he was able to live in peace and quiet. Then the Prince took back his sword and his loaf, and the three brothers rode on. But they had to pass through two more countries where war and famine were raging, and each time the Prince gave his sword and his loaf to the King, and in this way he saved three kingdoms.

After that they took a ship and crossed the sea. During the passage the two elder brothers said to each other, 'Our youngest brother found the Water of Life, and we did not, so our father will give him the kingdom which we ought to have, and he will take away our fortune from us.'

This thought made them very vindictive, and they made up their minds to get rid of him. They waited till he was asleep, and then they emptied the Water of Life from his goblet and took it themselves, and filled up his cup with salt sea water.

As soon as they got home the youngest Prince took his goblet to the King, so that he might drink of the water which was to make him well; but after drinking only a few drops of the sea water he became more ill than ever. As he was bewailing himself, his two elder sons came to him and accused the youngest of trying to poison him, and said that they had the real Water of Life, and gave him some. No sooner had he drunk it than he felt better, and he soon became as strong and well as he had been in his youth.

Then the two went to their youngest brother, and mocked him, saying, 'It was you who found the Water of Life; you had all the trouble, while we have the reward. You should have been wiser, and kept your eyes open; we stole it from you while you were asleep on the ship. When the end of the year comes, one of us will go and bring away the beautiful Princess. But don't dare to betray us. Our father will certainly not believe you, and if you say a single word you will lose your life; your only chance is to keep silence.'

The old King was very angry with his youngest son, thinking that he had tried to take his life. So he had the Court assembled to give judgment upon him, and it was decided that he must be secretly got out of the way.

One day when the Prince was going out hunting, thinking no evil, the King's huntsman was ordered to go with him. Seeing the huntsman look sad, the Prince said to him, 'My good huntsman, what is the matter with you?'

The huntsman answered, 'I can't bear to tell you, and yet I must.'

The Prince said, 'Say it out; whatever it is I will forgive you.'

'Alas!' said the huntsman, 'I am to shoot you dead; it is the King's command.'

The Prince was horror-stricken, and said, 'Dear huntsman, do not kill me; give me my life. Let me have your dress, and you shall have my royal robes.'

The huntsman said, 'I will gladly do so; I could never have shot you.' So they changed clothes, and the huntsman went home, but the Prince wandered away into the forest.

After a time three wagon-loads of gold and precious stones came to the King for his youngest son. They were sent by the Kings who had been saved by the Prince's sword and his miraculous loaf, and who now wished to show their gratitude.

Then the old King thought, 'What if my son really was innocent?' and said to his people, 'If only he were still alive! How sorry I am that I ordered him to be killed.'

'He is still alive,' said the huntsman. 'I could not find it in my heart to carry out your commands,' and he told the King what had taken place.

A load fell from the King's heart on hearing the good news, and he sent out a proclamation to all parts of his kingdom that his son was to come home, where he would be received with great favour.

In the meantime, the Princess had caused a road to be made of pure shining gold leading to her castle, and told her people that whoever came riding straight along it would be the true bridegroom, and they were to admit him. But anyone who came either on one side of the road or the other would not be the right one, and he was not to be let in.

When the year had almost passed, the eldest Prince thought that he would hurry to the Princess, and by giving himself out as her deliverer would gain a wife and a kingdom as well. So he rode away, and when he saw the beautiful golden road he thought it would be a thousand pities to ride upon it; so he turned aside, and rode to the right of it. But when he reached the gate the people told him that he was not the true bridegroom, and he had to go away.

Soon after the second Prince came, and when he saw the golden road he thought it would be a thousand pities for his horse to tread upon it; so he turned aside, and rode up on the left of it. But when he reached the gate he was also told that he was not the true bridegroom, and, like his brother, was turned away.

When the year had quite come to an end, the third Prince came out of the wood to ride to his beloved, and through her to forget all his past sorrows. So on he went, thinking only of her, and wishing to be with her; and he never even saw the golden road. His horse cantered right along the middle of it, and when he reached the gate it was flung open and the Princess received him joyfully, and called him her deliverer, and the lord of her kingdom. Their marriage was celebrated without

delay, and with much rejoicing. When it was over, she told him that his father had called him back and forgiven him. So he went to him and told him everything; how his brothers had deceived him, and how they had forced him to keep silence. The old King wanted to punish them, but they had taken a ship and sailed away over the sea, and they never came back as long as they lived.

Seven Swabians were once together. The first was Master Schulz; the second, Jackli; the third, Marli; the fourth, Jergli; the fifth, Michal; the sixth, Hans; the seventh, Veitli: all seven had made up their minds to travel about the world to seek adventures and perform great deeds. But in order that they might go in security and with arms in their hands, they thought it would be advisable that they should have one solitary, but very strong and very long, spear made for them. This spear all seven of them took in their hands at once; in front walked the boldest and bravest, and that was Master Schulz; all the others followed in a row, and Veitli was the last.

Then it came to pass one day in the haymaking month (July), when they had walked a long distance and still had a long way to go before they reached the village where they were to pass the night, that as they were in a meadow in the twilight a great beetle or hornet flew by them from behind a bush and hummed in a menacing manner. Master Schulz was so terrified that he all but dropped the spear, and a cold perspiration broke out over his whole body. 'Hark! hark!' cried he to his comrades, 'Good heavens! I hear a drum.'

Jackli, who was behind him holding the spear, and who perceived some kind of a smell, said, 'Something is most certainly going on, for I taste powder and matches.'

At these words Master Schulz began to take to flight, and in a trice jumped over a hedge, but as he just happened to jump on to the teeth of a rake which had been left lying there after the haymaking, the handle of it struck against his face and gave him a tremendous blow. 'Oh dear! Oh dear!' screamed Master Schulz. 'Take me prisoner; I surrender! I surrender!'

The other six all leapt over, one on top of the other, crying, 'If you surrender, I surrender too! If you surrender, I surrender too!' At length, as no enemy was there to bind and take them away, they saw that they had been mistaken, and in order that the story might not be known and they be treated as fools and ridiculed, they all swore to each other to hold their peace about it until one of them accidentally spoke of it.

Then they journeyed onwards. The second danger which they survived cannot be compared with the first. Some days afterwards, their path led them through a fallow-field where a hare was sitting sleeping in the sun. Her ears were standing straight up, and her great glassy eyes were wide open. All of them were alarmed at the sight of the horrible wild beast, and they consulted together as to what it would be the least dangerous to do. For if they were to run away, they knew that the

140

monster would pursue and swallow them whole. So they said, 'We must go through a great and dangerous struggle. Boldly ventured is half won,' and all seven grasped the spear, Master Schulz in front, and Veitli behind. Master Schulz was always trying to keep the spear back, but Veitli had become quite brave while behind, and wanted to dash forward and cried:

> 'Strike home, in every Swabian's name,
> Or else I wish ye may be lame.'

But Hans knew how to meet this, and said:

> 'Thunder and lightning, it's fine to prate,
> But for dragon-hunting thou'rt aye too late.'

Michal cried:

> 'Nothing is wanting, not even a hair,
> Be sure the Devil himself is there.'

Then it was Jergli's turn to speak:

> 'If it be not, it's at least his mother,
> Or else it's the Devil's own step-brother.'

And now Marli had a bright thought, and said to Veitli:

> 'Advance, Veitli, advance, advance,
> And I behind will hold the lance.'

Veitli, however, did not attend to that, and Jackli said:

> ' 'Tis Schulz's place the first to be,
> No one deserves the honour but he.'

Then Master Schulz plucked up his courage, and said gravely:

> 'Then let us boldly advance to the fight,
> And thus we shall show our valour and might.'

Hereupon they all together set on the dragon. Master Schulz crossed himself and prayed for God's assistance, but as all this was of no avail, and he was getting nearer and nearer to the enemy, he screamed, 'Oho! Oho! ho! ho! ho!' in the greatest anguish. This awakened the hare, which in great alarm darted swiftly away. When Master Schulz thus saw her flying from the field of battle, he cried in his joy:

'Quick, Veitli, quick, look there, look there,
The monster's nothing but a hare.'

But the Swabian allies went in search of further adventures, and came to the Moselle, a mossy, quiet, deep river, over which there are few bridges and which in many places people have to cross in boats. As the seven Swabians did not know this, they called to a man who was working on the opposite side of the river, to know how people contrived to get across. The distance and their way of speaking made the man unable to understand what they wanted, and he said, 'What? what?' in the way people speak in the neighbourhood of Trêves. Master Schulz thought he was saying, 'Wade, wade through the water,' and as he was the first, began to set out and went into the Moselle. It was not long before he sank in the mud, and the deep waves which drove against him, but his hat was blown on the opposite shore by the wind, and a frog sat down beside it and croaked, 'Wat, wat, wat.' The other six on the opposite side heard that, and said, 'Oho, comrades, Master Schulz is calling us; if he can wade across, why cannot we?' So they all jumped into the water together in a great hurry and were drowned, and thus one frog took the lives of six of them, and not one of the Swabian allies ever reached home again.

CLEVER GRETHEL

There was once a cook called Grethel, who wore shoes with red rosettes; and when she went out in them, she turned and twisted about gaily, and thought, 'How fine I am!'

After her walk she would take a draught of wine in her light-heartedness; and as wine gives an appetite, she would then taste some of the dishes that she was cooking, saying to herself, 'The cook is bound to know how the food tastes.'

It so happened that one day her master said to her, 'Grethel, I have a guest coming tonight; roast me two fowls in your best style.'

'It shall be done, sir!' answered Grethel. So she killed the chickens, scalded and plucked them, and then put them on the spit; towards evening she put them down to the fire to roast. They got brown and crisp, but still the guest did not come. Then Grethel called to her master, 'If the guest does not come I must take the fowls from the fire; but it will be a thousand pities if they are not eaten soon while they are juicy.'

Her master said, 'I will go and hasten the guest myself.'

Hardly had her master turned his back before Grethel laid the spit with the fowls on it on one side, and said to herself, 'It's thirsty work standing over the fire so long. Who knows when he will come. I'll go down into the cellar in the meantime and take a drop of wine.'

She ran down and held a jug to the tap, then said, 'Here's to your health, Grethel,' and took a good pull. 'Drinking leads to drinking,' she said, 'and it's not easy to give it up,' and again she took a good pull. Then she went upstairs and put the fowls to the fire again, poured some butter over them, and turned the spit round with a will. It smelt so good that she thought, 'There may be something wanting; I must have a taste.' And she passed her finger over the fowls and put it in her mouth. 'Ah, how good they are; it's a sin and a shame that there's nobody to eat them.' She ran to the window to see if her master was coming with the guest, but she saw nobody. Then she went back to the fowls again, and thought, 'One wing is catching a little, better to eat it—and eat it I will.' So she cut it off and ate it with much enjoyment. When it was finished, she thought, 'The other must follow, or the master will notice that something is wanting.' When the wings were consumed she went back to the window again to look for her master, but no one was in sight.

'Who knows,' she thought. 'I dare say they won't come at all; they must have dropped in somewhere else.' Then she said to herself, 'Now, Grethel, don't be afraid, eat it all up; why should good food be wasted? When it's all gone you can rest; run and have another drink and then finish it up.' So she went down to the cellar, took a good drink, and contentedly ate up the rest of the fowl. When it had all disappeared and still no master came, Grethel looked at the other fowl and said, 'Where one is gone the other must follow. What is good for one is right for the other. If I have a drink first I shall be none the worse.' So she took another hearty pull at the jug, and then she sent the other fowl after the first one.

In the height of her enjoyment, her master came back, and cried, 'Hurry, Grethel, the guest is just coming.'

'Very well, sir, I'll soon have it ready,' answered Grethel.

Her master went to see if the table was properly laid, and took the big carving-knife with which he meant to cup up the fowls, to sharpen it. In the meantime the guest came and knocked politely at the door. Grethel ran to see who was there, and, seeing the guest, she put her finger to her lips and said, 'Be quiet, and get away quickly; if my master catches you it will be the worse for you. He certainly invited you to supper, but only with the intention of cutting off both your ears. You can hear him sharpening his knife now.'

The guest heard the knife being sharpened, and hurried off down the steps as fast as he could.

Grethel ran with great agility to her master, shrieking, 'A fine guest you have invited, indeed!'

'Why, what's the matter, Grethel? What do you mean?'

'Well,' she said, 'he has taken the two fowls that I had just put upon the dish, and run off with them.'

'That's a clever trick!' said her master, regretting his fine fowls. 'If he had only left me one so that I had something to eat.'

He called out to him to stop, but the guest pretended not to hear. Then he ran after him, still holding the carving-knife, and cried, 'Only one, only one!'—meaning that the guest should leave him one fowl; but the guest only thought that he meant he was to give him one ear, and he ran as if he were pursued by fire, and so took both his ears safely home.

HANSEL AND GRETHEL

Close to a large forest there lived a woodcutter with his wife and his two children. The boy was called Hansel and the girl Grethel. They were always very poor and had very little to live on, and at one time, when there was famine in the land, he could no longer procure daily bread.

One night he lay in bed worrying over his troubles, and he sighed and said to his wife: 'What is to become of us? How are we to feed our poor children when we have nothing for ourselves?'

'I'll tell you what, husband,' answered the woman, 'tomorrow morning we will take the children out quite early into the thickest part of the forest. We will light a fire, and give each of them a piece of bread; then we will go to our work and leave them alone. They won't be able to find their way back, and so we shall be rid of them.'

'Nay, wife,' said the man, 'we won't do that. I could never find it in my heart to leave my children alone in the forest; the wild animals would soon tear them to pieces.'

'What a fool you are!' she said. 'Then we must all four die of hunger. You may as well plane the boards for our coffins at once.'

She gave him no peace till he consented. 'But I grieve over the poor children all the same,' said the man.

The two children could not go to sleep for hunger either, and they heard what their stepmother said to their father.

Grethel wept bitterly, and said: 'All is over with us now!'

'Be quiet, Grethel!' said Hansel. 'Don't cry; I will find some way out of it.'

When the old people had gone to sleep, he got up, put on his little coat, opened the door, and slipped out. The moon was shining brightly, and the white pebbles round the house shone like newly-minted coins. Hansel stooped down and put as many into his pockets as they would hold.

Then he went back to Grethel, and said: 'Take comfort, little sister, and go to sleep. God won't forsake us.' And then he went to bed again.

When the day broke, before the sun had risen, the woman came and said, 'Get up, you lazy-bones; we are going into the forest to fetch wood.'

Then she gave them each a piece of bread, and said, 'Here is something for your dinner, but mind you don't eat it before, for you'll get no more.'

Grethel put the bread under her apron, for Hansel had the stones in his pockets. Then they all started for the forest.

When they had gone a little way, Hansel stopped and looked back at the cottage, and he did the same thing again and again.

His father said: 'Hansel, what are you stopping to look back at? Take care, and put your best foot foremost.'

'O Father!' said Hansel, 'I am looking at my white cat; it is sitting on the roof, wanting to say good-bye to me.'

'Little fool! that's no cat, it's the morning sun shining on the chimney.'

But Hansel had not been looking at the cat, he had been dropping a pebble on to the ground each time he stopped. When they reached the middle of the forest, their father said:

'Now, children, pick up some wood, I want to make a fire to warm you.'

Hansel and Grethel gathered the twigs together and soon made a huge pile. Then the pile was lighted, and when it blazed up, the woman said, 'Now lie down by the fire and rest yourselves while we go and cut wood; when we have finished we will come back to fetch you.'

Hansel and Grethel sat by the fire, and when dinner-time came they each ate their little bit of bread, and they thought their father was quite near because they could hear the sound of an axe. It was no axe, however, but a branch which the man had tied to a dead tree, and which blew backwards and forwards against it. They sat there such a long time that they got tired, their eyes began to close, and they were soon fast asleep.

When they woke it was dark night. Grethel began to cry: 'How shall we ever get out of the wood!'

But Hansel comforted her, and said, 'Wait a little till the moon rises, then we will soon find our way.'

When the full moon rose, Hansel took his little sister's hand, and they walked on, guided by the pebbles, which glittered like newly-coined money. They walked the whole night, and at daybreak they found themselves back at their father's cottage.

They knocked at the door, and when the woman opened it and saw Hansel and Grethel, she said, 'You bad children, why did you sleep so long in the wood? We thought you did not mean to come back any more.'

But their father was delighted, for it had gone to his heart to leave them behind alone.

Not long after they were again in great destitution, and the children heard the woman at night in bed say to their father: 'We have eaten up everything. The children must go away; we will take them further into the forest so that they won't be able to find their way back. There is nothing else to be done.'

The man took it much to heart, and said, 'We had better share our last crust with the children.'

But the woman would not listen to a word he said; she only scolded and reproached him. Anyone who once says A must also say B, and as he had given in the first time, he had to do so the second also. The children were again wide awake and heard what was said.

When the old people went to sleep, Hansel again got up, meaning to go out and get some more pebbles, but the woman had locked the door and he couldn't get out. But he consoled his little sister, and said: 'Don't cry, Grethel; go to sleep. God will help us.'

In the early morning the woman made the children get up and gave them each a piece of bread, but it was smaller than the last. On the way to the forest Hansel crumbled it up in his pocket, and stopped every now and then to throw a crumb on to the ground.

'Hansel, what are you stopping to look about you for?' asked his father.

'I am looking at my dove which is sitting on the roof and wants to say good-bye to me,' answered Hansel.

'Little fool!' said the woman, 'that is no dove, it is the morning sun shining on the chimney.'

Nevertheless, Hansel strewed the crumbs from time to time on the ground. The woman led the children far into the forest where they had never been in their lives before. Again they made a big fire, and the woman said:

'Stay where you are, children, and when you are tired you may go to sleep for a while. We are going further on to cut wood, and in the evening when we have finished we will come back and fetch you.'

At dinner-time Grethel shared her bread with Hansel, for he had crumbled his up on the road. Then they went to sleep, and the evening passed, but no one came to fetch the poor children.

It was quite dark when they woke up, and Hansel cheered his little sister, and said:

'Wait a bit, Grethel, till the moon rises, then we can see the bread-crumbs which I scattered to show us the way home.'

When the moon rose they started, but they found no bread-crumbs, for all the thousands of birds in the forest had pecked them up and eaten them.

Hansel said to Grethel: 'We shall soon find the way.'

But they could not find it. They walked the whole night, and all the next day from morning till night, but they could not get out of the wood. They were very hungry, for they had nothing to eat but a few berries which they found. They were so tired that their legs would not carry them any further, and they lay down under a tree and went to sleep.

When they woke in the morning it was the third day since they had left their father's cottage.

They started to walk again, but they only got deeper and deeper into the wood, and if no help came they must perish.

At midday they saw a beautiful snow-white bird sitting on a tree. It sang so beautifully that they stood still to listen to it. When it stopped, it fluttered its wings and flew round them. They followed it till they came to a little cottage, on the roof of which it settled itself.

When they got quite near, they saw that the little house was made of bread, and it was roofed with cake; the windows were transparent sugar.

'This will be something for us,' said Hansel. 'We will have a good meal. I will have a piece of the roof, Grethel, and you can have a bit of the window; it will be nice and sweet.'

Hansel stretched up and broke off a piece of the roof to try what it was like. Grethel went to the window and nibbled at that. A gentle voice called out from within:

> 'Nibbling, nibbling, like a mouse,
> Who's nibbling at my little house?'

The children answered:

> 'The wind, the wind doth blow
> From heaven to earth below,'

and went on eating without disturbing themselves. Hansel, who found the roof very good, broke off a large piece for himself; and Grethel pushed a whole round pane out of the window, and sat down on the ground to enjoy it.

All at once the door opened and an old, old woman, supporting herself on a crutch, came hobbling out. Hansel and Grethel were so frightened that they dropped what they held in their hands.

But the old woman only shook her head and said: 'Ah, dear children, who brought you here? Come in and stay with me; you will come to no harm.'

She took them by the hand and led them into the little house. A nice dinner was set before them, pancakes and sugar, milk, apples and nuts. After this she showed them two little white beds into which they crept, and felt as if they were in heaven.

Although the old woman appeared to be so friendly, she was really a wicked old witch who was on the watch for children, and she had built the bread house on purpose to lure them to her. Whenever she could get a child into her clutches she cooked it and ate it, and considered it a grand feast. Witches have red eyes, and can't see very far, but they have keen scent like animals, and can perceive the approach of human beings.

When Hansel and Grethel came near her, she laughed wickedly to herself, and said scornfully, 'Now I have them; they shan't escape me.'

She got up early in the morning, before the children were awake, and when she saw them sleeping, with their beautiful rosy cheeks, she murmured to herself, 'They will be dainty morsels.'

She seized Hansel with her bony hand and carried him off to a little stable, where she shut him up with a barred door; he might shriek as loud as he liked, she took no notice of him. Then she went to Grethel and shook her till she woke, and cried:

'Get up, little lazy-bones, fetch some water and cook something nice for your brother; he is in the stable, and has to be fattened. When he is nice and fat, I will eat him.'

Grethel began to cry bitterly, but it was no use, she had to obey the witch's orders. The best food was now cooked for poor Hansel, but Grethel only had the shells of crayfish.

The old woman hobbled to the stable every morning, and cried: 'Hansel, put your finger out for me to feel how fat you are.'

Hansel put out a knuckle-bone, and the old woman, whose eyes were dim, could not see and thought it was his finger, and she was much astonished that he did not get fat.

When four weeks had passed, and Hansel still kept thin, she became very impatient and would wait no longer.

'Now then, Grethel,' she cried, 'bustle along and fetch the water. Fat or thin, tomorrow I will kill Hansel and eat him.'

Oh, how his poor little sister grieved! As she carried the water, the tears streamed down her cheeks.

'Dear God, help us!' she cried. 'If only the wild animals in the forest had devoured us, we should, at least, have died together.'

'You may spare your lamentations; they will do you no good,' said the old woman.

Early in the morning Grethel had to go out to fill the kettle with water, and then she had to kindle a fire and hang the kettle over it.

'We will bake first,' said the old witch. 'I have heated the oven and kneaded the dough.' She pushed poor Grethel towards the oven, and said: 'Creep in and see if it is properly heated, and then we will put the bread in.'

She meant, when Grethel had got in, to shut the door and roast her. But Grethel saw her intention, and said, 'I don't know how to get in. How am I to manage it?'

'Stupid goose!' cried the witch. 'The opening is big enough; you can see that I could get into it myself.'

She hobbled up, and stuck her head into the oven. But Grethel gave her a push which sent the witch right in, and then she banged the door and bolted it.

'Oh! oh!' she began to howl horribly. But Grethel ran away and left the wicked witch to perish miserably

Grethel ran as fast as she could to the stable. She opened the door, and cried: 'Hansel, we are saved. The old witch is dead.'

Hansel sprang out, like a bird out of a cage when the door is set open. How delighted they were! They fell upon each other's necks, and kissed each other, and danced about for joy.

As they had nothing more to fear, they went into the witch's house, and they found chests in every corner full of pearls and precious stones.

'These are better than pebbles,' said Hansel, as he filled his pockets.

Grethel said, 'I must take something home with me too.' And she filled her apron.

'But now we must go,' said Hansel, 'so that we may get out of this enchanted wood.'

Before they had gone very far they came to a great piece of water.

'We can't get across it,' said Hansel; 'I see no stepping-stones and no bridge.'

'And there are no boats either,' answered Grethel. 'But there is a duck swiming; it will help us over if we ask it.' So she cried:

> 'Little duck, that cries quack, quack,
> Here Grethel and here Hansel stand.
> Quickly, take us on your back,
> No path nor bridge is there at hand!'

The duck came swimming towards them, and Hansel got on its back and told his sister to sit on his knee.

'No,' answered Grethel, 'it will be too heavy for the duck; it must take us over one after the other.'

The good creature did this, and when they had got safely over and walked for a while, the wood seemed to grow more and more familiar to them, and at last they saw their father's cottage in the distance. They began to run, and rushed inside, where they threw their arms round their father's neck. The man had not had a single happy moment since he had deserted his children in the wood, and in the meantime his wife was dead.

Grethel shook her apron and scattered the pearls and precious stones all over the floor, and Hansel added handful after handful out of his pockets.

So all their troubles came to an end, and they lived together as happily as possible.

THE FROG PRINCE

In the olden times, when wishing was some good, there lived a King whose daughters were all beautiful, but the youngest was so lovely that even the sun, that looked on many things, could not but marvel when he shone upon her face.

Near the King's palace there was a large dark forest, and in the forest, under an old lime-tree, was a well. When the day was very hot the Princess used to go into the forest and sit upon the edge of this cool well; and when she was tired of doing nothing she would play with a golden ball, throwing it up in the air and catching it again, and this was her favourite game. Now on one occasion it so happened that the ball did not fall back into her hand stretched up to catch it, but dropped to the ground and rolled straight into the well. The Princess followed it with her eyes, but it disappeared, for the well was so very deep that it was quite impossible to see the bottom. Then she began to cry bitterly, and nothing would comfort her.

As she was lamenting in this manner, someone called out to her, 'What is the matter, Princess? Your lamentations would move the heart of a stone.'

She looked round towards the spot whence the voice came, and saw a frog stretching its broad, ugly face out of the water.

'Oh, it's you, is it, old splasher? I am crying for my golden ball which has fallen into the water.'

'Be quiet then, and stop crying,' answered the frog. 'I know what to do; but what will you give me if I get you back your plaything?'

'Whatever you like, you dear old frog,' she said, 'my clothes, my pearls and diamonds, or even the golden crown upon my head.'

The frog answered, 'I care not for your clothes, your pearls and diamonds, nor even your golden crown; but if you will be fond of me, and let me be your playmate, sit by you at table, eat out of your plate, drink out of your cup, and sleep in your little bed—if you will promise to do all this, I will go down and fetch your ball.'

'I will promise anything you like to ask, if only you will get me back my ball.'

She thought, 'What is the silly old frog chattering about? He lives in the well, croaking with his mates, and he can't be the companion of a human being.'

As soon as the frog received her promise, he ducked his head under the water and disappeared. After a little while, back he came with the ball in his mouth, and threw it on to the grass beside her.

The Princess was full of joy when she saw her pretty toy again, picked it up, and ran off with it.

'Wait, wait,' cried the frog. 'Take me with you; I can't run as fast as you can.'

But what was the good of his crying 'Croak, croak,' as loud as he could? She did not listen to him, but hurried home, and forgot all about the poor frog; and he had to go back to his well.

The next day, as she was sitting at dinner with the King and all the courtiers, eating out of her golden plate, something came flopping up the stairs, flip, flap, flip, flap. When it reached the top it knocked at the door, and cried: 'Youngest daughter of the King, you must let me in.' She ran to see who it was. When she opened the door and saw the frog she shut it again very quickly and went back to the table, for she was very much frightened.

The King saw that her heart was beating very fast, and he said: 'My child, what is the matter? Is there a giant at the door wanting to take you away?'

'Oh no!' she said, 'it's not a giant, but a hideous frog.'

'What does the frog want with you?'

'Oh, father dear, last night when I was playing by the well in the forest my golden ball fell into the water. And I cried, and the frog got it out for me; and then, because he insisted on it, I promised that he should be my playmate. But I never thought that he would come out of the water; but there he is, and he wants to come in to me.'

He knocked at the door for the second time, and sang:

> 'Youngest daughter of the King,
> Take me up, I sing;
> Know'st thou not what yesterday
> Thou to me didst say
> By the well in forest dell.
> Youngest daughter of the King,
> Take me up, I sing.'

Then said the King, 'What you have promised you must perform. Go and open the door for him.'

So she opened the door, and the frog shuffled in, keeping close to her feet, till he reached her chair. Then he cried, 'Lift me up beside you.' She hesitated, till the King ordered her to do it. When the frog was put on the chair, he demanded to be placed upon the table, and then he said, 'Push your golden plate nearer that we may eat together.' She did as he asked her, but very unwillingly, as could easily be seen. The frog made a good dinner, but the Princess could not swallow a morsel. At last he said, 'I have eaten enough, and I am tired, carry me into your bedroom and arrange your silken bed, that we may go to sleep.'

The Princess began to cry, for she was afraid of the clammy frog, which she did not dare to touch and which was now to sleep in her pretty little silken bed.

But the King grew very angry, and said, 'You must not despise anyone who has helped you in your need.'

So she seized him with two fingers and carried him upstairs, where she put him in a corner of her room. When she got into bed, he crept up to her and said, 'I am tired, and I want to go to sleep as well as you. Lift me up, or I will tell your father.'

She was very angry, picked him up, and threw him with all her might against the wall, saying, 'You may rest there as well as you can, you hideous frog.' But when he fell to the ground he was no longer a hideous frog, but a handsome Prince with beautiful friendly eyes.

And at her father's wish he became her beloved companion and husband. He told her that he had been bewitched by a wicked fairy, and nobody could have released him from the spells but she herself.

Next morning, when the sun rose, a coach drove up drawn by eight milk-white horses, with white ostrich plumes on their heads, and a golden harness. Behind stood faithful Henry, the Prince's body-servant. The faithful fellow had been so distressed when his master was changed into a frog that he had caused three iron bands to be placed round his heart, lest it should break from grief and pain.

The coach had come to carry the young pair back into the Prince's own kingdom. The faithful Henry helped both of them into the coach and mounted again behind, delighted at his master's deliverance.

They had only gone a little way when the Prince heard a cracking behind him, as if something were breaking. He turned round, and cried:

> 'Henry, the coach is giving way!'
> 'No, Sir, the coach is safe, I say,
> A band from my heart has fall'n in twain,
> For long I suffered woe and pain.
> While you a frog within a well
> Enchanted were by witch's spell!'

Once more he heard the same snapping and cracking, and then again. The Prince thought it must be some part of the carriage breaking, but it was only the bands round faithful Henry's heart which were snapping, because of his great joy at his master's deliverance and happiness.

HANS CHRISTIAN ANDERSEN'S
FAIRY TALES

THE TINDER-BOX

A soldier came marching along the road: 'Left, right! Left, right!' He had his knapsack on his back and a sword by his side, for he had been to the wars, and was now returning home. On the road he met an old witch—a horrid-looking creature. Her under-lip hung down quite to her breast.

'Good evening, soldier!' said she. 'What a bright sword, and what a large knapsack you have! You're the right sort of soldier, and you shall have as much money as you can wish for!'

'Thank you, old witch!' said the soldier.

'Do you see that large tree?' said she, pointing to a tree that stood by the wayside. 'It is quite hollow. Climb up to the top, and you will find a hole large enough for you to creep through, and so let yourself down into the tree. I will tie a rope round your waist, so that I can pull you up again when you call me.'

'But what am I to do down there in the tree?' asked the soldier. 'Why, fetch money, to be sure!' answered the witch. 'As soon as you get to the bottom, you will find yourself in a large, well lit hall, for more than three hundred lamps are burning there. Then you will see three doors which you can open easily, for the keys are in the locks. On opening the first door you will enter a room. In the middle of it, on the floor, stands a large chest with a dog seated on it whose eyes are as large as tea-cups. But don't trouble about him. I will lend you my blue checked apron, and you must spread it on the floor, and then go briskly up to the dog, and seize him, and set

163

him down on it. When that is done, you can open the chest and take as many pennies as you choose. That chest contains only copper coins. If you like silver better, you must go into the next room, and there you will find a dog with eyes as large as mill-wheels. Don't be afraid of him; you have only to set him down on my apron, and then rifle the chest at your leisure. But if you would rather have gold than either silver or copper, that is to be had too, and as much of it as you can carry, if you pass on into the third chamber. The dog that sits on this third money-chest is very terrible, and has eyes as big as towers. But don't be afraid; if you set him down on my apron, he will do you no harm, and you can take as much gold from the chest as you like.'

'That sounds all right,' said the soldier. 'But what am I to give you for all this, old woman? For, of course, you don't intend to tell me this for nothing.'

'Not a penny will I take,' answered the witch. 'I wish you only to bring me an old tinder-box which my grandmother left there by mistake the last time she was down in the tree.'

'Well, then, give me the rope and I'll be gone,' said the soldier.

'Here it is,' said the witch, 'and here is my blue apron.'

So the soldier climbed the tree, let himself down through the hole in the trunk, and found himself in the wide hall lit up by more than three hundred candles, as the witch had said.

He opened the first door. Faugh! There sat the dog with eyes as large as tea-cups, staring at him as though in utter amazement.

'There's a good dog!' said the soldier, as he spread the witch's apron on the floor, and lifted the animal on to it. He then filled his pockets with the copper coins in the chest, shut the lid, put the dog back in his place, and passed on into the second room.

There, right enough, sat the dog with eyes as large as mill-wheels.

'You had really better not stare so,' said the soldier. 'Your eyes might start out of your head altogether, you know.' With that he lifted the dog and set it down on the witch's apron. But when he saw the vast quantity of silver there was in the chest, he threw his pence away in disgust, and filled his pockets and his knapsack with the silver. Then he passed on into the third chamber. The dog in this chamber actually had a pair of eyes each as large as a tower, and they kept rolling round and round in his head like wheels.

'Good evening!' said the soldier, saluting respectfully, for such a dog as this he had never before seen or heard of. He stood still for a minute or two, looking at him, then thinking: 'The sooner it's done the better!' he took hold of the immense creature, removed him from the chest to the apron, and raised the lid of the chest. Oh, what a heap of gold was there, enough to buy all the cakes and sugar-plums, all the tin soldiers, whips, and rocking-horses in the world, and to buy the whole town as well! Hastily the soldier threw away all the silver money he had stuffed into his pockets and knapsack, and filled not only them, but even his cap and boots with gold. He could hardly walk for the weight he carried. He lifted the dog on to the chest again, banged the door of the room behind him, and called up the tree: 'Halloo, you old witch! Pull me up!'

'Have you got the tinder-box?' asked the witch.

'Upon my honour, I'd quite forgotten it!' shouted the soldier, and back he went to fetch it. The witch then drew him up, and now he stood again in the highroad, with his pockets, boots, knapsack, and cap stuffed with gold-pieces.

'What are you going to do with the tinder-box?' asked the soldier.

'That's no business of yours,' said the witch. 'You've got your money; give me my tinder-box!'

'Well, take your choice!' said the soldier. 'Tell me this instant what you want with the tinder-box, or I'll cut off your head.'

'I won't tell you!' screamed the witch.

So the soldier drew his sword and cut off her head. Then he made haste to tie all his money securely in her blue apron, slung it across his back, put the tinder-box into his pocket, and went on to the nearest town.

It was a large, handsome city. He walked into the first hotel in the place, called for the best rooms, and ordered the choicest dishes for his supper, for he was now a rich man, with plenty of gold to spend.

The man who cleaned his boots thought them too old and shabby for such a grand gentleman; but next day the soldier provided himself with new boots, and very gay clothes besides. Our soldier was now a fine gentleman, and the people came to visit him and gave him information about all the places of amusement in the city, and about their King, and the beautiful Princess, his daughter.

'I should rather like to see her,' said the soldier.

'No one can see her at all,' was the reply. 'She lives in a great stone castle, with ever so many walls and towers round it. No one but the King may go and visit her there, because it has been foretold that she will marry a common soldier, and our King cannot bear to think of that!'

'I should very much like to see her, though, just for once!' thought the soldier; but he could not get permission to do so.

And now he lived a gay life, went constantly to theatres, drove in the royal parks and gardens, and gave much money to the poor. He knew of old what a wretched thing it was not to have a shilling in one's pocket. He was always gaily dressed, and had a crowd of friends, who, one and all, declared he was a capital fellow, a real gentleman; and that pleased our soldier very much. But, as he kept on giving and spending every day, and never received anything in return, his money began to run out; and at last he had only a couple of shillings left, so he was forced to exchange his beautiful rooms for an attic, where he had to brush his own boots, and darn his own clothes, and where none of his friends ever came to see him, because there were so many stairs to go up that it was too fatiguing.

It was a very dark night, and he could not even afford to buy himself a rush-light;

then all at once he remembered that there was a bit of candle in the tinder-box that the old witch had bade him fetch out of the hollow tree. So he brought out the tinder-box and began to strike a light. But no sooner had he struck a few sparks from the flint, than the door burst open, and the dog with eyes as large as tea-cups, the one he had seen in the cavern beneath the tree, stood before him and said, 'What commands has my master for his slave?'

'What's this?' cried the soldier. 'This is a splendid sort of tinder-box, if it will furnish me with whatever I want. Fetch me some money,' said he to the dog. The creature vanished, and in half a minute was back again, with a large bag of coppers in his mouth.

Soon the soldier began to understand the rare virtues of this charming tinder-box. If he struck the flint only once, the dog that sat on the chest full of copper came to him; if he struck it twice, the dog that watched over the silver, and if he struck it three times, the dog with eyes like towers who kept guard over the gold.

The soldier now had plenty of money. He went back to his fine rooms, and dressed himself in fine clothes, so that all his friends knew him again, and thought as highly of him as ever.

One day he thought how ridiculous it was that no one should be allowed to see the Princess. Everyone said she was so very beautiful that it was a shame she should be shut up in that great stone castle surrounded by high walls. 'I do so want to see her if it could be managed,' thought he; 'but where's my tinder-box?' He struck the flint, and the dog with eyes as large as tea-cups stood before him.

'It is rather late, I know,' began the soldier, 'but I do wish to see the Princess so much, if only for a moment!'

The dog was out of the door, and, before the soldier could even look round, he was back again with the Princess sitting asleep on his back. She was so beautiful, so wonderfully beautiful, that everyone who saw her knew her at once for a real princess.

The soldier could not help himself; like a true soldier he knelt and kissed her hand. Then the dog ran back to the palace with the Princess that very minute.

Next morning, while at breakfast with the King and Queen, the Princess told what a strange dream she had of riding on a large dog, and of a soldier who had knelt and kissed her hand.

'A pretty sort of dream indeed!' said the Queen. And she made one of the old ladies of the court watch by the Princess's bedside next night, to find out whether it was really a dream or what was the meaning of it.

Next evening the soldier longed very much to see the Princess again, so he sent the dog to fetch her. Off he went, and ran as fast as before, but not so fast that the old lady watching by the couch was unable to follow. She put on goloshes and ran behind them, and saw the dog carry the Princess into a large house. Then, thinking to herself, 'Now I know what to do,' she took out a piece of chalk and made a great white cross on the door. Then she went home to bed and the dog carried back the

Princess. But when the dog saw that a cross had been put on the door of the house where the soldier lived, he took another piece of chalk and set crosses on every door throughout the town.

Early next morning the King and Queen came with the old court dame, and all the officers of the royal household, to see where the Princess had been. 'Here it is!' said the King, when he came to the first street-door with a cross chalked on it. 'My dear,' cried the Queen, 'where are your eyes?—this must be the house,' pointing to a second door with a cross. 'No, this is it surely—Why, here's a cross too!' cried all of them together, on discovering that there were crosses on all the doors.

It was evident that their search would be in vain, and they gave it up.

But the Queen was a very wise and clever woman who could do other things besides ride in a carriage. So she took her gold scissors, cut a large piece of silk into strips, and sewed these together, to make a pretty little bag. This bag she filled with the finest white flour, tied it to the Princess's waist, and then she cut a little hole in the bag, just large enough to let the flour drop out all the time the Princess was moving.

That evening the dog came again, took the Princess on his back, and ran away with her to the soldier, who now loved her very much, and wished himself a prince, so that he might marry her. The dog did not notice how the flour went drip, drip, dripping, all the way from the palace to the soldier's house, and from the soldier's house back to the palace. So next morning the King and Queen easily found where their daughter had been carried, and they took the soldier and cast him into prison.

And there he had to stay. Oh! how dark it was, how dreary! And the keeper kept coming in to remind him that he was to be hanged on the morrow. This piece of news was by no means agreeable; and besides, the tinder-box had been left in his rooms at the hotel.

When morning came, he could see through his narrow iron grating all the people hurrying out of the town to see him hanged. He could hear the drums beating, and presently, too, he saw the soldiers marching to the place of execution. What a crowd there was rushing by! Among the crush was a shoemaker's apprentice; he was running with such speed that one of his slippers flew off and struck the bars of the soldier's prison window.

'Stop, stop, little 'prentice!' cried the soldier; 'it's of no use to be in such a hurry. The fun will not begin till I come; but if you'll run to my lodgings and fetch me my tinder-box, I'll give you a shilling. But you must run for your life.' The boy liked the idea of earning a shilling, so away he raced and brought the tinder-box to the soldier. And then—well, now we shall hear what happened then!

Outside the city a gibbet had been built; round it stood the soldiers and many thousands of people. The King and Queen sat on magnificent thrones, and opposite them sat judges and the whole council.

The soldier was brought out. He already stood on the ladder and the executioner was on the point of putting the rope round his neck, when, turning to their Majesties, he said that the last harmless request of a poor wretch was always granted, and begged them to let him smoke a pipe of tobacco; it would be the last he should ever smoke in the world.

The King could not refuse this harmless request, so the soldier took out his tinder-box and struck the flint—once he struck it, twice he struck it, three times he struck it; and in an instant the three wizard dogs stood there—the one with eyes as big as tea-cups, the one with eyes as big as mill-wheels, and the third with eyes like towers.

'Now, help me; don't let me be hanged,' cried the soldier. And the three terrible dogs fell upon the judges and councillors, tossing them high into the air—so high that in falling again they were broken in pieces.

'We will not——' began the King. But the monster dog with eyes as large as towers did not wait to hear what His Majesty would not. He seized both him and the Queen, and flung them up into the air after the councillors. And the soldiers and all the people were frightened, and shouted out with one voice: 'Good soldier, you shall be our King, and the beautiful Princess shall be your wife and our Queen!'

So the soldier was taken to the palace, and the Princess was made Queen, which she liked much better than living as a prisoner in the stone castle.

THE NIGHTINGALE

The palace of the Emperor of China was the most beautiful palace in the world. It was made entirely of fine porcelain, which was so brittle that whoever touched it had to be very careful.

The choicest flowers were to be seen in the garden; and to the prettiest of these little silver bells were fastened, in order that their tinkling might prevent anyone from passing by without noticing them. Yes! Everything in the Emperor's garden was wonderfully well arranged; and the garden itself stretched so far that even the gardener did not know the end of it. Whoever walked farther than the end of the garden, however, came to a beautiful wood with very high trees, and beyond that to the sea. The tall trees went down quite to the sea, which was very deep and blue, so that large ships could sail close under their branches; and among the branches dwelt a nightingale, who sang so sweetly that even the poor fishermen, who had so much else to do when they came out at night-time to cast their nets, would stand still to listen to her song.

Travellers came from all parts of the world to the Emperor's city, and they admired the city, the palace, and the garden; but if they heard the nightingale they all said, 'This is the best.' And they talked about her after they went home, and learned men who wrote books about the city, the palace, and the garden, praised the nightingale above everything else. Poets also wrote the most beautiful verse about the nightingale of the wood near the sea.

These books went round the world, and one of them at last reached the Emperor. He read and read, and nodded his head every moment, for these splendid descriptions of the city, the palace, and the garden, pleased him greatly. But at last he saw something that surprised him. The words: 'But the nightingale is the best of all,' were written in the book.

'What in the world is this?' said the Emperor. 'The nightingale! I do not know it at all! Can there be such a bird in my empire, in my garden even, without my having ever heard of it? Truly one may learn something from books.'

So he called his Prime Minister. Now this was so grand a personage that no one of inferior rank might speak to him, and if one did venture to ask him a question, his only answer was 'Pooh!' which has no particular meaning.

'There is said to be a very remarkable bird here, called the nightingale,' began the Emperor; 'her song, they say, is worth more than anything else in all my dominions. Why has no one ever told me of her?'

'I have never before heard her mentioned,' said the Prime Minister, 'she has never been presented at court.'

'I wish her to come and sing before me this evening,' said the Emperor. 'The whole world, it seems, knows what I have, better than I do myself!'

'I have never before heard of her,' said the Prime Minister, 'but I will seek her, and try to find her.'

But where was she to be found? The Prime Minister ran up one flight of steps, down another, through halls, and through passages, but not one of all the people he met had ever heard of the nightingale. So he went back to the Emperor, and said, 'It must be a fable invented by the man who wrote the book. Your Imperial Majesty must not believe all that is written in books; much in them is pure invention.'

'But the book in which I have read it,' said the Emperor, 'was sent me by the high and mighty Emperor of Japan, and therefore it cannot be untrue. I wish to hear the nightingale; she must be here this evening, and if she does not come, after supper the whole court shall be flogged.'

In great alarm, the Prime Minister again ran upstairs and downstairs, through halls and through passages — and half the court ran with him, for no one liked the idea of being flogged. Many were the questions asked about the wonderful nightingale, of whom the whole world talked, and about whom no one at court knew anything.

At last they met a poor little girl in the kitchen, who said, 'Oh, yes! the nightingale! I know her very well. Oh! how she can sing! Every evening I carry the fragments left at table to my poor sick mother. She lives by the sea-shore; and when I come back, and stay to rest a little while in the wood, I hear the nightingale sing. It makes the tears come into my eyes!'

'Little kitchen-maiden,' said the Prime Minister, 'I will get you a good place in the kitchen, and you shall have permission to see the Emperor dine, if you will take us to the nightingale; for she is expected at court this evening.'

So they went together to the wood where the nightingale was accustomed to sing, and half the court went with them. Whilst they were on the way, a cow began to low.

'Oh!' said the court pages, 'now we have her! It is certainly a wonderful voice for so small an animal; surely we have heard it somewhere before.'

'No, those are cows you hear lowing,' said the little kitchen-maid, 'we are still far from the place.'

The frogs were now croaking in the pond.

'There she is now!' said the chief court-preacher, 'her voice sounds just like little church-bells.'

'No, those are frogs,' said the little kitchen-maid, 'but we shall soon hear her.'

Then the nightingale began to sing.

'There she is!' said the little girl. 'Listen! Listen! There she sits,' she added, pointing to a little brown bird up in the branches.

'Is it possible?' said the Prime Minister. 'I should not have thought it. How simple she looks! She must certainly have changed colour at the sight of so many distinguished personages.'

'Little nightingale!' called out the kitchen-maid, 'our gracious Emperor wishes you to sing something to him.'

'With the greatest pleasure,' said the nightingale, and she sang so beautifully that everyone was enchanted.

'It sounds like glass bells,' said the Prime Minister. 'And look at her throat, how it moves! It is singular that we should never have heard her before; she will have great success at court.'

'Shall I sing again to the Emperor?' asked the nightingale, for she thought the Emperor was among them.

'Most excellent nightingale!' said the Prime Minister. 'I have the honour to invite you to a court festival which is to take place this evening, when His Imperial Majesty will be delighted to hear you sing.'

'My song would sound far better among the green trees,' said the nightingale, but she followed willingly when she heard that the Emperor wished it.

In the centre of the grand hall where the Emperor sat, a golden perch had been fixed, on which the nightingale was to sit. The whole court was present, and the little kitchen-maid received permission to stand behind the door, for she now had the rank and title of 'Maid of the Kitchen'. All were dressed in their finest clothes, and all eyes were fixed upon the little brown bird, to whom the Emperor nodded as a signal for her to begin.

The nightingale sang so sweetly that tears came into the Emperor's eyes and tears rolled down his cheeks. Then the nightingale sang more sweetly still, and touched the hearts of everyone who heard her; and the Emperor was so very pleased that he said:

'The nightingale shall have my golden slippers, and wear them round her neck.' Bu the nightingale thanked him, and said she was already sufficiently rewarded.

'I have seen tears in the Emperor's eyes; that is the greatest reward I can have. The tears of an Emperor have a special value. I feel myself highly honoured.' And then she sang again more beautifully than ever.

'That singing is the most charming gift ever known,' said the ladies present; and they put water into their mouths, and tried when they spoke to move their throats as she did. They thought to become nightingales also. Indeed, even the footmen and chamber-maids declared that they were quite satisfied, which was a great thing to say, for of all people they are the most difficult to please. Yes indeed! the nightingale's success was complete. She was now to remain at court, to have her own cage, with permission to fly out twice in the day and once in the night. Twelve servants were set apart to wait on her on these occasions, who were each to hold the end of a silken band fastened round her foot. There was not much pleasure in that kind of flying.

All the city was talking of the wonderful bird; and when two people met, one would say only 'nightin' and the other 'gale'; and then they sighed, and understood each other perfectly. Indeed, eleven of the children of the citizens were named after the nightingale, but not one of them could sing a note.

One day a large parcel arrived for the Emperor, on which was written 'The Nightingale'.

'Here we have another new book about our far-famed bird,' said the Emperor. But it was not a book; it was a little piece of mechanism lying in a box—an artificial nightingale, which was intended to look like the living one, but covered all over with diamonds, rubies, and sapphires. When this artificial bird had been wound up, it could sing one of the tunes that the real nightingale sang; and its tail, all glittering with silver and gold, went up and down all the time.

'That is splendid!' said everyone, and he who had brought the bird was given the title of 'Chief Imperial Nightingale-Bringer'.

Then the Emperor ordered that the real and the toy nightingales should sing together. But it did not succeed, for the real nightingale sang in her own natural way, and the artificial bird produced its tones by wheels.

'It is not his fault,' said the music master, 'for he keeps exact time, and quite according to method.'

So the artificial bird now sang alone. He was quite as successful as the real nightingale, and then he was so much prettier to look at—his plumage sparkled with jewels.

Three-and-thirty times he sang one and the same tune, and yet he was not weary. Everyone would willingly have heard him again. The Emperor, however, now wished the real nightingale to sing something—but where was she? No one had noticed that she had flown out of the open window—flown away to her own green wood.

'What is the meaning of this?' said the Emperor, and all the courtiers abused the nightingale, and called her a most ungrateful creature. 'We have the best bird at all events,' said they, and for the four-and-thirtieth time they heard the same tune, but still they did not quite know it, because it was so difficult. The music master praised the bird very highly. 'Indeed,' he declared, 'it was superior to the real nightingale in every way.'

'For see,' he said, 'with the real nightingale one could never reckon on what was coming, but everything is settled with the artificial bird. He will sing in this one way, and no other. This can be proved; he can be taken to pieces, and the works can be shown—where the wheels lie, how they move, and how one follows from another.'

'That is just what I think,' said everybody, and the artist received permission to show the bird to the people on the following Sunday. 'They too shall hear him sing,' the Emperor said. So they heard him, and were as well pleased as if they had all been drinking tea, for it is tea that makes the Chinese merry. But the fisherman, who had heard the real nightingale, said, 'It sounds very pretty, almost like the real bird. But yet there is something wanting, I do not know what.'

The real nightingale was banished from the empire.

The artificial bird had his place on a silken cushion, close to the Emperor's bed; all the presents he received, gold and precious stones, lay around him. He had been given the rank and title of 'High Imperial Court Singer'.

And the music master wrote five-and-twenty volumes about the artificial bird, with the longest and most difficult words that are to be found in the Chinese language. So, of course, all said they had read and understood them, otherwise they would have been stupid, and perhaps would have been flogged.

Thus it went on for a year. The Emperor, the court, and all the Chinese knew every note of the artificial bird's song by heart; but that was the very reason why they enjoyed it so much—they could now sing with him. The little boys in the street sang 'zizizi cluck, cluck, cluck!' and the Emperor himself sang too.

But one evening, when the bird was in full voice and the Emperor was lying in bed listening, there was suddenly a 'whizz' inside the bird. Then a spring cracked. 'Whir—r—r' went all the wheels running round, and the music stopped.

The Emperor jumped quickly out of bed, and had his chief physician called, but of what use could he be? Then a clockmaker was fetched; and at last, after a great deal of discussion and consultation, the bird was in some measure put to rights again. But the clockmaker said he must be spared much singing, for the pegs were almost worn out, and it was impossible to put in new ones, at least without spoiling the music.

There was great lamentation, for now the artificial bird was allowed to sing only once a year, and even then there were difficulties. However, the music master made a short speech full of his favourite long words, and said the bird was as good as ever, and, of course, no one contradicted him.

When five years were passed away, a great affliction visited the whole empire, for the Emperor was ill, and it was reported that he could not live. A new Emperor had already been chosen, and the people stood in the street, outside the palace, and asked the Prime Minister how the Emperor was.

'Pooh!' said he, and shook his head.

Cold and pale lay the Emperor in his magnificent bed. All the court believed him to be already dead, and everyone ran away to greet the new Emperor.

But the Emperor was not yet dead. He could scarcely breathe, however, and it appeared to him as though something was sitting on his chest. He opened his eyes, and saw that it was Death. He had put on the Emperor's crown, and in one hand held the golden scimitar and in the other the splendid imperial banner. From under the folds of the thick velvet hangings the strangest-looking heads were peering forth, some with very ugly faces, and others with looks that were extremely gentle and lovely. These were the bad and good deeds of the Emperor, which were now all fixing their eyes upon him, whilst Death sat on his heart.

'Do you know this?' they whispered one after another. 'Do you remember that?' And they began reproaching him in such a manner that the sweat broke out upon his forehead.

'I have never known anything like it,' said the Emperor. 'Music, music, the great Chinese drum!' cried he; 'Let me not hear what they are saying.'

They went on, however, and Death, quite in the Chinese fashion, nodded his head to every word.

'Music, music!' cried the Emperor. 'You dear little golden bird, sing! I pray you, sing!—I have given you gold and precious stones, I have even hung my golden slippers round your neck—sing, I pray you, sing!'

But the bird was silent. There was no one there to wind him up, and without that he could not sing. Death continued to stare at the Emperor with his great hollow eyes, and everywhere it was still, fearfully still!

All at once came the sweetest music through the window. It was the living nightingale who was sitting on a branch outside. She had heard of her Emperor's severe illness, and was come to sing to him of comfort and hope. As she sang, the spectral forms became paler and paler. The blood flowed more and more quickly through the Emperor's feeble limbs; and even Death quietly listened, and said, 'Go on, little nightingale, go on.'

'Will you give me the beautiful golden sword? Will you give me the rich banner? And will you give me the Emperor's crown?' said the bird.

And Death gave up all these treasures for a song. And the nightingale sang on. She sang of the quiet churchyard where white roses blossom, where the lilac sends forth its fragrance, and the fresh grass is bedewed with the tears of the sorrowing friends of the departed. Then Death was seized with a longing to see his garden, and, like a cold white shadow, flew out at the window.

'Thanks, thanks, little bird,' said the Emperor, 'I know you well. I banished you

from my realm, and you have sung away those evil faces from my bed, and Death from my heart. How can I reward you?'

'You have already rewarded me,' said the nightingale. 'I have seen tears in your eyes, as when I sang to you for the first time. Those I shall never forget; they are the jewels that gladden a minstrel's heart! But sleep now, and wake fresh and healthy. I will sing to you again!'

And she sang—and the Emperor fell into a sweet sleep. Oh, how soft and refreshing it was!

The sun shone in at the window when he awoke, strong and healthy. Not one of the servants had returned, for they all believed him dead; only the nightingale still sat beside him and sang.

'You shall always stay with me,' said the Emperor. 'You shall only sing when it pleases you, and the artificial bird I will break into a thousand pieces.'

'Do not so,' said the nightingale, 'he has done what he could; take care of him. I cannot stay in the palace, but let me come when I like. I will sit on the branches close to the window, in the evening, and sing to you, that you may become happy and have thoughts full of joy. I will sing to you of those who rejoice and of those who suffer. I will sing to you of all that is good or bad which is hidden from you. The little minstrel flies afar to the fisherman's hut, to the peasant's cottage, to all which are far distant from you and your court. I love your heart more than your crown, and yet the crown has an odour of something holy about it. I will come; I will sing. But you must promise me one thing.'

'Everything,' said the Emperor. And now he stood in his imperial splendour, which he had put on himself, and held to his heart the scimitar so heavy with gold.

'One thing I beg of you: let no one know that you have a little bird who tells you everything; then all will go on well.' And the nightingale flew away.

The attendants came in to look at their dead Emperor—and the Emperor said, 'Good morning!'

THE SNOW QUEEN

The Mirror

and Its Fragments

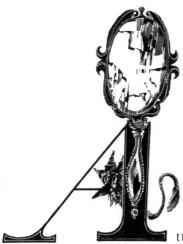

ttend! We are now beginning. When we get to the end of the story we shall know more than we do now. Once, then, there was a very wicked magician. He was one of the most wicked of all, a real demon. Great was his delight at having made a mirror which could at once cause everything good and beautiful reflected in it to shrink up almost to nothing, whilst ugly and useless things were made to appear ten times larger and worse than they were. The loveliest landscapes looked in this mirror like boiled spinach; and the handsomest persons became hideous, and looked as if they stood on their heads and had no bodies, and their features so distorted that their friends could never have recognized them. Moreover, if one of them had a freckle, it seemed to spread over the nose and mouth; and if a good or pious thought passed through his mind, a wrinkle was seen in the mirror. The magician thought all this very amusing, and chuckled with delight at his own clever invention. Those who went to the school of magic where he taught, spread its fame abroad, and declared that now for the first time the world and its inhabitants might be seen as they really were. They carried the mirror everywhere, till at last there was no country or person that had not been looked at through the mirror. They even wished to fly up to the sky with it to see the angels in the mirror; but the higher they flew the more slippery did the glass become. They could scarcely hold it. They flew on and on, higher and higher, till at last the mirror shivered so fearfully that it slipped from their hands and fell to the earth, breaking into millions, billions and trillions of pieces. And then it caused far greater unhappiness than before, for fragments of it scarcely as large as a grain of sand flew about in the air and sometimes got into people's eyes, making them view everything the wrong way, or have eyes only for the worst side of what they looked at; for each little fragment had just the same effect as the entire mirror. Some people were so unfortunate as to receive a little splinter into their hearts—that was terrible! The heart became cold and hard, like a lump of ice. Some pieces were large enough to be used as window-panes, but it was of no use to look at one's friends through such panes as these. Other fragments were made into spectacles, and then what trouble people had with setting and re-setting them!

The wicked magician was greatly amused with all this, and he laughed till his sides ached.

There are still some little splinters of this mirror flying about in the air. We shall hear more about them very soon.

A Little Boy

and a Little Girl

In a large town where there are so many houses and
people that there is not room enough for everyone to have even a little garden, and
where many have to be content with a few plants in pots, there dwelt two poor
children, whose garden was somewhat larger than a flower-pot. They were not
brother and sister, but they loved each other as much as if they had been, and their
parents lived in two attics which were exactly opposite each other. The roof of one
house nearly joined the other, the gutter ran along between, and there was in each
roof a little window, so that you could stride across the gutter from one window to
the other. The parents of these children each had a large wooden box in which grew
herbs for kitchen use, and they had placed these boxes upon the gutter, so near that
they almost touched each other. A beautiful little rose-tree grew in each box; scarlet-
runners clustered over the boxes, and the rose-bushes threw out shoots that were
trained round the windows. The whole looked almost like a triumphal arch of leaves
and flowers. The boxes were very high, and the children were always forbidden to
climb over them, but they often got leave to sit, on their little stools, under the rose-
trees, and thus passed many a delightful hour.

In winter there was an end to these pleasures. The windows were often quite
frozen over, and then they heated pennies on the stove, held the warm copper against
the frozen pane, and thus made a little round peep-hole through which they could
see each other.

185

The little boy was called Kay, the little girl's name was Gerda. In summer they could be together with one jump from the window, but in winter there were stairs to run down and stairs to run up, and sometimes there was wind and snow out of doors.

'Those are the white bees swarming there!' said Kay's old grandmother one day when it was snowing.

'Have they a Queen bee?' asked the little boy, for he knew that the real bees have one.

'They have,' said the grandmother. 'She flies yonder where they swarm so thickly; she is the largest of them, and never remains upon the earth, but flies up again into the black cloud. Often at midnight she flies through the streets of the town, and looks in at the windows, and then they are covered with strange and beautiful forms like trees and flowers.'

'Yes, I have seen them!' said both the children. They knew that this was true.

'Can the Snow Queen come in here?' asked the little girl.

'If she does come in,' said the boy, 'I will put her on the warm stove, and then she will melt.'

And the grandmother stroked his hair and told him stories.

One evening when little Kay was at home and half undressed, he crept upon the chair by the window and peeped through the little hole. Just then a few snowflakes fell, and one, the largest of them, remained lying on the edge of one of the flower-boxes. This snowflake grew larger and larger, till at last it took the form of a lady dressed in the finest white crape, which looked like millions of star-like snowflakes joined together. She was wonderfully fair and beautiful, but made entirely of ice, glittering, dazzling ice. She was alone and her eyes sparkled like two bright stars, but there was no rest or repose in them. She nodded at the window, and beckoned with her hand. The little boy was frightened and jumped down from the chair, and at that moment he seemed to see a large bird fly past the window.

There was a clear frost next day, and soon afterwards came spring—the trees and flowers budded, the swallows built their nests, the windows were opened, and the little children sat once more in their little garden upon the gutter that ran along the roofs of the houses.

The roses blossomed beautifully that summer, and the little girl had learned a hymn in which there was something about roses; it reminded her of her own. So she sang it to the little boy, and he sang it with her:

> 'Though roses bloom, then fade away and die,
> The Christ-Child's face we yet shall see on high.'

And the little ones held each other by the hand, kissed the roses, and looked up at the bright sunshine and talked to themselves as if the Christ-Child were there.

What glorious summer days were those! How delightful it was to sit under those rose-trees, which seemed as if they never meant to leave off blossoming!

One day Kay and Gerda were sitting looking at their picture-books full of birds and animals, when, just as the clock in the church tower struck twelve, Kay said, 'Oh, dear! what a pain I have in my heart!' and soon after, 'Oh, something has got into my eye.'

The little girl put her arm round his neck and looked into his eye, but there was nothing to be seen.

'I think it is gone,' said he, but gone it was not. It was one of those splinters from the magic mirror, the wicked glass that made everything great and good appear little and hateful, and that magnified everything ugly and mean. Poor Kay had also got a splinter in his heart. His heart would now become hard and cold like a lump of ice. He felt the pain no longer, but the splinter was there.

'Why do you cry?' asked he. 'You look so ugly when you cry! There is nothing the matter with me. Fie!' he exclaimed again, 'this rose is worm-eaten, and this one is crooked. After all, they are ugly roses, and it is an ugly box they grow in!' Then he kicked the box, and tore off the roses.

'Oh, Kay, what are you doing?' cried the little girl. But when he saw how it grieved her, he tore off another rose, and jumped down through his own window, away from his once-dear little Gerda.

Ever afterwards, when she brought forward the picture-book, he called it a baby's book, and when his grandmother told stories, he interrupted her with a 'but'; and when he could, he would get behind her, put on her spectacles, and mimic her to make people laugh. Very soon he could mimic everybody in the street. All that was singular and awkward about them Kay could imitate, and his neighbours said, 'What a boy that is!' But it was the glass splinter in his eye, the glass splinter in his heart, that made him careless whose feelings he wounded, and even made him tease little Gerda.

One winter day Kay came in with thick gloves on his hands and with his sledge at his back. He called to Gerda, 'I have got leave to go into the great square where the other boys play!' and away he went.

The boldest boys in the square used to fasten their sledges to the country people's carts, and thus drive a good way along with them. This they thought great fun. Whilst they were playing, a large sledge painted white passed by. In it sat someone wrapped in a rough white fur, and wearing a white cap. When the sledge had driven twice round the square, Kay fastened his little sledge to it, so that when it went away he followed it. On they went, faster and faster, into the next street. The person who drove turned round and nodded kindly to Kay, just as if they had been old acquaintances, and every time Kay was going to loose his little sledge, the driver turned and nodded again. So Kay sat still, and they passed through the gates of the town. Then the snow began to fall so thickly that the little boy could not see a handbreadth before him, but he was still carried on. He tried hastily to unloose the cords and free himself from the large sledge, but it was of no use; his little carriage held fast, and on they flew like the wind. Then he cried out as loud as he could, but no one heard him. The snow fell and the sledge flew. Every now and then it made a spring as if driving over hedges and ditches. He was very much frightened; he would have repeated 'Our Father', but he could remember nothing but the multiplication table.

The snowflakes seemed larger and larger, till at last they looked like great white fowls. All at once they fell aside, the large sledge stopped, and the person who drove it rose from the seat. Kay saw that the cap and coat were entirely of snow, that it was a lady, tall and slender, and dazzlingly white—it was the Snow Queen!

'We have driven fast!' said she, 'but no one likes to be frozen. Creep under my bearskin.' And she seated him in the sledge by her side, and spread her cloak around him—he felt as if he were sinking into a drift of snow.

'Are you still cold?' asked she, and then she kissed his brow. Oh! her kiss was colder than ice. It went to his heart, although that was half frozen already; he thought he should die. It was, however, only for a moment; directly afterwards he was quite well, and no longer felt the intense cold around.

'My sledge! Do not forget my sledge!' He thought first of that. It was fastened to one of the white fowls, which flew behind with it on his back. The Snow Queen kissed Kay again, and he entirely forgot little Gerda, his grandmother, and all at home.

'Now you must have no more kisses!' said she, 'else I should kiss you to death.'

Kay looked at her. She was very beautiful; he could not imagine a more intelligent or a more lovely face. She no longer seemed to him made of ice, as when she sat outside the window and beckoned to him. In his eyes she was perfect. He felt no fear; he told her how well he could reckon in his head as far as fractions, that he knew the number of square miles of every country, and the number of inhabitants in different towns. She always smiled, so then he thought that, after all, he did not yet know so very much. He looked up into the wide, wide space, and she flew with him high up into the black cloud while the storm was raging; it seemed now to Kay to be singing songs of olden times.

They flew over woods and lakes, over sea and land. Beneath them the cold wind whistled, the wolves howled, the snow glittered, and the black crow flew cawing over the plain, whilst above them shone the moon, clear and bright.

Thus did Kay spend the long winter night, and all day he slept at the feet of the Snow Queen.

The Enchanted

Flower Garden

ut how fared little Gerda when Kay did not come back? Where could he be? No one knew. The boys said he had tied his sledge to a larger, more handsome one which had driven into the street, and thence through the gate of the town. No one knew where he was, and many were the tears that were shed. Little Gerda wept bitterly for a long time. The boys said he must have been drowned in the river that flowed not far from the town. Oh, how long and dismal those winter·days were! At last the spring came with its warm sunshine.

'Alas! Kay is dead and gone,' said little Gerda.

'I don't believe it,' said the sunshine.

'He is dead and gone,' she said to the sparrows.

'We don't believe it,' they answered, and at last little Gerda herself did not believe it.

'I will put on my new red shoes,' said she one morning, 'those that Kay has never seen, and then I will go down to the river and ask after him.'

It was quite early. She kissed her old grandmother, who was still sleeping, put on her red shoes, and went alone through the gates of the town towards the river.

'Is it true that you have taken my little playfellow away?' she said to the river. 'I will give you my red shoes if you will give him back to me!'

And the waves of the river seemed to nod to her in a strange way. So she took off her red shoes, which she liked better than anything else she had, and threw them into the stream, but the little waves bore them back to her, as if they would not take from her what she loved most when they could not give her back little Kay. But she thought she had not thrown the shoes far enough out, so she stepped into a little boat that lay among the reeds, and standing at the farthest end of it, threw them again into the water. The boat was not fastened, and her movements sent it gliding away from the shore. She saw this, and hastened to the other end of the boat, but when she reached it she could not get out, for it was more than a yard from the land, and was gliding farther and farther away.

Little Gerda was much frightened and began to cry, but no one save the sparrows heard her, and they could not carry her back to the land; however, they flew along the banks, and sang, as if to comfort her, 'Here we are, here we are!' The boat floated with the stream.

'Perhaps the river will carry me to Kay,' thought Gerda, and then she became more cheerful, and amused herself for hours looking at the lovely country around her. At last she glided past a large cherry-garden, wherein stood a little cottage with thatched roof and curious red and blue windows. Two wooden soldiers stood at the door, who presented arms as she floated past. Gerda called to them, thinking that they were alive, but of course they made no answer. She came close to them, for the stream drifted the boat to the land, and then Gerda called still louder, and an old lady came out of the house, leaning on a crutch. She wore a large hat, with beautiful flowers painted on it.

'Poor little child!' said the old woman; 'what a long way the quick-rolling stream has carried you!' And then she walked into the water, seized the boat with her crutch, drew it to land, and lifted the little girl out.

Gerda was glad to be on dry land again, although she was a little afraid of the strange old woman.

'Come and tell me who you are, and how you came here,' said she.

Gerda told her all, and the old woman shook her head, and said, 'Hem, hem!' And when Gerda asked if she had seen little Kay, the old woman said that he had not come yet, but that he would be sure to come soon, and that in the meantime Gerda must not be sad; that she might stay with her, and eat the cherries and look at the flowers, which were prettier than any picture-book, for each could tell a story.

Then she took Gerda by the hand, and they went together into the cottage, and the old woman shut the door. The windows were very high, and as the panes were red, blue, and yellow, the daylight shone through them in all sorts of various and beautiful colours. Upon a table in the centre was a plate of very fine cherries, and of these Gerda was allowed to eat as many as she liked. Whilst she was eating them, the old dame combed her hair with a golden comb, and the bright flaxen ringlets fell on each side of her pretty, gentle face, which looked as fresh and blooming as a rose.

'I have long wished for such a dear little girl,' said the old woman. 'We shall see now if we cannot live very happily together.' And, as she combed little Gerda's hair, the child thought less and less of Kay, for the old woman was an enchantress, though not a wicked one. She did not practise magic for mischief, but merely for amusement, and now because she wished very much to keep little Gerda. So, fearing that if Gerda saw her roses she would think of those at home and of little Kay, and might run away, she went out into the garden, and stretched her crutch over all the rose-bushes, upon which, although they were full of leaves and blossoms, they immediately sank into the dark earth.

Then she led Gerda into this flower-garden. Every flower of every season of the year was there in full bloom; no picture-book could compare with it. Gerda jumped for joy, and played among the flowers till the sun set behind the tall cherry-trees. Then a pretty little bed, with crimson silk cushions, stuffed with blue violet-leaves, was prepared for her, and there she slept so sweetly and had such dreams as a queen might have on her bridal eve.

The next day and for many days she played among the flowers in the warm sunshine. Gerda knew every flower in the garden, but though they were so many, it seemed to her that one was wanting, she could not tell which. She was sitting one day, looking at the old woman's hat, with the flowers painted on it, and she saw that the loveliest among them was a rose! The old woman had forgotten the painted rose on her hat when she made the real roses sink into the ground. But it is not easy to re-member everything, and a little oversight will often upset the most careful arrangements.

'What,' cried Gerda, 'are there no roses in the garden?' She ran from one bed to another, sought and sought again, but no rose was to be found. She sat down and wept, and her tears fell on a spot where a rose-tree had stood, and as soon as her warm tears had moistened the earth, the bush shot up anew, as fresh and as blooming as when it had sunk; and Gerda threw her arms round it, kissed the flowers, and thought of the beautiful roses at home, and of little Kay. 'Oh, how could I stay here so long!' she cried. 'I left my home to seek for Kay. Do you know where he is?' she asked the roses. 'Is he dead?'

'Dead he is not,' said the roses. 'We have been in the ground where the dead lie, but Kay is not there.'

'Thank you,' said little Gerda, and then she went to the other flowers, and asked, 'Do you know where little Kay is?'

But each flower stood in the sunshine dreaming its own little tale. They told their stories to Gerda, but none of them knew anything of Kay.

So she ran away to the other end of the garden.

The gate was shut, but she pressed upon the rusty latch till it gave way. The gate sprang open, and little Gerda, with bare feet, ran out into the wide world. Three times she looked back, but there was no one following her. She ran till she could run no longer, and then sat down to rest upon a large stone, and when she looked round her she saw that the summer was past, that it was now late in the autumn. She had known nothing of this when she was in the garden, where there were sunshine and flowers all the year round.

'How long I must have stayed there!' said little Gerda. 'It is autumn now! There is no time to lose!' And she rose up to go on.

Oh, how sore and weary were her little feet! And all around looked so cold and bleak. The long willow-leaves had already turned yellow, and the dew trickled down from them like water. Leaf after leaf fell from the trees; the sloe alone bore fruit, and its berries were sharp and bitter. Oh, how cold, and grey, and sad the world seemed!

The Prince

and the Princess

erda was again obliged to rest. Suddenly a large raven hopped upon the snow in front of her, saying, 'Caw!—Caw!—Good day!—Good day!' He sat for some time on the withered branch of a tree opposite, eyeing the little maiden, and wagging his head, and now he came forward to make her acquaintance and to ask her whither she was going all alone. Gerda told the raven her story and asked if he had seen Kay.

And the raven nodded his head, half doubtfully, and said, 'I may. It is possible.'

'Do you think you have?' cried the little girl, and she kissed the raven, and in her joy almost hugged him to death.

'Gently, gently!' said the raven. 'I think I know. I think it may be little Kay, but he has certainly forsaken you for the Princess.'

'Does he dwell with a princess?' asked Gerda.

'Listen to me,' said the raven, 'but it is so difficult to speak your language! If you understand raven speech, then I can explain things so much better. Do you?'

'No! I have never learned it,' said Gerda, 'but my grandmother knew it, and used to speak it to me. Oh, how I wish I had learned it!'

'Never mind,' said the raven, 'I will tell my story as well as I can;' and he told her all he had heard.

'In the kingdom wherein we now are sitting, there lives a Princess so clever that she has read all the newspapers of the world, and forgotten them too. Not long ago she was sitting on her throne and began to sing a new song, the burden of which was, "Why should I not marry?" "Why not, indeed?" said she, and she determined to marry if she could find a man who knew what to say when people spoke to him and not one who could only look grand, for that was tiresome. So she called her ladies together and told them what she meant to do. "We are glad to hear it," said they, "we were talking about it only the other morning." You may believe that every word I say is true,' continued the raven, 'for I have a tame sweetheart who hops freely about the palace, and she told me all this.

'Proclamations with borders of hearts and the initials of the Princess were immediately issued. They gave notice that every well-favoured youth was free to go to the palace, and that he who could talk best with the Princess and show himself most at home would be the one the Princess would choose for her husband.

'You may believe what I say,' said the raven. 'It is as true as I sit here.

'The folks came in crowds, but it was no use. The young men could speak well enough while they were outside the palace gates, but when they entered, and saw the royal guard in silver uniform, and the lackeys on the staircase in gold, and the spacious saloon all lighted up, they became quite confused. They stood before the throne where the Princess sat, and when she spoke to them they could only repeat the last word she had said. It was just as if they had been struck dumb the moment they entered the palace, for as soon as they got out they could talk fast enough. There was quite a long line of them reaching from the gates of the town to the palace.'

'But Kay, little Kay, when did he come?' asked Gerda. 'Was he among the crowd?'

'Presently, presently; we are just coming to him. On the third day there came a youth with neither horse nor carriage. He marched gaily up to the palace. His eyes sparkled like yours. He had long beautiful hair, but his clothes were very shabby.'

'That was Kay!' said Gerda joyfully. 'Oh, then I have found him!' and she clapped her hands.

'He carried a knapsack on his back,' said the raven.

'No, not a knapsack,' said Gerda, 'a sledge, for he had a sledge with him when he left home.'

'It is possible,' answered the raven, 'I did not look very closely. But I heard from my sweetheart that when he entered the palace gates and saw the royal guard in silver, and the lackeys in gold upon the staircase, he did not seem in the least confused, but nodded pleasantly and said to them, "It must be very tedious standing out here; I prefer to go in." The rooms were blazing with light. Ministers and ambassadors were walking about barefooted carrying golden vessels; enough to make a man solemn and silent. His boots creaked horribly, yet he was not at all afraid.'

'That most certainly was Kay!' said Gerda. 'I know he had new boots; I have heard them creak in my grandmother's room.'

'They really did creak,' said the raven; 'but he went boldly up to the Princess, who was sitting upon a pearl as large as a spinning-wheel, whilst all the ladies of the court, with the maids of honour and their handmaidens, stood on one side, and all the gentlemen-in-waiting, with their gentlemen, and their gentlemen's gentlemen, who also kept pages, stood on the other side, and the nearer they were to the door the prouder they looked.'

'It must have been quite awful,' said Gerda. 'Did Kay win the Princess?'

'The young man spoke as well as I do myself when I use the raven tongue,' said the bird. 'At least my sweetheart said so. He was quite lively and agreeable. He did not come to woo her, he said, he had only come to hear her wisdom. And he liked her very much, and she liked him in return.'

'Yes, to be sure, that was Kay,' said Gerda. 'He was so clever, he could reckon in his head, even fractions! Oh, will you not take me into the palace?'

'Ah! that is easily said,' replied the raven, 'but how is it to be done? I will talk it over with my sweetheart, and ask her advice. It is no easy thing, I may tell you, to get permission for a little girl like you to enter the palace.'

'Oh, but I shall get permission easily!' cried Gerda. 'When Kay knows that I am here, he will come out at once and fetch me.'

'Wait for me at the trellis yonder,' said the raven, wagging his head as he flew away.

The raven did not return till late in the evening. 'Caw, caw,' said he. 'My sweetheart greets you kindly, and sends you this piece of bread which she took from the kitchen; there is plenty of bread there, and she thinks you must be hungry. As you have bare feet, the royal guard in silver uniform, and the lackeys in gold, would never let you enter the palace; but do not weep, you shall go there. My sweetheart knows a little back staircase leading to the sleeping apartments, and where to find the key.'

So they went into the garden, and down the grand avenue, and, when the lights in the palace one by one had all been put out, the raven led Gerda to a back door that stood half open. Oh, how Gerda's heart beat with fear and longing! It was just as if she were doing something wrong, yet she only wished to know if Kay really was there. She would see if his smile were the same as it used to be when they sat together under the rose-trees. He would be so glad to see her, to hear how far she had come for his sake, and how sorry all at home were when he did not come back. Her heart trembled with fear and joy.

They went up the stairs. A lamp was burning in a small closet at the top, and in the middle of the floor stood the tame raven, who first turned her head on all sides, and then looked at Gerda, who made her curtsy, as her grandmother had taught her to do.

'My betrothed has told me a great deal about you, little maiden,' said the tame raven. 'Your adventures are extremely interesting! If you will take the lamp, I will show you the way. We will go straight along this way, and we shall meet no one.'

They now entered the first hall. Its walls were covered with rose-coloured satin, embroidered with gold flowers. Each room they passed through seemed more splendid than the last. At length they reached the sleeping-hall. In the centre of this room stood a pillar of gold like the stem of a large palm-tree whose leaves of costly crystal made the ceiling; and from the tree hung, near the door, on thick golden stalks, two beds in the form of lilies. One was white, and in it lay the Princess. The other was red, and in this Gerda sought her playfellow, Kay. She bent aside one of the red leaves and saw a little brown neck. Oh, it must be Kay! She called his name, and held the lamp over him. He awoke, turned his head, and behold! it was not Kay.

The Princess looked out from her white lily bed, and asked what was the matter Then little Gerda wept, and told her story, and what the ravens had done to help her, 'Poor child!' said the Prince and Princess, and they praised the ravens, and said they were not at all angry with them for what they had done. Such a thing must never happen again, but this time they should be rewarded.

'Would you like to have your freedom?' asked the Princess, 'or to become Court Ravens with the right to all that is left in the royal kitchen?'

And both the ravens bowed low and chose the appointment at court, for they thought of their old age, and said it would be so comfortable to be well provided for in their declining years. Then the Prince rose and made Gerda sleep in his bed.

The next day she was dressed from head to foot in silk and velvet, and she was invited to stay at the palace and enjoy herself; but she begged only for a little carriage and a horse, and a pair of boots. All she desired was to go again into the wide world to seek Kay.

They gave her the boots and also a muff. And as soon as she was ready, there drove up to the door a new carriage of pure gold with the arms of the Prince and Princess glittering upon it like a star, and the coachman, the footman, and outriders, all wearing gold crowns. The Prince and Princess themselves helped her into the carriage and wished her success. The wood-raven, who was now married, went with her the first three miles. The carriage was well provided with sugar-plums, fruit, and gingerbread nuts.

'Farewell! farewell!' cried the Prince and Princess; and little Gerda wept, and the raven wept out of sympathy. Then he flew up to the branch of a tree and dapped his black wings at the carriage till it was out of sight.

hey drove through the dark forest, and the carriage shone like a torch. Unluckily its brightness attracted the notice of some forest robbers, who could not bear to let it pass without plundering it.

'It is gold; it is gold!' they cried, and then they rushed forward, seized the horses, stabbed the outriders, coachman, and footman to death, and dragged little Gerda out of the carriage.

'She is plump, she is pretty, she has been fed on nut-kernels,' said the old robber-wife, who had a long, bristly beard, and eyebrows hanging like bushes over her eyes. 'She is like a little fat lamb. How nice she will taste!' and saying this, she drew out her bright dagger, which glittered most terribly.

'Oh, oh!' shrieked the woman—for at the very moment she had lifted her dagger to stab Gerda, her own wild daughter jumped upon her back and bit her ear violently—'you naughty child!'

'She shall play with me,' said the little robber-maiden. 'She shall give me her muff and her pretty frock, and sleep with me in my bed!' And then she bit her mother again, till the robber-wife sprang up and shrieked with pain, and all the robbers laughed, saying: 'See how she is playing with her cub!'

The little robber-maiden was a spoilt child, and always had her own way; and she and Gerda sat in the carriage, and drove farther and farther into the wood. She was about as tall as Gerda, but much stronger. She had broad shoulders, and a very dark skin; her eyes were quite black, and she had a sad look. She put her arm round Gerda's waist, and said, 'She shall not kill you so long as I love you! Are you not a princess?'

'No,' said Gerda, and then she told her all that had happened to her, and how much she loved little Kay.

The robber-maiden looked earnestly in her face, shook her head, and said, 'She shall not kill you even if I do quarrel with you; then, indeed, I would rather do it myself!' And she dried Gerda's tears, and put both her hands into the pretty muff that was so soft and warm.

The carriage at last stopped in the courtyard of the robbers' castle. This castle was half ruined; crows and ravens flew out of the holes in it and large bulldogs, looking as if they could devour a man in a moment, jumped round the carriage. They did not bark, for that was forbidden.

The maidens entered a large smoky hall, where a big fire was blazing on the stone floor. A large cauldron full of soup was boiling over the fire, and hares and rabbits were roasting on the spit.

'You shall sleep with me and my little pets tonight,' said the robber-maiden. Then they had some food, and afterwards went to the corner where lay straw and a piece of carpet. More than a hundred pigeons were perched on staves and laths around them; they all seemed to be asleep, but were startled when the little maidens drew near.

'These all belong to me,' said the robber-maiden, and seizing hold of the nearest she held the poor bird by the feet and swung it till it flapped its wings. 'Kiss it,' said she, flapping it in Gerda's face. 'The wood-pigeons sit up there,' continued she, pointing to a number of laths and a cage fixed across a hole in the wall; 'they would fly away if I did not keep them shut up. And here is my old favourite!' and she pulled forward by the horn a reindeer who wore a bright copper ring round his neck, and was tied to a large stone. 'We are obliged to chain him up, or he would run away from us. Every evening I tickle his neck with my sharp dagger; it makes him fear me so much!' And then the robber-maiden drew out a long dagger from a chink in the wall and passed it over the reindeer's throat. The poor animal struggled and kicked, but the girl laughed, and then she pulled Gerda into bed with her.

'Will you keep the dagger in your hand whilst you sleep?' asked Gerda, looking very much afraid.

'I always sleep with my dagger by my side,' replied the little robber-maiden. 'One never knows what may happen. But now tell me all over again what you told me before about Kay, and why you came into the world all by yourself.'

Gerda told her story over again, and the wood-pigeons above cooed, but the others slept. The little robber-maiden threw one arm round Gerda's neck, and holding the dagger with the other, was soon fast asleep; but Gerda could not close her eyes, for she did not know what would become of her, or whether the robbers would let her live. The robbers sat round the fire drinking and singing. Oh, it was a dreadful night for the poor little girl!

Then the wood-pigeons said, 'Coo, coo, coo! we have seen little Kay. A white fowl carried his sledge, and he sat in the Snow Queen's chariot, which drove through the wood while we sat in our nest. She breathed upon us as she passed, and all the young ones died excepting us two—coo, coo, coo!'

'What are you saying?' cried Gerda. 'Where was the Snow Queen going? Do you know anything about it?'

'She travelled most likely to Lapland, where there is always ice and snow. Ask the reindeer bound to the rope up there.'

'Yes, there is always ice and snow there; it is a glorious land!' said the reindeer. 'There, free and happy, one can roam through the wide sparkling valleys! There the Snow Queen has her summer-tent, but her strong castle is near the North Pole, on the island called Spitzbergen.'

'O Kay, dear Kay!' sighed Gerda.

When morning came Gerda told the little robber-maiden what the wood-pigeons had said, and she looked grave and nodded her head. 'Do you know where Lapland is?' she asked of the reindeer.

'Who should know better?' said the animal, his eyes sparkling. 'There was I born and bred; and there I used to bound over the wild, icy plains!'

'Listen to me!' said the robber-maiden. 'You see all our men are gone, but my mother is still here, and here she will remain. At noon she will drink out of the great flask, and after that she will sleep a little—then I will do something for you!'

When her mother was fast asleep, the robber-maiden went to the reindeer and said, 'I should very much like to tickle your neck a few more times with my sharp dagger, for then you do look so droll, but never mind, I will untie your cord and let you go free, on condition that you run as fast as you can to Lapland, and take this little girl to the castle of the Snow Queen, where her playfellow is. You must have heard her story, for she speaks loud enough, and you know how to listen.'

The reindeer jumped for joy, and the robber-maiden lifted Gerda on his back, taking care to bind her on firmly, as well as to give her a little cushion to sit on. 'And here', said she, 'are your fur boots. You will need them for it will be very cold. The muff I must keep; it is so pretty. But you shall not be frozen for want of it, for here are my mother's big gloves; they reach up to the elbow. Put them on. Now your hands look as clumsy as my old mother's!'

Gerda shed tears of joy.

'I cannot bear to see you crying!' said the little robber-maiden. 'You ought to look glad. See, here are two loaves and a piece of bacon for you, so that you may not be hungry on the way.' She fastened these on the reindeer's back, opened the door, called away the great dogs, and then, cutting with her dagger the rope which bound the reindeer, shouted to him, 'Now then, run! but take good care of the little girl.'

Gerda stretched out her hands to the robber-maiden and bade her farewell, and the reindeer bounded through the forest, over stock and stone, over desert and heath, over meadow and moor. The wolves howled and the ravens shrieked 'Isch! Isch!'— a red light flashed—one might have fancied the sky was sneezing.

'Those are my dear old Northern Lights!' said the reindeer. 'See, how beautiful they are!' And he ran on night and day faster than ever; but the loaves were eaten and so was the bacon when at last they came to Lapland.

The Lapland Woman

and the Finland Woman

They stopped at a little hut. A wretched hut it was; the roof nearly touched the ground, and the door was so low that whoever wished to go in or out had to crawl upon hands and knees. No one was at home except an old Lapland woman who was busy boiling fish over a lamp. The reindeer told her Gerda's whole history—not, however, till after he had told her his own, which seemed to him of much more importance. Poor Gerda was so pinched with the cold that she could not speak.

'Poor thing!' said the Lapland woman, 'you have still a long way to go! You have a hundred miles to run before you can reach Finland. The Snow Queen lives there now and burns blue lights every night. I will write for you a few words on a piece of dried stock-fish—paper I have none—and you may take it with you to the wise Finland woman who lives there; she will advise you better than I can.'

So when Gerda was warmed, and had taken some food, the Lapland woman wrote a few words on a dried stock-fish and bade Gerda take care of it; she bound her once more firmly on the reindeer's back, and away they went at full speed.

The beautiful blue Northern Lights shone all through the night, and at length they reached Finland, and knocked at the chimney of the wise woman's hut, for there was no door above ground.

They crept in, but it was very hot within, so hot that the wise woman wore scarcely any clothes. She was small and very dirty looking. She loosened little Gerda's dress, took off her fur boots and thick gloves, laid a piece of ice on the reindeer's head, and then read what was written on the stock-fish. She read it three times. After the third reading she knew it by heart, so she threw the fish into the porridge-pot, for she knew it was good to eat, and she never wasted anything.

The reindeer then told his own story first, and next little Gerda's, and the wise woman twinkled her wise eyes but spoke not a word.

'Will you not mix for this little maiden that wonderful draught which will give her the strength of twelve men, and so make her able to overcome the Snow Queen?' said the reindeer.

'The strength of twelve men!' said the wise woman; 'that would not be of much use!' And she walked away, drew forth a large parchment roll from a shelf, and began to read. She read till the perspiration ran down her forehead.

At last her eyes began to twinkle again, and she drew the reindeer into a corner, and putting a fresh piece of ice upon his head, whispered: 'Little Kay is still with the Snow Queen, and he finds everything so much to his taste that he thinks it the best place in the world. But that is because he has a glass splinter in his heart and a glass splinter in his eye. Until he has got rid of them he will never feel like a human being, and the Snow Queen will always have power over him.'

'But can you not give something to little Gerda to help her to conquer this evil power?' asked the reindeer.

'I can give her no power as great as she has already,' answered the woman. 'Her power is greater than ours, because it comes from a pure and loving heart. If with this she cannot gain access to the Snow Queen's palace and free Kay's eye and heart from the glass splinters, we can do nothing for her! Two miles from here is the Snow Queen's garden; you can carry the little maiden there, and put her down close by the bush bearing red berries and half covered with snow. Don't waste time gossiping, and hasten back as fast as you can.' Then the wise woman lifted Gerda on the reindeer's back and away they went.

'Oh, I have left my boots and my gloves behind!' cried little Gerda, when she felt the biting cold; but the reindeer dared not stop. On he ran until he reached the bush with the red berries. Here he set Gerda down and kissed her, while the tears rolled down his cheeks. Then he ran back again fast—which was the best thing he could do. And there stood poor Gerda, without shoes, without gloves, alone in that dreary, desolate, ice-bound Finland.

She ran forward as fast as she could, and a whole regiment of snowflakes came to meet her. They did not fall from the sky, which was cloudless and bright with the Northern Lights; they ran straight along the ground, and the farther Gerda advanced the larger they grew. Gerda then remembered how large and curious the snowflakes had appeared to her when one day she had looked at them through a burning-glass. These, however, were very much larger and much more terrible, for they were alive. They were, in fact, the Snow Queen's guards, and their shapes were the strangest you could think of. Some looked like great ugly porcupines, others like snakes rolled into knots with their heads stretching out, and others like little fat bears with bristling hair, but all were dazzlingly white, and all were living snowflakes. Little Gerda began to repeat the Lord's Prayer, and it was so cold she could see her own breath coming out of her mouth like steam as she spoke the words. The steam seemed to grow thicker as she kept on praying, and at length it took the shape of little bright angels which, as they touched the earth, became larger and more distinct. They wore helmets on their heads and carried shields and spears. Their number increased so quickly that, by the time Gerda had finished her prayer, a whole legion stood round her. They thrust their spears into the horrible snowflakes, which broke into thousands of pieces, and little Gerda walked on unhurt and unafraid. The angels touched her hands and feet, and then she scarcely felt the cold, and went on boldly to the Snow Queen's palace.

But before we go further with her, let us see what Kay is doing. He is certainly not thinking of little Gerda, and least of all can he imagine that she is now standing at the palace gate.

The walls of the palace were formed of the drifted snow, its doors and windows of the cutting winds. There were more than a hundred rooms in the palace, the largest of them many miles in length. They were all lit up by the Northern Lights, and were all alike vast, empty, icily cold, and dazzlingly white. In the midst of the empty, endless hall of snow lay a frozen lake; it was broken into a thousand pieces, each piece so exactly like the others that the breaking of them might well be deemed a work of more than human skill. The Snow Queen, when at home, always sat in the middle of this lake.

Little Kay was quite blue, nay, almost black with cold, but he did not feel it, for the Snow Queen had kissed away the shiverings and his heart was already a lump of ice. He was busied among the sharp icy fragments, laying and joining them together in every possible way, just as people do with what are called Chinese puzzles. Kay could form the most curious and complete figures—and in his eyes they were of the utmost importance. He often formed whole words, but there was one word he could never succeed in forming—it was Eternity. The Snow Queen said to him 'When you can put that together, you shall be your own master and I will give you the whole world, and a new pair of skates besides.' But he could never do it.

'Now I am going to the warmer countries,' said the Snow Queen. 'I shall flit through the air, and look into the black craters, as they are called, of Etna and

Vesuvius. I shall whiten them a little. That will be good for the lemons and the vines.' So away flew the Snow Queen, leaving Kay sitting all alone in the large, empty hall of ice.

He looked at the pieces of ice and thought and thought till his head ached. He sat so still and so stiff that one might have thought that he too was frozen.

Cold and cutting blew the winds when little Gerda passed through the palace gates, but she repeated her evening prayer, and they at once sank to rest. She entered the large empty hall and saw Kay. She knew him at once. She flew to him and fell upon his neck, and held him fast, and cried, 'Kay! Dear, dear Kay! I have found you at last!'

But he sat still, quite stiff and cold and motionless. His unkindness wounded poor Gerda. She wept bitterly and her hot tears fell on his breast and thawed the ice, and penetrated to his heart and washed out the splinter of glass. He looked at her whilst she sang:

'Though roses bloom, then fade away and die,
The Christ-Child's face we yet shall see on high.'

Then Kay burst into tears. He wept till the glass splinter floated in his eye and fell with his tears. Then he knew his old companion, and cried with joy, 'Gerda, my dear little Gerda, where have you been all this time?—and where have I been?'

He looked around him. 'How cold it is here! How wide and empty!' Then he embraced Gerda, and she laughed and wept by turns. Even the pieces of ice took part in their joy; they danced about merrily, and when they were wearied and lay down they formed of their own accord the letters of which the Snow Queen had said that when Kay could put them together he should be his own master, and that she would give him the whole world, with a new pair of skates besides.

And Gerda kissed his cheeks, and they became fresh and glowing as ever. She kissed his eyes, and they sparkled like her own. She kissed his hands and feet, and he was once more healthy and merry. The Snow Queen might now come home as soon as she liked—it mattered not; Kay's charter of freedom stood written on the lake in bright icy characters.

They took each other by the hand, and went forth out of the ice palace, and as they walked on, the winds were hushed into a calm, and the sun burst forth in splendour from among the dark storm clouds. When they got to the bush with the red berries, they found the reindeer standing by waiting for them, and he had brought with him another and younger reindeer, whose udders were full, and who gladly gave her warm milk to refresh the young travellers.

The old reindeer and the young hind carried Kay and Gerda on their backs, first to the little hot room of the wise woman of Finland, where they warmed themselves and received advice about their journey home, and afterwards to the home of the Lapland woman, who made them some new clothes and provided them with a sledge.

The whole party ran on together till they came to the boundary of the country, and just where the green leaves began to sprout, the Lapland woman and the two reindeers took their leave. 'Farewell! farewell!' they all said. And the birds, the first they had seen for many a long day, began to chirp their pretty songs; and the trees of the forest were covered with variously tinted green leaves. Suddenly the boughs parted, and a spirited horse galloped up. Gerda knew it, for it was one which had drawn her gold coach. On it sat a young girl wearing a bright scarlet cap, and with pistols on the holster before her. It was the robber-maiden, who, weary of her home in the forest, was going on her travels, first to the North and afterwards to other parts of the world. She knew Gerda at once, and Gerda had not forgotten her. Most joyful was their greeting.

'A fine gentleman you are, to be sure, you graceless young truant!' said she to Kay. 'I should like to know if you deserved that anyone should be running to the end of the world on your account!'

But Gerda patted her cheeks, and asked after the Prince and Princess.

'They are gone to foreign countries,' replied the robber-maiden.

'And the raven?' asked Gerda.

'Ah! the raven is dead,' answered she. 'His sweetheart is now a widow, so she hops about with a piece of black worsted round her leg; she moans most piteously, and chatters more than ever! But tell me now how you managed to get back your old playfellow.'

So Gerda and Kay told their story.

'Snip-snap-snurre-basselurre!' said the robber-maiden. Then she took the hands of both, and promised that if ever she passed through their town she would pay them a visit; and then she bade them farewell, and rode away out into the wide world.

Then Kay and Gerda walked on hand in hand, and wherever they went it was spring, beautiful spring, with its bright flowers and green leaves.

They came to a large town, where the church bells were ringing merrily, and they knew at once the high towers rising into the sky, for it was the town wherein they had lived. Joyfully they passed through the streets, and stopped at the door of Gerda' grandmother. They walked up the stairs and entered the well-known room. The clock said 'Tick, tick!' and the hands moved as before. Only one change could they find, and that was in themselves, for they saw that they were now both grown up. The rose-trees on the roof blossomed in front of the open window, and there beneath them stood the children's stools. Kay and Gerda went and sat down upon them, still holding each other by the hand. The cold, hollow splendour of the Snow Queen's palace they had forgotten; it seemed to them only an unpleasant dream. The grandmother meanwhile sat in the bright sunshine, and read from the Bible these words: 'Unless ye become as little children, ye shall not enter into the kingdom of heaven.'

And Kay and Gerda gazed on each other; they now understood the words of their hymn:

<blockquote>
'Though roses bloom, then fade away and die,
The Christ-Child's face we yet shall see on high.'
</blockquote>

THE SHEPHERDESS

AND THE CHIMNEY-SWEEP

Have you ever seen an old-fashioned oak cabinet, black with age and covered, every inch of it, with carved foliage and curious figures? Just such a cabinet, an heirloom, once the property of its present mistress's great-grandmother, stood in a parlour. It was covered from top to bottom with carved roses and tulips, and little stags' heads with long branching antlers peered forth from the curious scrolls and foliage surrounding them. In the middle of the cabinet was carved the full-length figure of a man, who seemed to be perpetually grinning, perhaps at himself, for in truth he was a most ridiculous figure. He had crooked legs like a goat, small horns on his forehead, and a long beard. The children of the house used to call him 'Field-Marshal-Major-General-Corporal-Sergeant Billy-goat's legs'. This was a long, hard name, and not many figures, in wood or stone, could boast of such a title. There he stood, his eyes always fixed upon the table under the mirror, for on this table stood a pretty little porcelain shepherdess, her mantle gathered gracefully round her and fastened with a red rose. Her shoes and hat were gilt, her hand held a crook; she was a most charming figure. Close by her stood a little chimney-sweep as black as coal, and made, like the shepherdess, of porcelain. He was as clean and neat as any other china figure. Indeed, the manufacturer might just as well have made a prince of him as a chimney-sweep, for though elsewhere black as a coal, his face was as fresh and rosy as a girl's which was certainly a mistake—it ought to have been black. With his ladder in his hand, he kept his place close by the little shepherdess. They had been put side by side from the first, had always remained on the same spot, and so had plighted their troth to each other. They suited each other well, for they were both young, both of the same kind of china, and both alike fragile and delicate.

Near them stood another figure three times as large as they were, and also made of porcelain. He was an old Chinese mandarin who could nod his head, and he declared that he was grandfather of the little shepherdess. He could not prove this, but he insisted that he had authority over her, and so, when 'Field-Marshal-Major-General-Corporal-Sergeant Billy-goat's legs' made proposals to the little shepherdess, he nodded his head in token of his consent.

'Now you will have a husband,' said the old mandarin to her, 'who, I verily believe, is made of mahogany. You will be the wife of a Field-Marshal-Major-General-Corporal-Sergeant, of a man who has a whole cabinet full of silver plate, besides a store of no one knows what in the secret drawers.'

'I will not go into that dismal cabinet,' said the little shepherdess. 'I have heard that he has eleven china wives already imprisoned there.'

'Then you shall be the twelfth, and you will be in good company,' said the mandarin. 'This very night, as soon as you hear a noise in the old cabinet, you shall be married, as sure as I am a mandarin,' and then he nodded his head and fell asleep.

But the little shepherdess wept, and turned to her betrothed, the china chimney-sweep.

'I believe I must beg you,' said she,' to go out with me into the wide world, for we cannot stay here.'

'I will do everything you wish,' said the little chimney-sweep, 'let us go at once, I think I can support you by my profession.'

'If we could but get safely off the table!' sighed she. 'I shall never be happy till we are really out in the world.'

Then he comforted her, and showed her how to set her little foot on the curved edges and gilded foliage twining round the leg of the table. He helped her with his little ladder, and at last they reached the floor. But when they turned to look at the old cabinet, they saw that it was all astir: the carved stags were putting their little heads farther out, raising their antlers and moving their throats, whilst 'Field-Marshal-Major-General-Corporal-Sergeant Billy-goat's legs' was jumping up and down and shouting to the old Chinese mandarin, 'Look, they are running away! They are running away!' The runaways were dreadfully frightened, and jumped into an open drawer under the window-sill.

In this drawer there were three or four packs of cards, none of them complete, and also a little puppet-theatre which had been set up as neatly as it could be. A play was then going on, and all the queens, whether of diamonds, hearts, clubs, or spades, sat in the front row fanning themselves with the flowers they held in their hands, while behind them stood the knaves, showing that they had each two heads, one above and one below, as most cards have. The play was about two persons who were crossed in love, and the shepherdess wept over it, for it was just like her own story.

'I cannot bear this!' said she. 'Let us leave the drawer.' But when they again got to the floor, on looking up at the table they saw that the old Chinese mandarin was awake, and that his whole body was shaking to and fro with rage.

'Oh, the old mandarin is coming!' cried the little shepherdess and down she fell on one knee in the greatest distress.

'A thought has struck me,' said the chimney-sweep. 'Let us creep into the large potpourri vase that stands in the corner; there we can rest upon roses and lavender, and throw salt in his eyes if he comes near us.'

'That will not do at all,' said she, 'for many years ago the mandarin was betrothed to the potpourri vase, and there is always a kindly feeling between people who have been as intimate as that. No, there is no help for it; we must wander forth together into the wide world!'

'Have you indeed the courage to go with me into the wide world?' asked the chimney-sweep. 'Have you thought how large it is, and that we may never return?'

'I have,' replied she.

The chimney-sweep looked fixedly at her, and when he saw that she was firm, he said, 'My path leads through the chimney. Have you indeed the courage to creep with me through the fire-box and up the pipe? I know the way well! We shall climb up so high that they cannot come near us, and at the top there is a hole that leads into the wide world.'

He led her to the door of the stove.

'How black it looks!' sighed she, but she went on with him, through the fire-box and up the pipe, where it was dark, pitch dark.

'Now we are in the chimney,' said he, 'and look, what a lovely star shines over us.'

And it really was a star, shining right down upon them as if to show them the way. So they climbed and crawled; it was a fearful path, so dreadfully steep and seemingly endless, but the little sweep lifted her and held her, and showed her the best places to plant her tiny porcelain feet on, till at last they reached the edge of the chimney. There they sat down to rest, for they were very tired.

The sky with all its stars was above them, and the town with all its roofs lay beneath them. They could see all round them far out into the wide world. The poor little shepherdess had never dreamt of anything like this; she leant her little head on the chimney-sweep's arm, and wept so bitterly that the gilding broke off from her waistband.

'This is too much!' she cried. 'The world is all too large! Oh that I were once more upon the little table under the mirror! I shall never be happy till I am there again. I have followed you into wide world; surely if you love me you can follow me home again.'

The chimney-sweep talked sensibly to her, reminding her of the old mandarin and 'Field-Marshal-Major-General-Corporal-Sergeant Billy-goat's legs'. But she wept so bitterly, and kissed her little chimney-sweep so fondly, that at last he could not but yield to her request, foolish as it was.

So with great trouble they crawled down the chimney, crept through the pipe and through the fire-box and into the dark stove. They lurked for a little behind the door, listening, before they would venture to return to the room. Everything was quite still. They peeped out. Alas! on the floor lay the old mandarin. In trying to follow the runaways, he had jumped down from the table and had broken into three pieces. His head lay shaking in a corner. The 'Field-Marshal-Major-General-Corporal-Sergeant Billy-goat's legs' stood where he had always stood, thinking over what had happened.

'Oh, how shocking!' exclaimed the little shepherdess. 'My old grandfather is broken in pieces, and it is all our fault! I shall never get over it!' and she wrung her little hands.

'He can be put together again,' said the chimney-sweep. 'He can very easily be put together; only don't be so impatient! If they glue his back together, and put a strong rivet in his neck, then he will be as good as new, and will be able to say plenty of unpleasant things to us.'

'Do you really think so?' asked she. And then they climbed up the table to the place where they had stood before.

'Well, we're not much farther on,' said the chimney-sweep; 'we might have spared ourselves all the trouble.'

'If we could but have old grandfather put together!' said the shepherdess. 'Will it cost very much?'

He was put together. The family had his back glued and his neck riveted. He was as good as new, but could no longer nod his head.

'We have certainly grown very proud since we were broken in pieces,' said 'Field-Marshal-Major-General-Corporal-Sergeant Billy-goat's legs', 'but I must say, for my part, I do not see that there is anything to be proud of. Am I to have her or am I not? Just answer me that!'

The chimney-sweep and the little shepherdess looked imploringly at the old mandarin; they were so afraid lest he should nod. But nod he could not, and it was disagreeable for him to have to tell a stranger that he had a rivet in his neck. So the young porcelain people were left together, and they blessed the grandfather's rivet, and loved each other till they broke in pieces.

THE FIR-TREE

Far away in the deep forest there once grew a pretty little fir-tree. The sun shone full upon him, the breezes played freely round him, and near him grew many other fir-trees, some older, some younger; but the little fir-tree was not happy, for he was always longing to be tall like the others. He thought not of the warm sun and the fresh air; he cared not for the merry, prattling peasant children who came to the forest to look for strawberries and raspberries. Sometimes, after having filled their pitchers, or threaded the bright berries on a straw, they would sit down near the little fir-tree and say, 'What a pretty little tree this is!' and then the fir-tree would feel more unhappy than ever.

'Oh that I were as tall as the other trees,' sighed the little fir, 'then I should spread my branches on every side, and my top should look out over the wide world! The birds would build their nests among my branches, and when the wind blew I should bend my head so grandly, just as the others do!' He had no pleasure in the sunshine, in the song of the birds, or in the rosy clouds that sailed over him every morning and evening.

In winter, when the ground was covered with the white glistening snow, a hare would sometimes come scampering along, and jump right over the little tree's head, and then how miserable he felt! However, two winters passed away, and by the third the tree was so tall that the hare was obliged to run round it. 'Oh, if I could but grow

217

and grow, and become tall and old!' thought the tree. 'That is the only thing in the world worth living for.'

The wood-cutters came in the autumn and felled some of the largest of the trees. This happened every year, and our young fir, who was by this time a good height, shuddered when he saw those grand trees fall with a crash to the earth. Their branches were then cut off; the stems looked so terribly naked and lanky that they could hardly be recognised. They were laid one upon another in waggons, and horses drew them away, far, far away from the forest.

Where could they be going? What would happen to them? The fir-tree wished very much to know, so in the spring, when the swallows and the stork returned, he asked them if they knew where the felled trees had been taken.

The swallows knew nothing, but the stork looked thoughtful for a moment, then nodded his head and said, 'Yes, I believe I have seen them! As I was flying from Egypt I met many ships, and they had fine new masts that smelt like fir. I have little doubt that they were the trees that you speak of. They were stately, very stately, I assure you!'

'Oh, that I too were tall enough to sail upon the sea! Tell me, what is this sea, and what does it look like?'

'That,' said the stork, 'would take too long!' and away he stalked.

'Rejoice in your youth!' said the sunbeams; 'rejoice in your fresh youth, in the young life that is within you!'

And the wind kissed the tree, and the dew wept tears over him, but the fir-tree did not understand them.

When Christmas drew near, many quite young trees were felled, some of them not so tall as the young fir-tree who was always longing to be away. These young trees were chosen for their beauty. Their branches were not cut off. They too were laid in a waggon, and horses drew them away from the forest.

'Where are they going?' asked the fir-tree. 'They are no taller than I; indeed, one of them is much less. Why do they keep all their branches? Where can they be going?'

'We know! We know!' twittered the sparrows. 'We peeped through the windows in the town below! We know where they are gone. Oh, you cannot think what honour is done to them! We looked through the windows and saw them planted in a warm room, and decked out with such beautiful things: gilded apples, sweetmeats, play-things, and hundreds of bright candles!'

'And then?' asked the fir-tree, trembling in every branch, 'and then? What happened then?'

'Oh, we saw no more. That was beautiful, beautiful beyond compare!'

'Is such a glorious lot to be mine?' cried the delighted fir-tree. 'This is far better than sailing over the sea. How I long for the time. Oh that Christmas were come! I am now tall and have many branches, like those trees that were carried away last year. Oh that I were even now in the waggon! that I were in the warm room, honoured and adorned! and then—yes, then, something still better will happen, else why should they take trouble to decorate me? It must be that something still greater, still more splendid, must happen—but what? Oh I suffer, I suffer with longing! I know not what it is that I feel.'

'Rejoice in our love!' said the air and the sunshine. 'Rejoice in your youth and your freedom!'

But rejoice he would not. He grew taller every day. In winter and in summer he stood there clothed in green, dark green foliage. The people that saw him said, 'That is a beautiful tree!' And next Christmas he was the first that was felled. The axe cut through the wood and pith, and the tree fell to the earth with a deep groan. The pain was so sharp he felt faint. He quite forgot to think of his good fortune, he felt so sorry at having to leave his home in the forest. He knew that he would never again see those dear old comrades, or the little bushes and flowers that had flourished under his shadow, perhaps not even the birds. Neither did he find the journey by any means pleasant.

The tree first came to himself when, in the courtyard to which he had been taken with the other trees, he heard a man say, 'This is a splendid one, the very thing we want!'

Then came two smartly-dressed servants, and carried the fir-tree into a large and handsome drawing-room. Pictures hung on the walls, and on the mantelpiece stood large Chinese vases with lions on the lids. There were rocking-chairs, silken sofas, tables covered with picture-books, and toys. The fir-tree was placed in a large tub filled with sand, but no one could know that it was a tub, for it was hung with green cloth and stood on a rich, gaily coloured carpet. Oh, how the tree trembled! What was to happen next? Some young ladies, helped by servants, began to adorn him. On some branches they hung little nets cut out of coloured paper, every net filled with sugar-plums; from others gilded apples and walnuts were hung, looking just as if they had grown there; and hundreds of little wax tapers, red, blue, and white, were placed here and there among the branches. Dolls that looked almost like men and women—the tree had never seen such things before—seemed to dance to and fro among the leaves, and high up, on the top of the tree, was fastened a large star of gold tinsel. This was indeed splendid, beyond compare.

'This evening,' they said, 'this evening it will be lighted up.'

'Would that it were evening,' thought the tree. 'Would that the lights were kindled, for then—what will happen then? Will the trees come out of the forest to see me? Will the sparrows fly here and look in through the window-panes? Shall I stand here adorned both winter and summer?'

He thought much of it. He thought till he had barkache with longing, and barkaches with trees are as bad as headaches with us.

The candles were lighted—oh, what a blaze of splendour! The tree trembled in all his branches so that a candle caught one of the twigs and set it on fire. 'Oh dear!' cried the young ladies, and put it out at once.

So the tree dared not tremble again: he was so fearful of losing any of his beautiful ornaments. He felt bewildered by all this glory and brightness. And now, all of a sudden, both folding-doors were flung open, and a troop of children rushed in as if they had a mind to jump over him; the older people followed more quietly. The little ones stood quite silent, but only for a moment. Then they shouted with delight. They shouted till the room rang again; they danced round the tree, and one present after another was torn down.

'What are they doing?' thought the tree. 'What will happen now?' The candles burnt down to the branches, and as each burnt down it was put out. The children were given leave to strip the tree. They threw themselves on him till all his branches creaked, and had he not been fastened with the gold star to the ceiling he would have been overturned.

The children danced about with their beautiful playthings. No one thought of the tree any more except the old nurse. She came and peeped among the branches, but it was only to see if, perchance, a fig or an apple had been left among them.

'A story! a story!' cried the children, pulling a little fat man towards the tree. 'It is pleasant to sit under the shade of green boughs,' said he, sitting down; 'besides, the tree may be benefited by hearing my story. But I shall only tell one tale. Would you like to hear about Ivedy Avedy, or about Humpty Dumpty, who fell downstairs and yet came to the throne and won the Princess?'

'Ivedy Avedy!' cried some; 'Humpty Dumpty!' cried others. There was a great uproar. The fir-tree alone was silent thinking to himself. 'Ought I to make a noise as they do? or ought I to do nothing at all?' For he most certainly was one of the company, and had done all that had been required of him.

And the little fat man told the story of Humpty Dumpty, who fell downstairs and yet came to the throne and won the Princess. And the children clapped their hands and called out for another; they wanted to hear the story of Ivedy Avedy also, but they did not get it. The fir-tree stood meanwhile quite silent and thoughtful; the birds in the forest had never related anything like this. 'Humpty Dumpty fell downstairs and yet was raised to the throne and won the Princess! Yes, yes, strange things come to pass in the world!' thought the fir-tree, who believed it must all be true, because such a pleasant man had told it. 'Who knows but I, too, may fall downstairs and win a princess?' And he thought with delight of being next day again decked out with candles and playthings, gold and fruit. 'Tomorrow I will not tremble,' thought he. 'I will thoroughly enjoy my splendour. Tomorrow I shall hear again the story of Humpty Dumpty, and perhaps also that about Ivedy Avedy.' And the tree mused upon this all night.

In the morning the maids came in. 'Now begins my state anew!' thought the tree. But they dragged him out of the room, up the stairs, and into a garret, and there

220

they thrust him into a dark corner where little light could enter. 'What can be the meaning of this?' thought the tree. 'What am I to do here? What shall I hear in this place?' And he leant against the wall, and thought, and thought. And he had plenty of time for thinking it over, for day after day and night after night passed away, and yet no one ever came into the room. At last somebody did come in, but it was only to push some old trunks into the corner. The tree was now entirely hidden from sight and apparently quite forgotten.

'It is now winter,' thought the tree. 'The ground is hard and covered with snow; they cannot plant me now, so I am to stay here in shelter till the spring. Men are so thoughtful! I only wish it were not so dark and so lonely!'

'Squeak! squeak!' cried a little mouse, just then gliding forward. Another followed; they snuffed about the fir-tree, and then slipped in and out among the branches.

'It is horribly cold!' said a little mouse, 'or it would be quite comfortable here. Don't you think so, you old fir-tree?'

'I am not old,' said the fir-tree; 'there are many who are much older than I.'

'How came you here?' asked the mice, 'and what do you know?' They were most uncommonly inquisitive. 'Tell us about the most delightful place on earth! Have you ever been there? Have you been into the store-room, where cheeses lie on the shelves, and hams hang from the ceiling; where one can dance over tallow candles; where one goes in thin and comes out fat?'

'I know nothing about that,' said the tree, 'but I know the forest, where the sun shines and where the birds sing!' And then he spoke of his youth and its pleasures. The little mice had never heard anything like it before. They listened very closely and said, 'Well, to be sure! How much you have seen! How happy you have been!'

'Happy!' said the fir-tree, in surprise, and he thought a moment over all that he had been saying—'yes, on the whole those were pleasant times!' He then told them about the Christmas Eve when he had been dressed up with cakes and candles.

'Oh!' cried the little mice, 'how happy you have been, you old fir-tree!'

'I am not old at all!' returned the fir. 'It was only this winter that I left the forest; I am just in the prime of life!'

'How well you can talk!' said the little mice, and the next night they came again and brought with them four other little mice, who wanted also to hear the tree's history. And the more the tree spoke of his youth in the forest, the more clearly he remembered it. 'Yes,' said he, 'those were pleasant times! but they may come back, they may come back! Humpty Dumpty fell downstairs, and yet for all that he won the Princess; perhaps I, too, may win a princess!' And then the fir thought of a pretty little delicate birch that grew in the forest, a real, and, to the fir-tree, a very lovely, princess.

'Who's Humpty Dumpty?' asked the mice. In answer, the fir told the tale. He could remember every word of it perfectly; and the little mice were ready to jump with joy. Next night more mice came; and on Sunday there came also two rats. The rats, however, did not find the story at all amusing, and this annoyed the little mice, who, after hearing their opinion, could not like it so well either.

'Do you know only that one story?' asked the rats.

'Only that one!' answered the tree. 'I heard it on the happiest evening of my life, though I did not then know how happy I was.'

'It is a miserable story! Do you know none about pork and tallow? No store-room story?'

'No,' said the tree.

'Well, then, we have heard enough of it!' returned the rats, and they went away.

The mice, too, never came again. The tree sighed, 'It was pleasant when those busy little mice sat round me, listening to my words. Now that, too, is past! However, I shall have pleasure in remembering it, when I am taken from this place.'

But when would that be? One morning, people came and routed out the lumber-room. The trunks were taken away; the tree, too, was dragged out of the corner. They threw him on the floor, but one of the servants picked him up and carried him downstairs. Once more he beheld the light of day. 'Now life begins again!' thought the tree. He felt the fresh air, the warm sunbeams—he was out in the court. All happened so quickly that the tree quite forgot to look at himself—there was so much to look at all round. The court joined a garden. Everything was so fresh and blooming: roses so bright and so fragrant clustered round the trellis-work, the lime-trees were in full blossom, and the swallows flew backwards and forwards, twittering.

'I shall live! I shall live!' He was filled with delight and hope. He tried to spread out his branches, but alas! they were all dried up and yellow. He was thrown down on a heap of weeds and nettles. The star of gold tinsel that had been left on his crown now sparkled in the sunshine. Some children were playing in the court, the same merry youngsters who at Christmas-time had danced round the tree. One of the youngest of them saw the gold star, and ran to tear it off.

'Look at this, still fastened to the ugly old Christmas Tree!' cried he, trampling upon the boughs till they broke under his boots.

And the tree looked on the flowers of the garden now blooming in the freshness of their beauty; he looked upon himself, and he wished from his heart that he had been left to wither alone in the dark corner of the lumber-room. He called to mind his happy forest life, the merry Christmas Eve, and the little mice who had listened so eagerly when he related the story of Humpty Dumpty.

'Past, all past!' said the poor tree. 'Had I but been happy, as I might have been! Past, all past!'

And the servant came and cut the tree into small pieces, heaped them up, and set fire to them. And the tree groaned deeply, and every groan sounded like a little explosion. The children all ran up to the place and jumped about in front of the blaze. But at each of those heavy groans the fir-tree thought of a bright summer's day, of

224

Christmas Eve, or of Humpty Dumpty, the only story that he knew and could tell. And at last the tree was burned.

The boys played about in the court. On the chest of the youngest sparkled the gold star that the tree had worn on the happiest evening of his life; but that was past, and the tree was past and the story also, past! past! for all stories must come to an end some time or other.

THE REAL PRINCESS

There was once a Prince who wished to marry a Princess; but then she must be a real Princess. He travelled all over the world in hopes of finding such a one, but there was always something wrong. Princesses he found in plenty, but he could not make up his mind that they were real Princesses, for now one thing, now another, seemed to him not quite right about them. At last he went back to his palace quite downcast, because he wished so much to have a real Princess for his wife, and he had not been able to find one.

One evening a fearful tempest arose, with thunder and lightning, and the rain came down in torrents. Besides, it was as dark as pitch. All at once there was a violent knocking at the door, and the old King, the Prince's father, went out himself to open it.

It was a Princess who was standing outside. What with the rain and the wind, she was in a sad state; the water trickled from her hair, and her clothes clung to her body. She said she was a real Princess.

'Ah, we shall soon see about that!' thought the old Queen-mother. She gave no

hint, however, of what she was going to do, but went quietly into the bedroom, took all the bed-clothes off the bed, and put three little peas on the bedstead. Then she laid twenty mattresses one upon another over the three peas, and put twenty feather-beds over the mattresses.

Upon this bed the Princess was to pass the night.

The next morning she was asked how she had slept. 'Oh, very badly indeed!' she replied. 'I have scarcely closed my eyes the whole night through. I do not know what was in my bed, but I had something hard under me, and am all over black and blue. It has hurt me so much!'

Now it was plain that this must be a real Princess, since she had been able to feel the three little peas through the twenty mattresses and twenty feather-beds. None but a real Princess could have had such a delicate sense of feeling.

So the Prince made her his wife, being now convinced that he had found a real Princess. The three peas were, however, put into the royal museum, where they are still to be seen, if they have not been stolen.

Notice that this is a true story.

THE UGLY DUCKLING

How beautiful it was in the country! It was summer time; the wheat was yellow, the oats were green, the hay was stacked up in the verdant meadows, and the stork strutted about on his long red legs, chatting in Egyptian, the language he had learned from his mother. The fields and meadows were skirted by thick woods, and in the midst of the woods lay a deep lake. Yes, it was indeed beautiful in the country! The sunshine fell warmly on an old country house, surrounded by deep canals, and from the walls down to the water's edge there grew large burdock-leaves, so high that children could stand upright among them without being seen. This place was as wild and lonely as the thickest part of the wood, and on that account a duck had chosen to make her nest there. She was sitting on her eggs, but the pleasure she had felt at first was now almost gone, because she had been there so long, and had so few visitors, for the other ducks preferred swimming about in the canals to climbing up the slippery banks and sitting gossiping with her.

At last the eggs began to crack, and one little head after another appeared. 'Quack, quack!' said the duck, and all got up as well as they could, and peeped about from under the green leaves.

'How large the world is!' said the little ones.

'Do you think this is the whole of the world?' said the mother. 'It stretches far away beyond the other side of the garden down to the pastor's field, but I have never been there. Are you all here?' And then she got up. 'No, I have not got you all; the largest egg is still here. How long, I wonder, will this last? I am so weary of it!' And then she sat down again.

'Well! and how are you getting on?' asked an old duck, who had come to pay her a visit.

'This one egg keeps me so long,' said the mother, 'it will not break; but you should see the others! They are the prettiest little ducklings I have seen in all my days.'

'Depend upon it,' said the old duck, 'it is a turkey's egg. I was cheated in the same way once myself, and I had such trouble with the young ones. They were so afraid of the water that I could not get them to go near it. I called and scolded, but it was all of no use. But let me see the egg. Ah, yes! to be sure, that is a turkey's egg. Leave it, and teach the other little ones to swim.'

'I will sit on it a little longer,' said the duck. 'I have been sitting so long, that a day or two will not matter much.'

'It is no business of mine,' said the old duck, and away she waddled.

The great egg burst at last. 'Peep, peep!' said the little one, and out it tumbled. But oh! how large and ugly it was! The duck looked at it. 'That is a great, strong creature,' said she, 'none of the others are at all like it. Can it be a young turkey-cock? Well, we shall soon find out. Into the water it must go, though I shall have to push it in myself.'

The next day there was delightful weather, and the sun was shining warmly upon all the green leaves when mother-duck with her family went down to the canal. Splash! she went into the water. 'Quack, quack!' cried she, and one duckling after another jumped in. The water closed over their heads, but all came up again, and swam quite easily. All were there; even the ugly grey one was swimming about with the rest.

'No, it is not a turkey,' said the mother-duck; 'only see how prettily it moves its legs, how upright it holds itself. It is my own child, and it is really very pretty when one looks more closely at it. Quack! quack! now come with me, I will take you into the world; but keep close to me, or someone may tread on you. And beware of the cat.'

When they came into the duck-yard, two families were quarrelling about the head of an eel, which in the end was carried off by the cat.

'See, my children, that is the way of the world,' said the mother-duck, whetting her beak, for she too was fond of roasted eels. 'Now use your legs,' said she, 'keep together, and bow to the old duck you see yonder. She is the noblest born of them all, and is of Spanish blood, which accounts for her dignified appearance and manners. And look, she has a red rag on her leg; that is considered a special mark of distinction, and is the greatest honour a duck can have.'

The other ducks who were in the yard looked at them and said aloud, 'Only see! now we have another brood, as if there were not enough of us already. And fie! how ugly that one is; we will not endure it.' And immediately one of the ducks flew at him, and bit him on the neck.

'Leave him alone,' said the mother; 'he is doing no one any harm.'

'Yes, but he is so large, and so ungainly.'

'Those are fine children that our good mother has,' said the old duck with the red rag on her leg. 'All are pretty except that one, who certainly is not at all well favoured. I wish his mother could improve him a little.'

'Certainly he is not handsome,' said the mother, 'but he is a very good child, and swims as well as the others, indeed rather better. I think in time he will grow like the others, and perhaps will look smaller.' And she stroked the duckling's neck, and smoothed his ruffled feathers. 'Besides,' added she, 'he is a drake; I think he will be very strong, so he will fight his way through.'

'The other ducks are very pretty,' said the old duck. 'Pray make yourselves at home, and if you find an eel's head you can bring it to me.'

And accordingly they made themselves at home.

But the poor duckling, who had come last out of his eggshell, and who was so ugly was bitten, pecked, and teased by both ducks and hens. And the turkey-cock, who had come into the world with spurs on, and therefore fancied he was an emperor, puffed himself up like a ship in full sail, and marched up to the duckling quite red with passion. The poor thing scarcely knew what to do; he was quite distressed because he was so ugly.

So passed the first day, and afterwards matters grew worse and worse. Even his brothers and sisters behaved unkindly, and were constantly saying, 'May the cat take you, you ugly thing!' while his mother said she wished he had never been born. The ducks bit him, the hens pecked him, and the girl who fed poultry kicked him. He ran through the hedge, and the little birds in the bushes were frightened and flew

away. 'That is because I am so ugly,' thought the duckling, and ran on. At last he came to a wide moor, where lived some wild ducks. There he lay the whole night, feeling very tired and sorrowful. In the morning the wild ducks flew up, and then they saw their new companion. 'Pray who are you?' asked they, and the duckling greeted them as politely as possible.

'You are really very ugly,' said the wild ducks; 'but that does not matter to us if you do not wish to marry into our family.'

Poor thing! he had never thought of marrying. He only wished to lie among the reeds, and drink the water of the moor. There he stayed for two whole days. On the third day there came two wild geese, or rather goslings, for they had not long been out of their eggshells, which accounts for their impertinence.

'Hark ye,' said they, 'you are so ugly that we like you very well. Will you go with us and become a bird of passage? On another moor, not far from this, are some dear, sweet, wild geese, as lovely creatures as have ever said "hiss, hiss". It is a chance for you to get a wife; you may be lucky, ugly as you are.'

Bang! a gun went off, and both goslings lay dead among the reeds. Bang! another gun went off, and whole flock of wild geese flew up from the rushes. Again and again the same alarming noise was heard.

There was a great shooting party. The sportsmen lay in ambush all around; some were even sitting in the trees, whose huge branches overshadowed the rushes. The dogs splashed about in the mud, bending the reeds and rushes in all directions. How frightened the poor little duck was! He turned away his head, thinking to hide it under his wing, and at the same moment a fierce-looking dog passed close to him, his tongue hanging out of his mouth, his eyes sparkling fearfully. His jaws were wide open. He thrust his nose close to the duckling, showing his sharp, white teeth, and then—splash splash! he was gone—gone without hurting him.

'Well! let me be thankful,' sighed the duckling. 'I am so ugly that even a dog will not bite me.'

And so he lay still though the shooting continued among the reeds. The noise did not cease till late in the day, and even then the poor little thing dared not stir. He waited several hours before he looked round him, and then hastened away from the moor as fast as he could. He ran over fields and meadows, though the wind was so high that he could hardly go against it.

Towards evening he reached a wretched little hut, so wretched that it knew not on which side to fall, and therefore remained standing. He noticed that the door had lost one of its hinges, and hung so much awry that there was a space between it and the wall wide enough to let him through. So, as the storm was becoming worse and worse, he crept into the room.

In this room lived an old woman, with her tom-cat and her hen. The cat, whom she called her little son, knew how to set up his back and purr. He could even throw out sparks when his fur was stroked the wrong way. The hen had very short legs, and was therefore called 'Chickie Shortlegs'; she laid very good eggs, and the old woman loved her as her own child.

The next morning the cat began to mew and the hen to cackle when they saw the new guest.

'What is the matter?' asked the old woman, looking round. Her eyes were not good, so she took the duckling to be a fat duck who had lost her way. 'This is a capital catch,' said she. 'I shall now have duck's eggs, if it be not a drake. We must wait and see.' So the duckling was kept on trial for three weeks, but no eggs made their appearance.

Now the cat was the master of the house, and the hen was the mistress, and they used always to say, 'We and the world,' for they imagined themselves to be not only the half of the world, but also by far the better half. The duckling thought it was possible to be of a different opinion, but that the hen would not allow.

'Can you lay eggs?' asked she.

'No.'

'Well, then, hold your tongue.'

And the cat said, 'Can you set up your back? can you purr?'

'No.'

'Well, then you should have no opinion at all when sensible people are speaking.'

So the duckling sat in a corner feeling very much dispirited till the fresh air and bright sunshine came into the room through the open door, and these gave him such a strong desire to swim that he could not help telling the hen.

'What ails you?' said the hen. 'You have nothing to do, and therefore brood over these fancies; either lay eggs, or purr, then you will forget them.'

'But it is so delicious to swim,' said the duckling, 'so delicious when the waters close over your head, and you plunge to the bottom.'

'Well, that is a queer sort of pleasure,' said the hen; 'I think you must be crazy. Not to speak of myself, ask the cat—he is the wisest creature I know—whether he would like to swim, or to plunge to the bottom of the water. Ask your mistress: no one is cleverer than she. Do you think she would take pleasure in swimming, and in the waters closing over her head?'

'You do not understand me,' said the duckling.

'What! we do not understand you! So you think yourself wiser than the cat and the old woman, not to speak of myself! Do not fancy any such thing, child, but be thankful for all the kindness that has been shown you. Are you not lodged in a warm room, and have you not the advantage of society from which you can learn something? But you are a chatterbox and it is wearisome to listen to you. Believe me, I wish you well. I tell you unpleasant truths, but it is thus that real friendship is shown. Come, for once give yourself the trouble either to learn to purr, or to lay eggs.'

'I think I will take my chance and go out into the wide world again,' said the duckling.

'Well, go then,' said the hen.

So the duckling went away. He soon found water and swam on the surface and plunged beneath it, but all other animals passed him by, on account of his ugliness. The autumn came: the leaves turned yellow and brown, the wind caught them and danced about, the air was very cold, the clouds were heavy with hail or snow, and the raven sat on the hedge and croaked. The poor duckling was certainly not very comfortable!

One evening, just as the sun was setting, a flock of large birds rose from the brush-wood. The duckling had never seen anything so beautiful before; their plumage was of dazzling white, and they had long, slender necks. They were swans. They uttered a singular cry, spread out their long, splendid wings, and flew away from these cold regions to warmer countries, across the sea. They flew so high, so very high, and the ugly duckling's feelings were very strange! He turned round and round in the water like a wheel, strained his neck to look after them, and sent forth such a loud and strange cry, that it almost frightened him. Ah! he could not forget them, those noble birds, those happy birds! The duckling knew not what the birds were called, knew not whither they were flying, yet he loved them as he had never before loved anything. He envied them not. It would never have occurred to him to wish such beauty for himself. He would have been quite contented if the ducks in the duck-yard had but endured his company.

And the winter was so cold, so cold! The duckling had to swim round and round in the water to keep from freezing. But every night the opening in which he swam became smaller and smaller; the duckling had to make good use of his legs to prevent the water from freezing entirely. At last, wearied out, he lay stiff and cold in the ice.

Early in the morning there passed by a peasant, who saw him, broke the ice in pieces with his wooden shoes, and carried the duckling home to his wife.

The duckling soon revived. The children would have played with him, but he thought they wished to tease him, and in his terror jumped into the milk-pail, so that the milk was splashed about the room. The good woman screamed and clapped her hands. He flew first into the tub where the butter was kept, and thence into the meal-barrel, and out again.

The woman screamed, and struck at him with the tongs; the children ran races with each other trying to catch him, and laughed and screamed likewise. It was well for him that the door stood open; he jumped out among the bushes into the new-fallen snow, and lay there as in a dream.

But it would be too sad to relate all the trouble and misery he had to suffer during the winter. He was lying on a moor among the reeds when the sun began to shine warmly again. The larks were singing, and beautiful spring had returned.

Once more he shook his wings. They were stronger than formerly, and bore him forward quickly, and, before he was well aware of it, he was in a large garden where the apple-trees stood in full bloom, where the syringas sent forth their fragrance, and hung their long green branches down into the winding canal. Oh! everything was so lovely, so full of the freshness of spring!

Out of the thicket came three beautiful white swans. They displayed their feathers so proudly, and swam so lightly, so lightly! The duckling knew the glorious creatures, and was seized with a strange sadness.

'I will fly to them, those kingly birds!' said he. 'They will kill me, because, I, ugly as I am, have presumed to approach them, but it matters not. Better be killed by them than be bitten by the ducks, pecked by the hens, kicked by the girl who feeds the poultry, and have so much to suffer during the winter!' He flew into the water, and swam towards the beautiful creatures. They saw him and shot forward to meet him. 'Only kill me,' said the poor duckling, and he bowed his head low, expecting death. But what did he see in the water? He saw beneath him his own form, no longer that of a plump, ugly grey bird—it was that of a swan!

It matters not to have been born in a duck-yard, if one has been hatched from a swan's egg.

The larger swans swam round him, and stroked him with their beaks, and he was very happy.

Some little children were running about in the garden. They threw grain and bread into the water, and the youngest exclaimed, 'There is a new one!' The others also cried out, 'Yes, a new swan has come!' and they clapped their hands, and ran and told their father and mother. Bread and cake were thrown into the water, and everyone said, 'The new one is the best, so young, and so beautiful!' and the old swans bowed before him. The young swan felt quite ashamed, and hid his head under his wing. He was all too happy, but still not proud, for a good heart is never proud.

He remembered how he had been laughed at and cruelly treated, and he now heard everyone say he was the most beautiful of all beautiful birds. The syringas bent down their branches towards him, and the sun shone warmly and brightly. He shook his feathers, stretched his slender neck, and in the joy of his heart said, 'How little did I dream of so much happiness when I was the ugly, despised duckling!'

There were lots and lots of toys in the children's nursery. A money-box stood on top of the wardrobe; it was made in the shape of an earthenware pig and, of course, it had a slot in its back. The slot had been made larger with a knife-blade so that even big coins, like half-crowns and florins, could be put in —and two had been put in, as well as a lot of pennies. The money-pig was stuffed so full that the money couldn't rattle any more—and a money-pig can't do better than that!

There it stood, up there on the wardrobe, staring down at everything else in the room; it knew that it had enough money in its belly to buy up the whole show. There's self-confidence for you!

All the rest thought so as well, even if they didn't say so. In one of the half-open drawers of the chest of drawers a large doll was poking its head out. It was rather old and had a screw in its neck. 'Let's play at men and women,' it suggested. 'That's always fun.' So then there was a great stirring and bustling. Even the pictures turned round and faced the wall, though this wasn't because they minded.

It was midnight. The moon shone through the window and lit up the room for nothing. Now the game was ready to begin. All the toys had been asked to join in, even the pram, which was really one of the rougher toys. But as the pram said, 'Everyone has his good points. We can't all be gentlefolk. Somebody has got to do the work.'

The money-pig was the only person who got a written invitation. The toys were afraid he was too high up to hear if they just called to him. In any case he didn't answer; in fact he didn't come. If he was going to join in, he would have to do it where he was. The toys would have to arrange that, so they did.

The toy theatre was set up so that the money-pig could watch it from the wardrobe. The toys had meant to start with a play, then there was to be tea and a discussion. As it was, they began with the discussion first of all. The rocking-horse talked about racing and thoroughbreds, the pram talked about railways and steam-engines. You see, they all talked about something in their own line. The clock talked about politic-tic-tics. It knew what time it was, though the toys said it was never right. The walking-stick boasted about his ferrule and handle, for he was tipped with silver top and bottom. On the settee sat two embroidered cushions, pretty but rather feather-brained. Now the play was ready to begin.

They all sat round and looked on. They were asked to smack and clap and rattle to show they were enjoying themselves. But the riding-whip declared he never cracked for old people, only for young folk who weren't yet engaged. 'I crack for everyone,' said the cracker.

Well, the play wasn't very good; still it was well acted. All the actors turned their painted side to the audience. They were only meant to be seen on their best side. They all acted terrifically well and the doll was so excited that her screw came loose. As for the money-pig, he was so excited in his own way that he decided there and then to do something for one of the actors—to put him in his will and arrange to have a public funeral with him when the time arrived.

They enjoyed it all so much that they forgot about tea and began another discussion. This is what they called playing at 'men and women' and everybody wondered what the money-pig was thinking. Well, he was still thinking about his will and his funeral and when that would happen. It always happens before it's expected...

Crash! All of a sudden the money-pig fell from the top of the wardrobe. He lay on the floor in pieces, while the coins went rolling here and there. One of the half-crowns rolled all over the place, he was so keen to see the world. And so he did see the world, and so did all the other coins, while the broken pieces of the money-pig found their way into the dustbin.

The next day a brand-new earthenware money-pig stood on top of the wardrobe. There wasn't a single penny in it yet, and so this money-pig couldn't rattle either, just as the other couldn't because it had been full. Anyway, the new one had made a start—and with that we must come to an end.

THE FLYING TRUNK

There was once a merchant who was so rich that he could have paved the whole street with pieces of silver and, perhaps, an alley besides. But he did not do so; he knew another way of using his money. Such a good trader was he that whenever he laid out a shilling he gained a crown in return—till he died.

All his money went to his son, and he lived merrily, went to a masquerade every evening, made bank-notes into paper kites, and played at ducks and drakes in the pond with gold-pieces instead of stones. In this manner he soon spent all his money. At last he had nothing but four shillings left, and no other clothes but a pair of slippers and an old dressing-gown. His friends cared no more about him now that they could no longer walk abroad with him. One of them, however, more good-natured than the rest, sent him an old trunk, with this advice, 'Pack up, and be off!' This was all very fine, but he had nothing to pack up, so he himself got into the trunk.

It was a wonderful trunk. When the lock was pressed, it could fly. He did press the lock, and lo! up flew the trunk with him through the chimney, high into the clouds, on and on, higher and higher. Whenever the trunk creaked he was in a terrible fright, for if it had broken in two he would have made a tremendous somersault.

Only fancy it! in such manner he came to the country of the Turks. There he hid the trunk under a heap of dry leaves in a wood, and walked into the next town; and there he found that everybody was clad as he was, in dressing-gown and slippers. He met a nurse carrying a little child in her arms. 'Pardon me, Turkish nurse,' said he, can you tell me what that great castle is, close to the town, the castle where the windows are so high up?'

'The Sultan's daughter dwells there,' replied the nurse; 'it has been prophesied of her that she shall be made very unhappy by a lover, and therefore no one may visit her, except when the Sultan and Sultana are with her.'

'Thank you,' said the merchant's son, and he went back into the wood, sat down in his trunk, flew up to the roof of the palace, and crept through the window into the Princess's room.

She was lying asleep on the sofa, and she was so lovely that the merchant's son could not help kissing her. At this she awoke, and was dreadfully frightened till her visitor told her that he was the Turkish prophet and had come down from the sky to see her, and this pleased her greatly. They sat down side by side, and he talked to her about her eyes, calling them beautiful dark-blue seas where thoughts and feelings floated like mermaidens; and he spoke of her brow as a fair snowy mountain. And many other such things he said to her, and when he proposed to her she at once said 'Yes'.

'But you must come here on Saturday,' said she; 'the Sultan and Sultana are to drink tea with me that evening. They will be very proud when they hear that I am to marry the Turkish prophet! And you must tell them a very pretty story, for they are fond of stories; my mother likes them to be rather highflown and with a moral; father likes them to be funny, so as to make him laugh.'

'Very well, then; I shall bring you no other wedding present than a story,' replied the merchant's son.

Then they parted, but not before the Princess had given him a sabre all covered with gold. He knew right well what use to make of this present.

So he flew away, bought a new dressing-gown, and then sat down in the wood to make up the story which was to be ready by Saturday.

At last he was ready, and at last Saturday came.

The Sultan and the Sultana and the whole court were at tea with the Princess, and received him with much ceremony.

'Will you not tell us a story,' asked the Queen, a 'story that is instructive and full of deep meaning?'

'But let it make us laugh,' said the King.

'With pleasure,' replied the merchant's son. And this is what he told them:

There was once a bundle of matches that were extremely proud of their high descent. They traced their family to the tall fir-tree of which each of them was a splinter and which had been a tree of great age and size in the wood. The matches were now lying on the mantelpiece, between a tinder-box and an old iron saucepan, and to these two they often talked about their youth. 'Ah, when we were upon the green branches,' said they, 'when we really lived upon green branches—that was a happy time! Every morning and evening we had diamond tea—that is dew; the whole day long we had

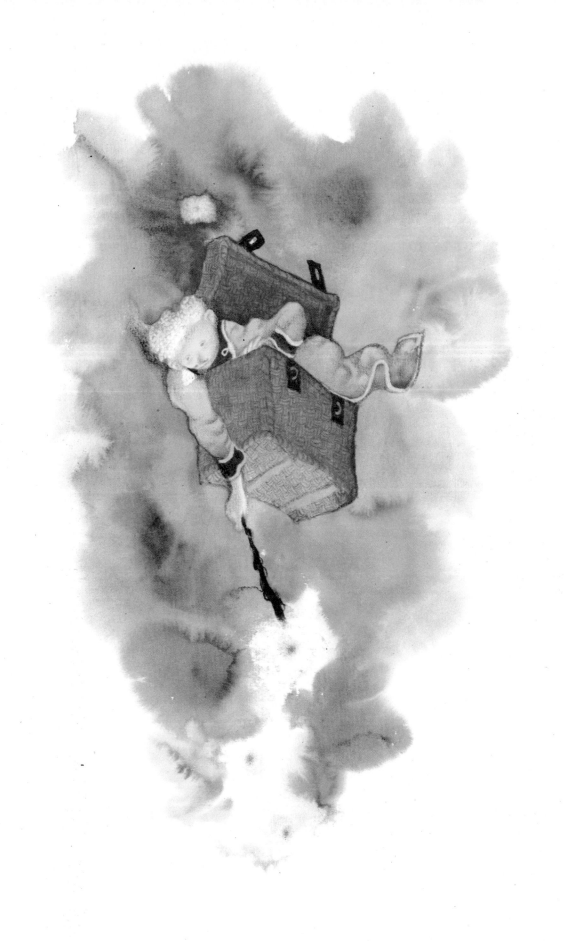

sunshine, at least whenever the sun shone, and all the little birds used to tell us stories. It might easily be seen, too, that we were rich, for the other trees were clothed with leaves only during the summer, whereas our family wore green clothes both summer and winter. At last came the wood-cutter—what a revolution that was!—and our family was broken up. The head of the family got a situation as mainmast to a magnificent ship, and can sail round the world when he will; the other branches of our family were scattered in different directions, and to us was given the task of enlightening the common people. Now you will understand how it comes to pass that persons of our class are living in a kitchen.'

'Mine has been a very different history,' said the iron saucepan, near which the matches were lying. 'From the moment I came into the world, I have been rubbed and scrubbed, and boiled over and over again. I love to have to do with what is solidly good, and am really of the first importance in this house. My chief pleasure is to stand clean and bright upon this mantelpiece after dinner and to have some sensible talk with my companions. But except the water-pail, who now and then goes out into the court, we all of us lead a very quiet life here. Our only newsmonger is the market-basket, but he talks in such an alarming way about "government" and the "people"— why, not long ago, there was an old jar standing here who was so much shocked by what he heard, that he fell down and broke to pieces. That market-basket is a Liberal, that's a fact.'

'Now, you talk too much,' broke in the tinder-box, and the steel struck the flint, so that the sparks flew out. 'Why should we not spend a pleasant evening?'

'Yes, let us settle who is of highest rank among us!' proposed the matches.

'Oh, no; for my part, I would rather not speak of myself,' said the saucepan, 'let us have some other kind of amusement. I will begin. Let us tell something that has happened to ourselves. It will be easy to throw ourselves into that, and very interesting. Near the Baltic, among the Danish beech-groves——'

'That is a capital beginning!' cried all the plates at once; 'it will certainly be just the sort of story for us!'

'Yes, there I spent my youth in a very quiet family; the furniture was rubbed, the floors were washed, clean curtains were hung up every fortnight.'

'What a charming way you have of describing things!' said the carpet-broom. 'Anyone might guess at once that it is someone who has been much in the company of ladies who is speaking; such a pure tone runs through the story.'

'Very true; one feels that!' cried the water-pail, and he gave a little leap of joy, so that some of the water splashed upon the floor.

And the saucepan went on with his tale, and the end was just as good as the beginning.

All the plates clattered applause, and the carpet-broom took some green parsley out of the sand-hole and crowned the saucepan, for she knew that this would vex the others; and she thought, 'If I crown him today, he will crown me tomorrow.'

'Now I will dance,' said the tongs, and accordingly she did dance, and oh! it was wonderful to see how she spun round on one leg; the old chair-cover in the corner split with surprise at the sight. 'Am I not to be crowned too?' asked the tongs, and she was crowned.

'These are the vulgar rabble!' thought the matches.

The tea-urn was now called upon to sing; but she said she had a cold, and could only sing when she was boiling, which, of course, was all pride and affectation. The fact was she never cared to sing except when she was standing on the parlour table before company.

In the window lay an old quill with which the maids used to write. There was nothing remarkable about her, except that she had been dipped too deep in the ink; but she was proud of that. 'If the tea-urn does not choose to sing,' said she, 'she may let it alone; there is a nightingale in a cage outside that can sing. To be sure, he has never learnt the notes—but we will not speak evil of anyone this evening!'

'I think it highly improper that a foreign bird should be listened to,' said the tea-kettle, who was the vocalist of the kitchen and a half-brother of the tea-urn. 'Is it patriotic? I appeal to the market-basket.'

'I am vexed,' said the market-basket, 'I am inwardly vexed more than anyone can think. Is this a becoming way of spending the evening? Would it not be much more sensible to put the house in order? Then everyone would get into his right place. What do you say? I would lead the game. That would be something worth doing!'

'Well, then, let us set about it at once!' they all cried. Just then the door opened—it was the servant-maid. They all stood still; not one dared stir, yet there was not a single pot there but was thinking about the great things he could have done, and how great was his superiority over the others.

'Ah, if I had chosen it,' thought each of them, 'what a merry evening we might have had!'

The maid took the matches and struck a light—oh, how they sputtered and blazed up!

'Now everyone may see,' thought they, 'that we are of highest rank; what a splendid light we give!' And while they were speaking they were burnt out.

'That is a capital story,' said the Sultana; 'I feel quite as if I were in the kitchen listening to the matches. Yes, you shall have our daughter!'

'With all my heart,' said the Sultan; 'on Monday you shall marry our daughter,' and from that moment they treated the young man as one of the family.

On the evening before the wedding the whole city was illuminated; cakes, buns, and sugar-plums were thrown out among the people; all the little boys in the streets stood upon tiptoe, shouting 'Hurrah!' and whistling through their fingers. Altogether it was a splendid affair.

'Well, I suppose I ought to do my part too,' thought the merchant's son. So he went and bought sky-rockets, squibs, Catherine-wheels, Roman-candles, and all kinds of fireworks conceivable, put them all into his trunk, and flew up into the air, letting them off as he flew.

All the Turks jumped up to look, so hastily that their slippers flew about their ears. Such a meteor they had never seen before. Now they might be sure that it was indeed the prophet who was to marry their Princess.

As soon as the merchant's son had returned in his trunk to the wood, he said to himself, 'I will go into the city and hear what people say about me, and what sort of figure they think I made in the air.' It was quite natural that he should wish to know.

Oh, what strange accounts were given! Everyone to whom he spoke had beheld the bright vision in a way of his own, but all agreed that it was a very beautiful sight.

'I saw the great prophet with my own eyes,' declared one. 'He had eyes like sparkling stars, and a beard like foaming water.'

'He flew away in a mantle of fire,' said another, 'and the prettiest little cherubs were peeping forth from under its folds.'

He heard many other wonderful things about himself; and next day was to be his wedding-day.

He now went back to the wood, intending to get into his trunk again, but, alas! the trunk was burnt. One spark from the fireworks had been left in it, and had set it on fire; the trunk now lay in ashes. The poor merchant's son could never fly again—could never again visit his bride.

She sat the livelong day upon the roof of her palace expecting him; she expects him still. He, meantime, goes about the world telling stories, but none of his stories now are so pleasant as that one which he told in the Princess's palace about the brimstone matches.

There were once five-and-twenty tin soldiers, all brothers, for all had been made out of one old tin spoon. They carried muskets in their arms and held themselves very upright, and their uniforms were red and blue. The first words they heard in this world were, 'Tin soldiers!' It was a little boy who uttered them, when the lid was taken off the box where they lay; and he clapped his hands with delight. They had been given to him because it was his birthday. Then he set them out on the table.

The soldiers were like each other to a hair; all but one, who had only one leg, because he had been made last, when there was not quite enough tin left. He stood as firmly, however, upon his one leg as the others did upon their two, and it is this one-legged tin soldier's fortunes that seem to us worthy of being told.

On the table where the tin soldiers stood there were other playthings, but the most charming of them all was a pretty pasteboard castle. Through its little windows one could look into the rooms. In front of the castle stood some tiny trees, clustering round a little mirror intended to represent a lake. Some waxen swans swam on the lake and were reflected in it.

All this was very pretty, but prettiest of all was a little lady standing in the open doorway of the castle. She, too, was cut out of pasteboard, but she had on a frock of the softest muslin, and a narrow sky-blue riband was flung across her shoulders like a scarf, and in the middle of this scarf was set a glittering tinsel rose. The little lady was a dancer, and she stretched out both her arms, and raised one of her legs so high in the air that the tin soldier could not see it, and thought she had, like himself, only one leg.

'That would be just the wife for me,' thought he, 'but then she is of too high a rank. She lives in a castle, and I have only a box, and even that is not my own, for all our five-and-twenty men live in it; so it is no place for her. Still, I must make her acquaintance.' Then he laid himself down at full length behind a snuff-box that stood on the table so that he had a full view of the delicate little lady still standing on one leg without losing her balance.

When evening came, all the other tin soldiers were put into the box, and the people of the house went to bed. Then the playthings began to have their own games,

to pay visits, fight battles and to give balls. The tin soldiers rattled in the box, for they wished to play too, but the lid would not open. The nut-crackers cut capers, and the slate-pencil danced about on the table. There was such a noise that the canary woke up and began to talk too, but he always talked in verse. The only two who did not move from their places were the tin soldier and the dancer. She remained standing on the very tip of her toes, with outstretched arms, and he stood just as firmly on his one leg, never for a moment taking his eyes off her.

Twelve o'clock struck, and with a crash the lid of the snuff-box sprang open—there was no snuff in it, it was only a toy puzzle—and out jumped a little black conjurer. 'Tin soldier!' said the conjurer, 'please keep your eyes to yourself!'

But the tin soldier pretended not to hear.

'Well, just wait till tomorrow!' said the conjurer.

When the children got up next morning the tin soldier was placed on the window-ledge, and, whether the conjurer or the wind caused it, all at once the window flew open and out fell the tin soldier head foremost, from the third storey to the ground. It was a dreadful fall, for he fell head first into the street, and at last rested with his cap and bayonet between two paving-stones, and with his one leg in the air.

The servant-maid and the little boy came downstairs directly to look for him; but though they very nearly trod on him they could not see him. If the tin soldier had but called out, 'Here I am!' they might easily have found him, but he thought it would not be becoming for him to cry out, as he was in uniform.

Presently it began to rain; soon the drops were falling thicker, and there was a perfect downpour. When it was over, two little street arabs came by.

'Look,' said one, 'there is a tin soldier. Let him have a sail for once in his life.'

So they made a boat out of newspaper, and put the soldier into it. Away he sailed down the gutter, both the boys running along by the side of it and clapping their hands. The paper boat rocked to and fro, and every now and then was whirled round so quickly that the tin soldier became quite giddy. Still he did not move a muscle but looked straight before him, and held his musket tightly clasped.

All at once the boat was carried into a long drain, where the tin soldier found it as dark as in his own box.

'Where can I be going now?' thought he. 'It is all that conjurer's doing. Ah! if only the little maiden were sailing with me I would not mind its being twice as dark.'

Just then a great water-rat that lived in the drain darted out. 'Have you a passport?' asked the rat. 'Show me your passport!' But the tin soldier was silent, and held his musket tighter than ever. The boat sailed on, and the rat followed. How he gnashed his teeth, and cried out to the sticks and the straws: 'Stop him, stop him, he has not paid the toll; he has not even shown his passport.' But the stream grew stronger and

stronger. The tin soldier could already catch a glimpse of the daylight where the tunnel ended, but at the same time he heard a roaring noise that might have made the boldest tremble. Where the tunnel ended, the water of the gutter fell into a great canal. This was as dangerous for the tin soldier as a waterfall would be for us.

The fall was now so close that he could no longer stand upright. The boat darted forward; the poor tin soldier held himself as stiffly as possible, so that no one could accuse him of having even blinked. The boat spun round three or four times, and was filled with water to the brim; it must sink now.

The tin soldier stood up to his neck in water, but deeper and deeper sank the boat, and softer and softer grew the paper till the water stood over the soldier's head. He thought of the pretty little dancer whom he should never see again, and these words rang in his ears:

'Fare on, thou soldier brave!
Life must end in the grave.'

The paper now split in two, and the tin soldier fell through the rent and was at once swallowed up by a large fish. Oh, how dark it was! darker even than in the tunnel and much narrower too! But the tin soldier was as constant as ever and lay there at full length, still shouldering his arms.

The fish swam to and fro, and made the strangest movements, but at last he became quite still. After a while a flash of lightning seemed to dart through him and the daylight shone brightly, and someone cried out, 'I declare, here is the tin soldier!' The fish had been caught, taken to the market, sold, and brought into the kitchen, where the servant-girl was cutting him up with a large knife. She seized the tin soldier by the middle with two of her fingers, and took him into the parlour, where everyone was eager to see the wonderful man who had travelled in the maw of a fish. But the tin soldier was not proud.

They set him on the table, and—what strange things do happen in the world!— the tin soldier was in the very room in which he had been before. He saw the same children, the same playthings on the table—among them the beautiful castle with the pretty little dancing maiden, who was still standing upon one leg while she held the other high in the air; she too was constant. It quite touched the tin soldier; he could have found it in his heart to weep tin tears, but such weakness would have been unbecoming in a soldier. He looked at her and she looked at him, but neither spoke a word.

And now one of the boys took the soldier and threw him into the stove. He gave no reason for doing so, but no doubt it was the fault of the conjurer in the snuff-box.

The tin soldier now stood in a blaze of light. He felt extremely hot, but whether from the fire or from the flames of love he did not know. He had entirely lost his colour. Whether this was the result of his travels, or the effect of strong feeling, I know not. He looked at the little lady, and she looked at him, and he felt that he was melting, but, constant as ever, he still stood shouldering his arms. A door opened, and the draught caught the dancer, and, like a sylph, she flew straightway into the stove, to the tin soldier. Instantly she was in a blaze and was gone. The soldier was melted and dripped down among the ashes, and when the maid cleaned out the fireplace the next day she found his remains in the shape of a little tin heart. Of the dancer all that was left was the tinsel rose, and that was burnt as black as of coal.

THUMBYKIN

Once upon a time there was a woman who wished very much for a little child, but did not know where to find one. So at last she went to a witch and said to her: 'I do so much wish to have a little child; can you, who are so wise, tell me where I can find one?'

'I can readily do so,' said the witch. 'There is nothing easier. Here is a barley corn, but it is quite unlike those that grow in the farmers' fields and that the fowls eat. Put it into a flowerpot and wait and see what takes place.'

'Oh, thank you so much,' said the woman, giving the witch twelve shillings, which was the price she asked for her barley corn. Thereafter she went straight home and planted the barley corn, and at once a large handsome flower sprang up. It looked something like a tulip, but its leaves were as tightly closed as if they were the leaves of a bud. 'What a lovely flower!' said the woman, kissing its red and golden-coloured leaves. At her kiss the leaves burst open with a crack and she saw that it was really a tulip such as one can see almost anywhere. But lo! in the very centre of the blossom, on one of the green velvety stamens, sat a tiny maiden, a delicate and graceful little creature, scarcely half as long as a thumb, and when the woman saw her she called her Thumbykin, because she was so small.

A finely polished walnut-shell formed her cradle, and therein, on a bed of violets, under a rose-leaf coverlet, Thumbykin slept soundly at night. During the day she amused herself by floating across a plate full of water in a large tulip-leaf which served her for a boat. The woman had placed the plate of water on a table, and put a wreath of flowers round the edge of it, and from side to side of the plate the little maiden rowed herself with two oars made of white horse-hair. It was pretty to see her and prettier still to hear her singing in a voice as clear as a tiny silver bell. Such singing certainly had never before been heard.

One night as she lay asleep in her pretty little bed, a large ugly old toad crept through a broken pane in the window and leapt up on the table. 'What a lovely little creature this is!' she thought, 'and what a charming wife she would make for my son!' So she took up the walnut-shell in which the little maiden lay asleep under her coverlet of rose-leaf, and leapt with it through the window, and so hopped back again into the garden.

Now through the garden a broad stream flowed, and in its marshy banks the old toad lived with her son. He was uglier even than his mother, and when he saw the pretty little maiden in her beautiful bed he was able only to cry in his harsh voice, 'Croak, croak, croak.'

'Don't make such a noise,' said the old toad, 'or you will wake her and then she may fly away, for she is as light as thistledown. We will put her on one of the large water-lily leaves that grow in the middle of the stream. It will seem an island to her, she is so small. She will not be able to get away from it, and we shall have plenty of time to get ready the state-room under the marsh, where you are to live when you are married.'

Out in the middle of the stream grew a number of water-lilies, with broad green leaves that floated on the top of the water. The largest of these leaves seemed much farther off than any of the rest, and thither the old toad swam, carrying with her the walnut-shell in which Thumbykin still lay sound asleep.

Very early in the morning the poor little creature awoke, and when she saw where she was she began to cry bitterly, for all round the leaf on which she was there was water, and she could see no way of ever reaching the land.

Meanwhile, down in the marsh the old toad was as busy as possible decking out her room with sedge and yellow rushes, so as to make it pretty and comfortable for her new daughter-in-law. When she had finished her work she swam out with her ugly son to the leaf where she had placed poor Thumbykin. She wished to carry off the pretty bed, that she might put it in the bridal chamber to be ready for the bride. To the little maiden the old toad in the water bowed low and said, 'Here is my son. He is to be your husband, and you will have a very happy life together in the fine house I have prepared for you down in the marsh by the stream.'

'Croak, croak, croak,' was all the ugly son could say for himself.

So the old toad and her son took up the pretty little cradle and swam away with it, leaving Thumbykin sitting weeping all alone on the green lily-leaf. She could not bear to think of living all alone with the old toad, and of having her ugly son for a husband.

Now the little fishes, who had been swimming about in the water, and had seen the old toad and had heard every word she said, leaped up till their heads were above the water, so that they might see the little girl; and when they caught sight of her they saw that she was very pretty, and they felt very sorry that any one so pretty should have to go and live with the ugly toads.

'No, no!' said they. 'Such a thing must never be allowed.'

So all the little fishes gathered together in the water round the green stalk of the leaf on which the little maiden sat, and they bit the stalk with their teeth until at last they bit it through. Then away went the leaf sailing quickly down the stream, and carrying Thumbykin far away where the toad could never reach her.

Past many towns she sailed, and when the birds in the bushes saw her they sang: 'What a lovely little girl!' On floated the leaf, carrying her farther and farther away, until at last she came to another land. Round her head a pretty little white butterfly kept fluttering constantly, till at last he settled on the leaf. He was greatly pleased with Thumbykin, and she was glad of it, for it was not possible now that the ugly toad could ever reach her, and the land through which she was sailing was very beautiful, and the sun shone on the water till it glowed and sparkled like silver. So Thumbykin took off her sash and tied one end of it round the butterfly, and fixed the other end to the leaf, which now sped on much faster than before, having the butterfly for a sail, and took the little maiden with it.

Presently a great cockchafer flew past. The moment he caught sight of the maiden he seized her, putting his claws round her slim waist, and away he flew with her into a tree. But the green leaf floated on down the river, and the butterfly flew with it, for he was tied to the leaf, and could not get away.

Oh, how frightened Thumbykin was when the cockchafer flew away with her into the tree! She was sorry, too, for the pretty white butterfly which she had tied to the leaf, for if he could not free himself, he would certainly die of hunger. But the cockchafer did not worry himself about that. He sat down beside her on one of the leaves of the tree, and gave her some honey from a flower to eat, and told her that she was very pretty, though not like a cockchafer. In a little while all the cockchafers that lived in the tree came to visit her. They stared their hardest at Thumbykin, and one young lady cockchafer said, 'Why, she has only two legs! How ugly that looks!' 'She has no feelers,' said another; 'how stupid she must be!' 'How slender her waist is!' said a third. 'Pooh! she looks just like a human being.'

'How ugly she is!' said all the lady cockchafers. Thumbykin was really very lovely, and the cockchafer who had carried her off thought so; but when they all said she was ugly, he began to think that it must be true. So he would have nothing more to say to Thumbykin, but told her that she might go where she pleased. Then the cockchafers flew down with her from the tree, and placed her on a daisy, and Thumbykin wept because she thought she was so ugly that the cockchafers would have nothing to say to her. And all the time she was in reality one of the loveliest creatures in the world, and as tender and delicate as a rose-leaf.

All the summer through poor Thumbykin lived all alone in the forest. She wove for herself a little bed with blades of grass, and she hung it up under a clover-leaf so that she might be sheltered from the rain. For food she sucked the honey from the flowers, and from the leaves every morning she drank the dew. So the summer and the autumn passed away, and then came the long cold winter. The birds that had sung to her so sweetly had all flown away; the trees had lost their leaves, and the flowers were withered. The great clover-leaf under whose shelter she had lived was now rolled together and shrivelled up, and nothing of it was left but a yellow withered stalk.

Poor Thumbykin felt very, very cold, for her clothes were torn, and she was such a frail, delicate little thing that she nearly died. The snow, too, began to fall, and each flake, as it fell on her, was like a whole shovelful falling on one of us, for we are tall, and she was only about an inch high. Then she rolled herself up in a dry leaf, but it cracked in the middle, and there was no warmth in it, so she shivered with cold. Very near the wood in which she had been living there was a large corn-field, but the corn had been cut long before this, and there was nothing left but the hard, dry stubble standing up out of the frozen ground. To Thumbykin, going through it, it was like struggling through another forest; and, oh, how bitterly cold it was! At last she came to the door of the house of a field-mouse, who lived in a hole under the stubble. It was a warm, cosy house, and the mouse was very happy, for she had a whole roomful of corn, besides a kitchen and a fine dining-room. Poor little Thumbykin stood before the door of the house, just like a beggar girl, and prayed the mouse for a small bit of barley corn, because she was starving, having had nothing to eat for the last two days.

'Poor little thing!' said the field-mouse, who was really a kind-hearted old creature, 'come into my warm room and have dinner with me.' The mouse was greatly pleased with Thumbykin, so she said, 'If you like, you can spend the winter with me; of course you will keep my rooms tidy and tell me stories. I am very fond of hearing stories.'

Thumbykin did all the kind old mouse asked her, and in return she was well treated and very comfortable. 'We shall have a visitor soon,' said the field-mouse to Thumbykin one day; 'my neighbour pays me a visit once a week. He is much richer than I am; he has fine large rooms and wears a beautiful black velvet fur. If you could get him for a husband you would indeed be well off. He is blind though, poor man! so you must tell him some of your prettiest stories.' But Thumbykin knew that the neighbour she had spoken of was only a mole, and she did not mean to trouble herself about him.

The mole, however, came and paid his visit. He was dressed in his black velvet coat.

264

'He is very learned and very rich,' whispered the old field-mouse to Thumbykin, and his house is twenty times larger than mine.'

Rich no doubt he was, and learned too, but never having seen the sun or the beautiful flowers, he always spoke slightingly regarding them. Thumbykin found that she had to sing to him, so she sang, 'Lady-bird, lady-bird, fly away home,' and 'As I was going along, long, long,' and other pretty songs, and the mole at once fell deeply in love with her because she had such a sweet voice; but, being a prudent man, he said nothing about his feelings.

A short time before this visit, the mole had dug a long underground passage between the two houses, and he gave the field-mouse and Thumbykin permission to walk in this passage whenever they pleased. But he told them that there was a dead bird lying in the passage, and he begged them not to be frightened by it. 'The bird,' he said, 'was perfect, with beak and feathers all complete. It could not have been dead long, and had been buried just where he had made the passage.' Then the mole took a piece of rotten wood in his mouth, and it shone like fire in the darkness, and he went before them to light them through the long dark passage. When they came to where the dead bird lay the mole pushed his broad nose through the ceiling so as to make a hole.

The daylight fell through the hole and shone on the body of a dead swallow. Its pretty wings were closely folded, and its head and claws were hidden under its feathers. The poor bird had undoubtedly died of cold. It made the little girl very sad to see it, for she dearly loved the little birds. All the summer through they had chirped and sung to please her.

But the unfeeling mole thrust the swallow aside with his crooked legs, and said, 'He will sing no more now. What a wretched thing it must be to be born a bird. Thank Heaven, none of my children will ever be birds. Birds can do nothing but cry tweet, tweet! and they always starve to death in the winter.'

'Indeed, as a sensible man, you may well say so,' cried the field-mouse. 'What does his chirping and twittering do for a bird when the winter comes? Can his tweet, tweet, appease his hunger, or keep him from being frozen to death? And yet it is thought to be very well bred!'

Thumbykin did not speak, but when the other two turned their backs on the dead bird, she stooped down and smoothed aside the feathers that covered the head, and kissed the closed eyelids.

'Perhaps it was you who sang so sweetly to me in the summer,' she said, 'and how much pleasure you gave me, you dear pretty bird!'

The mole then stopped up the hole through which the daylight came, and walked home with the ladies. But at night Thumbykin could not sleep; so she got out of bed, and wove a fine large rug of soft hay. When she had finished it, she gathered together some soft flower down that she found in the field-mouse's sitting-room, and she carried the rug and the down to the dead bird. The down was soft and warm like wool, and she put it carefully round him and spread the coverlet over him, that he might lie warm in the cold earth.

'Good-bye! you dear, pretty little bird,' said she, 'good-bye. Thank you for all the sweet songs you sang in the summer when the trees were green and the sun shone down warmly upon us.' Sorrowfully she laid her head on the breast of the bird, but almost at once she raised it in surprise. It seemed as if something inside the bird was going 'thump, thump'. It was the swallow's heart. The swallow was not really dead but only numbed with the cold, and when the warmth again stole over him his life came back.

In autumn all the swallows fly away to warmer lands. But if one of them stays behind too long, the cold freezes it and it falls to the ground as if dead. It lies where it falls and the cold snow covers it.

Thumbykin trembled with fear, for the bird seemed very large in comparison with a little thing like herself, only an inch long. But her pity was stronger than her fear, and being a brave little girl, she covered the poor swallow more thickly with the down, and ran and brought a balsam leaf that she herself used as a coverlet and spread it over the bird's head.

Next night she again stole into the passage to see him. He was still alive, but he was very weak, and could only open his eyes to look for a moment at his kind little nurse, who stood over him, holding in her hand a rotten piece of wood, for she had no other light.

'Thank you, pretty little maiden,' whispered the sick swallow. 'I am so nice and warm now that I shall soon get back my strength, and be able to fly about again in the warm sunshine.'

'Alas!' said she. 'You must wait for some time. It is too cold out of doors just now; it snows and freezes. You must stay in your warm bed, and I will take care of you.'

Then she brought him some water in a flower-leaf; and when he had drunk it he told her how he had wounded one of his wings in a thorn-bush and was not able to fly as fast as the other swallows; how they flew away without him; and how he fell senseless to the ground. He could not remember any more, and did not know how he came to be where he then lay. All the winter the swallow remained underground, and Thumbykin nursed him with the tenderest care. She did not say a word about the sick swallow to the mole or to the field-mouse, for they did not like birds. Soon the spring came. The sun warmed the earth, and the swallow said good-bye to his kind little nurse. She opened the hole in the ceiling which the mole had made. The glorious sunshine poured into the passage, and the swallow begged her to go away with him. She could sit on his back, he said, and he would fly away with her into the green woods. But the little maiden knew that it would vex the old field-mouse if she left her in that way, so she said, 'No, I cannot come.'

'Good-bye, then good-bye, you pretty little darling,' said the swallow, and away

he flew into the sunshine. Thumbykin gazed after him and tears filled her eyes. She dearly loved the pretty swallow, whose life she had saved.

'Joy, joy!' sang the bird as he flew away into the green woods. But poor Thumbykin was very sorrowful. She was not able to get out into the warm sunshine, for the corn which the farmer had sown in the field over the house of the field-mouse had grown up so high that it seemed a lofty and pathless wood to the little maiden.

'Now,' said the field-mouse to her one day, 'you are going to be married, Thumbykin. My neighbour, the mole, has proposed to you. What a piece of luck for a poor girl like you! You must begin at once to get your wedding clothes ready. You must have both woollen and linen, for nothing must be wanting in the wedding outfit of a mole's bride.'

Thumbykin had to set to work with the spindle, and the field-mouse hired four spiders who had to weave day and night. Every evening the mole came to pay his visit, and he always spoke of the time when the summer would be over. Then, he said, they would be married. Just now the sun was so hot that it burned up the ground and made it as hard as a stone. But the little maiden was not at all happy. She thought the mole tiresome and did not like him. In the morning when the sun rose, and in the evening when it set, she used to creep out at the door, and when the wind blew aside the ears of corn so that she could catch a glimpse of the blue sky, she used to think how lovely it was in the light, and long to see her dear swallow once more. But he never came back again, for by this time he had flown far, far away into the green woods. When the autumn came Thumbykin had her wedding outfit quite ready, and the field-mouse said, 'Well, Thumbykin, in a month from now you shall be married.' But the girl cried, and said she would never marry the tiresome mole.

'Nonsense, nonsense!' said the mouse. 'Don't be foolish or I shall bite you with my white teeth. The mole will make you a very handsome husband. The Queen herself does not wear such a fine black velvet coat. He has, besides, a full kitchen and cellar. You ought to be very thankful for your good fortune.'

At length the wedding-day arrived. The mole came to fetch his bride. Thumbykin would have to go away and live with him deep under the earth, and never again see the warm sun because he did not like it. The poor little maid was very sad at the thought of saying farewell to the beautiful sun, and as the field-mouse had permitted her to stand at the door, she went out to look at it once more, and to say farewell to it.

'Farewell, dear bright sun,' she cried, stretching out her arms towards it. Then she walked a little away from the house, for the corn had been cut, and there was only the dry stubble left in the fields. 'Farewell, farewell!' she said again, throwing her arms round a little red flower that grew close beside her. 'Give my love to the swallow, if you should ever see him again.'

Suddenly a 'tweet, tweet' sounded over her head. She looked up, and there was the swallow himself flying past. As soon as he spied Thumbykin he flew to her with delight, and she told him her story, told him how unwilling she was to marry the stupid mole, and to live always under the earth, and never again see the bright sun. As she told him about her marriage she could not help weeping.

'The cold winter is coming now,' said the swallow, 'and I am going to fly away to a warmer land. Will you come with me? You can sit on my back. Tie yourself on with your girdle. Then we will fly away from the ugly mole and his gloomy abode, fly far away over the hills to warmer lands—lands where the sunshine is brighter than it is here, where there are lovely flowers, and where it is always summer. Fly away with me now, dear little Thumbykin. You saved my life when I lay frozen in yonder black tunnel.'

'Yes, I will come with you,' said the little maiden. Then she sat down on the bird's back with her feet resting on his outspread wings, and she fastened her girdle to one of his stronger feathers; and the swallow rose high into the air, and flew fast over forest and lake, and over the snow-capped mountains. Poor Thumbykin would have been frozen but she crept under the bird's warm feathers, peeping out from time to time so that she might catch a glimpse of the beautiful lands over which they were passing. At last they reached the warm countries, where the sun shines much more brightly than it does here, and where the sky seems twice as high above the earth. There by the wayside and on the hedges there grew purple and green and white grapes, and pale lemons and golden oranges hung from the trees in the woods. The air was fragrant with the scent of myrtle and balm, and along the country lanes ran beautiful children, playing with large gay butterflies. The farther the swallow flew the more beautiful every place seemed to grow. At last they came to a lovely blue lake, and by the side of it, shaded by stately green trees, stood a pure white marble castle. It was an old building, and the vine leaves twined round its lofty columns. At the top of these there were many swallows' nests, and one of these was the nest of the swallow who carried Thumbykin.

'This is my house,' said the swallow; 'but it would not do for you to live here. Will you choose for yourself one of those beautiful flowers?—and I will put you down on it, and then you shall have everything you can wish to make you happy.'

'That will be charming,' cried the little maiden, and she clapped her tiny hands.

On the ground lay a large white marble pillar, which had fallen and been broken into three pieces. Between the pieces grew the most beautiful large white flowers. The swallow flew down with Thumbykin and set her on one of the broad leaves. But how surprised she was to see in the middle of the flower a tiny little man as white and transparent as glass! On his head was a graceful golden crown, and at his shoulders a pair of delicate wings. He was not much larger than the little maid herself. He was the flower-elf. An elf-man and an elf-maid live in every flower, and this was the King of all the flower-elves.

'Oh, how beautiful he is!' whispered Thumbykin to the swallow.

The little flower-king was at first quite frightened at the bird. Compared with a little man like himself, it was a giant. But when he saw Thumbykin he was charmed.

270

Never had he seen such a pretty girl. He took the gold crown from his head and placed it on hers; he asked her name, and begged her to marry him, and become the Queen of all the flowers.

This was certainly a very different kind of husband from the son of the toad or from the mole with his black velvet coat, so she said 'yes' to this handsome prince, her new suitor. Then all the flowers opened, and out of each came a tiny lady and gentleman. They were all so graceful that it was a pleasure to look at them. They each brought Thumbykin a present, but the present she loved most of all was a pair of lovely white wings from a big white fly. When these were fastened to her shoulders she could fly from flower to flower.

Then there were great rejoicings, and the little swallow who sat in his nest overhead was asked to sing a wedding song for them. He sang as well as he could, but his heart was sad, for he was very fond of the little maiden, and had hoped never again to part from her.

'You must no longer be called Thumbykin,' said the flower-elf to her. 'It's an ugly name, and you are very beautiful. We will call you Maia.'

'Good-bye, good-bye,' sang the swallow, sad at heart, as he left the warm lands and flew away to the colder North. There he had a nest outside the window of a man who could tell fairy tales. For him the swallow sang 'tweet, tweet', and that's how we came to hear the whole story.

THE TRAVELLING COMPANION

Poor Johannes was sorely afflicted, for his father was ill, past all hope of recovery. Besides their two selves, not a soul was present in the little room. The lamp on the table was flickering, and it was late at night.

'You have been a good son, Johannes,' said the sick father, 'and God will, no doubt, help you on in the world.' And he gazed at him with mild and thoughtful eyes, fetched a deep sigh, and then died—though he only looked as if he had gone to sleep. But Johannes wept, for now he had nobody in the wide world—neither father, mother, sister, nor brother. Poor Johannes! He knelt down beside the bed, kissed his dead father's hand, and shed many, many bitter tears! But at length his eyes closed, and he fell asleep against the hard bed-post.

Then he had a strange dream. He thought the sun and moon came down to him, and he saw his father again in health and freshness, and heard him laugh as he used to do when he was pleased. A pretty girl, with a gold crown on her long, shining hair, presented her hand to him, and his father said: 'Look what a bride you have won. She is the loveliest maid upon earth.' He then woke, and all these fine things vanished; his father lay dead and cold in his bed, and nobody was near them. Poor Johannes!

In the following week, the dead man was buried. The son followed close behind the coffin, for he was never again to behold the father who had loved him so dearly. He heard them fling the earth down upon the coffin, and still saw a little corner of it left, but, at the next shovelful, even that disappeared. Then he felt as though his heart would break, so afflicted was he. They sang a psalm round the grave, and it sounded so beautiful that it brought tears to Johannes's eyes. He wept, and felt relieved. The sun shone down gloriously on the green trees, just as if it meant to say: 'You must not be so mournful, Johannes. Look how beautifully blue the sky is yonder! Your father is up above, and is begging of the All-merciful that you may thrive at all times!'

'I will always be good,' said Johannes, 'then I shall join my father in heaven, and what joy it will be to meet him again! How much I shall have to tell him, and how much he will have to teach me about the delights of heaven, just as he used to teach me here on earth. Oh, what joy that will be!'

He fancied it all so plainly that he smiled, while the tears still ran down his cheeks. The birds in the chestnut trees kept twittering, 'Twit! twit!' They were gay, although they had been at the funeral; but they knew that the dead man was now in heaven, and had wings much larger and more beautiful than their own, and that he was happy, because he had been good here on earth, and, therefore, they were pleased. Johannes saw how they flew from the green trees out into the wide world, and then he wished to fly away also. But he first cut out a large wooden cross to place on his father's grave, and when he brought it thither in the evening, he found the grave decked with gravel and flowers. This had been done by strangers, who all esteemed the worthy man who had gone to his last home.

Early the next morning, Johannes packed up his little bundle, and put into his pouch his whole legacy, consisting of fifty gilders and a couple of silver shillings, with which he meant to wander forth into the world. But first of all he repaired to his father's grave in the churchyard, where he repeated the Lord's Prayer, and then said, 'Farewell!'

Abroad in the fields through which he passed, all the flowers looked fresh and lovely in the warm sunshine. And they nodded in the wind, just as if they meant to say: 'Welcome to the greenwood! Is it not delightful here?' But Johannes turned round to give a last look at the old church, in which he was christened as an infant, and where he used to go with his father every Sunday to hear the service and to sing his psalm, and in so doing he perceived, in one of the upper loopholes of the church tower, the little goblin belonging to it, who stood with his little pointed red cap on his head, shading his countenance with his arm, so that the sun might not stream into his eyes. Johannes nodded farewell to him, and the little goblin waved his red cap, laid his hand on his heart, and then kissed his hand to him, to show that he was kindly disposed towards him, and wished him a happy journey.

Johannes now thought of how many beautiful things he should see in the wide world, so large and so magnificent as it was; and he went on and on much farther than he had ever been before. He did not know the places through which he passed, nor the people whom he met. He was now abroad in a foreign land.

The first night he was obliged to lie on a haycock in the open fields, for he had no other bed. But this, he thought, was so nice a bed that the king himself could not be better off. The field, and the haycock, with the blue sky above, certainly formed a very pretty bedchamber. The green grass, dotted with little red and white flowers, was the carpet, the elder bushes and hedges of wild roses were the nosegays that decorated the room, and his washing-basin was the brook, with its clear, pure waters, where the reeds were nodding to bid him good-night and good-morning. The moon was a large lamp, high up in the blue ceiling, and one that could not set fire to the curtains. Johannes might sleep in peace, and he did so; nor did he wake till the sun rose, and all the little birds around were singing: 'Good-morrow! Good-morrow! Are you not yet up?'

The bells were ringing for church, for it was Sunday. The people were going to hear the preacher, and Johannes followed them, sang a psalm, and heard the word of God. He felt just as if he were in his own parish church, in which he had been christened, and where he sang psalms with his father.

In the churchyard were several graves, some of which were overgrown with very high grass. And he thought how his father's grave would grow to look the same in the end, as he would not be there to weed it and deck it. So he fell to work and tore up the grass, and set up the wooden crosses that had fallen down, and replaced the wreaths that had been blown away by the wind, thinking all the time, 'Perhaps some-one is doing the same for my father's grave, as I am unable to take care of it.'

Before the church door stood an aged beggar, leaning on a crutch. Johannes gave him his silver shillings, and then went forth on his way, lighter and happier than he had felt before.

Towards evening there arose a violent storm, which made him hasten to find a shelter. Darkness soon came on, but at length he reached a small and lonely church that stood on a little hill.

'I will sit down in a corner,' said he, as he went in; 'I am so tired that I need rest.' He then sat down and folded his hands, and said his evening prayer; and before he perceived it, he was fast asleep and dreaming, while a thunder-storm was raging abroad.

When he awoke it was in the middle of the night, but the fearful storm was over, and the moon shone in through the window to greet him. In the middle of the church stood an open coffin, in which lay the body of a man, that was awaiting burial. Johannes was not fearful, for he had a good conscience, and, besides, he knew that the dead never injure anyone. It is only living, wicked men that do any harm. Two

274

such bad characters stood beside the dead man who was lying in the church awaiting burial, and they wanted to vent their spite, by not letting him rest in his coffin, and casting his poor body outside the church door.

'Why do you want to do so?' asked Johannes. 'It would be very wicked. In Christ's name, let him rest in peace!'

'Oh, stuff and nonsense!' said the two hideous men; 'he has taken us in. He owed us money, and couldn't pay it, and now he is dead into the bargain, and we shan't recover a penny! Therefore we will take our revenge, and he shall lie outside the church door like a dog.'

'I have nothing in the world but fifty gilders,' said Johannes, 'which form my whole patrimony; yet will I willingly give them to you, provided you promise truly to leave the dead man in peace. I shall manage without the money. I have strong and healthy limbs, and a merciful God will assist me in times of need!'

'Of course,' said the ugly men, 'if you pay his debt, we will neither of us lay a finger on him—you may depend on that.' And thereupon they took the money which he gave them, laughed aloud at his simple good nature, and went their ways. Then he laid the body carefully back into the coffin, folded the dead man's hands, took leave of him, and continued his way through a large forest, in a contented frame of mind.

All around him, wherever the moon shone through the trees, he saw numbers of elegant little elves at play. His presence did not disturb them, for they knew him to be a good and harmless son of the earth; for it is only bad people who are not privileged to see the elves. Some of them were not taller than the breadth of one's finger, and wore their long yellow hair fastened up with gold combs. They were rocking themselves, two by two, on the large dew-drops that sparkled on the leaves and the tall grass. Now and then the drop would roll away, and down they fell between the long blades, occassioning a deal of laughter and merriment amongst the tiny folk. It was a pretty sight. Then they sang, and Johannes recognised distinctly all the pretty songs he had learned as a little boy. Large speckled spiders, with silver crowns upon their heads, were set to build suspension bridges and palaces from one hedge to another, which, when spangled by the dew, glittered like glass in the moonshine. These frolics continued till sunrise, when the little elves crept into the flower-buds and the wind took possession of their bridges and palaces, which were tossed upon the air as cobwebs.

Johannes had just left the forest, when the full-toned voice of a man cried out to him, 'Ho there, comrade! whither are you going?'

'Into the wide world,' said he, 'I have neither father nor mother, and am a poor boy, but the Lord will help me in time of need.'

'I am likewise going into the wide world,' said the stranger. 'Shall we keep each other company?'

'Willingly,' said he; and so they walked on together. They soon felt a mutual liking for each other, for both were good; only Johannes soon found out that the stranger was much wiser than himself. He had travelled throughout nearly the whole world, and could tell of everything that existed.

The sun was already high when they sat down under a tree to eat their breakfast, just as an old woman was coming up to them. She was very aged, and almost bent double, and supported herself on a crutch-stick, while she carried on her back a bundle of firewood which she had gathered in the forest. Her apron was tucked up, and Johannes saw three large rods of fern and willow twigs peeping out at each end. When she was quite close to our travellers, her foot slipped, and she fell with a loud scream, for she had broken her leg—poor old woman!

Johannes at once proposed that they should carry the old woman home, but the stranger opened his knapsack and took out a box, saying that he had an ointment which would immediately make her leg whole again, and so strong that she would be able to walk home by herself, just as if the accident had never happened; only he required that she should give him in return the three rods she carried in her apron.

'That would be well paid,' said the old woman, nodding her head in a peculiar manner. She did not like giving up the rods, but, on the other hand, it was still more disagreeable to be lying there with a broken limb. So she gave him the rods, and the moment he had rubbed her leg with the ointment the old dame got up, and walked much better than before. Such were the effects of the ointment; and truly it was not of a sort to be purchased at the apothecary's.

'What do you want with these rods?' asked Johannes of his fellow-traveller.

'They are three very pretty herb-brooms,' said he, 'and I like them, because I am a foolish fellow.'

They then went on a good deal farther.

'Look how overcast the sky appears!' said Johannes, pointing before them. 'Those are frightfully heavy clouds.'

'No,' said his fellow-traveller, 'they are not clouds; they are mountains—fine, large mountains—at the top of which one may overlook the clouds, and breathe fresh air. And delightful it is, believe me, to stand there! Tomorrow we shall assuredly be far out in the wide world.'

But they were not so near as they looked, and it took a full day before they had reached the mountains, where the black forests were towering up to the sky, and where blocks of stone might be found as huge as a large town. It seemed a somewhat difficult undertaking to cross them; therefore, Johannes and his fellow-traveller turned in to an inn, in order to rest and gather strength for the next day's excursion.

A number of persons were assembled in the tap-room of the inn, where a man was exhibiting a puppet show. He had just set up his little theatre, and the people were sitting round to see the play. But, right in front, a stout butcher had sat himself down in the very best place, while his great bulldog, by his side—who looked wondrously snappish—sat staring like the rest of the audience.

The play now began. It was a very pretty piece, with a king and queen, who sat on a splendid throne, with gold crowns on their heads and long trains to their robes, for their means allowed them to indulge in such luxuries. The prettiest little puppets, with glass eyes and large moustaches, stood at all the doors, and opened and shut them, to let in fresh air. It was a very agreeable play, and not at all mournful. But, just as the queen got up and passed across the stage, no one knows what the huge bulldog took into his head; but, being no longer held by the butcher, he jumped right into the theatre and seized the queen by the middle of her slender waist, so that it cracked again and again. It was quite shocking to hear.

The poor man who exhibited the show was both frightened and sorry for the loss of his queen, for she was the most elegant puppet in his stock, and the ugly bulldog had bitten her head off. But when the rest of the spectators had retired, the stranger who travelled with Johannes said that he would set her to rights, and, taking out his box, he smeared the puppet with the same ointment that had cured the old woman's broken leg. The moment this was done, the puppet was whole again, and could even move all her limbs of herself, and no longer required to be pulled by wires. The puppet was like a human being, except that she could not speak. The showman was vastly delighted, for now he had no longer any occasion to hold this puppet, who could dance of her own accord, which none of the others could do.

Late at night, when all the folks at the inn had gone to bed, somebody was heard to sigh so dreadfully deeply, and so frequently, that the whole household got up to see what could be the matter. The showman went to his little theatre, for it was from thence the sighing proceeded. All the wooden puppets were lying in a heap; the king and his body-guard it was who were sighing so piteously, and staring with their glass eyes, because they wished so to be smeared a little like the queen, in order that they might move of themselves. The queen knelt down and lifted up her pretty crown, saying, 'Take this, but do smear my husband and my courtiers.' The poor showman could not then help crying, for he was really sorry for his puppets. He immediately promised Johannes's fellow-traveller all the money he might earn on the following evening through his puppet-show if he would only smear four or five of his prettiest puppets. But the fellow-traveller said he did not require anything but the large sword that he wore at his side, on receiving which, he besmeared six puppets, that immediately danced so gracefully that all living girls that beheld them were irresistibly impelled to dance likewise. The coachman and the cook began dancing, then the waiters and the chambermaids, and all the strangers present, as well as the shovel and the tongs—only the latter fell down at the very first leap. They had, indeed, a merry night of it!

Next morning, Johannes started with his fellow-traveller, before any of the others were astir, and crossed the large forest of fir-trees, on the way up the high mountains. They climbed to such a height that the church steeples below looked like little blue berries in the green grass, and they could see for miles and miles around, where they had never yet been. Johannes had never before seen so much at once of the beauties of this lovely world. And then the sun shone so warmly through the fresh blue air, and the huntsmen's horns echoed so beautifully between the mountains, that tears came to his eyes, and he could not forbear exclaiming, 'All-merciful God! what a kind Father Thou art to us, to have given us all the fine things to be seen in the world!'

His fellow-traveller likewise stood with folded hands, and gazed upon the forest, and the towns that lay in the bright sunshine. At the same moment, they heard a lovely sound above their heads, and, on looking up, they perceived a large white swan hovering in the air, and singing as no bird ever sang before. But its voice grew weaker and weaker, till its head dropped, and it slowly dropped down at their feet, where the poor bird lay quite dead.

'Two such beautiful wings,' said the fellow-traveller, 'so white and so large as this bird's are worth some money; so I will take them with me. You see it was well that I obtained a sword.' And he cut off the two wings of the dead swan at a single blow, and kept them.

They now travelled many miles across the mountains, till they at length reached a large city, containing hundreds of towers, that shone like silver in the sunshine. In the midst of the town stood a handsome marble palace, roofed with pure red gold, in which dwelt the King.

Johannes and his fellow-traveller did not care to enter the town immediately, but went into an inn, situated on the outskirts, in order to dress themselves, for they wished to look tidy when they walked through the streets. The landlord informed them how good a man the King was, and that he never injured anybody; but as to this daughter—Heaven defend us!—she was a bad Princess indeed! Beauty she possessed in abundance; nobody was prettier or more elegant than herself. But what of that? She was a wicked witch, and was the cause of many accomplished princes having lost their lives. She had given leave to everybody to woo her. Anyone might present himself, be he a prince or a beggar; it was all the same to her. Only he must guess three things that she had thought of and questioned him about. If he succeeded, he was to marry her, and become king over all the land at her father's death, but if he could not guess the three things, he was then to be hanged, or to have his head struck off. Her father, the old King, was deeply concerned at all this, but he could not forbid her being so wicked, because he had once declared that he would never meddle with her lovers, and that she might do as she liked about them. Every time a prince came to try his luck at guessing, in order to obtain the Princess's hand, he was sure to fail and was, therefore, hanged or beheaded. He had been warned betimes that it would be safer to desist from his suit. The old King was so afflicted at the mourning and wretchedness thus occasioned that, for one whole day in the year, he and all his soldiers used to kneel and pray that the Princess might grow good; but she would not. The old women who tippled brandy used to colour it quite black before they drank it; this was their way of mourning, and they could not well do more.

'What a shocking Princess!' said Johannes. 'She deserves the rod, and it would do her good. If I were the old King, she should have been thrashed long ago.'

They now heard the mob cheering outside the inn. The Princess was passing, and she was really so beautiful that everybody forgot how wicked she was, and therefore cheered. Twelve beautiful maidens, dressed in white silk clothes and holding golden tulips in their hands, rode by her side on coal-black horses. The Princess herself was mounted on a snow-white steed, with diamond and ruby trappings. Her riding-dress was of gold brocade, and the whip she held in her hand looked like a sunbeam. The gold crown on her head resembled the little stars twinkling in the heavens, while her mantle consisted of thousands of splendid butterflies' wings stitched together. Yet, in spite of this magnificence, she was herself far more beautiful than her clothes.

When Johannes caught sight of her, his face grew as red as a drop of blood, and he was struck completely dumb, for the Princess exactly resembled the beautiful girl with the golden crown whom he had dreamed of the night his father died. He thought her most beautiful, and could not help loving her passionately. It could not be possible, thought he, that she was a wicked witch, who ordered people to be hanged or beheaded when they were unable to guess what she asked. 'But since everyone, down to the poorest beggar, is free to woo her,' said he, 'I will repair to the palace, for I cannot resist doing so.' Everybody advised him not to attempt such a thing, as he must inevitably fail like the rest. His fellow-traveller, likewise, warned him to desist, but Johannes thought he should succeed. He brushed his shoes and his coat, washed his hands and face, combed his pretty, flaxen hair, and then went alone into the town, and proceeded to the palace.

'Come in,' said the old King, when Johannes knocked at the door. Johannes opened it, and the old King came forward to meet him in his dressing-gown and embroidered slippers; he wore his crown on his head, and bore his sceptre in one hand and his orb in the other. 'Wait a bit,' said he, putting the orb under his arm, to leave one hand free to present to Johannes. But the moment he heard he came as a suitor, he began to weep so violently that both orb and sceptre fell on the floor, and he was fain to wipe his eyes with the skirts of his dressing-gown. Poor old King!

'Think not of it,' said he, 'you will fare as badly as all the others. Come, you shall see.'

He then led him into the Princess's pleasure-garden, and a frightful sight was there to behold! From every tree hung three of four kings' sons who wooed the Princess, but had been unable to guess her riddles. At every breeze that blew, all these skeletons rattled till the little birds were frightened, and never dared to come into the garden. All the flowers were propped with human bones, and human skulls might be seen grinning in flower-pots. It was an odd garden for a princess.

'Now, you see,' said the old King, 'your fate will be just the same as that of all the others whose remains you behold. Therefore give up the attempt. You really make me quite unhappy, for I take it so to heart.'

Johannes kissed the good old King's hand, and assured him that all would be well, for he was quite enchanted with the lovely Princess.

As the Princess then rode into the palace-yard accompanied by all her ladies, they went out to greet her. She was marvellously fair to look upon, as she presented her hand to Johannes. And he thought a great deal more of her than he did before, and felt certain she could not be a wicked witch, as everybody said she was. They then went into a room where little pages handed them sweetmeats and gingerbread-nuts. But the old King was so out of sorts, he could not eat at all. Besides, the gingerbread-nuts were too hard for him.

It was agreed that Johannes should return to the palace on the following morning, when the judges and the whole council would be assembled to see and hear how the guessing was carried on. If he succeeded, he was then to return twice more; but there never yet had been anybody who had been able to solve any question the first time, and in each case his life was forfeited.

Johannes felt no anxiety as to how he should fare. On the contrary, he was pleased, and thought only of the beautiful Princess, and was quite confident that God would help him through his trials. Though how this was to be accomplished he knew not, and preferred not to trouble himself to think about the matter. He capered along on the highroad, as he went back to the inn where his fellow-traveller was waiting for his return.

Johannes could not cease expatiating on the gracious reception he had met with

from the Princess, and on her extreme beauty. He quite longed for the morrow, when he was to go to the palace and try his luck at guessing.

But his fellow-traveller shook his head mournfully. 'I wish you so well!' said he. 'We might have remained together a good deal longer, and now I must lose you! Poor, dear Johannes! I could weep, only I will not spoil your joy on the last evening that we may ever spend together. We will be merry—right merry! Tomorrow, when you are gone, I shall be able to weep undisturbed.'

All the inhabitants of the town had immediately heard that there was a new suitor for the Princess's hand, and there prevailed universal consternation. The theatre was closed, the pastry-cooks put crape round their sugar-husbands, and the King and the priests were on their knees in the church. This sadness was occasioned by the conviction that Johannes could not fare better than all the other suitors had.

Towards evening Johannes's fellow-traveller prepared a goodly bowl of punch, and said: 'Now let us be merry, and drink the Princess's health.' But after drinking a couple of glasses, Johannes proved so sleepy that he could not possibly keep his eyes open, and fell fast asleep. His fellow-traveller then lifted him gently out of his chair, and laid him in bed; and when it was quite dark, he took the two large wings he had cut off from the dead swan, and fastened them firmly to his own shoulders. He then put into his pocket the largest rod that he had obtained from the old woman who fell and broke her leg, and opening the window, he flew over the town, straight to the palace, where he placed himself in an upper corner of the building right under the Princess's bedchamber.

The whole town was perfectly quiet. The clock now struck a quarter to twelve, when the window opened, and the Princess, wrapped in a flowing white mantle, and provided with a pair of black wings, flew over the city towards a large mountain. But the fellow-traveller made himself invisible; and as he flew behind the Princess he thrashed her with his rod till she bled. What a strange flight through the air it was! The wind caught her mantle, which swelled out on all sides like the large sail of a ship, and the moon shone through it.

'How it does hail, to be sure!' said the Princess, at every blow she received from the rod; and such weather suited her. At last she reached the mountain, and knocked for admittance. Then came a noise like a clap of thunder, while the mountain opened, and the Princess went in. The fellow-traveller followed her, for nobody could see him, as he was invisible. They went through a long, wide passage, where the walls shone brilliantly from the light of above a thousand glittering spiders that were running up and down and illuminating them like fire. They next entered a large hall built of silver and gold; red and blue flowers, as large as sunflowers, were beaming from the walls, but nobody could pluck them, for the stems were ugly, venomous serpents, and the flowers were the flames their jaws kept vomiting forth. The whole ceiling was covered with glow-worms and light-blue bats that were flapping their thin wings. It looked quite frightful. In the middle of the floor stood a throne that was supported by the skeletons of four horses, whose harness had been furnished by the red, fiery spiders. The throne itself was of milk-white glass, and the cushions were little black mice that kept biting each other's tails. Above it was a canopy of a deep-red cobweb, dotted with the prettiest little green flies that sparkled like precious stones. On the throne sat an old magician, with a crown on his ugly head and a sceptre in his hand. He kissed the Princess on her forehead, and placed her beside him on his splendid throne, and then the music struck up. Huge black grasshoppers played the jew's-harp, while the owl beat a tattoo on its own body, having no better drum. It was a ludicrous concert. Little dark-coloured goblins, with a will-o'-the-wisp in their caps, danced about the room. But nobody could see the fellow-traveller, who had placed himself right behind the throne, where he could see and hear everything. The courtiers, who now came in, were very delicate and genteel. But anybody who could see what is what, would quickly perceive what they were made of. They were nothing better than broomsticks with cabbages for their heads, that the magician had conjured into life, and that he had decked out in embroidered clothes. However, they did just as well, as they were only wanted for show.

After dancing a little, the Princess related to the magician that she had a new suitor, and consulted him as to what she should ask him next morning when he came to the palace.

'I will tell you what,' said the magician; 'you must choose something easy, and then he'll never hit upon it. Think of one of your shoes. He'll never guess that. Then you will have him beheaded, and mind you don't forget to bring me his eyes to-morrow night.'

The Princess bowed, and said she would not forget to bring them. The magician then opened the mountain, and she flew back; but the fellow-traveller followed her, and struck her so smartly with the rod, that she sighed most deeply over such a hail-storm, and hastened all she could to reach her bedchamber through the window. The fellow-traveller then returned to the inn, where Johannes was still asleep, took off his wings, and went to bed likewise, for he might well be tired.

Johannes woke at an early hour next morning. His fellow-traveller got up, and told him that he had had a strange dream that night about the Princess and her shoe, and therefore urged him to ask whether it was not her shoe that the Princess was thinking about. For this he had learned from the magician in the mountain.

'I may as well ask that as anything else,' said Johannes. 'Perhaps your dream may turn out to be the truth, for I trust in God to help me through. Still,

I will take leave of you, because should I guess wrong, I shall never see you again.'

They then embraced one another, and Johannes went into the town, and walked to the palace. The whole hall was filled with people. The judges sat in their arm-chairs, with their heads propped up by eider-down cushions, because they had so much to think about. The old King stood wiping his eyes with a white pocket-handkerchief. The Princess now entered. She looked more beautiful even than the day before, and saluted the assembly with charming grace. But she extended her hand to Johannes, saying: 'Good morning to you.'

Johannes was now called upon to guess what she had thought of. Bless me! how kindly she did look at him! But no sooner had he pronounced the single word 'shoe', than she turned as pale as chalk, and trembled all over. Still, this did not serve her much, since he had guessed correctly.

But, goodness! how pleased the old King was—he cut a caper that was quite pleasant to behold! And all present clapped their hands, to cheer both him and Johannes, who had been successful in this, his first ordeal.

The fellow-traveller was likewise much rejoiced on hearing how matters had turned out. But Johannes folded his hands and thanked his God, who he felt certain would help him through the two next times. On the following day, he was to make a second attempt at guessing.

The evening passed much the same as the foregoing one. When Johannes had gone to sleep, his fellow-traveller flew after the Princess to the mountain, and thrashed her more violently than before, having taken two rods with him. Nobody saw him, and he heard all that was said. The Princess was to think of her glove, and this he repeated to Johannes, as if it had been a dream. And so he was able to guess correctly, which occasioned great joy amongst the inmates of the palace. The whole court cut capers as they had seen the King do the first time. But the Princess lay on the sofa and would not speak a word. All now depended on whether Johannes could guess right the third time. If he succeeded, he was to marry the beautiful Princess, and reign over the land at the old King's death. But if he guessed wrong, he was to forfeit his life, and the magician would have his beautiful blue eyes.

On the preceding evening, Johannes went to bed early, said his prayers, and then fell into a quiet sleep. But his fellow-traveller tied his wings to his back, and put his sword at his side, and taking the three rods with him, flew towards the palace.

It was as dark as pitch, and there was such a storm that the tiles were flying off the roofs of the houses, and the trees in the garden, in which the skeletons hung, bent like so many reeds beneath the wind. Forked lightning lit the sky and thunder rolled along as though it were a single clap that lasted through the whole night. The window now opened, and the Princess flew out. She was as pale as death, but she laughed at the bad weather, and thought it was scarcely bad enough. And her white mantle fluttered in the wind like a large sail, while the fellow-traveller thrashed her with the three rods till her blood flowed, and she could scarcely fly any farther. She managed, however, to reach the mountain.

'This is a violent hail-storm,' said she; 'I was never out in such weather before.'

'There may be too much of a good thing,' observed the magician.

She now told him that Johannes had guessed aright the second time, and should he succeed again on the following morning, he would then have won, and she would never again be able to come to the mountain, or to practise magic arts as she had hitherto done; therefore she was quite out of spirits.

'He shall not be able to guess it,' said the magician, 'for I will seek out something that he will never hit upon, unless he is a greater conjurer than myself. But now let's be merry!' And then he took both the Princess's hands, and they danced about with all the little goblins wearing will-o'-the-wisp lights that were in the room. The red spiders jumped just as merrily up and down the walls; it looked as if the fiery flowers were emitting sparks. The owl beat the drum, the crickets whistled, and the black grasshoppers played on the jew's-harp. It was a frolicsome ball.

When they had danced enough the Princess was obliged to go home, for fear of being missed in the palace. The magician said he would accompany her, that they might be together a little longer.

They then flew away through the bad weather, while the fellow-traveller broke his three rods across their shoulders. The magician had never been out in such a hail-storm before. Just on reaching the palace, and on bidding the Princess farewell, he whispered, 'Think of my head.' But the fellow-traveller heard him, and just as the Princess slipped in at her bedroom window, and the magician was about to turn round, he seized him by his long black beard, and cut off his ugly head at a single stroke with his sword, so that the magician had not even time to see him. He then threw the body into the sea, to serve as food for the fishes; but he merely dipped the head in the waters, and then tied it up in his silk handkerchief, and took it to the inn, and went to bed.

Next morning he gave the bundle to Johannes, bidding him not to open it till the Princess should ask him what she was thinking of.

There were so many spectators in the large hall of the palace, that they stood as thick as radishes tied in a bunch. The council sat on their arm-chairs with the soft cushions, and the old King was dressed in new clothes; his golden crown and sceptre had been furbished up, and the whole scene looked very solemn. But the Princess was pale as ashes, and wore a coal-black dress, as though she were attending a funeral.

'What have I thought of?' asked she of Johannes. And he immediately opened the silk handkerchief, when he was himself quite startled on beholding the ugly magician's head. Everybody shuddered, for it was frightful to look at, but the Princess sat like a statue and could not speak. At length she rose and gave her hand to Johannes, for he had guessed aright. She looked neither to the right nor the left, but sighed out: 'Now you are my master! Our wedding will be celebrated this evening.'

'So much the better,' said the old King, 'that's just what I wish.' All present cried 'Hurrah!' The soldiers on parade struck up their music in the streets, the bells were set a-ringing, the pastry-cooks took the black crape off their sugar-husbands, and rejoicings were held everywhere. Three oxen, stuffed with ducks and chickens, and roasted whole, were placed in the middle of the market-place, and everyone was free to cut a slice; the fountains spouted the most delicious wine, and if one bought a penny cracknel at the baker's, one received six large biscuits as a present—and the biscuits had raisins in them!

Towards night the whole town was illuminated, the soldiers fired cannons, and the boys let off pop-guns, and there was a deal of eating, and drinking, and crushing, and capering at the palace. All the fine gentlemen and the beautiful young ladies danced together, and one might hear them from afar singing the following song:

'Here are many maidens fair,
  Who twirl like any spinning-wheel,
And tread the floor as light as air;
  Still round and round, sweet maiden, reel,
And dance away the mazes through,
  Until the sole has left your shoe.'

But the Princess was still a witch, and could not endure Johannes. His fellow-traveller saw this, and therefore he gave Johannes three feathers out of the swan's wings, and a small phial containing only a few drops, and told him to place a large vat full of water in front of the Princess's bed, and when the Princess was about to get into bed, he must give her a slight push, so that she should fall into the water, into which he must dip her three times, having taken care first to shake in the feathers and the contents of the phial. The magic spell would then be broken, and she would love him tenderly.

Johannes did all that his fellow-traveller suggested. The Princess shrieked aloud when he dipped her into the water, and struggled out of his hands under the form of a coal-black swan with fiery eyes. The second time she rose to the surface the swan had become white, all but a black ruff round its neck. Johannes prayed to God, and made the bird dive down a third time, when it was suddenly transformed into the most beautiful Princess. She was far lovelier than before, and thanked him, with tears in her eyes, for having broken the spell that bound her.

On the following morning, the old King came with all his court, and the congratulations lasted till late in the day. Last of all came Johannes's fellow-traveller, with his stick in his hand and his knapsack at his back. Johannes embraced him affectionately, and said that he must not go away, but stay with him, for he was the cause of all his happiness. But his fellow-traveller shook his head, and said in a mild and friendly voice: 'No; my time is now up. I have but paid a debt. Do you remember the dead man whom his wicked creditors would fain have ill-used? You gave all you possessed that he might rest in peace in his grave. I am that dead man!'

And at the same moment he vanished.

The wedding rejoicings now lasted a full month. Johannes and the Princess loved each other dearly, and the old King lived to see many a happy day, and dandled his little grandchildren on his knee, and let them play with his sceptre. And Johannes became King over the whole land.

THE EMPEROR'S NEW CLOTHES

Many years ago there was an Emperor who was so very fond of new clothes that he spent all his money on dress. He did not trouble himself in the least about his soldiers, nor did he care to go either to the theatre or to hunt, except for the occasion they gave him for showing off his new clothes. He had a different suit for each hour of the day; and as one is accustomed to say of any other king or emperor, 'He is sitting in council,' it was always said of him, 'The Emperor is sitting in his wardrobe.'

Time passed merrily in the large town that was his capital. Strangers arrived at the court every day. One day two rogues, calling themselves weavers, made their appearance. They gave out that they knew how to weave stuffs of the most beautiful colours and patterns, but that the clothes made from these had the wonderful property of remaining invisible to every one who was either stupid or unfit for the office he held.

'Those would indeed be splendid clothes!' thought the Emperor. 'Had I such a suit, I might at once find out what men in my realms are unfit for their office, and be able to distinguish the wise from the foolish. This stuff must be woven for me immediately.' And he caused large sums of money to be given to the weavers, that they might begin their work at once.

So the rogues set up two looms, and made a show of working very busily, though in reality they had nothing at all on the looms. They asked for the finest silk and the purest gold thread, put both into their own knapsacks, and then continued their pretended work at the empty looms until late at night.

'I should like to know how the weavers are getting on with my cloth,' thought the Emperor after some time. He was, however, rather nervous when he remembered that a stupid person, or one unfit for his office, would be unable to see the stuff. 'To be sure,' he thought, 'I have nothing to risk in my own person; but yet I would prefer sending somebody else to bring me news about the weavers and their work, before I trouble myself in the affair.' All the city had heard of the wonderful property the cloth was to possess, and all were anxious to learn how worthless and stupid their neighbours were.

'I will send my faithful old minister to the weavers,' concluded the Emperor at last. 'He will be best able to see how the cloth looks, for he is a man of sense, and no one can be better fitted for his post than he is.'

So the faithful old minister went into the hall where the knaves were working with all their might at their empty looms. 'What can be the meaning of this?' thought the old man, opening his eyes very wide. 'I can't see the least bit of thread on the looms!' However, he did not speak aloud.

The rogues begged him most respectfully to be so good as to come nearer, and then asked whether the design pleased him and whether the colours were not very beautiful, pointing at the same time to the empty frames. The poor old minister looked and looked; he could see nothing on the looms, for there was nothing there. 'What!' thought he, 'is it possible that I am silly? I have never thought so myself; and no one must know it now. Can it be that I am unfit for my office? It will never do for me to say that I could not see the stuff.'

'Well, Sir Minister!' said one of the knaves, still pretending to work, 'you do not say whether the stuff pleases you.'

'Oh, it's very fine!' said the old minister, looking at the loom through his spectacles. 'The pattern and the colours are wonderful. Yes, I will tell the Emperor without delay how very beautiful I think them.'

'We are glad they please you,' said the cheats, and then they named the different colours and described the pattern of the pretended stuff. The old minister paid close attention, that he might repeat to the Emperor what they said.

Then the knaves asked for more silk and gold, saying it was needed to complete what they had begun. Of course, they put all that was given them into their knapsacks, and kept on as before working busily at their empty looms.

The Emperor now sent another officer of his court to see how the men were getting on, and to find out whether the cloth would soon be ready. It was just the same with him as with the first. He looked and looked, but could see nothing at all but the empty looms.

'Isn't it fine stuff?' asked the rogues. The minister said he thought it beautiful.

Then they began as before, pointing out its beauties and talking of patterns and colours that were not there.

'I certainly am not stupid,' thought the officer. 'It must be that I am not fit for my post. That seems absurd. However, no one shall know it.' So he praised the stuff he could not see, and said he was delighted with both colours and patterns. 'Indeed, Your Majesty,' said he to the Emperor when he gave his report, 'the cloth is magnificent.'

The whole city was talking of the splendid cloth that the Emperor was having woven at his own cost.

And now the Emperor thought he would like to see the cloth while it was still on the loom. Accompanied by a select number of officials, among whom were the two honest men who had already admired the cloth, he went to the cunning weavers who, when aware of the Emperor's approach, went on working more busily than ever, although they did not pass a single thread through the looms.

'Is it not absolutely magnificent?' said the two officers who had been there before. 'If Your Majesty will only be pleased to look at it! What a splendid design! What glorious colours!' And at the same time they pointed to the empty looms, for they thought that everyone else could see the cloth.

'How is this?' said the Emperor to himself; 'I can see nothing! Oh, this is dreadful. Am I a fool? Am I unfit to be an Emperor? That would be the worst thing that could happen to me.—Oh! the cloth is charming,' said he aloud. 'It has my complete approval.' And he smiled most graciously, and looked closely at the empty looms; for on no account would he say that he could not see what two of the officers of his court had praised so much. All the retinue now looked and looked, but they could see nothing more than the others. Nevertheless, they all exclaimed, 'Oh how beautiful!' and advised His Majesty to have some new clothes made from this splendid material for the approaching procession. 'Magnificent! Charming! Excellent!' resounded on all sides; and everyone seemed greatly pleased. The Emperor showed his satisfaction by making the rogues knights, and giving them the title of 'Gentlemen Weavers to the Emperor'.

The two rogues sat up the whole of the night before the day of the procession. They had sixteen candles burning, so that everyone might see how hard they were working to finish the Emperor's new suit. They pretended to roll the cloth off the looms; they cut the air with great scissors, and sewed with needles without any thread in them. 'See!' cried they at last; 'the Emperor's new clothes are ready!'

And now the Emperor, with all the grandees of his court, came to the weavers. The rogues raised their arms, as if holding something up, and said, 'Here are Your Majesty's trousers! here is the scarf! here is the mantle! The whole suit is as light as a cobweb. You might fancy you had on nothing at all when dressed in it; that, however, is the great virtue of this fine cloth.'

'Yes, indeed!' said all the courtiers, although not one of them could see anything, because there was nothing to be seen.

'If Your Imperial Majesty will be graciously pleased to take off your clothes, we will fit on the new suit in front of the large looking-glass,' said the swindlers.

The Emperor accordingly took off his clothes, and the rogues pretended to put on him separately each article of his new suit, the Emperor turning round from side to side before the looking-glass.

'How splendid His Majesty looks in his new clothes, and how well they fit!' everyone cried out. 'What a design! What colours! These are indeed royal robes!'

'The attendants are waiting outside with the canopy which is to be borne over Your Majesty in the procession,' announced the chief master of the ceremonies.

'I am quite ready,' answered the Emperor. 'Do my new clothes fit well?' he asked, turning himself round again before the looking-glass as if he were carefully examining his handsome suit.

The lords of the bedchamber, who were to carry His Majesty's train, felt about on the ground, as if they were lifting up the ends of the mantle, and walked as if they were holding up a train; for they feared to show that they saw nothing and so be thought stupid or unfit for their office.

So in the midst of the procession the Emperor walked under his high canopy through the streets of his capital. And all the people standing by, and those at the windows, cried out, 'Oh! how beautiful are our Emperor's new clothes! What a train there is to the mantle! and how gracefully the scarf hangs!' In short, no one would allow that he could not see those much admired clothes, because, in doing so, he would have declared himself either a fool or unfit for his office. Certainly, none of the Emperor's previous suits had made such an impression as this.

'But the Emperor has nothing on at all!' said a little child.

'Listen to the voice of innocence!' exclaimed her father; and what the child had said was whispered from one to another.

'But he has nothing on at all!' at last cried out all the people. The Emperor was vexed, for he felt that the people were right; but he thought the procession must go on now. And the lords of the bedchamber took greater pains than ever to appear to be holding up a train, although, in reality, there was no train to hold.

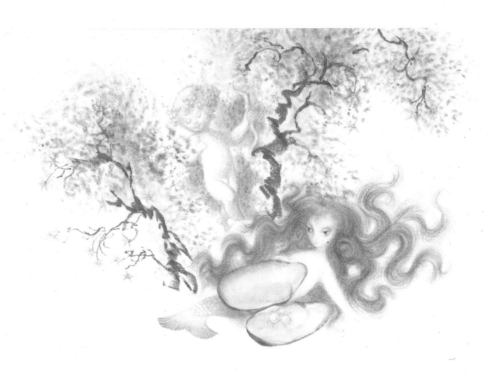

THE LITTLE MERMAID

Far out in the wide sea—where the water is blue as the loveliest cornflower, and clear as the purest crystal, where it is so deep that very many church towers must be heaped one upon another, in order to reach from the lowest depth to the surface above—dwell the mer-people.

Now you must not imagine that there is nothing but sand below the water: no, indeed, far from it! Trees and plants of wondrous beauty grow there, whose stems and leaves are so light that they are waved to and fro by the slightest motion of the water, almost as if they were living beings. Fishes, great and small, glide in and out among the branches, just as birds fly about among our trees.

Where the water is deepest, stands the palace of the Mer-king. The walls of this palace are of coral, and the high, pointed windows are of amber; the roof, however, is composed of mussel-shells, which, as the billows pass over them, are continually opening and shutting. This looks exceedingly pretty, especially as each of these mussel-shells contains a number of bright, glittering pearls, any one of which would be a costly ornament in the diadem of a king in the upper world.

The Mer-king had been for years a widower; his old mother managed the household affairs for him. She was, on the whole, a sensible sort of lady, although extremely proud of her high birth and station; on which account she wore twelve oysters on her tail, whilst the other inhabitants of the sea were allowed only six. In every other respect she merited unlimited praise, especially for the affection she showed to the six little Princesses, her granddaughters. These were all very beautiful children; the youngest was, however, the most lovely. Her skin was as soft and delicate as a rose-leaf, her eyes were of as deep a blue as the sea; but, like all other mermaids, she had no feet, and her body ended in a tail like that of a fish.

The whole day long the children used to play in the spacious apartments of the palace, where beautiful flowers grew out of the walls on all sides round them. When the great amber windows were opened, fishes would swim into these apartments as swallows fly into our rooms. But the fishes were bolder than the swallows; they swam straight up to the little Princesses, ate from their hands, and allowed themselves to be caressed.

In front of the palace there was a large garden full of fiery red and dark blue trees, whose fruit glittered like gold, and whose flowers resembled a bright, burning sun. The sand that formed the soil of the garden was of a bright blue colour, something like flames of sulphur, and a strangely beautiful blue was spread over the whole, so that one might have fancied oneself raised very high in the air, with the sky at once above and below—certainly not at the bottom of the sea. When the waters were quite still, the sun might be seen to look like a purple flower, out of whose cup streamed forth the light of the world.

Each of the little Princesses had her own plot in the garden, where she might plant and sow at her pleasure. One chose hers to be made in the shape of a whale; another preferred the figure of a mermaid. But the youngest had hers quite round like the sun, and planted in it only those flowers that were red, as the sun seemed to her. She was certainly a singular child, very quiet and thoughtful. Whilst her sisters were adorning themselves with all sorts of gay things that came out of a ship which had been wrecked, she asked for nothing but a beautiful white marble statue of a boy, which had been found in it. She put the statue in her garden, and planted a red weeping willow by its side.

The tree grew up quickly, and let its long boughs fall upon the bright blue ground, where ever-moving shadows played in violet hues, as if boughs and root were embracing.

Nothing pleased the little Princess more than to hear about the world of human beings living above the sea. She made her old grandmother tell her everything she knew about ships, towns, men and land animals, and was particularly pleased when she heard that the flowers of the upper world had a pleasant fragrance—for the flowers of the sea are scentless—and that the woods were green, and the fishes fluttering among the branches were of various colours, and that they could sing with a loud clear voice. The old lady meant birds, but she called them fishes, because her grandchildren, having never seen a bird, would not otherwise have understood her.

'When you have attained your fifteenth year,' she added, 'you will be permitted to rise to the surface of the sea; you will then sit by moonlight in the clefts of the rocks, see the ships sail by, and learn to distinguish towns and men.'

The next year the eldest of the sisters reached this happy age, but the others—alas! The second sister was a year younger than the eldest, the third a year younger than the second, and so on; the youngest had still five whole years to wait till that joyful time should come, when she also might rise to the surface of the water and see what was going on in the upper world. However, the eldest promised to tell the others of everything she might see when the first day of her being of age arrived; for the grandmother gave them but little information, and there was so much that they wished to hear.

But none of all the sisters longed so keenly for the day when she should be released from childish restraint as the youngest—she who had longest to wait, and was so quiet and thoughtful. Many a night she stood by the open window, looking up through the clear blue water, whilst the fishes were leaping and plying around her. She could see the sun and the moon; their light was pale, but they appeared larger than they do to those who live in the upper world. If a shadow passed over them, she knew it must be either a whale or a ship sailing by full of human beings, who, indeed, little thought that, far beneath them, a little mermaiden was passionately stretching forth her white hands towards their ship's keel.

The day had now arrived when the eldest Princess had attained her fifteenth year, and was therefore allowed to rise up to the surface of the sea.

When she returned she had a thousand things to relate. Her chief pleasure had been to sit upon a sandbank in the moonlight, looking at the large town which lay on the coast, where lights were beaming like stars, and where music was playing. She had heard the distant noise of men and carriages; she had seen the high church-towers, had listened to the ringing of the bells. And, just because she could not go there, she longed the more for all these things.

How attentively did her youngest sister listen to her words! And when she next stood at night-time by her open window, gazing upward through the blue waters, she thought so intensely of the great noisy city that she fancied she could hear the church-bells ringing.

Next year the second sister received permission to swim wherever she pleased. She rose to the surface of the sea just when the sun was setting, and this sight so delighted her that she declared it to be more beautiful than anything else she had seen above the waters.

'The whole sky seemed tinged with gold,' said she, 'and it is impossible for me to describe to you the beauty of the clouds: now red, now violet, they glided over me. But still more swiftly flew over the water a flock of white swans, just where the sun was descending; I looked after them, but the sun disappeared, and the bright rosy light of the surface of the sea and on the edges of the clouds was gradually extinguished.'

It was now time for the third sister to visit the upper world. She was the boldest of the six, and ventured up a river. On its shore she saw green hills covered with woods and vineyards, from among which rose houses and castles; she heard the birds singing, and the sun shone with so much power that she was continually obliged to plunge below, in order to cool her burning face. In a little bay she met with a number of children who were bathing and jumping about; she would have joined in their gambols, but the children fled back to the land in great terror, and a little black animal barked at her in such a manner that she herself was frightened at last, and swam back to the sea. She could not, however, forget the green woods, and the hills, and the pretty children, who, although they had no fins, were swimming about in the river so fearlessly.

The fourth sister was not so bold. She remained in the open sea, and said, on her return home, she thought nothing could be more beautiful. She had seen ships sailing by, so far off that they looked like sea-gulls; she had watched the merry dolphins gambolling in the water, and the enormous whales, sending up into the air a thousand sparkling fountains.

The year after, the fifth sister attained her fifteenth year. Her birthday happened at a different season from that of her sisters; it was winter, the sea was of a green colour, and immense icebergs were floating on its surface. These, she said, looked like pearls; they were, however, much larger than the church towers in the land of human beings. She sat down upon one of these pearls, and let the wind play with her long hair, but then all the ships hoisted their sails in terror, and escaped as quickly as possible.

In the evening the sky was covered with sails, and whilst the great mountains of ice alternately sank and rose again, and beamed with a reddish glow, flashes of lightning burst forth from the clouds, and the thunder rolled on, peal after peal. The sails of all the ships were instantly furled, and horror and fright reigned on board, but the Princess sat still on the iceberg, looking unconcernedly at the blue zigzags of the flashes.

The first time that any of these sisters rose out of the sea, she was quite enchanted at the sight of so many new and beautiful objects, but the novelty was soon over and it was not long ere their own home appeared more attractive than the upper world, for there only did they find everything agreeable.

Many an evening would the five sisters rise hand in hand from the depths of the ocean. Their voices were far sweeter than any human voice, and when a storm was coming on they would swim in front of the ships and sing—oh! how sweetly did they sing, describing the happiness of those who lived at the bottom of the sea, and entreating the sailors not to be afraid, but to come down to them!

The mariners, however, did not understand their words; they fancied the song was only the whistling of the wind, and thus they lost the hidden glories of the sea. For if their ships were wrecked all on board were drowned, and none but dead men ever entered the Mer-king's palace.

Whilst the sisters were swimming at evening time, the youngest would remain motionless and alone, in her father's palace, looking up after them. She would have wept, but mermaids cannot weep, and therefore, when they are troubled, suffer infinitely more than human beings do.

'Oh! if I were but fifteen,' sighed she, 'I know that I should love the upper world and its inhabitants so much.'

At last the time she had so longed for arrived.

'Well, now it is your turn,' said the grandmother; 'come here that I may adorn you like your sisters.' And she wound round her hair a wreath of white lilies, whose every petal was the half of a pearl, and then commanded eight large oysters to fasten themselves to the Princess's tail, in token of her high rank.

'But that is so very uncomfortable!' said the little Princess.

'One must not mind slight inconveniences when one wishes to look well,' said the old lady.

The Princess would have given up all this splendour and exchanged her heavy crown for the red flowers of her garden, which were so much more becoming to her, but she dared not do so. 'Farewell,' said she, and she rose from the sea, light as a flake of foam.

When, for the first time in her life, she appeared on the surface of the water, the sun had just sunk below the horizon, the clouds were beaming with bright golden and rosy hues, the evening star was shining in the pale western sky, the air was mild and refreshing, and the sea as smooth as a looking-glass.

A large ship with three masts lay on the still waters; only one sail was unfurled, but not a breath was stirring, and the sailors were quietly seated on the cordage and ladders of the vessel. Music and song resounded from the deck, and after it grew dark hundreds of lamps, all of a sudden, burst forth into light, whilst innumerable flags were fluttering overhead.

The little mermaid swam close up to the captain's cabin, and every now and then, when the ship was raised by the motion of the water, she could look through the clear window-panes. She saw within many richly-dressed men; the handsomest among them was a young Prince with large black eyes. He could certainly not be more than sixteen years old, and it was in honour of his birthday that a grand festival was being celebrated. The crew were dancing on the deck, and when the young Prince appeared among them a hundred rockets were sent up into the air, turning night into day, and so terrifying the little mermaid that for some minutes she plunged beneath the water.

However, she soon raised her little head again, and then it seemed as if all the stars were falling down upon her. Such a fiery shower she had never even seen before; never had she heard that men possessed such wonderful powers. Large suns revolved around her, bright fishes swam in the air, and everything was reflected perfectly on the clear surface of the sea. It was so light in the ship that everything could be seen distinctly. Oh! how happy the young Prince was! He shook hands with the sailors, laughed and jested with them, whilst sweet notes of music mingled with the silence of night.

It was now late, but the little mermaid could not tear herself away from the ship and the handsome young Prince. She remained looking through the cabin window, rocked to and fro by the waves. There was a foaming in the depths, and the ship began to move on faster; the sails were spread, the waves rose high, thick clouds gathered over the sky, and the noise of distant thunder was heard.

The sailors perceived that a storm was coming on, so they again furled the sails. The great vessel was tossed about on the stormy ocean like a light boat, and the waves rose to an immense height, towering over the ship, which alternately sank beneath and rose above them.

To the little mermaid this seemed most delightful, but the ship's crew thought very differently. The vessel cracked, the stout masts bent under the violence of the billows, the waters rushed in. For a minute the ship tottered to and fro, then the main mast broke, as if it had been a reed; the ship turned over, and was filled with water. The little mermaid now saw that the crew was in danger, for she herself was forced to beware of the beams and splinters torn from the vessel and floating about on the waves.

But at the same time it became pitch dark, so that she could not distinguish anything. Presently, however, a dreadful flash of lightning disclosed to her the whole of the wreck. Her eyes sought the young Prince—the same instant the ship sank to the bottom. At first she was delighted, thinking that the Prince must now come to her abode, but she soon remembered that man cannot live in water, and therefore if the Prince ever entered her palace it would be as a corpse.

'Die! No, he must not die!' She swam through the fragments with which the water was strewn, regardless of the danger she was incurring, and at last found the Prince all but exhausted, and with great difficulty keeping his head above water. He had already closed his eyes, and must surely have been drowned, had not the little mermaid come to his rescue. She seized hold of him and kept him above water, and the current bore them on together.

Towards morning the storm was hushed; no trace, however, remained of the ship. The sun rose like fire out of the sea; its beams seemed to restore colour to the Prince's cheeks, but his eyes were still closed.

The mermaid kissed his high forehead, and stroked his wet hair away from his face. He looked like the marble statue in her garden. She kissed him again, and wished most fervently that he might recover.

She now saw the dry land with its mountains glittering with snow. A green wood extended along the coast, and at the entrance to the wood stood a chapel or convent— she could not be sure which. Orange and lemon trees grew in the garden adjoining it; an avenue of tall palm-trees led up to the door. The sea here formed a little bay, in which the water was quite smooth but very deep, and under the cliffs there were dry, firm sands. Hither swam the little mermaid with the Prince seemingly dead; she laid him upon the warm sand, and took care to place his head high, and turn his face to the sun.

The bells began to ring in the large white building which stood before her, and a number of young girls came out to walk in the garden. The mermaid went away from the shore, hid herself behind some rocks, covered her head with foam, so that her little face could not be seen, and watched the Prince.

It was not long before one of the young girls approached. She seemed quite frightened at finding the Prince in this state, apparently dead. Soon, however, she recovered herself, and ran back to call her sisters. The little mermaid saw that the Prince revived, and that they all smiled kindly and joyfully upon him. For her, however, he looked not; he knew not that it was she who had saved him. And when the Prince was taken into the house, she felt so sad that she immediately plunged beneath the water, and returned to her father's palace.

If she had before been quiet and thoughtful, she now grew still more so. Her sisters asked her what she had seen in the upper world, but she made no answer.

Many an evening she rose to the place where she had left the Prince. She saw the snow melt on the mountains, the fruit ripen in the garden, but the Prince she never saw; so she always returned sorrowfully to her home in the deep. Her only pleasure was to sit in her little garden gazing on the beautiful statue so like the Prince. She cared no longer for her flowers; they grew up in wild luxuriance, covered the steps, and entwined their long stems and tendrils among the boughs of the trees, so that her whole garden became a bower.

At last, being unable to conceal her sorrow any longer, she revealed the secret to one of her sisters, who told it to the other Princesses, and they to some of their friends. Among them was a young mermaid who recollected the Prince, having been an eye-witness herself to the festivities on the ship; she knew also in what country the Prince lived, and the name of its King.

'Come, little sister!' said the Princesses, and embracing her, they rose together, arm-in-arm, out of the water, just in front of the Prince's palace.

This palace was built of bright yellow stones; a flight of white marble steps led from it down to the sea. A gilded cupola crowned the building, and white marble figures, which might almost have been taken for real men and women, were placed among the pillars surrounding it. Through the clear glass of the high windows one might look into grand apartments hung with silken curtains, the walls adorned with magnificent paintings. It was a real treat to the little royal mermaids to behold so splendid an abode; they gazed through the windows of one of the largest rooms, and in the centre saw a fountain playing, whose waters sprang up to the glittering cupola above, through which the sunbeams fell dancing on the water and brightening the pretty plants which grew around it.

The little mermaid now knew where her beloved Prince dwelt, and henceforth she went there almost every evening. She often approached nearer the land than her sisters had ventured and even swam up the narrow channel that flowed under the marble balcony. Here, on a bright moonlight night, she would watch the young Prince, who believed himself alone.

Sometimes she saw him sailing on the water in a gaily-painted boat with many-coloured flags waving above. She would then hide among the green reeds which grew on the banks, listening to his voice; and if anyone in the boat heard the rustling of her long silver veil, which was caught now and then by the light breeze, they only fancied it was a swan flapping his wings.

Many a night, when the fishermen were casting their nets by the beacon's light, she heard them talking of the Prince, and telling the noble deeds he had performed. She was then so happy, thinking how she had saved his life when he was struggling with the waves, and remembering how his head had rested on her bosom, and how she had kissed him when he knew nothing of it and could never even dream of such a thing.

Human beings became more and more dear to her every day; she wished that she were one of them. Their world seemed to her much larger than that of the mer-people. They could fly over the ocean in their ships, as well as climb to the summits

of those high mountains that rose above the clouds, and their wooded domains extended much farther than a mermaid's eye could see.

There were many things that she wished to hear explained, but her sisters could not give her any satisfactory answer. She was again obliged to have recourse to the old Queen-mother, who knew a great deal about the upper world, which she used to call 'the country above the sea'.

'Do men when they are not drowned live for ever?' she asked one day. 'Do they not die as we do, who live at the bottom of the sea?'

'Yes,' was the grandmother's reply; 'they must die like us, and their life is much shorter than ours. We live to the age of three hundred years, but when we die, we become foam on the sea, and are not allowed even to share a grave among those that are dear to us. We have no immortal souls; we can never live again, and are like the grass which, when cut down, is withered for ever. Human beings, on the contrary, have souls that continue to live when their bodies become dust, and as we rise out of the water to admire the homes of man, they ascend to glorious unknown dwellings in the skies which we are not permitted to see.'

'Why have *we* not souls?' asked the little mermaid. 'I would willingly give up my three hundred years to be a human being for only one day, thus to become entitled to that heavenly world above.'

'You must not think of that,' answered her grandmother; 'it is much better as it is; we live longer and are far happier than human beings.'

'So I must die, and be dashed like foam over the sea, never to rise again and hear the gentle murmur of the ocean—never again see the beautiful flowers and the bright sun! Tell me, dear grandmother, are there no means by which I may obtain an immortal soul?'

'No!' replied the old lady. 'It is true that if you could so win the affections of a human being as to become dearer to him than either father or mother, if he loved you with all his heart, and promised whilst the priest joined his hands with yours to be always faithful to you, then his soul would flow into yours and you would then become partaker of human bliss. But that can never be! For what in our eyes is the most beautiful part of our body—the tail—the inhabitants of the earth think hideous—they cannot bear it. To appear handsome to them, the body must have two clumsy props which they call legs.'

The little mermaid sighed and looked mournfully at the scaly part of her form, otherwise so fair and delicate.

'We are happy,' added the old lady; 'we shall jump and swim about merrily for three hundred years—that is a long time—and afterwards we shall repose peacefully in death. This evening we have a court ball.'

The ball which the Queen-mother spoke of was far more splendid than any that earth has ever seen. The walls of the saloon were of crystal, very thick, but yet very clear. Hundreds of large mussel-shells were planted along them in rows; some of these shells were rose-coloured, some green as grass, but all sent forth a bright light which illuminated the whole apartment. They also shone through the glassy walls so as to light up the waters around for a great space, and made the scales of the fishes—great and small, crimson and purple, silver and gold-coloured—appear more brilliant than ever.

Through the centre of the saloon flowed a bright, clear stream, on the surface of which danced mermen and mermaids to the melody of their own sweet voices—voices far sweeter than those of the dwellers upon earth. The little Princess sang more harmoniously than any other, and they clapped their hands and applauded her.

She was pleased at this, for she knew well that there was neither on earth nor in the sea a more beautiful voice than hers. But her thoughts soon returned to the world above her. She could not forget the handsome Prince; she could not control her sorrow at not having an immortal soul. She stole away from her father's palace, and whilst all was joy within she sat alone, lost in thought, in her little neglected garden.

On a sudden she heard the tones of horns resounding over the water far away in the distance, and she said to herself, 'Now he is going out to hunt—he whom I love more than my father and my mother, with whom my thoughts are constantly occupied, and to whom I would so willingly trust the happiness of my life! All! all will I risk to win him—and an immortal soul. Whilst my sisters are still dancing in the palace, I will go to the enchantress whom I have hitherto feared so much, but who is, nevertheless, the only person who can advise and help me.'

So the little mermaid left the garden, and went to the foaming whirlpool beyond which dwelt the enchantress. She had never been this way before—neither flowers nor sea-grass bloomed along her path. She had to traverse an expanse of bare grey sand till she reached the whirlpool, whose waters were eddying and whizzing like mill-wheels, tearing everything they could seize along with them into the abyss below. She was obliged to make her way through this horrible place, in order to arrive at the territory of the enchantress. Then she had to pass through a boiling, slimy bog, which the enchantress called her turf-moor; her house stood in a wood beyond this, and a strange abode it was.

All the trees and bushes around were polypi, looking like hundred-headed serpents shooting up out of the ground; their branches were long slimy arms and fingers of worms, every member, from the root to the uttermost tip, ceaselessly moving and extending on all sides. Whatever they seized they fastened upon so that it could not loosen itself from their grasp.

The little mermaid stood still for a minute looking at this horrible wood; her heart beat with fear, and she would certainly have returned without attaining her object had she not remembered the Prince—and immortality. The thought gave her new courage. She bound up her long waving hair, that the polypi might not catch hold of it, crossed her delicate arms over her bosom, and, swifter than a fish can glide through the water, she passed these unseemly trees, which stretched their eager arms after her in vain.

She could not, however, help seeing that every polypus had something in its grasp, held as firmly by a thousand little arms as if enclosed by iron bands. The whitened skeletons of a number of human beings who had been drowned in the sea, and had sunk into the abyss, grinned horribly from the arms of these polypi; helms, chests, skeletons of land animals, were also held in their embrace. Among other things might be seen even a little mermaid whom they had seized and strangled! What a fearful sight for the unfortunate Princess!

But she got safely through this wood of horrors, and then arrived at a slimy place, where huge, fat snails were crawling about, and in the midst of this place stood a house built of the bones of unfortunate people who had been shipwrecked. Here sat the witch, caressing a toad in the same manner as some persons would a pet bird. The ugly fat snails she called her chickens, and she permitted them to crawl about her.

'I know well what you would ask of me,' said she to the little Princess. 'Your wish is foolish enough, but it shall be fulfilled, though its accomplishment is sure to bring misfortune on you, my fairest Princess. You wish to get rid of your tail, and to have instead two stilts like those of human beings, in order that a young Prince may fall in love with you, and that you may obtain an immortal soul. Is it not so?'

While the witch spoke these words, she laughed so violently that her pet toad and snails fell from her lap.

'You come just at the right time,' continued she; 'had you come after sunset, it would not have been in my power to have helped you before another year. I will prepare for you a drink with which you must swim to land; you must sit down upon the shore and swallow it and then your tail will fall and shrink up to the things which men call legs. This transformation will, however, be very painful; you will feel as though a sharp knife passed through your body. All who look on you after you have been thus changed will say that you are the loveliest child of earth they have ever seen. You will retain your graceful movements, and no dancer will move so lightly; but every step you take will cause you pain all but unbearable—it will seem to you as if you were walking on the sharp edges of swords—and your blood will flow. Can you endure all this suffering? If so, I will grant your request.'

'Yes, I can,' answered the Princess, with a faltering voice, for she remembered her dear Prince, and the immortal soul which her suffering might win.

'Only consider,' said the witch, 'that you can never again become a mermaid, when once you have received a human form. You may never return to your sisters, and your father's palace; and unless you shall win the Prince's love to such a degree that he shall leave father and mother for you, that you shall be mixed up with all his thoughts and wishes, and unless the priest join your hands, so that you become man and wife, you will never obtain the immortality you seek. The morrow of the day on which he is united to another, will see your death; your heart will break with sorrow, and you will be changed to foam on the sea.'

'Still I will venture!' said the little mermaid, pale and trembling as a dying person.

'Besides all this, I must be paid, and it is no slight thing that I require for my trouble. You have the sweetest voice of all the dwellers in the sea, and you think by its means to charm the Prince; this voice, however, I demand as my recompense. The best thing you possess I require in exchange for my magic drink; for I shall be obliged to sacrifice my own blood, in order to give it the sharpness of a two-edged sword.'

'But if you take my voice from me,' said the Princess, 'what have I left with which to charm the Prince?'

'Your graceful form,' replied the witch; 'your modest gait, and speaking eyes. With such as these, it will be easy to infatuate a vain human heart. Well now! have you lost courage? Put out your little tongue, that I may cut if off and take it for myself, in return for my magic drink.'

'Be it so!' said the Princess, and the witch took up the cauldron, in order to mix her potion. 'Cleanliness is a good thing,' remarked she, as she began to rub the cauldron with a handful of toads and snails. She then scratched her bosom, and let the black blood trickle down into the cauldron, every moment throwing in new ingredients. The smoke from the mixture assumed such horrible forms as would fill beholders with terror, and a moaning and groaning proceeded from it which might be compared to the weeping of crocodiles. The magic drink at length became clear and transparent as pure water; it was ready.

'Here it is!' said the witch to the Princess, cutting out her tongue at the same moment. The poor little mermaid was now dumb; she could neither sing nor speak. 'If the polypi should attempt to seize you, as you pass through my little grove,' said the witch, 'you have only to sprinkle some of this magic drink over them, and their arms will burst into a thousand pieces.'

But the Princess had no need of this counsel, for the polypi drew hastily back as soon as they perceived the bright phial that glittered in her hand like a star; thus she passed safely through the formidable wood, over the moor and across the foaming mill-stream.

She now looked once again at her father's palace; the lamps in the saloon were out, and all the family were asleep. She would not go in, for she could not speak if she did. She was about to leave her home for ever; her heart was ready to break with sorrow at the thought. She stole into the garden, plucked a flower from the bed of each of her sisters as a remembrance, kissed her hand again and again, and then rose through the dark blue water to the world above.

The sun had not yet risen when she arrived at the Prince's dwelling, and ascended those well-known marble steps. The moon still shone in the sky when the little mermaid drank of the wonderful liquid contained in her phial. She felt it run through her like a sharp knife, and she fell down in a swoon. When the sun rose she awoke, and felt a burning pain in all her limbs; but—she saw standing close to her the object of her love, the handsome young Prince, whose coal-black eyes were fixed inquiringly upon her. Full of shame, she cast down her own and perceived, instead of the long fish-like tail she had hitherto borne, two slender legs; but she was quite naked, and tried in vain to cover herself with her long, thick hair.

The Prince asked who she was, and how she had got there, and she, in reply, smiled and gazed upon him with her bright blue eyes, for alas! she could not speak. He then led her by the hand into the palace. She found that the witch had told her true; she felt as though she were walking on the edges of sharp swords, but she bore the pain willingly. On she passed, light as a zephyr, and all who saw her wondered at her light, graceful movements.

When she entered the palace, rich clothes of muslin and silk were brought to her; she was lovelier than all who dwelt there, but she could neither speak nor sing. Some female slaves, gaily dressed in silk and gold brocade, sang before the Prince and his royal parents; and one of them distinguished herself by her clear, sweet voice, which the Prince applauded by clapping his hands. This made the little mermaid very sad, for she knew that she used to sing far better than the young slave. 'Alas!' thought she, 'if he did but know that, for his sake, I have given away my voice for ever.'

The slaves began to dance; our lovely little mermaiden then arose, stretched out her delicate white arms, and hovered gracefully about the room. Every motion displayed more and more the perfect symmetry and elegance of her figure, and the expression which beamed in her eyes touched the hearts of the spectators far more than the song of the slaves.

All present were enchanted, but especially the young Prince, who called her his dear little foundling. And she danced again and again, although every step cost her excessive pain. The prince then said she should always be with him, and accordingly a sleeping-place was prepared for her on velvet cushions in the ante-room of his own apartment.

The Prince caused a suit of male apparel to be made for her, in order that she might accompany him on his rides; so together they traversed the fragrant woods, where green boughs brushed against their shoulders, and the birds sang merrily among the fresh leaves. With him she climbed up steep mountains, and although her tender feet bled, so as to be remarked by the attendants, she only smiled, and followed her dear Prince to the heights, whence they could see the clouds chasing each other beneath them, like a flock of birds migrating to other countries.

During the night she would, when all in the palace were at rest, walk down the marble steps, in order to cool her feet in the deep waters; she would then think of those beloved ones who dwelt in the lower world.

One night, as she was thus bathing her feet, her sisters swam together to the spot, arm-in-arm and singing, but alas! so mournfully! She beckoned to them, and they immediately recognised her, and told her how great was the mourning in her father's house for her loss. From this time the sisters visited her every night; and once they brought with them the old grandmother, who had not seen the upper world for a great many years. They likewise brought their father, the Mer-king, with his crown on his head; but these two old people did not venture near enough to land to be able to speak to her.

The little mermaid became dearer and dearer to the Prince every day; but he only looked upon her as a sweet, gentle child, and the thought of making her his wife never entered his head. And yet his wife she must be, ere she could receive an immortal soul; his wife she must be or she would change into foam, and be driven restlessly over the billows of the sea!

'Dost thou not love me above all others?' her eyes seemed to ask, as he pressed her fondly in his arms, and kissed her lovely brow.

'Yes,' the Prince would say; 'thou art dearer to me than any other, for no one is as good as thou art! Thou lovest me so much, and thou art so like a young maiden whom I have seen but once, and may never see again. I was on board a ship which was wrecked by a sudden tempest; the waves threw me on the shore near a holy temple where a number of young girls are occupied constantly with religious services. The youngest of them found me on the shore, and saved my life. I saw her only once, but her image is vividly impressed upon my memory, and her alone can I love. But she belongs to the holy temple, and thou who resemblest her so much hast been given to me for consolation. Never will we be parted!'

'Alas! he does not know that it was I who saved his life,' thought the little mermaid, sighing deeply. 'I bore him over the wild waves into the wooded bay where the holy temple stood; I sat behind the rocks, waiting till someone should come. I saw the pretty maiden approach, whom he loves more than me'—and again she heaved a deep sigh, for she could not weep. 'He said that the young girl belongs to the holy temple; she never comes out into the world—so they cannot meet each other again. And I am always with him, see him daily; I will love him, and devote my whole life to him.'

'So the Prince is going to be married to the beautiful daughter of the neighbouring King,' said the courtiers, 'that is why he is having that splendid ship fitted out. It is announced that he wishes to travel, but in reality he goes to see the Princess; a numerous retinue will accompany him.' The little mermaid smiled at these and similar conjectures, for she knew the Prince's intentions better than anyone else.

'I must go,' he said to her. 'I must see the beautiful Princess: my parents require me to do so; but they will not compel me to marry her, and bring her home as my bride. And it is quite impossible for me to love her, for she cannot be so like the beautiful girl in the temple as thou art; and if I were obliged to choose, I should prefer thee, my little silent foundling, with the speaking eyes.' And he kissed her rosy lips, played with her locks, and folded her in his arms where upon arose in her heart a sweet vision of human happiness and immortal bliss.

'Thou art not afraid of the sea, art thou, my sweet, silent child?' asked he tenderly as they stood together in the splendid ship which was to take them to the country of the neighbouring King. And then he told her of the storms that sometimes stir the waters, of the strange fishes that inhabit the deep, and of the wonderful things seen by divers. But she smiled at his words, for she knew better than any child of earth what went on in the depths of the ocean.

At night-time, when the moon shone brightly, and when all on board were fast asleep, she sat and looked down into the sea. It seemed to her, as she gazed through the foamy track made by the ship's keel, that she saw her father's palace, and her grandmother's silver crown. She saw her sisters rise out of the water, looking sorrowful and stretching out their hands towards her. She nodded to them, smiled, and would have explained that everything was going on quite according to her wishes, but just then the cabin-boy approached, upon which the sisters plunged beneath the water so suddenly that the boy thought what he had seen on the waves was nothing but foam.

The next morning the ship entered the harbour of the King's capital. Bells were rung, trumpets sounded, and soldiers marched in procession through the city, with waving banners, and glittering bayonets. Every day witnessed some new entertainments; balls and parties followed each other. The Princess, however, was not yet in the town; she had been sent to a distant convent for education, and had there been taught the practice of all royal virtues. At last she arrived at the palace.

The little mermaid had been anxious to see this wonderful Princess; and she was now obliged to confess that she had never before seen so beautiful a creature.

The skin of the Princess was so white and delicate that the veins might be seen through it, and her dark eyes sparkled beneath a pair of finely-formed eyebrows.

'It is herself!' exclaimed the Prince, when they met; 'it is she who saved my life, when I lay like a corpse on the seashore!' and he pressed his blushing bride to his beating heart—'Oh, I am all too happy!' said he to his dumb foundling. 'What I never dared to hope for has come to pass. Thou must rejoice in my happiness, for thou lovest me more than all others who surround me.'

And the little mermaid kissed his hand in silent sorrow; it seemed to her as if her heart was breaking already, although the morrow of his marriage day, which must of necessity see her death, had not yet dawned.

Again the church-bells rang, whilst heralds rode through the streets of the capital, to announce the approaching bridal. Odorous flames burned in silver candlesticks on all the altars, the priests swung their golden censers, and bride and bridegroom joined hands while the holy words that united them were spoken.

The little mermaid, clad in silk and cloth-of-gold, stood behind the Princess, and held the train of the bridal dress. But her ear heard nothing of the solemn music; her eye saw not the holy ceremony. She remembered her approaching end; she remembered that she had lost both this world and the next.

That very same evening, bride and bridegroom went on board the ship. Cannons were fired, flags waved with the breeze, and in the centre of the deck stood a magnificent pavilion of purple and cloth-of-gold, fitted up with the richest and softest couches. Here the princely pair were to spend the night. A favourable wind swelled the sails, and the ship glided lightly over the blue waters.

As soon as it was dark, coloured lamps were hung out, and dancing began on the deck. The little mermaid was thus reminded of what she had seen the first time she rose to the upper world. The spectacle that now presented itself was equally splendid—and she was obliged to join in the dance, hovering lightly as a bird over the ship boards. All applauded her, for never had she danced with more enchanting grace. Her little feet suffered extremely, but she no longer felt the pain; the anguish her heart suffered was much greater.

It was the last evening she might see him, for whose sake she had forsaken her home and all her family, had given away her beautiful voice, and suffered daily the most violent pain—all without his having the least suspicion of it. It was the last evening that she might breathe the same atmosphere in which he, the beloved one, lived, the last evening when she might behold the deep blue sea, and the starry heavens. An eternal night, in which she might neither think nor dream, awaited her. And all was joy in the ship; and she, her heart filled with thoughts of death and annihilation, smiled and danced with the others, till past midnight. Then the Prince kissed his lovely bride, and arm-in-arm they entered the magnificent tent prepared for their repose.

All was now still; the steersman alone stood at the ship's helm. The little mermaid leaned her white arms on the gallery, and looked towards the east watching for the dawn; she well knew that the first sunbeam would witness her death. She saw her sisters rise out of the sea; their features were deadly pale, and their long hair no more fluttered over their shoulders—it had all been cut off.

'We have given it to the witch,' said they, 'to induce her to help thee, so that thou mayest not die. She has given to us a penknife: here it is! Before the sun rises, thou must plunge it into the Prince's heart, and when his warm blood trickles down upon thy feet they will again be changed to a fish-like tail. Thou wilt once more become a mermaid, and wilt live thy full three hundred years, ere thou changest to foam on the sea. But hasten! either he or thou must die before sunrise.

'Our aged mother mourns for thee so much, her grey hair has fallen off through sorrow, as ours fell before the scissors of the witch. Kill the Prince, and come down to us! Hasten! hasten! dost thou not see the red streaks in the eastern sky, announcing the near approach of the sun? A few minutes more and he rises, and then all will be over with thee.'

At these words they sighed deeply and vanished.

The little mermaid drew aside the purple curtains of the pavilion, where lay the bride and bridegroom; bending over them, she kissed the Prince's forehead, and then glancing at the sky, she saw that the dawning light became every moment brighter. The Prince's lips murmured the name of his bride—he was dreaming of her, and her only, whilst the fatal penknife trembled in the hand of the unhappy mermaid.

All at once she threw far out into the sea that instrument of death; the waves rose like bright blazing flames around, and the water where it fell seemed tinged with blood. With eyes fast becoming dim and fixed, she looked once more at her beloved Prince, then plunged from the ship into the sea, and felt her body slowly but surely dissolving into foam.

The sun rose from his watery bed; his beams fell so softly and warmly upon her that our little mermaid was scarcely sensible of dying. She still saw the glorious sun, and over her head hovered a thousand beautiful transparent forms; she could still distinguish the white sails of the ship, and the bright red clouds in the sky. The voices of those airy creatures above her had a melody so sweet and soothing that a human ear would be as little able to catch the sounds as her eye was capable of distinguishing their forms; they hovered round her without wings, borne by their own lightness through the air. The little mermaid at last saw that she had a body as transparent as

313

theirs, and felt herself raised gradually from the foam of the sea to higher regions.

'Where are they taking me?' asked she, and her words sounded just like the voices of those heavenly beings.

'Speak you to the daughters of air?' was the answer. 'The mermaid has no immortal soul, and can only acquire that heavenly gift by winning the love of one of the sons of men; her immortality depends upon union with man.

'Neither do the daughters of air possess immortal souls, but they can acquire them by their own good deeds. We fly to hot countries, where the children of earth are sinking under sultry pestilential breezes; our fresh cooling breath revives them. We diffuse ourselves through the atmosphere; we perfume it with the delicious fragrance of flowers, and thus spread delight and health over the earth. By doing good in this manner for three hundred years we win immortality, and receive a share of the eternal bliss of human beings. And thou, poor little mermaid! who following the impulse of thine own heart, hast done and suffered so much—thou art now raised to the airy world of spirits, that by performing deeds of kindness for three hundred years, thou mayest acquire an immortal soul.'

The little mermaid stretched out her transparent arms to the sun, and, for the first time in her life, tears moistened her eyes.

And now again all were awake and rejoicing on the ship. She saw the Prince, with his pretty bride. They had missed her; they looked sorrowfully down on the foamy waters, as if they knew she had plunged into the sea. Unseen she kissed the bridegroom's forehead, smiled upon him, and then, with the rest of the children of air, soared high above the rosy cloud which was sailing so peacefully over the ship.

'After three hundred years we shall fly in the kingdom of Heaven!'

'We may arrive there even sooner,' whispered one of her sisters. 'We fly invisibly through the dwellings of men where there are children; and whenever we find a good child, who gives pleasure to his parents and deserves their love, the good God shortens our time of probation.

'No child is aware that we are flitting about his room, and that whenever joy draws from us a smile, a year is struck out of our three hundred. But when we see a rude, naughty child, we weep bitter tears of sorrow, and every tear we shed adds a day to our time of probation.'

THE SWINEHERD

There was once a poor Prince, who had a kingdom. His kingdom was small, but was still large enough to marry upon, and he wished to marry.

His name was known far and wide, and there were a hundred princesses who would each have answered 'Yes!' and 'Thank you kindly!' if he had asked her to be his wife, but he wished to marry the Emperor's daughter.

It happened that on the grave of the Prince's father there grew a rose-tree—a most beautiful rose-tree. It blossomed only once in every five years, and even then it bore only one rose—but what a rose! It was so sweet that whoever breathed its scent forgot all cares and sorrows.

And further, the Prince had a nightingale, who could sing as though all sweet melodies dwelt in her little throat. So he put the rose and the nightingale into silver caskets, and sent them to the Princess.

The Emperor had them brought into a large hall, where the Princess was playing at 'visiting' with her maids of honour, and when she saw the caskets with the presents she clapped her hands for joy.

'Oh, I do hope it is a little pussy-cat!' said she—but the rose-tree with its beautiful flower was brought out.

'Oh, how prettily it is made!' said all the court ladies.

But the Princess touched it, and was almost ready to cry.

315

'Fie! Papa,' said she, 'it is not made at all; it is natural!'

And all the court ladies said, 'Pah! it's a natural rose.'

'Let us see what is in the other casket, before we get into a bad humour,' said the Emperor. So the nightingale came forth, and sang so delightfully that at first no one could say anything ill-humoured of her.

'*Superbe! Charmant!*' cried the ladies, for they all used to chatter French, each one worse than her neighbour.

'How the bird reminds me of the musical-box that belonged to our blessed Empress!' said an old knight. 'Oh yes! these are the same tones, the same phrasing.'

'Yes! yes!' said the Emperor, and he wept at the remembrance.

'I do hope that it is not a real bird,' said the Princess.

'Yes, it is a real bird,' said those who had brought it.

'Well, then, let it fly,' said the Princess, and she refused to see the Prince.

However, he was not to be discouraged. He daubed his face over brown and black pulled his cap over his eyes, and knocked at the door.

'Good-day to my lord Emperor!' said he. 'Can I be taken into your service at the palace?'

'Why, yes,' said the Emperor. 'I want someone to take care of the pigs, for we have a great many of them.'

So the Prince was made 'Imperial Swineherd'. He had a dirty little room close by the pigsties, and there he sat the whole day, and worked. By the evening he had made a pretty little kitchen-pot with bells all round it. When the pot boiled, these bells tinkled in the most charming way, and played the old tune:

'Ah! my dearest Augustine,
All is gone, gone, gone!'

But what was still more curious, whoever held his finger in the steam of the kitchen-pot immediately smelt all the dishes that were cooking on every hearth in the city.

Now the Princess happened to walk that way, and when she heard the tune, she stood quite still, and seemed greatly pleased, for it was the only piece she knew, and she played it with one finger.

'Why, there is my piece!' said the Princess. 'That swineherd must have been well educated! Go in and ask him the price of the instrument.'

So one of the ladies ran in; but she drew on wooden slippers first.

'What will you take for the kitchen-pot?' said the lady.

'Ten kisses from the Princess,' said the swineherd.

'He is an impudent fellow!' said the Princess when she heard this, and she walked on. But when she had gone a little way, the bells tinkled so prettily that she had to stop.

316

'Stay,' said the Princess. 'Ask him if he will have ten kisses from the ladies of my court.'

'No, thank you!' said the swineherd, 'ten kisses from the Princess, or I keep the kitchen-pot myself.'

'That must not be either!' said the Princess; 'but do you all stand before me that no one may see us.'

So the court ladies placed themselves in front of her, and spread out their dresses; the swineherd got ten kisses and the Princess—the kitchen-pot.

That was delightful! the pot was boiling the whole evening, and the whole of the following day. They knew perfectly well what was cooking at every fire throughout the city, from the chamberlain's to the cobbler's. The court ladies danced, and clapped their hands.

The swineherd let not a day pass without making something. One day he made a rattle which, when it was swung round, played all the waltzes and jig tunes that have ever been heard.

'Ah, that is *superbe!*' said the Princess when she passed by. 'I have never heard prettier compositions! Go in and ask him the price of the instrument, but, mind, he shall have no more kisses!'

'He will have a hundred kisses from the Princess!' said the lady who had been to ask.

'I think he is out of his senses!' said the Princess, and walked on; but when she had gone a little way, she stopped again. 'One must encourage the fine arts,' said she. 'I am the Emperor's daughter. Tell him, he shall, as before, have ten kisses from me, and may take the rest from the ladies of the court.'

'Oh!—but we should not like that at all!' said they.

'Why are you muttering?' asked the Princess. 'If I can kiss him, surely you can!' So the ladies were obliged to go to him again.

'One hundred kisses from the Princess!' said he, 'or I keep the rattle.'

'Stand round us then!' said the Princess, and all the ladies stood round them whilst the kissing was going on.

'What can be the reason for such a crowd close by the pigsties?' said the Emperor, who happened just then to step out on the balcony. He rubbed his eyes and put on his spectacles. 'They are the ladies of the court; I must go down and see what they are about!'

The ladies were so much taken up with counting the kisses that they did not notice the Emperor. He rose on his tiptoes.

'What is all this?' said he, when he saw what was going on; and he boxed the Princess's ears, just as the swineherd was taking the eighty-sixth kiss.

'Begone!' said the Emperor, for he was very angry, and both Princess and swineherd were thrust out of the city.

The Princess wept, the swineherd scolded, and the rain poured down.

'Alas! unhappy creature that I am!' said the Princess. 'If I had but married the handsome young Prince! Ah, how unfortunate I am!'

The swineherd went behind a tree, washed the dirt from his face, threw off his old clothes, and stepped forth in all his princely robes; he looked so noble that the Princess could not help bowing before him.

'I have come to despise you,' said he. 'You would not have an honourable Prince! You could not prize the rose and the nightingale, but you were ready to kiss the swineherd for the sake of a trumpery plaything. You are rightly served.'

He then went back to his own little kingdom, and shut the door of his palace in her face. Now she might well sing:

'Ah! my dearest Augustine,
All is gone, gone, gone!'

THE WILD SWANS

Far, far away, in the land to which the swallows fly in our winter-time, there dwelt a King who had eleven sons and one daughter, named Elise. The eleven brothers were Princes, and went to school with stars on their breasts and swords by their sides; they wrote in golden copy-books with diamond pens, and learnt by heart just as they read. In short, it was easy to see that they were Princes. Their sister Elise used to sit upon a little glass stool, and had a picture book which had cost the half of a kingdom. Oh, the children were so happy. But happy they were not to remain always.

Their father, who was the King of the whole country, married a wicked Queen who was not at all kind to the poor children. They found this out on the first day after the marriage. There were great festivities at the palace, and the children played at receiving company, but instead of letting them have, as usual, as many cakes and burnt apples as were left, the Queen gave them only some sand in a teacup, and told them to play at make-believe with that.

The week after, she sent the little Elise to be brought up by some peasants in the country, and before long she told the King so many falsehoods about the poor Princes, that he would have nothing more to do with them.

'Away, out into the world, and take care of yourselves,' said the wicked Queen; 'fly away in the form of great speechless birds.' But she could not make them ugly, as she wished to do, for they were changed into eleven white swans. Sending forth a strange cry, they flew out of the palace windows, over the park and over the wood.

It was still early in the morning when they passed the peasant's cottage where Elise lay sleeping. They hovered over the roof, stretched their long necks, and flapped their wings; but no one heard or saw them, so they were forced to fly away. They flew up to the clouds and out into the wide world, far away into the dark forest, which stretched as far as the seashore.

Poor little Elise stood in the peasant's cottage, playing with a green leaf, for she had no other plaything. She pricked a hole in the leaf and peeped through it at the sun, and then she fancied she saw her brothers' bright eyes, and whenever the warm sunbeams shone full upon her cheeks, she thought of her brothers' kisses.

One day was just like another. When the wind blew through the thick hedge of rose-trees in front of the house, she would whisper to the roses, 'Who is more beautiful than you?' And the roses would shake their heads and say, 'Elise.' And when the peasant's wife sat on Sundays at the door of her cottage reading her hymn-book, the wind would rustle the leaves and say to the book, 'Who is more pious than you?' And the hymn-book would answer, 'Elise.' And what the roses and the hymn-book said was no more than the truth.

When she was fifteen years old she had to go home, and when the Queen saw how beautiful she was, she hated her more than ever, and would willingly have turned her, like her brothers, into a wild swan; but she dared not do so, because the King wished to see his daughter.

Early one morning the Queen went into the bathroom, which was made of marble and fitted up with soft pillows and the gayest carpets. She took three toads with her and kissed them, and said to one, 'When Elise comes to the bath settle thou upon her head that she may become dull and sleepy like thee.' 'Settle thou upon her forehead,' said she to another, 'and let her become ugly like thee, so that her father may not know her again.' And 'Do thou place thyself upon her bosom,' whispered she to the third, 'that her heart may become evil, and a torment to herself.' She then put the toads into clear water, which immediately turned green, and having called Elise, took off her clothes and made her get into the bath. As she dipped her head under the water, one toad settled in her hair, another on her forehead, and the third upon her bosom. But Elise seemed not at all aware of it; and when she rose up three poppies were seen swimming on the water. Had not the animals been poisonous and kissed by a witch, they would have been changed into roses because they had rested on Elise's head and heart. She was too good for magic to have any power over her.

When the Queen perceived this, she rubbed walnut juice all over the maiden's skin, so that it became quite swarthy, smeared a nasty salve over her lovely face, and entangled her long thick hair, till it was impossible to recognise the beautiful Elise. When her father saw her he was shocked, and said she could not be his daughter. No one knew her but the mastiff and the swallows, and they were only poor animals and could not say anything.

Poor Elise wept and thought of her eleven brothers who were all away. In great distress she stole away and wandered the whole day over fields and marshes, till she came to the great forest. She knew not where to go, but she was so sad, and longed so much to see her brothers, who like herself had been driven out into the world, that she made up her mind to seek for them and find them.

She had not been long in the forest when night came on, and she lost her way amid the darkness. So she lay down on the soft moss, said her evening prayer, and leaned her head against the trunk of a tree. It was very still in the forest. The air was mild, and from the grass and mould around gleamed the green lights of many hundred glow-worms; and when Elise touched one of the branches hanging over her, bright insects fell down upon her like falling stars.

All the night long she dreamed of her brothers. It seemed to her that they were all children again, playing together, writing with diamond pens in golden copy-books, and looking at the pictures in the beautiful book that had cost half of a kingdom. But they did not as formerly make straight strokes and pothooks upon the copy-books. No; they wrote of the noble deeds they had done, and the strange things they had seen. In the picture-book, too, everything seemed alive; the birds sang, and the men and women stepped from the pages and talked to Elise and her brothers, jumping back into their places, however, when she turned over the leaves, so that the pictures did not get confused.

When Elise awoke the sun was already high in the heavens. She could not see it, for the tall trees twined their thickly-leaved branches so closely together that, as the sunbeams played upon them, they looked like a golden veil waving to and fro. The air was fragrant, and the birds almost perched upon Elise's shoulders. She heard the noise of water, and when she went towards it she found a pool, formed by several springs, with the prettiest pebbles at the bottom. Bushes were growing thickly round, but the deer had trodden a broad path through them, and by this path Elise went down to the water's edge. The water was so clear that had not the boughs and bushes around been moved to and fro by the wind she might have fancied they were painted upon the smooth surface, so distinctly was each little leaf mirrored upon it, whether glowing in the sunlight or lying in the shade.

When Elise saw her own face in the water she was frightened, so brown and ugly did it look; but when she wetted her little hand, and rubbed her brow and eyes, the white skin again appeared. So she took off her clothes, stepped into the fresh water and bathed herself, and in the whole world there was not a king's daughter more beautiful than she then appeared.

After she had again dressed herself, and had braided her long hair, she went to the bubbling spring, caught some water in the hollow of her hand and drank it, and then wandered farther into the forest. She knew not where she was going, but she thought of her brothers, and of the good God who, she felt, would never forsake her. He it was who made the wild apples grow to feed the hungry, and who showed her a tree whose boughs bent under the weight of their fruit. She made her noonday meal under the shade of this tree, then propped up the boughs and walked on into the gloomiest depths of the forest. It was so still that she could hear her own footsteps, and the rustling of each little withered leaf that was crushed beneath her feet. Not a bird was to be seen, not a sunbeam penetrated the thick foliage, and the tall stems of the trees stood so close together that when she looked straight before her she seemed enclosed by trellis-work upon trellis-work. Oh! there was a solitariness in this forest such as Elise had never known before.

And the night was so dark! not a single glow-worm sent forth its light from the moss. Sorrowfully she lay down to sleep. Then it seemed to her as though the boughs above her opened, and she saw the angel of God smiling down upon her, and a thousand little cherubs all round him. When she awoke in the morning she could not tell whether this was a dream or whether it had really happened.

She walked on a little farther and met an old woman with a basket full of berries. The old woman gave her some of the berries, and Elise asked if she had not seen eleven Princes ride through the wood.

'No,' said the old woman, 'but I saw yesterday eleven swans with golden crowns on their heads swim down the brook near here.'

Then she led Elise on a little farther to a sloping bank at the foot of which ran a little brook. The trees on each side stretched their long leafy branches towards each other, and where they could not unite naturally the roots had torn themselves from the earth, so that the branches might mingle their foliage as they hung over the water.

Elise bade the old woman farewell, and wandered by the side of the stream till she came to the place where it reached the open sea.

The great, the beautiful sea lay before the maiden's eyes, but not a ship, not a boat was to be seen. How was she to go on? She noticed how the numberless little stones on the shore had all been washed into a round form by the waves; glass, iron, stone, everything that lay scattered there had been moulded into shape, and yet the water which had done this was much softer than Elise's delicate little hand.

'The water rolls on unweariedly,' said she, 'till it smooths all that is hard; I will be no less unwearied! Thank you for the lesson you have given me, ye bright rolling waves; some day, my heart tells me, you shall carry me to my dear brothers!'

Upon the wet sea-grass lay eleven white swan-feathers. Elise gathered them up and put them together. Drops of water hung about them, whether dew or tears she could not tell. She was quite alone on the seashore, but she did not mind that, for the sea was full of interest to her; it was always moving, always changing, always new, and so gave her more pleasure in a few hours than the gentle inland waters could have given in a whole year. When a black cloud passed over the sky, it seemed as if the sea would say, 'I too can look dark', and then the wind would blow and the waves fling out their white foam; but when the clouds shone with a bright red tint, and the winds were asleep, the sea became like a rose-leaf now green, now white. Yet however smooth its glassy surface was, there was always a slight motion near the shore as the waves rose and fell like the breast of a sleeping child.

At sunset Elise saw eleven wild swans with golden crowns on their heads fly towards the land; they flew one behind another, looking like a long white ribbon. Elise climbed the slope from the shore and hid herself behind a bush. The swans came down close to her, and flapped their long white wings.

As the sun sank beneath the water, the swans' feathers fell off, and beside her stood eleven handsome Princes, her brothers. She uttered a loud cry, for although they were very much changed, Elise knew and felt that they must be her brothers. Then she threw herself into their arms, calling them by their names, and the Princes were very happy to see their sister, now grown so tall and so beautiful! They laughed and wept, and soon told each other how wickedly their stepmother had acted towards them.

'We brothers,' said the eldest, 'fly or swim as long as the sun is in the sky, but when it sets we appear again in our human form; we are therefore bound to look out for a safe resting-place before sunset, for if we were flying among the clouds at the time, we should fall down into the sea when we recovered our human shape. We do not dwell here. A land quite as beautiful as this lies on the other side of the sea, but it is far off. To reach it we have to cross the deep waters, and there is no island midway on which we may rest at night. One little solitary rock rises from the waves, and upon it we only find room enough to stand side by side. There we spend the night in our human form; and when the sea is rough the foam dashes over us. But we thank God even for this rock, for without it we should never be able to visit our native country. Only once in the year are we allowed to make this visit to our home. We require two of the longest days for our flight, and can remain here only eleven days, during which time we fly over the large forest, whence we can see the palace in which we were born, where our father dwells, and the tower of the church in which our mother was buried.

Here even the trees and bushes seem of kin to us. The wild horses still race over the plains as in the days of our childhood. The charcoal-burner still sings the same old tunes to which we used to dance in our youth. This is our fatherland to which we are drawn by ties of love, and here we have found thee, thou dear little sister! We have yet two days longer to stay here, and then we must fly over the sea to a land beautiful indeed, but not our fatherland. How shall we take thee with us? We have neither ship nor boat!'

'How can I break this spell?' said the sister. And so they went on talking almost the whole of the night. They slept only a few hours.

Elise was awakened by the rustling of wings, and saw the swans fluttering above her. Her brothers were again changed into swans. For some time they flew round in wider and wider circles, till at last they flew far away. One of them remained behind; it was the youngest. He laid his head in her lap and she stroked his white wings; they remained the whole day together. Towards evening the others came back, and when the sun was set, again they stood on the firm ground in their natural form.

'Tomorrow we shall fly away,' they said, 'and may not return for a year, but we cannot leave you here. Have you courage to go with us? Our arms are strong enough to bear you through the forest, and will not our wings be strong enough to fly with you over the sea?'

'Yes, take me with you,' said Elise.

They spent the whole night in weaving a mat of the pliant willow bark and the tough rushes, and their mat was thick and strong. Elise lay down upon it, and when the sun had risen, and the brothers had been turned again into wild swans, they seized the mat with their beaks and flew up high among the clouds with their dear sister. She was still sleeping, and, as the sunbeams shone full upon her face, one of the swans flew over her head and shaded her with his broad wings.

They were already far from land when Elise awoke. She thought she was still dreaming, so strange did it seem to her to feel herself being carried so high up in the air over the sea. By her side lay a cluster of pretty ripe berries and a bundle of sweet roots. Her youngest brother had gathered them for her and laid them there, and she thanked him with a smile, for she knew him as the swan who flew over her head and shaded her with his wings.

They soared so high that the first ship they saw beneath them seemed like a white sea-gull hovering over the water. Elise saw behind her a large cloud, which looked like a mountain, and on it were gigantic shadows of herself and the eleven swans; altogether it formed a picture more beautiful than any she had ever yet seen. Soon, however, the sun rose higher, the cloud was left behind, and the shadowy picture disappeared.

The whole day they flew on like a winged arrow through the air, but yet they went slower than usual, for they had their sister to carry. There seemed a storm brewing, and the evening was drawing near. Anxiously did Elise watch the sun. It was

setting, and still the solitary rock could not be seen. It appeared to her that the swans plied their wings faster and faster. Alas! it would be her fault if her brothers did not arrive at the rock in time. They would become human beings when the sun set, and must fall into the sea and be drowned. She prayed to God most fervently. Still no rock was to be seen. The black clouds drew nearer, and gusts of wind told of a coming storm, while from a mass of clouds that seemed to move forward like a leaden, threatening wave flash after flash of lightning broke forth.

The sun was now on the rim of the sea. Elise's heart beat fast; the swans shot downward so swiftly that she thought she must fall, but in another moment they began to soar again. The sun was half sunk beneath the water, but now she saw the little rock below her; it looked like a seal's head when he raises it just above the water. The sun was sinking fast. It seemed scarce larger than a star as her foot touched the hard ground, and in a moment it vanished altogether, like the last spark on a burnt piece of paper. Arm in arm her brothers stood around her; there was just room for her and them. The sea beat wildly against the rock, flinging over them a shower of foam. The sky seemed ablaze with the continual flashes, and one clap of thunder followed close on another, but sister and brothers kept firm hold of each other's hands. They sang a psalm, and their psalm gave them comfort and courage.

By daybreak the air was pure and still, and, as soon as the sun rose, the swans flew away with Elise from the rock. The sea was still rough, and from the clouds the white foam that crested the blackish-green waves looked as if millions of swans were swimming on the waters.

As day advanced, Elise saw before her floating in the air a range of mountains, with masses of glittering ice on their summits. In their midst stood a castle at least a mile in length, with rows of columns, one above another, while around it grew palmtrees and gorgeous-looking flowers as large as mill-wheels. She asked if this was the land to which they were flying, but the swans shook their heads, for what she saw was the beautiful ever-changing cloud castle of the fairy Morgana, which no human being can ever enter. Whilst Elise still bent her eyes upon it, mountains, trees, and castle all disappeared, and in their place stood twenty stately churches with high towers and pointed windows—she fancied she heard the organ play, but it was only the murmur of the sea. As they drew nearer to these churches they too changed, into a large fleet sailing under them. She looked down and saw it was only a sea-mist passing rapidly over the water. Such strange scenes kept floating before her eyes, till at last she saw the actual land to which they were going with its blue mountains, its cedar woods, its towns and castles. Long before sunset Elise sat down among the mountains, in front of a large cavern round which delicate young creepers grew so thickly that the ground appeared covered with gay embroidered carpets.

'Now we shall see what thou wilt dream of tonight!' said her youngest brother, as he showed her the chamber where she was to sleep.

'Oh that I could dream how you might be freed from the spell!' said she, and she could think of nothing else. She prayed most earnestly for God's help, nay, even in dreams she continued praying, and it appeared to her that she was flying up high in the air towards the castle of the fairy Morgana. The fairy came forward to meet her, radiant and beautiful, and yet she thought she looked like the old woman who had given her berries in the forest, and told her of the swans with golden crowns.

'You can release your brothers,' said she; 'but have you courage and patience enough? The water is indeed softer than your delicate hands, and yet can mould the hard stones to its will, but then it cannot feel the pain which your tender fingers will feel; it has no heart, and cannot suffer the anxiety and grief which you must suffer. Do you see these stinging-nettles I have in my hand? There are many round the cave where you are sleeping; only those that grow there or on the graves in the churchyard are of use, remember that! You must pluck them though they sting your hand; you must trample on them with your feet, and get yarn from them, and with this yarn you must weave eleven shirts with long sleeves. When they are all made, throw them over the eleven wild swans, and the spell will be broken. But mark this: from the moment that you begin your work till it is completed, even should it occupy you for years, you must not speak a word. The first syllable that escapes your lips will fall like a dagger into the hearts of your brothers. On your tongue depend their lives. Mark well all this!'

At the same moment the fairy touched Elise's hands with a nettle, which made them burn like fire, and Elise awoke. It was broad daylight, and close to her lay a nettle like the one she had seen in her dream. She fell upon her knees, thanked God, and then went out of the cave to begin her work. She plucked with her own delicate hands the ugly stinging-nettles. They burned large blisters on her hands and arms, but she bore the pain willingly in the hope of freeing her dear brothers. Then she trampled on the nettles with her naked feet, and spun the green yarn.

At sunset came her brothers. Elise's silence quite frightened them; they thought it must be the effect of some fresh spell of their wicked stepmother. But when they saw her blistered hands, they found out what their sister was doing for their sake. The youngest brother wept, and when his tears fell upon her hands, Elise felt no more pain, and the blisters disappeared.

The whole night she spent in her work, for she could not rest till she had released her brothers. All the following day she sat in her solitude, for the swans had flown away, but never had time passed so quickly. One shirt was ready, and she now began the second.

Suddenly a hunting-horn echoed among the mountains and made her start with fear. The noise came nearer; she heard the hounds barking. In great terror she fled into the cave, bound up into a bundle the nettles she had gathered and combed, and sat down upon it.

She had just done so when a large dog sprang out from the bushes. Two others immediately followed; they barked loudly, ran away, and then returned. It was not long before the hunters stood in front of the cave. The handsomest among them was the King of that country, and he stepped up to Elise, for never had he seen a lovelier maiden.

'How came you here, beautiful child?' said he. Elise shook her head; she dared not speak, for a word might have cost her the lives of her brothers, and she hid her hands under her apron lest the King should see how she was suffering.

'Come with me,' said he. 'You must not stay here! If you are as good as you are beautiful, I will dress you in velvet and silk, I will put a gold crown upon your head and you shall dwell in my palace!' So he lifted her upon his horse, while she wept and wrung her hands; but the King said, 'I only desire your happiness! You shall thank me for this some day!' and away he rode over mountains and valleys, holding her on his horse in front, whilst the other hunters followed. When the sun set, the King's capital with its churches and domes lay before them, and the King led Elise into the palace, where, in a high marble hall, fountains were playing, and the walls and ceiling were covered with the most beautiful paintings. But Elise cared not for all this splendour. She wept and mourned in silence, even whilst some female attendants dressed her in royal robes, wove costly pearls into her hair, and drew soft gloves over her blistered hands.

And now as she stood before them in her rich dress, her beauty was so dazzling, that the courtiers all bowed low before her, and the King chose her for his bride although the Archbishop shook his head, and whispered that the 'beautiful lady of the wood was only a witch, who had blinded their eyes and bewitched the King's heart.'

But the King did not listen; he ordered that music should be played. The most costly dishes were served up, and the loveliest maidens danced round the bride. She was led through fragrant gardens into magnificent halls, but not a smile was seen to play upon her lips or beam from her eyes. She looked the very picture of grief. The King then opened a small room next her bedroom. The floor was covered with costly green tapestry, and looked exactly like the cave in which she had been found. On it lay the bundle of yarn which she had spun from the nettles, and by the wall hung the shirt she had made. One of the hunters had brought all this, thinking there must be something wonderful in it.

'Here you may dream of your former home,' said the King. 'Here is the work you were doing there. Amid all your present splendour it may sometimes give you pleasure to fancy yourself there again.'

When Elise saw what was so dear to her heart, she smiled, and the blood came back to her cheeks. She thought her brothers might still be freed from the spell, and she kissed the King's hand. He pressed her to his heart, and ordered the bells of all the churches in the city to be rung, to announce their marriage. The beautiful dumb maiden of the wood was to become the Queen of the land.

The Archbishop whispered evil words in the King's ear, but he paid no heed to them. He and Elise were married, and the Archbishop himself was obliged to put the crown upon her head. In his rage he pressed the narrow rim so firmly on her forehead that it hurt her, but a heavier weight of sorrow for her brothers lay upon her heart, and she did not feel bodily pain. She was still silent, because a single word would have killed her brothers, but her eyes beamed with heartfelt love to the King, so good and handsome, who had done so much to make her happy. She loved him more and more every day. Oh! how she wished she might tell him her sorrows, but she must remain silent, she could not speak until her work was finished. So she stole away every night, and went into the little room that was fitted up like the cave. There she worked at her shirts; but by the time she had begun the seventh, all her yarn was spent.

She knew that the nettles she needed grew in the churchyard, but she must gather them herself, and how to get them she knew not.

'Oh, what is the pain in my fingers compared with the anguish my heart suffers!' thought she. 'I must venture to the churchyard; the good God will still watch over me!

Fearful as though she were about to do something wrong, one moonlight night she crept down to the garden, and through the long avenues into the lonely road leading to the churyard. She saw sitting on one of the broadest tombstones a number of ugly old witches. They took off their ragged clothes as if they were going to bathe and digging with their long lean fingers into the fresh grass, drew up the dead bodies and devoured the flesh. Elise was obliged to pass close by them, and the witches fixed their wicked eyes upon her; but she repeated her prayer, gathered the stinging-nettles, and took them back with her into the palace. One person only had seen her. It was the Archbishop; he was awake when others slept. Now he felt sure that all was not right about the Queen; she must be a witch, who had, by her magic, won the hearts of the King and all the people.

In the Confessional he told the King what he had seen, and what he feared; and when the slanderous words came from his lips, the sculptured images of the saints shook their heads as though they would say, 'It is untrue, Elise is innocent!' But the Archbishop explained the omen quite otherwise; he thought it was a testimony against her, and that the holy images shook their heads at hearing of her sin.

Two large tears rolled down the King's cheeks, and he returned home in doubt. He pretended to sleep at night, though sleep never visited him, and he noticed that Elise rose from her bed every night, and every time he followed her secretly and saw her enter her little room.

His face grew darker every day. Elise perceived it, though she did not know the cause. She was much pained, and besides, what did she not suffer in her heart for her brothers! Her bitter tears ran down on the royal velvet and purple, looking like bright diamonds, and all who saw the grandeur that surrounded her wished themselves in her place. She had now nearly finished her work; only one shirt was wanting. Unfortunately, yarn was wanting also; she had not a single nettle left. Once more, only this one time, she must go to the churchyard and gather a few handfuls. She shuddered when she thought of the solitary walk and of the horrid witches, but her resolution was as firm as her trust in God.

Elise went, and the King and the Archbishop followed her. They saw her disappear at the churchyard door, and when they came nearer they saw the witches sitting on the tombstones as Elise had seen them; and the King turned away, for he believed her whose head had rested on his bosom that very evening to be amongst them. 'Let the people judge her!' said he. And the people condemned her to be burnt.

She was now dragged from the King's splendid palace into a dark, damp prison, where the wind whistled through the barred window. Instead of velvet and silk, they gave her the bundle of nettles she had gathered. On that she had to lay her head, and the shirts she had woven had to serve her as mattress and counterpane. But they could not have given anything more welcome to her, and she continued her work, at the same time praying earnestly to God. The boys sang shameful songs about her in front of her prison; not a soul comforted her with one word of love.

Towards evening she heard the rustling of swans' wings at the grating. It was the youngest of her brothers, who had at last found her, and she sobbed aloud for joy, although she knew that probably she had only one night to live; but then her work was almost finished and her brothers were near.

The Archbishop came in to spend the last hour with her as he had promised the King he would, but she shook her head and begged him with looks and signs to go away. For this night she must finish her work, or all she had suffered, her pain, her anxiety, her sleepless nights, would be in vain. The Archbishop went away with many angry words, but poor Elise knew herself to be perfectly innocent, and went on with her work.

Little mice ran busily about and dragged the nettles to her feet, wishing to help her, and a thrush perched on the iron bars of the window, and sang all night as merrily as he could, that she might not lose courage.

An hour before sunrise then eleven brothers stood before the palace gates, and begged to be shown to the King. But it could not be, they were told; it was still night, the King was asleep, and they dared not wake him. They prayed, they threatened, in vain. The guard came up. At last the King himself stepped out to ask what was the matter, but at that moment the sun rose, the brothers could be seen no longer, and eleven white swans flew away over the palace.

The people poured forth from the gates of the city to see the witch burnt. One wretched horse drew the cart in which Elise sat. She wore a coarse frock of sackcloth, her beautiful long hair hung loosely over her shoulders, her cheeks were of a deathly paleness, but her lips moved gently, and her fingers wove the green yarn, for even on her way to her cruel death she did not give up her work. The ten shirts lay at her feet, she was now labouring to complete the eleventh. The crowd insulted her.

'Look at the witch, how she mutters! She has no psalm-book in her hand—no, there she sits with her juggling! Tear it from her, tear it into a thousand pieces!'

333

And they all crowded about her, and were on the point of snatching away the shirts, when eleven white swans came flying towards the cart, settled all round her, and flapped their wings. The crowd gave way in terror.

'It is a sign from Heaven! she is certainly innocent!' whispered some; they dared not say so aloud.

The executioner now took hold of her hand to lift her out of the cart, but she hastily threw the eleven shirts over the swans, and eleven handsome Princes appeared in their place. The youngest had, however, only one arm, and a wing instead of the other, for one sleeve in his shirt had not been quite finished.

'Now I may speak,' said she; 'I am innocent!'

And the people who had seen what had happened bowed before her as before a saint. She, however, sank lifeless in her brothers' arms; suspense, fear, and grief had quite exhausted her.

'Yes, she is innocent,' said her eldest brother, and he told their wonderful story. Whilst he spoke a fragrance as from millions of roses spread itself around, for every piece of wood in the funeral pyre had taken root and sent forth branches, and a hedge of blooming red roses surrounded Elise, and above all the others blossomed a flower of a dazzling white colour, bright as a star. The King plucked it and laid it on Elise' bosom, and then she awoke with peace and joy in her heart.

And all the church-bells began to ring of their own accord, and birds flew to the spot in swarms, and there was a joyous procession back to the palace, such as no king has ever seen equalled.

MOTHER ELDER

Once there was a little boy who had caught a cold by getting his feet wet; how he had managed it no one could conceive, for the weather was perfectly fine and dry. His mother took off his clothes, put him to bed, and brought in the teapot, intending to make him a cup of good, warm elder-tea.

Just then the pleasant old man who lodged in the uppermost floor of the house came in. He lived quite alone, poor man! He had neither wife nor children of his own, but he loved all his neighbours' children very fondly, and had so many charming stories and fairy tales to tell them, that it was a pleasure to see him among them.

'Now drink your tea, like a good boy,' said the mother, 'and who knows but you may hear a story.'

'Ah, yes, if one could only think of something new!' said the old man, smiling and nodding his head. 'But where did the little one get his feet wet?' asked he.

'Where indeed?' said the mother, 'that's just what nobody can make out.'

'Mayn't I have a story?' asked the boy.

'Yes, if you can tell me exactly how deep the gutter is in the little street yonder, along which you go to school. I want to know that first.'

'The water just comes up to the middle of my boot,' replied the boy, 'but not unless I walk through the deep hole.'

337

'Ah, then, that's where we got our feet wet!' said the old man. 'And now, suppose, you will call upon me for a tale, but really I don't know any more.'

'But you can get one ready in a moment,' insisted the boy. 'Mother says that everything you look at quickly becomes a fairy tale, and that everything you touch you turn into a story.'

'Yes, but those stories and fairy tales are not good for much! The right sort come of their own accord; they tap at my forehead, and cry, "Here we are!"'

'I hope they will soon come and tap,' said the little boy, and his mother laughed, put some elder-flowers into the teapot, and poured boiling water over them. 'Come now for a story! Tell me one, pray!'

'Yes, if the stories would but come; but they are proud, and will only visit me when it so pleases them. Hush!' cried he, all of a sudden, 'here we have it! Keep a good lookout; now it is in the teapot!'

And the little boy looked at the teapot. He saw the lid rise up, and the elder-flowers spring forth, fresh and white. They shot out long, thick branches—even out of the spout they shot forth—spreading on all sides, and growing larger and larger, till at last there stood by the bedside a most charming elder-bush, a perfect tree, some of its boughs stretching over the bed and thrusting the curtains aside.

Oh, how full of blossoms was this tree, and how fragrant were those blossoms! In the midst of the tree sat a kind-looking old dame, wearing the strangest dress in the world. It was green like the elder-leaves with a pattern of large white elder-flower clusters spreading all over it. One could not be sure whether it was really a gown, or living green leaves and flowers.

'What is her name?' inquired the little boy.

'Why, those old Greeks and Romans,' replied the old man, 'used to call her a Dryad, but we don't understand those outlandish names. The sailors in the New Booths have a much better name for her; they call her Mother Elder, and that suits her very well. Now listen to me, and keep looking at the pretty elder-tree the while...

Just such another large tree as that stands among the New Booths; it has grown up in the corner of a miserable little courtyard. Under the shade of this tree there sat, one afternoon, with the glorious sunshine around them, two old people—a very old sailor, and his very old wife.

They were great-grandparents already, and would soon have to keep their golden wedding-day, but they could not exactly remember on what day it would fall; and Mother Elder sat in the tree above them, looking so pleased, just as she does now. 'Ah, I know which is the golden wedding-day!' said she, but they did not hear her. There they sat talking over old times.

'Can't you remember,' said the sailor, 'the days when we were little ones, and used to be always running and playing about in this very same yard where we are sitting now, and how we stuck slips in the ground to make a garden?'

'To be sure I remember it!' replied the old woman. 'We watered the slips every day, but only one of them took root, and that was an elder-slip, and it shot out its green shoots till it grew up to be this large tree that we old folks are now sitting under!'

'So it did!' said the sailor; 'and in the corner yonder used to stand a water-pail, where I sailed my boats. I carved them with my own hand—such famous boats they were! But I soon had to sail myself, in rather larger vessels than those, though.'

'Yes, but first we went to school to be made scholars of,' said his wife, 'and then we were confirmed. We both of us cried, I remember, and in the afternoon we went hand-in-hand up to the Round Tower, and looked out upon the world, out over all Copenhagen and the sea; and then we went to Fredericksberg, where the King and Queen were sailing about the canals in their magnificent barges.'

'But those barges were scarcely more like the great ships I sailed in than my poor little boats were, and oh, for how many, many years I was away on those long voyages!'

'Yes, and how often I wept for you!' said she. 'I believed you must be dead and gone for ever, lying low down beneath the deep waters. Many a night have I got up to look at the weather-cock, to see if the wind had changed; and change it did, over and over again, but still you did not return.

'There is one day I shall never forget. It was pouring with rain; the dustmen had come to the house where I was in service. I came down with the dust-box, and remained standing at the door. Oh, what weather it was! and while I stood there, the postman came up and gave me a letter; it was from you.

'What a journey that letter had made! I tore it open and read it; I laughed and cried by turns, I was so happy. The letter told me you were in the warm countries, where the coffee-trees grow—what charming countries those must be; it told me so many things, and I fancied I could see all that you had described. And the rain still kept pouring down in torrents, and there I stood at the door with the dust-box. Just then somebody came up behind me, and took hold of me—'

'Yes, indeed, and didn't you give him a good box on the ear! Didn't his ear tingle after it!'

'But I did not know that it was you. You had arrived as soon as your letter, and you were so handsome!—but that you are still, and you had a large yellow silk hand-kerchief in your pocket, and a new hat on your head. Oh, what weather it was; the streets were quite flooded.'

'And then we were married,' said the sailor; 'don't you remember that? And then we had our first little boy, and after him we had Marie, and Niels, and Peter and Hans Christian.'

'Ah! and how happy it was that they should all grow up to be good, and honest, and industrious, and to be loved by everybody.'

'And their children, too—they have little ones now,' added the old sailor. 'Yes, they are fine healthy babies, those great-grandchildren of ours. And so it was, I fancy, just about this time of year that we had our wedding.'

'Yes, this very day is your golden wedding-day!' said Mother Elder, putting out her head between the two old people, but they fancied she was their neighbour nodding to them. They gave little heed to her, but again looked at each other, and took hold of each other's hand.

Presently their children and grandchildren came out into the court; they knew well that this was the golden wedding-day, and had come that very morning to congratulate their parents. But the two old people had quite forgotten that, although they could remember so clearly things that had happened half a century ago.

And the elder-blossoms smelled sweetly; and the sun, which was near setting, shone full into the old couple's faces. A red rosy light he shed over their features; and the youngest of the grandchildren danced round them, shouting with glee that this evening there should be a grand feast, for they were all to have hot potatoes for supper. Mother Elder nodded her head to them from the tree, and shouted 'Hurrah!' as loudly as they did...

'But I don't call that a tale at all,' said the little boy in the bed.

'Don't you?' said the kind old story-teller. 'Well, suppose we ask Mother Elder what she thinks about it.'

'No, you are right, that was not a tale,' replied Mother Elder; 'but now you shall have one. I will show you how the most charming fairy tales spring out of the commonest incidents of everyday life; were it not so, you know, my pretty elder-bush could hardly have grown out of the tea-pot!'

And then she took the little boy out of bed, pillowing his head upon her bosom, and the elder-boughs laden with blossoms entwined round them, so that they seemed to be sitting in a thick-leaved, fragrant arbour, and the arbour flew away with them through the air—that was most delightful!

Mother Elder had, all of a sudden, changed into a pretty and graceful young girl; her robe was still of the same fresh green, white-flowered material that Mother Elder had worn. On her bosom rested a real elder-flower cluster, and a whole garland of elder-flowers was wreathed among her curling flaxen hair. Her eyes were large and blue—it was a delight to behold a creature so lovely! And she and the boy embraced, and immediately they were of the same age: they loved each other, and were unbelievably happy.

Hand in hand they walked out of the arbour, and were now in the pretty flower-garden of their home. On the grass plot they found their father's walking-stick. For the children, it seemed, there was life in this stick: as soon as they got astride it the bright knob of the handle became a fiery neighing head, a long black mane fluttered to and fro in the wind, four long, slender legs shot out. A fine spirited creature was their new steed, and off he galloped with them round the grass plot—hurrah!

'Now we will ride many miles away,' said the boy; 'let us ride to the dear old manor house we went to last year.' And still they rode round and round the grass plot, the little girl, who, as we know, was no other than Mother Elder, crying out all the

340

while: 'Now we are in the country. Seest thou not yonder pretty cottage? The elder-tree lowers its branches over it, and the cock is strutting about, and scraping up the ground for the hens. See how proudly he strides! And now we are close to the church; it stands high on the hill, among the great oak-trees, one of which is quite hollow. Now we are at the smithy; the fire is blazing, and the half-naked men are banging away with their hammers, and the sparks are flying about all round. Away, away, to the old manor house!'

And all that the little maiden riding on the stick described flew past them; the boy saw it all, and still they only rode round and round the grass plot. Then the children played in one of the walks, and marked out a tiny garden for themselves in the mould; and the girl took one of the elder-blossoms out of her hair and planted it, and it grew up, just as the elder-sprig grew which was planted among the New Booths by the old sailor and his wife when they were little ones, as has been told already.

And hand in hand the children now went on together, just as the children in the New Booths had done; but not up to the Round Tower or to the gardens of Fredericks-berg. No, the little girl threw her arms round the little boy's waist, and then away they flew over all Denmark; and spring deepened into summer, and summer mellowed into autumn, and autumn faded into pale, cold winter; and a thousand pictures were mirrored in the boy's eyes and heart; and still the little girl sang to him, 'Never, oh never, forget thou this!'

And wherever they flew, the sweet strong perfume of the elder-tree floated round them. The little boy could distinguish the delicious fragrance of the roses blooming in the gardens he flew past, and the wind wafted to him the fresh odour of the beech-trees; but the elder-perfume far excelled these, he thought, for its blossoms nestled to his fairy-like maiden's heart, and over those blossoms he continually bowed his head while flying.

'How beautiful is spring!' exclaimed the young girl, as they stood together in the beech-wood where the trees had newly burst into fresh loveliness, where the sweet-scented woodruff grew at their feet, the pale-tinted anemones looking so pretty amid its green. 'Oh, would it were always spring in the fragrant Danish beech-wood!'

'How beautiful is summer!' said she again, as they passed an ancient baronial castle, its red-stained walls and battlements mirrored in the moat encircling them, swans swimming in the moat, and peering up into the cool shady avenues. A sea of green corn waved to and fro in the fields, tiny red and golden blossoms peeped out of the ditches, and the hedges were wreathed with wild, wantoning hops, and the bell-flowered white bindweed. It was evening; the moon rose large and round, the meadows were odorous with the scent of haystacks. 'Never, oh never, forget thou this!'

'How beautiful is autumn!' exclaimed the little maiden, and the vault of heaven seemed to rise higher and to grow more intensely blue, and the woods became flushed with the richest and most varied hues of crimson, green, and yellow. The hounds bounded past in full cry; whole flocks of wildfowl flew screaming over the cairn-stones, to which luxuriant brambles were clinging. In the far distance lay the deep, blue sea, dotted over with white sails; old women, young maids, and children were assembled in a barn, picking hops into a great cask: the young ones of the party were singing, and the ancient dames were telling old legends of fairies and enchantments. What could be pleasanter than this?

'How beautiful is winter!' declared our young damsel, and behold! the trees stood around them all covered with hoar-frost—like white branching corals they looked; the snow crisped under the children's feet with a noise as if they had creaking new boots on, and falling stars, one after another, shot across the sky. The Christmas-tree was lighted up in the parlour; everybody had had presents given him, and everybody was in good humour. The peasant's cot in the country was merry with the sound of the violin, and the pancakes disappeared fast! Even the poorest child might have reason to echo the words, 'How beautiful is winter!'

Yes, truly it was beautiful! and it was our fairy maiden who showed all these fair sights to the little boy, and still the elder-perfume floated round him, when a new picture rose up before his eyes—the red flag with its white cross fluttering in the breeze, the very same flag under which the old mariner in the New Booths had sailed. And the boy felt that he was now grown up to be a youth, and that he must go to seek his fortune in the wide world; far away must he go to the warm countries, where grow the coffee-trees, but at their parting the young maiden took the cluster of elder-blossoms from her bosom, and gave it to him. And he kept it carefully; he kept it between the leaves of his hymn-book. And when he was in foreign lands he never took up the book but it opened upon the place where the flower of memory lay, and the oftener he looked at it the fresher, he fancied, it became. He seemed, while he looked at it, to breathe the sweet air of the Danish beech-groves, to see peeping among the tiny elder-flowerets the pretty maiden with her bright blue eyes, and to hear her low whisper, 'How beautiful is Denmark in spring, in summer, in autumn, and in winter!' and a hundred fair visions of the past flitted unbidden across his mind.

Many, very many, years passed away, and he was now an old man sitting with his old wife under a flowering tree. They each held other by the hand, just as the old couple in the New Booths had done, and they talked, too, of old times, and of their golden wedding-day. The little maiden, with the blue eyes and elder-blossoms in her hair, sat on the tree above, and nodded her head to them, saying, 'Today is your golden wedding-day!' and then she took two flower clusters out of her hair and kissed them twice: at the first kiss they shone like silver, after the second, like gold; and when she had set them on the two old people's heads each cluster became a gold crown. And thus the two sat there, like a crowned king and queen, under the fragrant elder-tree, and the old man began to tell his wife the story about Mother Elder, which had been told him when a little boy; and it seemed to them both that a great part of the story was very like their own real history—and they liked that part far the best.

'Yes, so it is!' said the little maiden in the tree. 'Some call me Mother Elder,

342

others call me a Dryad, but my proper name is Memory. Here I sit in the tree whilst it grows and grows; I never forget—I remember all things well—I could tell such famous stories. Now let me see if you still have your flower safe.'

And the old man opened his hymn-book; there lay the elder-flower, as fresh as though it had but just been laid between the leaves, and Memory nodded her head. And the two old people with their gold crowns sat under the tree, their faces flushed with the red evening sunlight. They closed their eyes, and then—and then—why then there was an end of the tale.

The little boy lay in his bed; he did not rightly know whether he had been dreaming all this, or whether it had been told him. The teapot stood on the table, but no elder-tree was growing out of it; and his friend the old story-teller was just on the point of going out at the door. Whilst the boy was rubbing his eyes he was gone.

'How pleasant that was!' said the little boy. 'Mother, I have been to the warm countries.'

'Yes, I have no doubt of that!' replied the mother, 'after you had drunk two brimful cups of good hot elder-tea, you were likely enough to get into the warm countries!' and she covered him up well for fear he should get chilled. 'You have had such a famous sound sleep, while I sat disputing with him as to whether it were a fairy tale, or a real, true history.'

'And where is Mother Elder?' asked the boy.

'She is in the teapot,' said his mother, 'and there she may stay.'

THE TOAD

It was a very deep well, and for that reason the rope which was used to pull up the pail full of water had to be very long too. When the pail was drawn up over the edge of the well, the crank was very difficult to turn. The sun never penetrated far enough to be reflected in the water, no matter how clear the water was, but wherever its rays touched, the stones became covered with a green film.

A family of toads lived in the well; they were newcomers and had actually got there head first with their old toad mother, who was still alive. The green frogs, who had settled there long before them and were swimming about in the water, recognised their kin and called them 'the well guests'.

The toads, however, decided to remain; they found it very pleasant indeed living in the dry, which was the way they described the damp stones.

One day Mother Toad went on a journey. She just happened to be in the pail when it was being pulled up, but the sudden light dazzled her and she fell out. She hit the water with a frightful splash, and then had to lie down for three days with a sprained back. And though she could not tell them anything about the outside world, she knew nevertheless—and she told all the others—that the well was not the whole world. Mother Toad, it is true, could have told them all manner of things, but she never replied when the frogs asked her anything, and so the frogs preferred not to ask.

'How fat and horrid, how ugly and repulsive she is!' said the young green frogs. 'And her young will be exactly the same!'

344

'Quite possibly,' replied Mother Toad. 'But one of them has a jewel in his head, or I have one.'

The green frogs listened awhile and their eyes bulged with amazement; but as they did not like to hear what Mother Toad was saying, they turned their backs on her and dived to the bottom of the well.

The young toads, on the other hand, stretched their hind legs out of sheer pride. Every one of them thought that *he* had that jewel, and so they held their heads erect and motionless. At last, however, they began to enquire what it was that they were so proud of; what *was* a jewel, they wanted to know.

'A jewel is something so beautiful and so precious,' said Mother Toad, 'that I cannot even describe it. It is something that you wear to please yourself and that others envy you. But ask me no more, for I will not answer.'

'I'm sure that I haven't got this jewel,' said the smallest of the toads, who was as ugly as you could possibly imagine. 'Why should I, of all frogs, have something as beautiful as that? And anyway, if it annoys others, it cannot please me. No, all I want is one day to be able to get up to the edge of the well and take a look outside. That must be wonderful.'

'Just you stay where you are,' Mother Toad rebuked him. 'At least you know what it's like here. Be careful of the pail, or it will crush you! And if you did manage to get inside it, you might fall out, and everyone isn't as fortunate as I was to survive such a fall with all four limbs unbroken.'

'Croak!' cried the little toad, which, in frog language, means something like 'Oh!' in our tongue.

He felt a great desire to sit on the edge of the well and to look outside. He longed for the greenery up there. Next morning, when the full pail was being hauled up and stopped for a moment in front of the stone upon which he was sitting, the little toad trembled, and then leaped into the pail. He fell to the bottom, and when the pail was emptied at the top, he was swept out by the water.

'Ugh! What a monster!' cried a boy who was standing by the well, when he saw the toad. 'That's the ugliest creature I've ever seen!' And he threw his wooden shoe at him. The little toad would have been completely crushed had he not quickly hidden behind some nettles.

The nettles stood stem after stem and then he looked up at the sky. The sun was shining upon the leaves and shining through them. To him it seemed very much as it does to us when we suddenly find ourselves in a huge forest in which the sun is shinning on the branches and leaves of the trees.

'How much nicer it is here than down there in the well! I should like to stay here all my life!' said the little toad to himself.

He lay there an hour, then two hours.

'I wonder what might be over there, outside?' it occurred to him. 'Since I have got this far, I must try and get farther still.'

He hopped out of the nettles as fast as he could go. Now he found himself on a road. The sun was shining down upon him and the dust settled on him as he crossed the highway.

'Here I am really in the dry,' said the toad. 'Indeed, it is perhaps even a little too much of a good thing, for it is making me itch.'

He hopped up to the ditch. Forget-me-nots grew there, and spiraea, and right beside the ditch there was a hedge of elder and hawthorn, with white bindweed creeping up it. There was a profusion of colour everywhere. A butterfly flew past, and the toad thought it was a blossom that had come loose to take a better look at the world, and he did not find this at all strange.

'If only I could fly like that!' thought the toad. 'Croak! Oh! How beautiful!'

He spent eight days and eight nights in the ditch, and was not wanting for food.

On the ninth day he thought: 'Right, and now I must get on!' But what could there be that would be finer than this? Perhaps another small toad, or some green frogs. Last night he had heard sounds in the air which seemed to indicate that some cousins might be near.

'How beautiful it is to be alive! To get out of the well, lie among the nettles, crawl over the dusty road, and rest in the damp ditch. But I must go on. I'll try and find some frogs, or a small toad—I miss them, so it seems that nature by itself is not enough.'

And he set out at once on his journey.

He went through a field and reached a large, reed-encircled pond. He looked enquiringly at the reeds and found that there were frogs in that place.

'Don't you find it too wet here?' they asked him. 'But you are very welcome. Are you a he-frog or a she-frog? But no matter, you are welcome just the same.'

That night the little toad was invited to a family concert. No food was served, only drink, and plenty of it: they were at liberty to drink up the whole pond, if they but could.

'And now I'll go on again,' said the little toad to himself. Something kept urging him on all the time to find a better place.

He saw the stars, enormous and bright; he saw the moon; he saw the sun rise in the sky, higher and higher.

'I am still in a well, a larger well perhaps, but a well just the same. I must get higher! I feel restless and full of a strange longing.'

And when there was a full moon, the poor little creature thought: 'That is probably a pail that is lowered down and into which I must jump if I want to get higher. Is the sun perhaps also a big pail? How big it is, and how it shines! We could all find a place in it—I'll just have to wait for a suitable opportunity. Oh, how clear my head is! I don't think that even a jewel could shine more brightly. But even though I haven't got one I'm not sad on that account; no, let me just get higher, nearer that bright glare where all is joy. I feel a longing and, at the same time, an anxiety. It is a difficult

step that I'm about to take, but it is a necessary one. Forward! Straight on to the road!'

He took a few steps the way frogs walk and he was on the road. People lived there and there were flower and vegetable gardens. Outside one vegetable garden he rested. 'How many various shapes there are here that I've never seen before. And how big and beautiful the world is! But one must look round in it and not just stay in one spot all the time.' And he hopped into the vegetable garden.

'How green everything is here! How beautiful!'

'I know it is,' said a green caterpillar sitting on a cabbage leaf. 'My leaf here is the largest of all. It covers half the world, but I can do without the other half.'

Then he heard the cackling of hens. They came and ran about the garden. The first hen was long-sighted; seeing the caterpillar on the leaf, she pecked at him and the caterpillar fell to the ground and lay there writhing. The hen looked at him, first with one eye, then with the other, for she did not know what the writhing might mean.

'I'm sure he's up to no good,' thought the hen and lifted her head to take another peck at the caterpillar. The little toad was so frightened that he crawled right towards the hen.

'Ah, he's got accomplices!' said the hen to herself. 'Well, well, what a creature!' She turned away, saying: 'I'm not interested in this small green morsel. It only tickles in the throat anyway.'

The other hens were of the same mind, and they went away.

'There, that's got rid of them!' said the caterpillar. 'It's fortunate that I have such presence of mind. But now how am I to get back on to my cabbage leaf? Where is it?'

The little toad came up to him and expressed his sympathy, saying he was happy that he had chased away the hens by his ugliness.

'What on earth do you mean?' asked the caterpillar. 'It was I myself who got rid of them. You really *are* very unpleasant to look at. And in any case I have a perfect right to stay in my place. I can smell cabbage already. Here is my leaf. There is nothing more beautiful than that which belongs to us. But I must get higher!'

'Yes, higher,' said the toad. 'Higher! He has the same feelings as I have. He's not in a good mood today, though; it must be the shock. We all of us want to get higher.'

And he looked as high up as he could.

A stork was sitting in his nest on the roof of a farmer's house. He was clapping his beak, and Mrs Stork was clapping hers as well.

'How high he lives!' thought the toad. 'Whoever can get up as high as that?'

Two young students lived on the farm; one was a poet and the other a naturalist. The one sang and wrote joyfully about everything that God had created and that had left a reflection in his heart; the other treated God's work as a huge mathematical sum.

He subtracted and multiplied, wishing to get to the bottom of everything and to speak sensibly. Both of them were good-natured and gay.

'Look, that's a fine specimen of a toad sitting over there,' said the naturalist. 'I must put him in alcohol.'

'Oh, but you have two already,' said the poet. 'Let him sit and enjoy life.'

'But he is so beautifully ugly,' said the other.

'Though, of course, if we could but find the jewel in his head,' said the poet, 'I'd gladly help you dissect him.'

'Jewel!' cried his friend. 'You know a lot about natural science!'

'But don't you think it's beautiful, this human belief that the toad, the ugliest of all animals, often has the most precious of jewels in his head? Isn't it exactly the same with people? After all, two of the wisest men of ancient times, Aesop and Socrates, possessed just such a jewel, though they were physically unattractive.'

That was all the toad heard, and of that he hardly understood half. The two friends went out, and he was saved from being preserved in alcohol.

'They, too, spoke of a jewel!' said the toad to himself. 'How fortunate I am not to have it, otherwise something unpleasant might easily befall me.'

Just then the stork's beak could be heard clapping up on the farmhouse roof. Father Stork was lecturing his family, who were stealing glances at the two young men in the garden below.

'People are the most conceited of all creatures,' said the stork. 'Listen to their beaks going nineteen to the dozen. And yet they can't even clap them properly. How proud they are of their gift of the gab, of their language! And what a strange language it is: a single day's flight from here and they cannot understand each other! We, on the other hand, can make ourselves understood with our language anywhere, even in Egypt. And they cannot fly, either. All they can do is to travel by the contraption they call 'railway', and even then they often come to grief; I get shivers down my spine and my beak begins to tremble at the mere thought of it. The world could easily do without people. We would certainly not miss them, as long as we have earthworms and frogs.'

'What a fine speech!' thought the little toad. 'What a great gentleman that is, and how high he sits! I've never in my life seen anyone sit so high before. And how he can swim!' he exclaimed when the stork spread his wings and flew up into the air.

Then Mother Stork spoke up, telling her children in the nest of the land called Egypt, of the waters of the Nile, and of all the wonderful marshes that are to be found in that far-off foreign land. All this was new to the toad, and he enjoyed it thoroughly.

'I must go to Egypt!' he decided. 'If only the stork or one of his young would take me with them! But of course I shall manage to get to Egypt. How happy I am! My longing is far better than any jewel in the head.'

And yet it was he who did have the jewel: and eternal longing and the desire to get higher. Always higher. It shone inside him; it shone with joy, with love of life.

Suddenly the stork swooped down. He saw the toad in the grass and he pounced on him, picking him up none too gently. He snapped his beak, his wings flapped noisily it was none too pleasant, but the toad was soaring up, up towards Egypt—that much the toad knew, that was why his eyes were shining as if sparks were about to fly out of them.

'Croak! Oh!'

The body was dead, the toad was killed. But where are the sparks from his eyes?

The sun's rays took them. The sun's rays carried away the jewel from the toad's head. Where to?

Don't ask the naturalist, ask the poet instead. He will tell it you in the form of a fairy-tale; it will include a caterpillar and a stork family. Just think! The caterpillar will turn into a beautiful butterfly! The stork family will fly over the mountains and over the seas to distant Africa, and yet it will find the shortest way back home again, to the same place, the very same roof! Yes, indeed, that sounds almost too much like a fairy-tale, yet it is perfectly true.

Ask the naturalist—he will confirm it.

And you yourself know it, for you have seen it.

But a jewel in the head of a toad?

Look for it in the sun, if you can!

The jewel is too bright, though. Our eyes are not yet good enough to see it in its full beauty as God made it. But one day we shall possess it, and that will be the most beautiful fairy-tale of all. Because we ourselves shall be in it.

THE END